THE WORKS OF
BENJAMIN DISRAELI
EARL OF BEACONSFIELD

VOLUME
20

AMS PRESS
NEW YORK

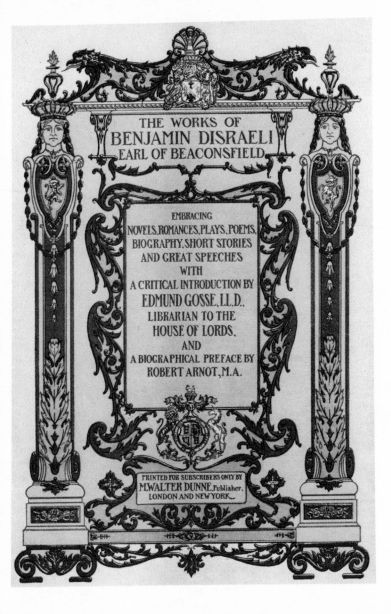

THE WORKS OF
BENJAMIN DISRAELI
EARL OF BEACONSFIELD

EMBRACING
NOVELS, ROMANCES, PLAYS, POEMS,
BIOGRAPHY, SHORT STORIES
AND GREAT SPEECHES
WITH
A CRITICAL INTRODUCTION BY
EDMUND GOSSE, LL.D.,
LIBRARIAN TO THE
HOUSE OF LORDS,
AND
A BIOGRAPHICAL PREFACE BY
ROBERT ARNOT, M.A.

PRINTED FOR SUBSCRIBERS ONLY BY
M. WALTER DUNNE, Publisher,
LONDON AND NEW YORK.

AFTER AN ORIGINAL DRAWING BY GEORGE ALFRED
WILLIAMS.

*' She enters the Catholic Church; the Archbishop
of Tyre has received her.'*

(See page 200.)

ENDYMION

BY

BENJAMIN DISRAELI

EARL OF BEACONSFIELD

VOLUME II.

M. WALTER DUNNE

NEW YORK AND LONDON

Library of Congress Cataloging in Publication Data

Beaconsfield, Benjamin Disraeli, Earl of, 1804-1881.
    Endymion.

    (The Works of Benjamin Disraeli, Earl of Beaconsfield;
v. 19-20)
    Vol. 2 includes the author's Miscellanea.
    Reprint of the 1904 ed. published by M. W. Dunne,
New York.
    I. Title.
PR4080.F76 vol. 19-20   [PR4084]   828'.8'09s   [823'.8]
ISBN 0-404-08800-7   (set)   76-12442

Reprinted from the edition of 1904, New York and London
First AMS edition published in 1976
Manufactured in the United States of America

International Standard Book Number:
Complete Set: 0-404-08800-7
Volume 20: 0-404-08820-1

AMS PRESS INC.
NEW YORK, N.Y.

CONTENTS

ENDYMION
(*Continued.*)

CONTENTS

CONTENTS

MISCELLANEA

CONTENTS

ILLUSTRATIONS

ENDYMION
(*CONTINUED*)

CHAPTER LXIV.

THE DECLINE OF TRADE.

THIS strangely-revived acquaintance with Job Thornberry was not an unfruitful incident in the life of Endymion. Thornberry was a man of original mind and singular energy; and, although of extreme views on commercial subjects, all his conclusions were founded on extensive and various information, combined with no inconsiderable practice. The mind of Thornberry was essentially a missionary one. He was always ready to convert people; and he acted with ardour and interest on a youth who, both by his ability and his social position, was qualified to influence opinion. But this youth was gifted with a calm, wise judgment, of the extent and depth of which he was scarcely conscious himself; and Thornberry, like all propagandists, was more remarkable for his zeal and his convictions than for that observation and perception of character which are the finest elements in the management of men and affairs.

'What you should do,' said Thornberry, one day, to Endymion, 'is to go to Scotland; go to the Glasgow district; that city itself, and Paisley, and Kilmarnock — keep your eye on Paisley. I am much mistaken if there will not soon be a state of things there which alone will break up the whole concern. It will burst it, sir; it will burst it.'

So Endymion, without saying anything, quietly went to Glasgow and its district, and noted enough to make him resolve soon to visit there again; but the cabinet reassembled in the early part of November, and he had to return to his duties.

In his leisure hours, Endymion devoted himself to the preparation of a report, for Mr. Sidney Wilton, on the condition and prospects of the manufacturing districts of the North of England, with some illustrative reference to that of the country beyond the Tweed. He concluded it before Christmas, and Mr. Wilton took it down with him to Gaydene, to study it at his leisure. Endymion passed his holidays with Lord and Lady Montfort, at their southern seat, Princedown.

Endymion spoke to Lady Montfort a little about his labours, for he had no secrets from her; but she did not much sympathise with him, though she liked him to be sedulous and to distinguish himself. 'Only,' she observed, 'take care not to be *doctrinaire*, Endymion. I am always afraid of that with you. It is Sidney's fault; he always was *doctrinaire*. It was a great thing for you becoming his private secretary; to be the private secretary of a cabinet minister is a real step in life, and I shall always be most grateful to Sidney, whom I love, for appointing you; but still, if I could have had my wish, you should have been

Lord Roehampton's private secretary. That is real politics, and he is a real statesman. You must not let Mr. Wilton mislead you about the state of affairs in the cabinet. The cabinet consists of the Prime Minister and Lord Roehampton, and, if they are united, all the rest is vapour. And they will not consent to any nonsense about touching the Corn Laws; you may be sure of that. Besides, I will tell you a secret, which is not yet Punchinello's secret, though I dare say it will be known when we all return to town—we shall have a great event when Parliament meets; a royal marriage. What think you of that? The young queen is going to be married, and to a young prince, like a prince in a fairy tale. As Lord Roehampton wrote to me this morning, "Our royal marriage will be much more popular than the Anti-Corn-Law League."'

The royal marriage was very popular; but, unfortunately, it reflected no splendour on the ministry. The world blessed the queen and cheered the prince, but shook its head at the government. Sir Robert Peel also—whether from his own motive or the irresistible impulse of his party need not now be inquired into—sanctioned a direct attack on the government, in the shape of a vote of want of confidence in them, immediately the court festivities were over, and the attack was defeated by a narrow majority.

'Nothing could be more unprincipled,' said Berengaria, 'after he had refused to take office last year. As for our majority, it is, under such circumstances, twenty times more than we want. As Lord Roehampton says, one is enough.'

Trade and revenue continued to decline. There was again the prospect of a deficiency. The ministry, too, was kept in by the Irish vote, and the Irish then were very unpopular. The cabinet itself generally was downcast, and among themselves occasionally murmured a regret that they had not retired when the opportunity offered in the preceding year. Berengaria, however, would not bate an inch of confidence and courage. 'You think too much,' she said to Endymion, 'of trade and finance. Trade always comes back, and finance never ruined a country, or an individual either if he had pluck. Mr. Sidney Wilton is a croaker. The things he fears will never happen; or, if they do, will turn out to be unimportant. Look to Lord Roehampton; he is the man. He does not care a rush whether the revenue increases or declines. He is thinking of real politics: foreign affairs; maintaining our power in Europe. Something will happen, before the session is over, in the Mediterranean;' and she pressed her finger to her lip, and then she added, 'The country will support Lord Roehampton, as they supported Pitt, and give him any amount of taxes that he likes.'

In the meantime, the social world had its incidents as well as the political, and not less interesting. Not one of the most insignificant, perhaps, was the introduction into society of the Countess of Beaumaris. Her husband, sacrificing even his hunting, had come up to town at the meeting of Parliament, and received his friends in a noble mansion on Piccadilly Terrace. All its equipments were sumptuous and refined, and everything had been arranged under the personal supervision of Mr. Waldershare. They commenced very quietly; dinners little but constant, and graceful and finished as a banquet of Watteau. No formal invitations; men were brought in to dinner from the House of Lords 'just up,' or picked up, as it were

carelessly, in the House of Commons by Mr. Waldershare, or were asked by Imogene, at a dozen hours'
notice, in billets of irresistible simplicity. Soon it was
whispered about, that the thing to do was to dine
with Beaumaris, and that Lady Beaumaris was 'something too delightful.' Prince Florestan frequently dined
there; Waldershare always there, in a state of corus-
cation; and every man of fashion in the opposite
ranks, especially if they had brains.

Then, in a little time, it was gently hoped that
Imogene should call on their wives and mothers, or
their wives and mothers call on her; and then she received, without any formal invitation, twice a week;
and as there was nothing going on in London, or
nothing half so charming, everybody who was anybody came to Piccadilly Terrace; and so as, after long
observation, a new planet is occasionally discovered
by a philosopher, thus society suddenly and indubit-
ably discovered that there was at last a Tory house.

Lady Roehampton, duly apprised of affairs by her
brother, had called on Lord and Lady Beaumaris, and
had invited them to her house. It was the first appearance of Imogene in general society, and it was
successful. Her large brown eyes, and long black
lashes, her pretty mouth and dimple, her wondrous
hair — which, it was whispered, unfolded, touched the
ground — struck every one, and the dignified simplicity of her carriage was attractive. Her husband
never left her side; while Mr. Waldershare was in
every part of the saloons, watching her from distant
points, to see how she got on, or catching the remarks of others on her appearance. Myra was kind
to her as well as courteous, and, when the stream of
arriving guests had somewhat ceased, sought her out

and spoke to her; and then put her arm in hers,
walked with her for a moment, and introduced her
to one or two great personages, who had previously
intimated their wish or their consent to that effect.
Lady Montfort was not one of these. When parties
are equal, and the struggle for power is intense,
society loses much of its sympathy and softness.
Lady Montfort could endure the presence of Tories,
provided they were her kinsfolk, and would join, even
at their houses, in traditionary festivities; but she
shrank from passing the line, and at once had a prejudice against Imogene, who she instinctively felt
might become a power for the enemy.

'I will not have you talk so much to that Lady
Beaumaris,' she said to Endymion.

'She is an old friend of mine,' he replied.

'How could you have known her? She was a
shop-girl, was not she, or something of that sort?'

'She and her family were very kind to me when
I was not much better than a shop-boy myself,' replied Endymion, with a mantling cheek. 'They are
most respectable people, and I have a great regard for
her.'

'Indeed! Well; I will not keep you from your
Tory woman,' said Berengaria rudely; and she walked
away.

Altogether, this season of '40 was not a very satisfactory one in any respect, as regarded society or the
country in general. Party passion was at its highest.
The ministry retained office almost by a casting
vote; were frequently defeated on important questions;
and whenever a vacancy occurred, it was filled by
their opponents. Their unpopularity increased daily,
and it was stimulated by the general distress. All

that Job Thornberry had predicted as to the state of
manufacturing Scotland duly occurred. Besides manufacturing distress, they had to encounter a series of
bad harvests. Never was a body of statesmen placed
in a more embarrassing and less enviable position.
There was a prevalent, though unfounded, conviction
that they were maintained in power by a combination
of court favour with Irish sedition.

Lady Montfort and Lord Roehampton were the
only persons who never lost heart. She was defiant;
and he ever smiled, at least in public. 'What nonsense!' she would say. 'Mr. Sidney Wilton talks
about the revenue falling off! As if the revenue
could ever really fall off! And then our bad harvests.
Why, that is the very reason we shall have an excellent harvest this year. You cannot go on always
having bad harvests. Besides, good harvests never
make a ministry popular. Nobody thanks a ministry
for a good harvest. What makes a ministry popular
is some great *coup* in foreign affairs.'

Amid all these exciting disquietudes, Endymion
pursued a life of enjoyment, but also of observation
and much labour. He lived more and more with the
Montforts, but the friendship of Berengaria was not
frivolous. Though she liked him to be seen where
he ought to figure, and required a great deal of attention herself, she ever impressed on him that his
present life was only a training for a future career,
and that his mind should ever be fixed on the at-
tainment of a high position. Particularly she impressed on him the importance of being a linguist.
'There will be a reaction some day from all this political economy,' she would say, 'and then there will
be no one ready to take the helm.'

Endymion was not unworthy of the interest which Berengaria took in him. The terrible vicissitudes of his early years had gravely impressed his character. Though ambitious, he was prudent; and, though born to please and be pleased, he was sedulous and self-restrained. Though naturally deeply interested in the fortunes of his political friends, and especially of Lord Roehampton and Mr. Wilton, a careful scrutiny of existing circumstances had prepared him for an inevitable change; and, remembering what was their position but a few years back, he felt that his sister and himself should be reconciled to their altered lot, and be content. She would still be a peeress, and the happy wife of an illustrious man; and he himself, though he would have to relapse into the drudgery of a public office, would meet duties the discharge of which was once the object of his ambition, coupled now with an adequate income and with many friends.

And among those friends, there were none with whom he maintained his relations more intimately than with the Neuchatels. He was often their guest both in town and at Hainault, and he met them frequently in society, always at the receptions of Lady Montfort and his sister. Zenobia used sometimes to send him a card; but these condescending recognitions of late had ceased, particularly as the great dame heard he was 'always at that Lady Beaumaris's.' One of the social incidents of his circle, not the least interesting to him, was the close attendance of Adriana and her mother on the ministrations of Nigel Penruddock. They had become among the most devoted of his flock; and this, too, when the rapid and startling development of his sacred offices had so alarmed the easy, though sagacious, Lord Roehampton, that he had absolutely expressed his wish to Myra that she should rarely attend them, and, indeed, gradually altogether drop a habit which might ultimately compromise her. Berengaria had long ago quitted him. This was attributed to her reputed caprice, yet it was not so. 'I like a man to be practical,' she said. 'When I asked for a deanery for him the other day, the Prime Minister said he could hardly make a man a dean who believed in the Real Presence.' Nigel's church, however, was more crowded than ever, and a large body of the clergy began to look upon him as the coming man.

Towards the end of the year the 'great *coup* in foreign affairs,' which Lady Montfort had long brooded over, and indeed foreseen, occurred, and took the world, who were all thinking of something else, entirely by surprise. A tripartite alliance of great powers had suddenly started into life; the Egyptian host was swept from the conquered plains of Asia Minor and Syria by English blue-jackets; St. Jean d'Acre, which had baffled the great Napoleon, was bombarded and taken by a British fleet; and the whole fortunes of the world in a moment seemed changed, and permanently changed.

'I am glad it did not occur in the season,' said Zenobia. 'I really could not stand Lady Montfort if it were May.'

The ministry was elate, and their Christmas was right merry. There seemed good cause for this. It was a triumph of diplomatic skill, national valour, and administrative energy. Myra was prouder of her husband than ever, and, amid all the excitement, he smiled on her with sunny fondness. Everybody congratulated her. She gave a little reception before the holidays, to which everybody came who was in town or passing through. Even Zenobia appeared; but she stayed a very short time, talking very rapidly. Prince Florestan paid his grave *devoirs*, with a gaze which seemed always to search into Lady Roehampton's inmost heart, yet never lingering about her; and Waldershare, full of wondrous compliments and conceits, and really enthusiastic, for he ever sympathised with action; and Imogene, gorgeous with the Beaumaris sapphires; and Sidney Wilton, who kissed his hostess's hand, and Adriana, who kissed her cheek.

'I tell you what, Mr. Endymion,' said Mr. Neuchatel, 'you should make Lord Roehampton your Chancellor of the Exchequer, and then your government might perhaps go on a little.'

CHAPTER LXV.

A STRUGGLE BETWEEN FACTIONS.

BUT, as Mr. Tadpole observed, with much originality, at the Carlton, they were dancing on a volcano. It was December, and the harvest was not yet all got in, the spring corn had never grown, and the wheat was rusty; there was, he well knew, another deficiency in the revenue to be counted by millions; wise men shook their heads and said the trade was leaving the country, and it was rumoured that the whole population of Paisley lived on the rates.

'Lord Roehampton thinks that something must be done about the Corn Laws,' murmured Berengaria one day to Endymion, rather crestfallen; 'but they will try sugar and timber first. I think it all nonsense, but nonsense is sometimes necessary.'

This was the first warning of that famous budget of 1841 which led to such vast consequences, and which, directly or indirectly, gave such a new form and colour to English politics. Sidney Wilton and his friends were at length all-powerful in the cabinet, because, in reality, there was nobody to oppose them. The vessel was waterlogged. The premier shrugged his shoulders; and Lord Roehampton said, 'We may as well try it, because the alternative is, we shall have to resign.'

Affairs went on badly for the ministry during the early part of the session. They were more than once in a minority, and on Irish questions, which then deeply interested the country; but they had resolved that their fate should be decided by their financial measures, and Mr. Sidney Wilton and his friends were still sanguine as to the result. On the last day of April the Chancellor of the Exchequer introduced the budget, and proposed to provide for the deficiency by reducing the protective duties on sugar and timber. A few days after, the leader of the House of Commons himself announced a change in the Corn Laws, and the intended introduction of grain at various-priced duties per quarter.

Then commenced the struggle of a month. Ultimately, Sir Robert Peel himself gave notice of a resolution of want of confidence in the ministry; and after a week's debate it was carried, in an almost complete house, by a majority of one!

It was generally supposed that the ministry would immediately resign. Their new measures had not revived their popularity, and the Parliament in which they had been condemned had been elected under their own advice and influence. Mr. Sidney Wilton had even told Endymion to get their papers in order; and all around the somewhat dejected private secretary there were unmistakable signs of that fatal flitting which is peculiarly sickening to the youthful politician.

He was breakfasting in his rooms at the Albany with not a good appetite. Although he had for some

time contemplated the possibility of such changes—
and contemplated them, as he thought, with philosophy—when it came to reality and practice, he found
his spirit was by no means so calm, or his courage
so firm, as he had counted on. The charms of office
arrayed themselves before him. The social influence,
the secret information, the danger, the dexterity, the
ceaseless excitement, the delights of patronage which
everybody affects to disregard, the power of bene-
fiting others, and often the worthy and unknown,
which is a real joy—in eight-and-forty hours or so,
all these, to which he had now been used for some
time, and which with his plastic disposition had become a second nature, were to vanish, and probably
never return. Why should they? He took the
gloomiest view of the future, and his inward soul
acknowledged that the man the country wanted was
Peel. Why might he not govern as long as Pitt?
He probably would. Peel! his father's friend! And
this led to a train of painful but absorbing memories,
and he sat musing and abstracted, fiddling with an
idle egg-spoon.

His servant came in with a note, which he eagerly
opened. It ran thus: 'I must see you instantly. I
am here in the brougham, Cork Street end. Come
directly. B. M.'

Endymion had to walk up half the Albany, and
marked the brougham the whole way. There was
in it an eager and radiant face.

'You had better get in,' said Lady Montfort, 'for
in these stirring times some of the enemy may be
passing. And now,' she continued, when the door was
fairly shut, 'nobody knows it, not five people. They
are going to dissolve.'

'To dissolve!' exclaimed Endymion. 'Will that help us?'

'Very likely,' said Berengaria. 'We have had our share of bad luck, and now we may throw in. Cheap bread is a fine cry. Indeed it is too shocking that there should be laws which add to the price of what everybody agrees is the staff of life. But you do nothing but stare, Endymion: I thought you would be in a state of the greatest excitement!'

'I am rather stunned than excited.'

'Well, you must not be stunned, you must act. This is a crisis for our party, but it is something more for you. It is your climacteric. They may lose; but you must win, if you will only bestir yourself. See the whips directly, and get the most certain seat you can. Nothing must prevent your being in the new Parliament.'

'I see everything to prevent it,' said Endymion. 'I have no means of getting into Parliament — no means of any kind.'

'Means must be found,' said Lady Montfort. 'We cannot stop now to talk about means. That would be a mere waste of time. The thing must be done. I am now going to your sister, to consult with her. All you have got to do is to make up your mind that you will be in the next Parliament, and you will succeed; for everything in this world depends upon will.'

'I think everything in this world depends upon woman,' said Endymion.

'It is the same thing,' said Berengaria.

Adriana was with Lady Roehampton when Lady Montfort was announced.

Adriana came to console; but she herself was not

without solace, for, if there were a change of government, she would see more of her friend.

'Well; I was prepared for it,' said Lady Roehampton. 'I have always been expecting something ever since what they called the Bed-Chamber Plot.'

'Well; it gave us two years,' said Lady Montfort; 'and we are not out yet.'

Here were three women, young, beautiful, and powerful, and all friends of Endymion — real friends. Property does not consist merely of parks and palaces, broad acres, funds in many forms, services of plate, and collections of pictures. The affections of the heart are property, and the sympathy of the right person is often worth a good estate.

These three charming women were cordial, and embraced each other when they met; but the conversation flagged, and the penetrating eye of Myra read in the countenance of Lady Montfort the urgent need of confidence.

'So, dearest Adriana,' said Lady Roehampton, 'we will drive out together at three o'clock. I will call on you.' And Adriana disappeared.

'You know it?' said Lady Montfort, when they were alone. 'Of course you know it. Besides, I know you know it. What I have come about is this: your brother must be in the new Parliament.'

'I have not seen him; I have not mentioned it to him,' said Myra, somewhat hesitatingly.

'I have seen him; I have mentioned it to him,' said Lady Montfort decidedly. 'He makes difficulties; there must be none. He will consult you. I came on at once that you might be prepared. No difficulty must be admitted. His future depends on it.'

'I live for his future,' said Lady Roehampton.

'He will talk to you about money. These things always cost money. As a general rule, nobody has money who ought to have it. I know dear Lord Roehampton is very kind to you; but, all his life, he never had too much money at his command; though why, I never could make out. And my lord has always had too much money; but I do not much care to talk to him about these affairs. The thing must be done. What is the use of diamond necklaces if you cannot help a friend into Parliament. But all I want now is that you will throw no difficulties in his way. Help him, too, if you can.'

'I wish Endymion had married,' replied Myra.

'Well; I do not see how that would help affairs,' said Lady Montfort. 'Besides, I dislike married men. They are very uninteresting.'

'I mean, I wish,' said Lady Roehampton musingly, 'that he had made a great match.'

'That is not very easy,' said Lady Montfort, 'and great matches are generally failures. All the married heiresses I have known have shipwrecked.'

'And yet it is possible to marry an heiress and love her,' said Myra.

'It is possible, but very improbable.'

'I think one might easily love the person who has just left the room.'

'Miss Neuchatel?'

'Adriana. Do not you agree with me?'

'Miss Neuchatel will never marry,' said Lady Montfort, 'unless she loses her fortune.'

'Well; do you know, I have sometimes thought that she liked Endymion? I never could encourage such a feeling; and Endymion, I am sure, would not. I wish, I almost wish,' added Lady Roehampton, trying to speak with playfulness, 'that you would use your magic influence, dear Lady Montfort, and bring it about. He would soon get into Parliament then.'

'I have tried to marry Miss Neuchatel once,' said Lady Montfort, with a mantling cheek, 'and I am glad to say I did not succeed. My match-making is over.'

There was a dead silence; one of those still moments which almost seem inconsistent with life, certainly with the presence of more than one human being. Lady Roehampton seemed buried in deep thought. She was quite abstracted, her eyes fixed, and fixed upon the ground. All the history of her life passed through her brain — all the history of their lives; from the nursery to this proud moment, proud even with all its searching anxiety. And yet the period of silence could be counted almost by seconds. Suddenly she looked up with a flushed cheek and a dazed look, and said, 'It must be done.'

Lady Montfort sprang forward with a glance radiant with hope and energy, and kissed her on both cheeks. 'Dearest Lady Roehampton,' she exclaimed, 'dearest Myra! I knew you would agree with me. Yes! it must be done.'

'You will see him perhaps before I do?' inquired Myra rather hesitatingly.

'I see him every day at the same time,' replied Lady Montfort. 'He generally walks down to the House of Commons with Mr. Wilton, and when they have answered questions, and he has got all the news of the lobby, he comes to me. I always manage to get home from my drive to give him half an hour before dinner.'

CHAPTER LXVI.

THE INFLUENCE OF WOMAN.

LADY MONTFORT drove off to the private residence of the Secretary of the Treasury, who was of course in the great secret. She looked over his lists, examined his books, and seemed to have as much acquaintance with electioneering details as that wily and experienced gentleman himself. 'Is there anything I can do?' she repeatedly inquired; 'command me without compunction. Is it any use giving any parties? Can I write any letters? Can I see anybody?'

'If you could stir up my lord a little?' said the secretary inquiringly.

'Well, that is difficult,' said Lady Montfort, 'perhaps impossible. But you have all his influence, and when there is a point that presses you must let me know.'

'If he would only speak to his agents?' said the secretary, 'but they say he will not, and he has a terrible fellow in ——shire, who I hear is one of the stewards for a dinner to Sir Robert.'

'I have stopped all that,' said Lady Montfort. 'That was Odo's doing, who is himself not very sound; full of prejudices about O'Connell, and all that stuff. But he must go with his party. You need not fear about him.'

'Well! it is a leap in the dark,' said the secretary.

'Oh! no,' said Lady Montfort, 'all will go right. A starving people must be in favour of a government who will give them bread for nothing. By-the-bye, there is one thing, my dear Mr. Secretary, you must remember, I must have one seat, a certain seat, reserved for my nomination.'

'A certain seat in these days is a rare gem,' said the secretary.

'Yes, but I must have it nevertheless,' said Lady Montfort. 'I don't care about the cost or the trouble —but it must be certain.'

Then she went home and wrote a line to Endymion, to tell him that it was all settled, that she had seen his sister, who agreed with her that it must be done, and that she had called on the Secretary of the Treasury, and had secured a certain seat. 'I wish you could come to luncheon,' she added, 'but I suppose that is impossible; you are always so busy. Why were you not in the Foreign Office? I am now going to call on the Tory women to see how they look, but I shall be at home a good while before seven, and of course count on seeing you.'

In the meantime, Endymion by no means shared the pleasurable excitement of his fair friend. His was an agitated walk from the Albany to Whitehall, where he resumed his duties moody and disquieted. There was a large correspondence this morning, which was a distraction and a relief, until the bell of Mr. Sidney Wilton sounded, and he was in attendance on his chief.

'It is a great secret,' said Mr. Wilton, 'but I think
I ought to tell you; instead of resigning, the government have decided to dissolve. I think it a mistake,
but I stand by my friends. They believe the Irish
vote will be very large, and with cheap bread will
carry us through. I think the stronger we shall be in
Ireland the weaker we shall be in England, and I
doubt whether our cheap bread will be cheap enough.
These Manchester associations have altered the aspect
of affairs. I have been thinking a good deal about
your position. I should like, before we broke up, to
have seen you provided for by some permanent office
of importance in which you might have been useful
to the state, but it is difficult to manage these things
suddenly. However, now we have time at any rate
to look about us. Still, if I could have seen you permanently attached to this office in a responsible position, I should have been glad. I impressed upon the
chief yesterday that you are most fit for it.'

'Oh! do not think of me, dear sir; you have been
always too kind to me. I shall be content with my
lot. All I shall regret is ceasing to serve you.'

Lady Montfort's carriage drove up to Montfort
House just as Endymion reached the door. She took
his arm with eagerness; she seemed breathless with
excitement. 'I fear I am very late, but if you had
gone away I should never have pardoned you. I have
been kept by listening to all the new appointments
from Lady Bellasyse. They quite think we are out;
you may be sure I did not deny it. I have so much
to tell you. Come into my lord's room; he is away
fishing. Think of fishing at such a crisis! I cannot
tell you how pleased I was with my visit to Lady
Roehampton. She quite agreed with me in every-

thing. "It must be done," she said. How very right! and I have almost done it. I will have a certain seat; no chances. Let us have something to fall back upon. If not in office we shall be in opposition. All men must sometime or other be in opposition. There you will form yourself. It is a great thing to have had some official experience. It will save you from mares' nests, and I will give parties without end, and never rest till I see you Prime Minister.'

So she threw herself into her husband's easy chair, tossed her parasol on the table, and then she said, 'But what is the matter with you, Endymion? you look quite sad. You do not mean you really take our defeat—which is not certain yet—so much to heart. Believe me, opposition has its charms; indeed I sometimes think the principal reason why I have enjoyed our ministerial life so much is, that it has been from the first a perpetual struggle for existence.'

'I do not pretend to be quite indifferent to the probably impending change,' said Endymion, 'but I cannot say there is anything about it which would affect my feelings very deeply.'

'What is it, then?'

'It is this business about which you and Myra are so kindly interesting yourselves,' said Endymion, with some emotion; 'I do not think I could go into Parliament.'

'Not go into Parliament!' exclaimed Lady Montfort. 'Why, what are men made for except to go into Parliament? I am indeed astounded.'

'I do not disparage Parliament,' said Endymion; 'much the reverse. It is a life that I think would suit me, and I have often thought the day might come'——

'The day has come,' said Lady Montfort, 'and not a bit too soon. Mr. Fox went in before he was of age, and all young men of spirit should do the same. Why! you are two-and-twenty!'

'It is not my age,' said Endymion hesitatingly; 'I am not afraid about that, for from the life which I have led of late years, I know a good deal about the House of Commons.'

'Then what is it, dear Endymion?' said Lady Montfort impatiently.

'It will make a great change in my life,' said Endymion calmly, but with earnestness, 'and one which I do not feel justified in accepting.'

'I repeat to you, that you need give yourself no anxiety about the seat,' said Lady Montfort. 'It will not cost you a shilling. I and your sister have arranged all that. As she very wisely said, "It must be done," and it is done. All you have to do is to write an address, and make plenty of speeches, and you are M.P. for life, or as long as you like.'

'Possibly; a parliamentary adventurer, I might swim or I might sink; the chances are it would be the latter, for storms would arise when those disappear who have no root in the country, and no fortune to secure them breathing time and a future.'

'Well, I did not expect, when you handed me out of my carriage to-day, that I was going to listen to a homily on prudence.'

'It is not very romantic, I own,' said Endymion, 'but my prudence is at any rate not a commonplace caught up from copy-books. I am only two-and-twenty, but I have had some experience, and it has been very bitter. I have spoken to you, dearest lady, sometimes of my earlier life, for I wished you to be acquainted with it, but I observed also you always seemed to shrink from such confidence, and I ceased from touching on what I saw did not interest you.'

'Quite a mistake. It greatly interested me. I know all about you and everything. I know you were not always a clerk in a public office, but the spoiled child of splendour. I know your father was a dear good man, but he made a mistake, and followed the Duke of Wellington instead of Mr. Canning. Had he not, he would probably be alive now, and certainly Secretary of State, like Mr. Sidney Wilton. But *you* must not make a mistake, Endymion. My business in life, and your sister's too, is to prevent your making mistakes. And you are on the eve of making a very great one if you lose this golden opportunity. Do not think of the past; you dwell on it too much. Be like me, live in the present, and when you dream, dream of the future.'

'Ah! the present would be adequate, it would be fascination, if I always had such a companion as Lady Montfort,' said Endymion, shaking his head. 'What surprises me most, what indeed astounds me, is that Myra should join in this counsel—Myra, who knows all, and who has felt it perhaps deeper even than I did. But I will not obtrude these thoughts on you, best and dearest of friends. I ought not to have made to you the allusions to my private position which I have done, but it seemed the only way to explain my conduct, otherwise inexplicable.'

'And to whom ought you to say these things if not to me,' said Lady Montfort, 'whom you called just now your best and dearest friend? I wish to be such to you. Perhaps I have been too eager, but, at any rate, it was eagerness for your welfare. Let us then be calm. Speak to me as you would to Myra. I cannot be your twin, but I can be your sister in feeling.'

He took her hand and gently pressed it to his lips; his eyes would have been bedewed, had not the dreadful sorrows and trials of his life much checked his native susceptibility. Then speaking in a serious tone, he said, 'I am not without ambition, dearest Lady Montfort; I have had visions which would satisfy even you; but partly from my temperament, still more perhaps from the vicissitudes of my life, I have considerable waiting powers. I think if one is patient and watches, all will come of which one is capable; but no one can be patient who is not independent. My wants are moderate, but their fulfilment must be certain. The break-up of the government, which deprives me of my salary as a private secretary, deprives me of luxuries which I can do without — a horse, a brougham, a stall at the play, a flower in my button-hole — but my clerkship is my freehold. As long as I possess it, I can study, I can work, I can watch and comprehend all the machinery of government. I can move in society, without which a public man, whatever his talents or acquirements, is in life playing at blind-man's-buff. I must sacrifice this citadel of my life if I go into Parliament. Do not be offended, therefore, if I say to you, as I shall say to Myra, I have made up my mind not to surrender it. It is true I have the misfortune to be a year older than Charles Fox when he entered the senate, but even with this great disadvantage I am sometimes conceited enough to believe that I shall succeed, and to back myself against the field.'

CHAPTER LXVII.

£20,000 in Consols.

M R. WALDERSHARE was delighted when the great secret was out, and he found that the ministry intended to dissolve, and not resign. It was on a Monday that Lord John Russell made this announcement, and Waldershare met Endymion in the lobby of the House of Commons. 'I congratulate you, my dear boy; your fellows, at least, have pluck. If they lose, which I think they will, they will have gained at least three months of power, and irresponsible power. Why! they may do anything in the interval, and no doubt will. You will see; they will make their chargers consuls. It beats the Bed-Chamber Plot, and I always admired that. One hundred days! Why, the Second Empire lasted only one hundred days. But what days! what excitement! They were worth a hundred years at Elba.'

'Your friends do not seem quite so pleased as you are,' said Endymion.

'My friends, as you call them, are old fogies, and want to divide the spoil among the ancient hands. It will be a great thing for Peel to get rid of

(25)

some of these old friends. A dissolution permits the powerful to show their power. There is Beaumaris, for example; now he will have an opportunity of letting them know who Lord Beaumaris is. I have a dream; he must be Master of the Horse. I shall never rest till I see Imogene riding in that golden coach, and breaking the line with all the honours of royalty.'

'Mr. Ferrars,' said the editor of a newspaper, seizing his watched-for opportunity as Waldershare and Endymion separated, 'do you think you could favour me this evening with Mr. Sidney Wilton's address? We have always supported Mr. Wilton's views on the Corn Laws, and if put clearly and powerfully before the country at this juncture, the effect might be great, perhaps even, if sustained, decisive.'

Eight-and-forty hours and more had elapsed since the conversation between Endymion and Lady Montfort; they had not been happy days. For the first time during their acquaintance there had been constraint and embarrassment between them. Lady Montfort no longer opposed his views, but she did not approve them. She avoided the subject; she looked uninterested in all that was going on around her; talked of joining her lord and going a-fishing; felt he was right in his views of life. 'Dear Simon was always right,' and then she sighed, and then she shrugged her very pretty shoulders. Endymion, though he called on her as usual, found there was nothing to converse about; politics seemed tacitly forbidden, and when he attempted small talk Lady Montfort seemed absent — and once absolutely yawned.

What amazed Endymion still more was, that, under these rather distressing circumstances, he did not find adequate support and sympathy in his sister. Lady Roehampton did not question the propriety of his decision, but she seemed quite as unhappy and as dissatisfied as Lady Montfort.

'What you say, dearest Endymion, is quite unanswerable, and I alone perhaps can really know that; but what I feel is, I have failed in life. My dream was to secure you greatness, and now, when the first occasion arrives, it seems I am more than powerless.'

'Dearest sister! you have done so much for me.'

'Nothing,' said Lady Roehampton; 'what I have done for you would have been done by every sister in this metropolis. I dreamed of other things; I fancied, with my affection and my will, I could command events, and place you on a pinnacle. I see my folly now; others have controlled your life, not I — as was most natural; natural, but still bitter.'

'Dearest Myra!'

'It is so, Endymion. Let us deceive ourselves no longer. I ought not to have rested until you were in a position which would have made you master of your destiny.'

'But if there should be such a thing as destiny, it will not submit to the mastery of man.'

'Do not split words with me; you know what I mean; you feel what I mean; I mean much more than I say, and you understand much more than I say. My lord told me to ask you to dine with us, if you called, but I will not ask you. There is no joy in meeting at present. I feel as I felt in our last year at Hurstley.'

'Oh! don't say that, dear Myra!' and Endymion sprang forward and kissed her very much. 'Trust me; all will come right; a little patience, and all will come right.'

'I have had patience enough in life,' said Lady Roehampton; 'years of patience, the most doleful, the most dreary, the most dark and tragical. And I bore it all, and I bore it well, because I thought of you, and had confidence in you, and confidence in your star; and because, like an idiot, I had schooled myself to believe that, if I devoted my will to you, that star would triumph.'

So, the reader will see that our hero was not in a very serene and genial mood when he was button-holed by the editor in the lobby, and, it is feared, he was unusually curt with that gentleman, which editors do not like, and sometimes reward with a leading article in consequence, on the character and career of our political chief, perhaps with some passing reference to jacks-in-office, and the superficial impertinence of private secretaries. These wise and amiable speculators on public affairs should, however, sometimes charitably remember that even ministers have their chagrins, and that the trained temper and imperturbable presence of mind of their aides-de-camp are not absolutely proof to all the infirmities of human nature.

Endymion had returned home from the lobby, depressed and dispirited. The last incident of our life shapes and colours our feelings. Ever since he had settled in London, his life might be said to have been happy, gradually and greatly prosperous. The devotion of his sister and the eminent position she had achieved, the friendship of Lady Montfort, and the kindness of society, who had received him with open arms, his easy circumstances after painful narrowness of means, his honourable and interesting position —

these had been the chief among many other causes which had justly rendered Endymion Ferrars a satisfied and contented man. And it was more than to be hoped that not one of these sources would be wanting in his future. And yet he felt dejected, even to unhappiness. Myra figured to his painful consciousness only as deeply wounded in her feelings, and he somehow the cause; Lady Montfort, from whom he had never received anything but smiles and inspiring kindness, and witty raillery, and affectionate solicitude for his welfare, offended and estranged. And as for society, perhaps it would make a great difference in his position if he were no longer a private secretary to a cabinet minister and only a simple clerk; he could not, even at this melancholy moment, dwell on his impending loss of income, though that increase at the time had occasioned him, and those who loved him, so much satisfaction. And yet, was he in fault? Had his decision been a narrow-minded and craven one? He could not bring himself to believe so — his conscience assured him that he had acted rightly. After all that he had experienced, he was prepared to welcome an obscure, but could not endure a humiliating position.

It was a long summer evening. The House had not sat after the announcement of the ministers. The twilight lingered with a charm almost as irresistible as among woods and waters. Endymion had been engaged to dine out, but had excused himself. Had it not been for the Montfort misunderstanding, he would have gone; but that haunted him. He had not called on her that day; he really had not courage to meet her. He was beginning to think that he might never see her again; never, certainly, on the same terms. She had the reputation of being capricious, though she had been constant in her kindness to him. Never see her again, or only see her changed! He was not aware of the fulness of his misery before: he was not aware, until this moment, that unless he saw her every day life would be intolerable.

He sat down at his table, covered with notes in every female handwriting except the right one, and with cards of invitation to banquets and balls and concerts, and 'very earlies,' and carpet dances — for our friend was a very fashionable young man — but what is the use of even being fashionable, if the person you love cares for you no more? And so out of very wantonness, instead of opening notes sealed or stamped with every form of coronet, he took up a business-like epistle, closed only with a wafer, and saying in drollery, 'I should think a dun,' he took out a scrip receipt for £20,000 consols, purchased that morning in the name of Endymion Ferrars, Esq. It was enclosed in half a sheet of note-paper, on which were written these words, in a handwriting which gave no clew of acquaintanceship, or even sex: 'Mind — you are to send me your first frank.'

CHAPTER LXVIII.

PERPLEXITY.

T WAS useless to ask who could it be? It could only be one person; and yet how could it have been managed? So completely and so promptly! Her lord, too, away; the only being, it would seem, who could have effected for her such a purpose, and he the last individual to whom, perhaps, she would have applied. Was it a dream? The long twilight was dying away, and it dies away in the Albany a little sooner than it does in Park Lane; and so he lit the candles on his mantel-piece, and then again unfolded the document carefully, and read it and re-read it. It was not a dream. He held in his hand firmly, and read with his eyes clearly, the evidence that he was the uncontrolled master of no slight amount of capital, and which, if treated with prudence, secured to him for life an absolute and becoming independence. His heart beat and his cheek glowed.

What a woman! And how true were Myra's last words at Hurstley, that women would be his best friends in life! He ceased to think; and, dropping

into his chair, fell into a reverie, in which the past
and the future seemed to blend, with some mingling
of a vague and almost ecstatic present. It was a
dream of fair women, and even fairer thoughts, domestic tenderness and romantic love, mixed up with
strange vicissitudes of lofty and fiery action, and passionate passages of eloquence and power. The clock
struck and roused him from his musing. He fell from
the clouds. Could he accept this boon? Was his doing so consistent with that principle of independence
on which he had resolved to build up his life? The
boon thus conferred might be recalled and returned;
not legally indeed, but by a stronger influence than
any law — the consciousness on his part that the feeling of interest in his life which had prompted it
might change — would, must change. It was the romantic impulse of a young and fascinating woman,
who had been to him invariably kind, but who had
a reputation for caprice, which was not unknown to
him. It was a wild and beautiful adventure; but only
that.

He walked up and down his rooms for a long
time, sometimes thinking, sometimes merely musing;
sometimes in a pleased but gently agitated state of
almost unconsciousness. At last he sat down at his
writing-table, and wrote for some time; and then, directing the letter to the Countess of Montfort, he resolved to change the current of his thoughts, and
went to a club.

Morning is not romantic. Romance is the twilight spell; but morn is bright and joyous, prompt
with action, and full of sanguine hope. Life has few
difficulties in the morning, at least none which we
cannot conquer; and a private secretary to a minis-

ter, young and prosperous, at his first meal, surrounded by dry toast, all the newspapers, and piles of correspondence, asking and promising everything, feels with pride and delight the sense of powerful and responsible existence. Endymion had glanced at all the leading articles, had sorted in the correspondence the grain from the chaff, and had settled in his mind those who must be answered and those who must be seen. The strange incident of last night was of course not forgotten, but removed, as it were, from his consciousness in the bustle and pressure of active life, when his servant brought him a letter in a handwriting he knew right well. He would not open it till he was alone, and then it was with a beating heart and a burning cheek.

LADY MONTFORT'S LETTER.

'What is it all about? and what does it all mean? I should have thought some great calamity had occurred if, however distressing, it did not appear in some sense to be gratifying. What is gratifying? You deal in conundrums, which I never could find out. Of course I shall be at home to you at any time, if you wish to see me. Pray come on at once, as I detest mysteries. I went to the play last night with your sister. We both of us rather expected to see you, but it seems neither of us had mentioned to you we were going. I did not, for I was too low-spirited about your affairs. You lost nothing. The piece was stupid beyond expression. We laughed heartily, at least I did, to show we were not afraid. My lord came home last night suddenly. Odo is going to stand for the county, and his borough is vacant.

What an opportunity it would have been for you! a certain seat. But I care for no boroughs now. My lord will want you to dine with him to-day; I hope you can come. Perhaps he will not be able to see you this morning, as his agent will be with him about these elections. Adieu!'

If Lady Montfort did not like conundrums, she had succeeded, however, in sending one sufficiently perplexing to Endymion. Could it be possible that the writer of this letter was the unknown benefactress of the preceding eve? Lady Montfort was not a mystifier. Her nature was singularly frank and fearless, and when Endymion told her everything that had occurred, and gave her the document which originally he had meant to bring with him in order to return it, her amazement and her joy were equal.

'I wish I had sent it,' said Lady Montfort, 'but that was impossible. I do not care who did send it; I have no female curiosity except about matters which, by knowledge, I may influence. This is finished. You are free. You cannot hesitate as to your course. I never could speak to you again if you did hesitate. Stop here, and I will go to my lord. This is a great day. If we can only settle to-day that you shall be the candidate for our borough, I really shall not much care for the change of ministry.'

Lady Montfort was a long time away. Endymion would have liked to have gone forth on his affairs, but she had impressed upon him so earnestly to wait for her return that he felt he could not retire. The room was one to which he was not unaccustomed, otherwise, its contents would not have been uninteresting; her portrait by more than one great master, a miniature of her husband in a Venetian dress upon her writing-table — a table which wonderfully indicated alike the lady of fashion and the lady of business, for there seemed to be no form in which paper could be folded and emblazoned which was there wanting; quires of letter paper, and note paper, and notelet paper, from despatches of state to billet-doux, all were ready; great covers with arms and supporters, more moderate ones with 'Berengaria' in letters of glittering fancy, and the destined shells of diminutive effusions marked only with a golden bee. There was another table covered with trinkets and precious toys: snuff-boxes and patch-boxes beautifully painted, exquisite miniatures, rare fans, cups of agate, birds glittering with gems almost as radiant as the tropic plumage they imitated, wild animals cut out of ivory, or formed of fantastic pearls — all the spoils of queens and royal mistresses.

Upon the walls were drawings of her various homes; that of her childhood, as well as of the hearths she ruled and loved. There were a few portraits on the walls also of those whom she ranked as her particular friends. Lord Roehampton was one, another was the Count of Ferroll.

Time went on; on a little table, by the side of evidently her favourite chair, was a book she had been reading. It was a German tale of fame, and Endymion, dropping into her seat, became interested in a volume which hitherto he had never seen, but of which he had heard much.

Perhaps he had been reading for some time; there was a sound, he started and looked up, and then, springing from his chair, he said, 'Something has happened!'

Lady Montfort was quite pale, and the expression of her countenance distressed, but when he said these words she tried to smile, and said, 'No, no, nothing, nothing,—at least nothing to distress you. My lord hopes you will be able to dine with him to-day, and tell him all the news.' And then she threw herself into a chair and sighed. 'I should like to have a good cry, as the servants say—but I never could cry. I will tell you all about it in a moment. You were very good not to go.'

It seems that Lady Montfort saw her lord before the agent, who was waiting, had had his interview, and the opportunity being in every way favourable, she felt the way about obtaining his cousin's seat for Endymion. Lord Montfort quite embraced the proposal. It had never occurred to him. He had no idea that Ferrars contemplated Parliament. It was a capital idea. He could not bear reading the Parliament reports, and yet he liked to know a little of what was going on. Now, when anything happened of interest, he should have it all from the fountain-head. 'And you must tell him, Berengaria,' he continued, 'that he can come and dine here whenever he likes, in boots. It is a settled thing that M.P.s may dine in boots. I think it a most capital plan. Besides, I know it will please you. You will have your own member.'

Then he rang the bell, and begged Lady Montfort to remain and see the agent. Nothing like the present time for business. They would make all the arrangements at once, and he would ask the agent to dine with them to-day, and so meet Mr. Ferrars.

So the agent entered, and it was all explained to him, calmly and clearly, briefly by my lord, but with fervent amplification by his charming wife. The agent several times attempted to make a remark, but for some time he was unsuccessful; Lady Montfort was so anxious that he should know all about Mr. Ferrars, the most rising young man of the day, the son of the late Right Honourable William Pitt Ferrars, who, had he not died, would probably have been Prime Minister, and so on.

'Mr. Ferrars seems to be everything we could wish,' said the agent, 'and as you say, my lady, though he is young, so was Mr. Pitt, and I have little doubt, after what you say, my lady, that it is very likely he will in time become as eminent. But what I came up to town particularly to impress upon my lord is, that if Mr. Odo will not stand again, we are in a very great difficulty.'

'Difficulty about what?' said Lady Montfort impatiently.

'Well, my lady, if Mr. Odo stands, there is great respect for him. The other side would not disturb him. He has been member for some years, and my lord has been very liberal. But the truth is, if Mr. Odo does not stand, we cannot command the seat.'

'Not command the seat! Then our interest must have been terribly neglected.'

'I hope not, my lady,' said the agent. 'The fact is, the property is against us.'

'I thought it was all my lord's.'

'No, my lady; the strong interest in the borough is my Lord Beaumaris. It used to be about equal, but all the new buildings are in Lord Beaumaris' part of the borough. It would not have signified if things had remained as in the old days. The grandfather of the present lord was a Whig, and always supported

the Montforts, but that's all changed. The present
earl has gone over to the other side, and, I hear, is
very strong in his views.'

Lady Montfort had to communicate all this to
Endymion. 'You will meet the agent at dinner, but
he did not give me a ray of hope. Go now; indeed,
I have kept you too long. I am so stricken that I
can scarcely command my senses. Only think of our
borough being stolen from us by Lord Beaumaris! I
have brought you no luck, Endymion; I have done
you nothing but mischief; I am miserable. If you had
attached yourself to Lady Beaumaris, you might have
been a member of Parliament.'

CHAPTER LXIX.

PLOTS AND COUNTERPLOTS.

IN THE meantime, the great news being no longer a secret, the utmost excitement prevailed in the world of politics. The Tories had quite made up their minds that the ministry would have resigned, and were sanguine, under such circumstances, of the result. The Parliament, which the ministry was going to dissolve, was one which had been elected by their counsel and under their auspices. It was unusual, almost unconstitutional, thus to terminate the body they had created. Nevertheless, the Whigs, never too delicate in such matters, thought they had a chance, and determined not to lose it. One thing they immediately succeeded in, and that was, frightening their opponents. A dissolution with the Tories in opposition was not pleasant to that party; but a dissolution with a cry of 'Cheap bread!' amid a partially starving population, was not exactly the conjuncture of providential circumstances which had long been watched and wished for, and cherished and coddled and proclaimed and promised, by the energetic army of conservative wire-pullers.

Mr. Tadpole was very restless at the crowded Carlton, speaking to every one, unhesitatingly answering every question, alike cajoling and dictatorial, and yet, all the time, watching the door of the morning-room with unquiet anxiety.

'They will never be able to get up the steam, Sir Thomas; the Chartists are against them. The Chartists will never submit to anything that is cheap. In spite of their wild fancies, they are real John Bulls. I beg your pardon, but I see a gentleman I must speak to,' and he rushed towards the door as Waldershare entered.

'Well, what is your news?' asked Mr. Tadpole affecting unconcern.

'I come here for news,' said Waldershare. 'This is my Academus, and you, Tadpole, are my Plato.'

'Well, if you want the words of a wise man, listen to me. If I had a great friend, which Mr. Waldershare probably has, who wants a great place, these are times in which such a man should show his power.'

'I have a great friend whom I wish to have a great place,' said Waldershare, 'and I think he is quite ready to show his power, if he knew exactly how to exercise it.'

'What I am saying to you is not known to a single person in this room, and to only one out of it, but you may depend upon what I say. Lord Montfort's cousin retires from Northborough to sit for the county. They think they can nominate his successor as a matter of course. A delusion; your friend Lord Beaumaris can command the seat.'

'Well, I think you can depend on Beaumaris,' said Waldershare, much interested.

'I depend upon you,' said Mr. Tadpole with a glance of affectionate credulity. 'The party already owes you much. This will be a crowning service.'

'Beaumaris is rather a queer man to deal with,' said Waldershare; 'he requires gentle handling.'

'All the world says he consults you on everything.'

'All the world, as usual, is wrong,' said Waldershare. 'Lord Beaumaris consults no one except Lady Beaumaris.'

'Well, then, we shall do,' rejoined Mr. Tadpole triumphantly. 'Our man that I want him to return is a connection of Lady Beaumaris, a Mr. Rodney, very anxious to get into Parliament, and rich. I do not know who he is exactly, but it is a good name; say a cousin of Lord Rodney until the election is over, and then they may settle it as they like.'

'A Mr. Rodney,' said Waldershare musingly; 'well, if I hear anything I will let you know. I suppose you are in pretty good spirits?'

'I should like a little sunshine. A cold spring, and now a wet summer, and the certainty of a shocking harvest combined with manufacturing distress spreading daily, is not pleasant, but the English are a discriminating people. They will hardly persuade them that Sir Robert has occasioned the bad harvests.'

'The present men are clearly responsible for all that,' said Waldershare.

There was a reception at Lady Roehampton's this evening. Very few Tories attended it, but Lady Beaumaris was there. She never lost an opportunity of showing by her presence how grateful she was to Myra for the kindness which had greeted Imogene when she first entered society. Endymion, as was his custom when the opportunity offered, rather hung about Lady Beaumaris. She always welcomed him with unaffected cordiality and evident pleasure. He talked to her, and then gave way to others, and then came and talked to her again, and then he proposed to take her to have a cup of tea, and she assented to the proposal with a brightening eye and a bewitching smile.

'I suppose your friends are very triumphant, Lady Beaumaris?' said Endymion.

'Yes; they naturally are very excited. I confess I am not myself.'

'But you ought to be,' said Endymion. 'You will have an immense position. I should think Lord Beaumaris would have any office he chose, and yours will be the chief house of the party.'

'I do not know that Lord Beaumaris would care to have office, and I hardly think any office would suit him. As for myself, I am obliged to be ambitious, but I have no ambition, or rather I would say, I think I was happier when we all seemed to be on the same side.'

'Well, those were happy days,' said Endymion, 'and these are happy days. And few things make me happier than to see Lady Beaumaris admired and appreciated by every one.'

'I wish you would not call me Lady Beaumaris. That may be, and indeed perhaps is, necessary in society, but when we are alone, I prefer being called by a name which once you always and kindly used.'

'I shall always love the name,' said Endymion, 'and,' he added with some hesitation, 'shall always love her who bears it.'

She involuntarily pressed his arm, though very slightly; and then in rather a hushed and hurried tone she said, 'They were talking about you at dinner to-day. I fear this change of government, if there is to be one, will be injurious to you—losing your private secretaryship to Mr. Wilton, and perhaps other things?'

'Fortune of war,' said Endymion; 'we must bear these haps. But the truth is; I think it not unlikely there may be a change in my life which may be incompatible with retaining my secretaryship under any circumstances.'

'You are not going to be married?' she said quickly.

'Not the slightest idea of such an event.'

'You are too young to marry.'

'Well, I am older than you.'

'Yes; but men and women are different in that matter. Besides, you have too many fair friends to marry, at least at present. What would Lady Roehampton say?'

'Well, I have sometimes thought my sister wished me to marry.'

'But then there are others who are not sisters, but who are equally interested in your welfare,' said Lady Beaumaris, looking up into his face with her wondrous eyes; but the lashes were so long, that it was impossible to decide whether the glance was an anxious one or one half of mockery.

'Well, I do not think I shall ever marry,' said Endymion. 'The change in my life I was alluding to is one by no means of a romantic character. I have some thoughts of trying my luck on the hustings, and getting into Parliament.'

'That would be delightful,' said Lady Beaumaris. 'Do you know that it has been one of my dreams that you should be in Parliament?'

'Ah! dearest Imogene, for you said I might call you Imogene, you must take care what you say. Remember, we are unhappily in different camps. You must not wish me success in my enterprise; quite the reverse; it is more than probable that you will have to exert all your influence against me; yes, canvass against me, and wear hostile ribbons, and use all your irresistible charms to array electors against me, or to detach them from my ranks.'

'Even in jest, you ought not to say such things,' said Lady Beaumaris.

'But I am not in jest, I am in dreadful earnest. Only this morning I was offered a seat, which they told me was secure; but when I inquired into all the circumstances, I found the interest of Lord Beaumaris so great, that it would be folly for me to attempt it.'

'What seat?' inquired Lady Beaumaris in a low tone.

'Northborough,' said Endymion, 'now held by Lord Montfort's cousin, who is to come in for his county. The seat was offered to me, and I was told I was to be returned without opposition.'

'Lady Montfort offered it to you?' asked Imogene.

'She interested herself for me, and Lord Montfort approved the suggestion. It was described to me as a family seat, but when I looked into the matter, I found that Lord Beaumaris was more powerful than Lord Montfort.'

'I thought that Lady Montfort was irresistible,' said Imogene; 'she carries all before her in society.'

'Society and politics have much to do with each other, but they are not identical. In the present case, Lady Montfort is powerless.'

'And have you formally abandoned the seat?' inquired Lady Beaumaris.

'Not formally abandoned it; that was not necessary, but I have dismissed it from my mind, and for some time have been trying to find another seat, but hitherto without success. In short, in these days it is no longer possible to step into Parliament as if you were stepping into a club.'

'If I could do anything, however little?' said Imogene. 'Perhaps Lady Montfort would not like me to interfere?'

'Why not?'

'Oh! I do not know,' and then after some hesitation she added, 'Is she jealous?'

'Jealous! why should she be jealous?'

'Perhaps she has had no cause.'

'You know Lady Montfort. She is a woman of quick and brilliant feeling, the best of friends and a dauntless foe. Her kindness to me from the first moment I made her acquaintance has been inexpressible, and I sincerely believe she is most anxious to serve me. But our party is not very popular at present; there is no doubt the country is against us. It is tired of us. I feel myself the general election will be disastrous. Liberal seats are not abundant just now, quite the reverse, and though Lady Montfort has done more than any one could under the circumstances, I feel persuaded, though you think her irresistible, she will not succeed.'

'I hardly know her,' said Imogene. 'The world considers her irresistible, and I think you do. Nevertheless, I wish she could have had her way in this matter, and I think it quite a pity that Northborough has turned out not to be a family seat.'

CHAPTER LXX.

FEMININE CONFIDENCES ABOUT HUSBANDS.

HERE was a dinner-party at Mr. Neuchatel's, to which none were asked but the high government clique. It was the last dinner before the dissolution: 'The dinner of consolation, or hope,' said Lord Roehampton. Lady Montfort was to be one of the guests. She was dressed, and her carriage in the courtyard, and she had just gone in to see her lord before she departed.

Lord Montfort was extremely fond of jewels, and held that you could not see them to advantage, or fairly judge of their water or colour, except on a beautiful woman. When his wife was in grand toilette, and he was under the same roof, he liked her to call on him in her way to her carriage, that he might see her flashing rivières and tiaras, the lustre of her huge pearls, and the splendour of her emeralds and sapphires and rubies.

'Well, Berengaria,' he said in a playful tone, 'you look divine. Never dine out again in a high dress. It distresses me. Bertolini was the only man who ever caught the tournure of your shoulders, and yet I am not altogether satisfied with his work. So, you are going to dine with that good Neuchatel. Remember me kindly to him. There are few men I like better. He is so sensible, knows so much, and so much of what is going on. I should have liked very much to have dined with him, but he is aware of my unfortunate state. Besides, my dear, if I were better I should not have strength for his dinners. They are really banquets; I cannot stand those ortolans stuffed with truffles and those truffles stuffed with ortolans. Perhaps he will come and dine with us some day off a joint.'

'The Queen of Mesopotamia will be here next week, Simon, and we must really give her what you call a joint, and then we can ask the Neuchatels and a few other people.'

'I was in hopes the dissolution would have carried everybody away,' said Lord Montfort rather woefully. 'I wish the Queen of Mesopotamia were a candidate for some borough; I think she would rather like it.'

'Well, we could not return her, Simon; do not touch on the subject. But what have you got to amuse you to-day?'

'Oh! I shall do very well. I have got the head of the French detective police to dine with me, and another man or two. Besides, I have got here a most amusing book, *Topsy-Turvy;* it comes out in numbers. I like books that come out in numbers, as there is a little suspense, and you cannot deprive yourself of all interest by glancing at the last page of the last volume. I think you must read *Topsy-Turvy,* Berengaria. I am mistaken if you do not hear of it. It is very cynical, which authors, who know a little of the world, are apt to be, and everything is exaggerated, which is another of their faults when they are only a trifle acquainted with manners. A little knowledge of the world is a very dangerous thing, especially in literature. But it is clever, and the man writes a capital style; and style is everything, especially in fiction.'

'And what is the name of the writer, Simon?'

'You never heard of it; I never did; but my secretary, who lives much in Bohemia, and is a member of the Cosmopolitan and knows everything, tells me he has written some things before, but they did not succeed. His name is St. Barbe. I should like to ask him to dinner if I knew how to get at him.'

'Well, adieu! Simon,' and, with an agitated heart, though apparent calmness, she touched his forehead with her lips. 'I expect an unsatisfactory dinner.'

'Adieu! and if you meet poor Ferrars, which I dare say you will, tell him to keep up his spirits. The world is a wheel, and it will all come round right.'

The dinner ought not to have been unsatisfactory, for though there was no novelty among the guests, they were all clever and distinguished persons and united by entire sympathy. Several of the ministers were there, and the Roehamptons, and Mr. Sidney Wilton, and Endymion was also a guest. But the general tone was a little affected and unnatural; forced gaiety, and a levity which displeased Lady Montfort, who fancied she was unhappy because the country was going to be ruined, but whose real cause of dissatisfaction at the bottom of her heart was the affair of 'the family seat.' Her hero, Lord Roehampton,

particularly did not please her to-day. She thought
him flippant and in bad taste, merely because he
would not look dismal and talk gloomily.

'I think we shall do very well,' he said. 'What
cry can be better than that of "Cheap bread?" It
gives one an appetite at once.'

'But the Corn-Law League says your bread will
not be cheap,' said Melchior Neuchatel.

'I wonder whether the League has really any
power in the constituencies,' said Lord Roehampton.
'I doubt it. They may have in time, but then in
the interval trade will revive. I have just been reading Mr. Thornberry's speech. We shall hear more of
that man. You will not be troubled about any of
your seats?' he said, in a lower tone of sympathy,
addressing Mrs. Neuchatel, who was his immediate
neighbour.

'Our seats?' said Mrs. Neuchatel, as if waking
from a dream. 'Oh, I know nothing about them,
nor do I understand why there is a dissolution. I
trust that Parliament will not be dissolved without
voting the money for the observation of the transit of
Venus.'

'I think the Roman Catholic vote will carry us
through,' said a minister.

'Talking of Roman Catholics,' said Mr. Wilton,
'is it true that Penruddock has gone over to Rome?'

'No truth in it,' replied a colleague. 'He has
gone to Rome — there is no doubt of that, and he
has been there some time, but only for distraction.
He has overworked himself.'

'He might have been a Dean if he had been a
practical man,' whispered Lady Montfort to Mr. Neuchatel, 'and on the high road to a bishopric.'

'That is what we want, Lady Montfort,' said Mr. Neuchatel; 'we want a few practical men. If we had a practical man as Chancellor of the Exchequer, we should not be in the scrape in which we now are.'

'It is not likely that Penruddock will leave the Church with a change of government possibly impending. We could do nothing for him with his views, but he will wait for Peel.'

'Oh! Peel will never stand those high-fliers. He put the Church into a Lay Commission during his last government.'

'Penruddock will never give up Anglicanism while there is a chance of becoming a Laud. When that chance vanishes, trust my word, Penruddock will make his bow to the Vatican.'

'Well, I must say,' said Lord Roehampton, 'if I were a clergyman I should be a Roman Catholic.'

'Then you could not marry. What a compliment to Lady Roehampton!'

'Nay; it is because I could not marry that I am not a clergyman.'

Endymion had taken Adriana down to dinner. She looked very well, and was more talkative than usual.

'I fear it will be a very great confusion — this general election,' she said. 'Papa was telling us that you think of being a candidate.'

'I am a candidate, but without a seat to captivate at present,' said Endymion; 'but I am not without hopes of making some arrangement.'

'Well, you must tell me what your colours are.'

'And will you wear them?'

'Most certainly; and I will work you a banner if you be victorious.'

'I think I must win with such a prospect.'

'I hope you will win in everything.'

When the ladies retired, Berengaria came and sat by the side of Lady Roehampton.

'What a dreary dinner!' she said.

'Do you think so?'

'Well, perhaps it was my own fault. Perhaps I am not in good cue, but everything seems to me to go wrong.'

'Things sometimes do go wrong, but then they get right.'

'Well, I do not think anything will ever get right with me.'

'Dear Lady Montfort, how can you say such things? You who have, and have always had, the world at your feet — and always will have.'

'I do not know what you mean by having the world at my feet. It seems to me I have no power whatever — I can do nothing. I am vexed about this business of your brother. Our people are so stupid. They have no resource. When I go to them and ask for a seat, I expect a seat, as I would a shawl at Howell and James' if I ask for one. Instead of that they only make difficulties. What our party wants is a Mr. Tadpole; he out-manœuvres them in every corner.'

'Well, I shall be deeply disappointed — deeply pained,' said Lady Roehampton, 'if Endymion is not in this Parliament, but if we fail I will not utterly despair. I will continue to do what I have done all my life, exert my utmost will and power to advance him.'

'I thought I had will and power,' said Lady Montfort, 'but the conceit is taken out of me. Your

brother was to me a source of great interest, from
the first moment that I knew him. His future was an
object in life and I thought I could mould it. What
a mistake! Instead of making his fortune I have only
dissipated his life.'

'You have been to him the kindest and the most
valuable of friends, and he feels it.'

'It is no use being kind, and I am valuable to no
one. I often think if I disappeared to-morrow no one
would miss me.'

'You are in a morbid mood, dear lady. To-morrow perhaps everything will be right, and then you
will feel that you are surrounded by devoted friends,
and by a husband who adores you.'

Lady Montfort gave a scrutinising glance at Lady
Roehampton as she said this, then shook her head.
'Ah! there it is, dear Myra. You judge from your
own happiness; you do not know Lord Montfort.
You know how I love him, but I am perfectly con-
vinced he prefers my letters to my society.'

'You see what it is to be a Madame de Sévigné,'
said Lady Roehampton, trying to give a playful tone
to the conversation.

'You jest,' said Lady Montfort; 'I am quite serious. No one can deceive me; would that they could!
I have the fatal gift of reading persons, and penetrating motives, however deep or complicated their character, and what I tell you about Lord Montfort is
unhappily too true.'

In the meantime, while this interesting conversation was taking place, the gentleman who had been
the object of Lady Montfort's eulogium, the gentleman who always out-manœuvred her friends in every
corner, was, though it was approaching midnight,

walking up and down Carlton Terrace with an agitated and indignant countenance, and not alone.

'I tell you, Mr. Waldershare, I know it; I have it almost from Lord Beaumaris himself; he has declined to support our man, and no doubt will give his influence to the enemy.'

'I do not believe that Lord Beaumaris has made any engagement whatever.'

'A pretty state of affairs!' exclaimed Mr. Tadpole. 'I do not know what the world has come to. Here are gentlemen expecting high places in the Household, and under-secretaryships of state, and actually giving away our seats to our opponents.'

'There is some family engagement about this seat between the Houses of Beaumaris and Montfort, and Lord Beaumaris, who is a young man, and who does not know as much about these things as you and I do, naturally wants not to make a mistake. But he has promised nothing and nobody. I know, I might almost say I saw the letter, that he wrote to Lord Montfort this day, asking for an interview to-morrow morning on the matter, and Lord Montfort has given him an appointment for to-morrow. This I know.'

'Well, I must leave it to you,' said Mr. Tadpole. 'You must remember what we are fighting for. The constitution is at stake.'

'And the Church,' said Waldershare.

'And the landed interest, you may rely upon it,' said Mr. Tadpole.

'And your Lordship of the Treasury *in posse,* Tadpole. Truly it is a great stake.'

CHAPTER LXXI.

LORD MONTFORT TAKES A HAND.

THE interview between the heads of the two great Houses of Montfort and Beaumaris, on which the fate of a ministry might depend, for it should always be recollected that it was only by a majority of one that Sir Robert Peel had necessitated the dissolution of Parliament, was not carried on exactly in the spirit and with the means which would have occurred to and been practised by the race of Tadpoles and Tapers.

Lord Beaumaris was a very young man, handsome, extremely shy, and one who had only very recently mixed with the circle in which he was born. It was under the influence of Imogene that, in soliciting an interview with Lord Montfort, he had taken for him an unusual, not to say unprecedented step. He had conjured up to himself in Lord Montfort the apparition of a haughty Whig peer, proud of his order, prouder of his party, and not over-prejudiced in favour of one who had quitted those sacred ranks, freezing with arrogant reserve and condescending politeness. In short, Lord Beaumaris was extremely nervous, when ushered by many servants through many chambers, there came forward to receive him the most sweetly mannered gentleman alive, who not only gave him his hand, but retained his guest's, saying, 'We are a sort of cousins, I believe, and ought to have been acquainted before, but you know perhaps my wretched state,' though what that was nobody exactly did know, particularly as Lord Montfort was sometimes seen wading in streams breast-high while throwing his skilful line over the rushing waters. 'I remember your grandfather,' he said, 'and with good cause. He pouched me at Harrow, and it was the largest pouch I ever had. One does not forget the first time one had a five-pound note.'

And then when Lord Beaumaris, blushing and with much hesitation, had stated the occasion of his asking for the interview, that they might settle together about the representation of Northborough in harmony with the old understanding between the families which he trusted would always be maintained, Lord Montfort assured him that he was personally obliged to him by his always supporting Odo, regretted that Odo would retire, and then said if Lord Beaumaris had any brother, cousin, or friend to bring forward, he need hardly say Lord Beaumaris might count upon him. 'I am a Whig,' he continued, 'and so was your father, but I am not particularly pleased with the sayings and doings of my people. Between ourselves, I think they have been in a little too long, and if they do anything very strong, if, for instance, they give office to O'Connell, I should not be at all surprised if I were myself to sit on the cross benches.'

It seems there was no member of the Beaumaris family who wished at this juncture to come forward,

and being assured of this, Lord Montfort remarked
there was a young man of promise who much
wished to enter the House of Commons, not unknown,
he believed, to Lord Beaumaris, and that was Mr.
Ferrars. He was the son of a distinguished man,
now departed, who in his day had been a minister
of state. Lord Montfort was quite ready to support
Mr. Ferrars, if Lord Beaumaris approved of the selection, but he placed himself entirely in his hands.

Lord Beaumaris, blushing, said he quite approved
of the selection; knew Mr. Ferrars very well, and
liked him very much; and if Lord Montfort sanctioned it, would speak to Mr. Ferrars himself. He
believed Mr. Ferrars was a Liberal, but he agreed
with Lord Montfort, that in these days gentlemen
must be all of the same opinion if not on the same
side, and so on. And then they talked of fishing
appropriately to a book of very curious flies that was
on the table, and they agreed if possible to fish together in some famous waters that Lord Beaumaris
had in Hampshire, and then, as he was saying farewell, Lord Montfort added, 'Although I never pay
visits, because really in my wretched state I cannot,
there is no reason why our wives should not know
each other. Will you permit Lady Montfort to have
the honour of paying her respects to Lady Beaumaris?'

Talleyrand or Metternich could not have conducted
an interview more skilfully. But these were just the
things that Lord Montfort did not dislike doing. His
great good nature was not disturbed by a single inconvenient circumstance, and he enjoyed the sense of his
adroitness.

The same day the cards of Lord and Lady Montfort were sent to Piccadilly Terrace, and on the next

day the cards of Lord and Lady Beaumaris were returned to Montfort House. And on the following day, Lady Montfort, accompanied by Lady Roehampton, would find Lady Beaumaris at home, and after a charming visit, in which Lady Montfort, though natural to the last degree, displayed every quality which could fascinate even a woman, when she put her hand in that of Imogene to say farewell, added, 'I am delighted to find that we are cousins.'

A few days after this interview, Parliament was dissolved. It was the middle of a wet June, and the season received its *coup de grâce*. Although Endymion had no rival, and apparently no prospect of a contest, his labours as a candidate were not slight. The constituency was numerous, and every member of it expected to be called upon. To each Mr. Ferrars had to expound his political views, and to receive from each a cordial assurance or a churlish criticism. All this he did and endured, accompanied by about fifty of the principal inhabitants, members of his committee, who insisted on never leaving his side, and prompting him at every new door which he entered with contradictory reports of the political opinions of the indwellers, or confidential intimations how they were to be managed and addressed.

The principal and most laborious incidents of the day were festivals which they styled luncheons, when the candidate and the ambulatory committee were quartered on some principal citizen with an elaborate banquet of several courses, and in which Mr. Ferrars' health was always pledged in sparkling bumpers. After the luncheon came two or three more hours of what was called canvassing; then, in a state of horrible repletion, the fortunate candidate, who had no contest, had to dine with another principal citizen, with real turtle soup, and gigantic turbots, *entrées* in the shape of volcanic curries, and rigid venison, sent as a compliment by a neighbouring peer. This last ceremony was necessarily hurried, as Endymion had every night to address in some ward a body of the electors.

When this had been going on for a few days, the borough was suddenly placarded with posting bills in colossal characters of true blue, warning the Conservative electors not to promise their votes, as a distinguished candidate of the right sort would certainly come forward. At the same time there was a paragraph in a local journal that a member of a noble family, illustrious in the naval annals of the country, would if sufficiently supported, solicit the suffrages of the independent electors.

'We think, by the allusion to the navy, that it must be Mr. Hood of Acreley,' said Lord Beaumaris' agent to Mr. Ferrars, 'but he has not the ghost of a chance. I will ride over and see him in the course of the day.'

This placard was of course Mr. Tadpole's last effort, but that worthy gentleman soon forgot his mortification about Northborough in the general triumph of his party. The Whigs were nowhere, though Mr. Ferrars was returned without opposition, and in the month of August, still wondering at the rapid, strange, and even mysterious incidents, that had so suddenly and so swiftly changed his position and prospects in life, took his seat in that House in whose galleries he had so long humbly attended as the private secretary of a cabinet minister.

His friends were still in office, though the country had sent up a majority of ninety against them, and

Endymion took his seat behind the Treasury bench, and exactly behind Lord Roehampton. The debate on the address was protracted for three nights, and then they divided at three o'clock in the morning, and then all was over. Lord Roehampton, who had vindicated the ministry with admirable vigour and felicity, turned round to Endymion, and smiling said in the sweetest tone, 'I did not enlarge on our greatest feat, namely, that we had governed the country for two years without a majority. Peel would never have had the pluck to do that.'

Notwithstanding the backslidings of Lord Beaumaris and the unprincipled conduct of Mr. Waldershare, they were both rewarded as the latter gentleman projected — Lord Beaumaris accepted a high post in the Household, and Mr. Waldershare was appointed Under-Secretary of State for Foreign Affairs. Tadpole was a little glum about it, but it was inevitable. 'That fact is,' as the world agreed, 'Lady Beaumaris is the only Tory woman. They have nobody who can receive except her.'

The changes in the House of Commons were still greater than those in the administration. Never were so many new members, and Endymion watched them, during the first days, and before the debate on the address, taking the oaths at the table in batches with much interest. Mr. Bertie Tremaine was returned, and his brother, Mr. Tremaine Bertie. Job Thornberry was member for a manufacturing town, with which he was not otherwise connected. Hortensius was successful, and Mr. Vigo for a metropolitan borough, but what pleased Endymion more than anything was the return of his valued friend Trenchard, who a short time before had acceded to the paternal estate; all these gentlemen were Liberals, and were destined to sit on the same side of the House as Endymion.

After the fatal vote, the Whigs all left town. Society in general had been previously greatly dispersed, but Parliament had to remain sitting until October.

'We are going to Princedown,' Lady Montfort said one day to Endymion, 'and we had counted on seeing you there, but I have been thinking much of your position since, and I am persuaded, that we must sacrifice pleasure to higher objects. This is really a crisis in your life, and much, perhaps everything, depends on your not making a mistake now. What I want to see you is a great statesman. This is a political economy Parliament, both sides alike thinking of the price of corn and all that. Finance and commerce are everybody's subjects, and are most convenient to make speeches about for men who cannot speak French and who have had no education. Real politics are the possession and distribution of power. I want to see you give your mind to foreign affairs. There you will have no rivals. There are a great many subjects which Lord Roehampton cannot take up, but which you could very properly, and you will have always the benefit of his counsel, and, when necessary, his parliamentary assistance; but foreign affairs are not to be mastered by mere reading. Bookworms do not make chancellors of state. You must become acquainted with the great actors in the great scene. There is nothing like personal knowledge of the individuals who control the high affairs. That has made the fortune of Lord Roehampton. What I think you ought to do, without doubt ought to do, is to take advantage of this long interval before the meeting of Parliament, and go to Paris. Paris is now the capital of diplomacy. It is not the best time of the year to go there, but you will meet a great many people of the diplomatic world, and if the opportunity offers, you can vary the scene, and go to some baths which princes and ministers frequent. The Count of Ferroll is now at Paris, and minister for his court. You know him; that is well. But he is my greatest friend, and, as you know, we habitually correspond. He will do everything for you, I am sure, for my sake. It is not pleasant to be separated; I do not wish to conceal that; I should have enjoyed your society at Princedown, but I am doing right, and you will some day thank me for it. We must soften the pang of separation by writing to each other every day, so when we meet again it will only be as if we had parted yesterday. Besides — who knows? — I may run over myself to Paris in the winter. My lord always liked Paris; the only place he ever did, but I am not very sanguine he will go; he is so afraid of being asked to dinner by our ambassador.'

CHAPTER LXXII.

ENDYMION IN PARIS.

N ALL lives, the highest and the humblest, there is a crisis in the formation of character, and in the bent of the disposition. It comes from many causes, and from some which on the surface are apparently even trivial. It may be a book, a speech, a sermon; a man or a woman; a great misfortune or a burst of prosperity. But the result is the same; a sudden revelation to ourselves of our secret purpose, and a recognition of our perhaps long shadowed, but now masterful convictions.

A crisis of this kind occurred to Endymion the day when he returned to his chambers, after having taken the oaths and his seat in the House of Commons. He felt the necessity of being alone. For nearly the last three months he had been the excited actor in a strange and even mysterious drama. There had been for him no time to reflect; all he could aim at was to comprehend, and if possible control, the present and urgent contingency; he had been called upon, almost unceasingly, to do or to say something sudden and unexpected; and it was only now, when the crest of the ascent had been reached, that he could look around him and consider the new world opening to his gaze.

The greatest opportunity that can be offered to an Englishman was now his — a seat in the House of Commons. It was his almost in the first bloom of youth, and yet after advantageous years of labour and political training, and it was combined with a material independence on which he never could have counted. A love of power, a passion for distinction, a noble pride, which had been native to his early disposition, but which had apparently been crushed by the enormous sorrows and misfortunes of his childhood, and which had vanished, as it were, before the sweetness of that domestic love which had been the solace of his adversity, now again stirred their dim and mighty forms in his renovated, and, as it were, inspired consciousness. 'If this has happened at twenty-two,' thought Endymion, 'what may not occur if the average life of man be allotted to me? At any rate, I will never think of anything else. I have a purpose in life, and I will fulfil it. It is a charm that its accomplishment would be the most grateful result to the two beings I most love in the world.'

So when Lady Montfort shortly after opened her views to Endymion as to his visiting Paris, and his purpose in so doing, the seeds were thrown on a willing soil, and he embraced her counsels with the deepest interest. His intimacy with the Count of Ferroll was the completing event of this epoch of his life.

Their acquaintance had been slight in England, for after the Montfort Tournament the Count had been appointed to Paris, where he was required; but he received Endymion with a cordiality which contrasted with his usual demeanour, which, though frank, was somewhat cynical.

'This is not a favourable time to visit Paris,' he said, 'so far as society is concerned. There is some business stirring in the diplomatic world, which has re-assembled the fraternity for the moment, and the King is at St. Cloud, but you may make some acquaintances which may be desirable, and at any rate look about you and clear the ground for the coming season. I do not despair of our dear friend coming over in the winter. It is one of the hopes that keep me alive. What a woman! You may count yourself fortunate in having such a friend. I do. I am not particularly fond of female society. Women chatter too much. But I prefer the society of a firstrate woman to that of any man; and Lady Montfort is a firstrate woman—I think the greatest since Louise of Savoy; infinitely beyond the Princesse d'Ursins.'

The business that was then stirring in the diplomatic world, at a season when the pleasures of Parisian society could not distract him, gave Endymion a rare opportunity of studying that singular class of human beings which is accustomed to consider states and nations as individuals, and speculate on their quarrels and misunderstandings, and the remedies which they require, in a tongue peculiar to themselves, and in language which often conveys a meaning exactly opposite to that which it seems to express. Diplomacy is hospitable, and a young Englishman of graceful mien, well introduced, and a member of the House of Commons—that awful assembly which produces those dreaded blue books which strike terror in the boldest of foreign statesmen—was not only received, but courted, in the interesting circle in which Endymion found himself.

There he encountered men grey with the fame and wisdom of half a century of deep and lofty action, men who had struggled with the first Napoleon, and had sat in the Congress of Vienna; others, hardly less celebrated, who had been suddenly borne to high places by the revolutionary wave of 1830, and who had justly retained their exalted posts when so many competitors with an equal chance had long ago, with equal justice, subsided into the obscurity from which they ought never to have emerged. Around these chief personages were others not less distinguished by their abilities, but a more youthful generation, who knew how to wait, and were always prepared or preparing for the inevitable occasion when it arrived — fine and trained writers, who could interpret in sentences of graceful adroitness the views of their chiefs; or sages in precedents, walking dictionaries of diplomacy, and masters of every treaty; and private secretaries reading human nature at a glance, and collecting every shade of opinion for the use and guidance of their principals.

Whatever their controversies in the morning, their critical interviews and their secret alliances, all were smiles and graceful badinage at the banquet and the reception; as if they had only come to Paris to show their brilliant uniforms, their Golden Fleeces and their grand crosses, and their broad ribbons with more tints than the iris.

'I will not give them ten years,' said the Count of Ferroll, lighting his cigarette, and addressing Endymion on their return from one of these assemblies; 'I sometimes think hardly five.'

'But where will the blow come from?'

'Here; there is no movement in Europe except in France, and here it will always be a movement of subversion.'

'A pretty prospect!'

'The sooner you realise it the better. The system here is supported by journalists and bankers; two influential classes, but the millions care for neither; rather, I should say, dislike both.'

'Will the change affect Europe?'

'Inevitably. You rightly say Europe, for that is a geographical expression. There is no State in Europe; I exclude your own country, which belongs to every division of the globe, and is fast becoming more commercial than political, and I exclude Russia, for she is essentially oriental, and her future will be entirely the East.'

'But there is Germany!'

'Where? I cannot find it on the maps. Germany is divided into various districts, and when there is a war, they are ranged on different sides. Notwithstanding our reviews and annual encampments, Germany is practically as weak as Italy. We have some kingdoms who are allowed to play at being firstrate powers; but it is mere play. They no more command events than the King of Naples or the Duke of Modena.'

'Then is France periodically to overrun Europe?'

'So long as it continues to be merely Europe.'

A close intimacy occurred between Endymion and the Count of Ferroll. He not only became a permanent guest at the official residence, but when the Conference broke up, the Count invited Endymion to be his companion to some celebrated baths, where they would meet not only many of his late distinguished colleagues, but their imperial and royal masters, seeking alike health and relaxation at this famous rendezvous.

'You will find it of the first importance in public life,' said the Count of Ferroll, 'to know personally those who are carrying on the business of the world; so much depends on the character of an individual, his habits of thought, his prejudices, his superstitions, his social weaknesses, his health. Conducting affairs without this advantage is, in effect, an affair of stationery; it is pens and paper who are in communication, not human beings.'

The brother-in-law of Lord Roehampton was a sort of personage. It was very true that distinguished man was no longer minister, but he had been minister for a long time, and had left a great name. Foreigners rarely know more than one English minister at a time, but they compensated for their ignorance of the aggregate body by even exaggerating the qualities of the individual with whom they are acquainted. Lord Roehampton had conducted the affairs of his country always in a courteous, but still in a somewhat haughty spirit. He was easy and obliging, and conciliatory in little matters, but where the credit, or honour, or large interests of England were concerned, he acted with conscious authority. On the continent of Europe, though he sometimes incurred the depreciation of the smaller minds, whose self-love he may not have sufficiently spared, by the higher spirits he was feared and admired, and they knew, when he gave his whole soul to an affair, that they were dealing with a master.

Endymion was presented to emperors and kings, and he made his way with these exalted personages.

He found them different from what he had expected. He was struck by their intimate acquaintance with affairs, and by the serenity of their judgment. The life was a pleasant as well as an interesting one. Where there are crowned heads, there are always some charming women. Endymion found himself in a delightful circle. Long days and early hours, and a beautiful country, renovate the spirit as well as the physical frame. Excursions to romantic forests, and visits to picturesque ruins, in the noon of summer, are enchanting, especially with princesses for your companions, bright and accomplished. Yet, notwithstanding some distractions, Endymion never omitted writing to Lady Montfort every day.

CHAPTER LXXIII.

'A Crust of Bread and Liberty.'

THE season at Paris, which commenced towards the end of the year, was a lively one, and especially interesting to Endymion, who met there a great many of his friends. After his visit to the baths he had travelled alone for a few weeks, and saw some famous places of which he had long heard. A poet was then sitting on the throne of Bavaria, and was realising his dreams in the creation of an ideal capital. The Black Forest is a land of romance. He saw Walhalla, too, crowning the Danube with the genius of Germany, as mighty as the stream itself. Pleasant it is to wander among the quaint cities here clustering together: Nuremberg with all its ancient art, imperial Augsburg, and Würzburg with its priestly palace, beyond the splendour of many kings. A summer in Suabia is a great joy.

But what a contrast to the Rue de la Paix, bright and vivacious, in which he now finds himself, and the companion of the Neuchatel family! Endymion had only returned to Paris the previous evening, and the Neuchatels had preceded him by a week; so they had seen everybody and could tell him everything.

Lord and Lady Beaumaris were there, and Mrs. Rodney their companion, her husband detained in London by some mysterious business; it was thought a seat in Parliament, which Mr. Tadpole had persuaded him might be secured on a vacancy occasioned by a successful petition. They had seen the Count of Ferroll, who was going to dine with them that day, and Endymion was invited to meet him. It was Adriana's first visit to Paris, and she seemed delighted with it; but Mrs. Neuchatel preferred the gay capital when it was out of season. Mr. Neuchatel himself was always in high spirits,—sanguine and self-satisfied. He was an Orleanist, had always been so, and sympathised with the apparently complete triumph of his principles—'real liberal principles, no nonsense; there was more gold in the Bank of France than in any similar establishment in Europe. After all, wealth is the test of the welfare of a people, and the test of wealth is the command of the precious metals. Eh! Mr. Member of Parliament?' And his eye flashed fire and he seemed to smack his lips at the very thought and mention of these delicious circumstances.

They were in a jeweller's shop, and Mrs. Neuchatel was choosing a trinket for a wedding present. She seemed infinitely distressed. 'What do you think of this, Adriana? It is simple and in good taste. I should like it for myself, and yet I fear it might not be thought fine enough.'

'This is pretty, mamma, and new,' and she held before her mother a bracelet of much splendour.

'Oh, no! that will never do, dear Adriana; they will say we are purse-proud.'

'I am afraid they will always say that, mamma.' and she sighed.

'It is a long time since we all separated,' said Endymion to Adriana.

'Months! Mr. Sidney Wilton said you were the first runaway. I think you were quite right. Your new life now will be fresh to you. If you had remained, it would only have been associated with defeat and discomfiture.'

'I am so happy to be in Parliament, that I do not think I could ever associate such a life with discomfiture.'

'Does it make you very happy?' said Adriana, looking at him rather earnestly.

'Very happy.'

'I am glad of that.'

The Neuchatels had a house at Paris — one of the fine hotels of the First Empire. It was inhabited generally by one of the nephews, but it was always ready to receive them with every luxury and every comfort. But Mrs. Neuchatel herself particularly disliked Paris, and she rarely accompanied her husband in his frequent but brief visits to the gay city. She had yielded on this occasion to the wish of Adriana, whom she had endeavoured to bring up in a wholesome prejudice against French taste and fashions.

The dinner to-day was exquisite, in a chamber of many-coloured marbles, and where there was no marble there was gold, and when the banquet was over, they repaired to saloons hung with satin of a delicate tint which exhibited to perfection a choice collection of Greuze and Vanloo. Mr. Sidney Wilton dined there, as well as the Count of Ferroll, some of the French ministers, and two or three illustrious Orleanist celebrities of literature, who acknowledged and emulated the matchless conversational powers of

Mrs. Neuchatel. Lord and Lady Beaumaris and Mrs. Rodney completed the party.

Sylvia was really peerless. She was by birth half a Frenchwoman, and she compensated for her deficiency in the other moiety, by a series of exquisite costumes, in which she mingled with the spell-born fashion of France her own singular genius in dress. She spoke not much, but looked prettier than ever; a little haughty, and now and then faintly smiling. What was most remarkable about her was her convenient and complete want of memory. Sylvia had no past. She could not have found her way to Warwick Street to save her life. She conversed with Endymion with ease and not without gratification, but from all she said, you might have supposed that they had been born in the same sphere, and always lived in the same sphere, that sphere being one peopled by duchesses and countesses and gentlemen of fashion and ministers of state.

Lady Beaumaris was different from her sister almost in all respects, except in beauty, though her beauty even was of a higher style than that of Mrs. Rodney. Imogene was quite natural, though refined. She had a fine disposition. All her impulses were good and naturally noble. She had a greater intellectual range than Sylvia, and was much more cultivated. This she owed to her friendship with Mr. Waldershare, who was entirely devoted to her, and whose main object in life was to make everything contribute to her greatness. 'I hope he will come here next week,' she said to Endymion. 'I heard from him to-day. He is at Venice. And he gives me such lovely descriptions of that city, that I shall never rest till I have seen it and glided in a gondola.

'Well, that you can easily do.'

'Not so easily. It will never do to interfere with my lord's hunting—and when hunting is over there is always something else—Newmarket, or the House of Lords, or rook-shooting.'

'I must say there is something delightful about Paris, which you meet nowhere else,' said Mr. Sidney Wilton to Endymion. 'For my part, it has the same effect on me as a bottle of champagne. When I think of what we were doing this time last year—those dreadful November cabinets—I shudder! By-the-bye, the Count of Ferroll says there is a chance of Lady Montfort coming here; have you heard anything?'

Endymion knew all about it, but he was too discreet even to pretend to exclusive information on that head. He thought it might be true, but supposed it depended on my lord.

'Oh! Montfort will never come. He will bolt at the last moment when the hall is full of packages. Their very sight will frighten him, and he will steal down to Princedown and read *Don Quixote*.'

Sidney Wilton was quite right. Lady Montfort arrived without her lord. 'He threw me over almost as we were getting into the carriage, and I had quite given it up when dear Lady Roehampton came to my rescue. She wanted to see her brother, and—here we are.'

The arrival of these two great ladies gave a stimulant to gaieties which were already excessive. The court and the ministers rivalled the balls and the banquets which were profusely offered by the ambassadors and bankers. Even the great faubourg relaxed, and its halls of high ceremony and mysterious splendour were open to those who in London had extended to many of their order a graceful and abounding hospitality. It was with difficulty, however, that they persuaded Lady Montfort to honour with her presence the embassy of her own court.

'I dined with those people once,' she said to Endymion, 'but I confess when I thought of those dear Granvilles, their *entrées* stuck in my throat.'

There was, however, no lack of diplomatic banquets for the successor of Louise of Savoy. The splendid hotel of the Count of Ferroll was the scene of festivals not to be exceeded in Paris, and all in honour of this wondrous dame. Sometimes they were feasts, sometimes they were balls, sometimes they were little dinners, consummate and select, sometimes large receptions, multifarious and amusing. Her pleasure was asked every morn, and whenever she was disengaged, she issued orders to his devoted household. His boxes at opera or play were at her constant disposal; his carriages were at her command, and she rode, in his society, the most beautiful horses in Paris.

The Count of Ferroll had wished that both ladies should have taken up their residence at his mansion.

'But I think we had better not,' said Lady Montfort to Myra. 'After all, there is nothing like "my crust of bread and liberty," and so I think we had better stay at the Bristol.'

CHAPTER LXXIV.

Berengaria in a Temper.

GO AND talk to Adriana,' said Lady Roehampton to her brother. 'It seems to me you never speak to her.'

Endymion looked a little confused.

'Lady Montfort has plenty of friends here,' his sister continued. 'You are not wanted, and you should always remember those who have been our earliest and kindest friends.'

There was something in Lady Roehampton's words and look which rather jarred upon him. Anything like reproach or dissatisfaction from those lips and from that countenance, sometimes a little anxious but always affectionate, not to say adoring, confused and even agitated him. He was tempted to reply, but, exercising successfully the self-control which was the result rather of his life than of his nature, he said nothing, and, in obedience to the intimation, immediately approached Miss Neuchatel.

About this time Waldershare arrived at Paris, full of magnificent dreams which he called plans. He was delighted with his office; it was much the most

important in the government, and more important because it was not in the cabinet. Well managed, it
was power without responsibility. He explained to
Lady Beaumaris that an Under-Secretary of State for
Foreign Affairs, with his chief in the House of Lords,
was 'master of the situation.' What the situation
was, and what the Under-Secretary was to master, he
did not yet deign to inform Imogene; but her trust
in Waldershare was implicit, and she repeated to
Lord Beaumaris, and to Mrs. Rodney, with an air of
mysterious self-complacency, that Mr. Waldershare
was 'master of the situation.' Mrs. Rodney fancied
that this was the correct and fashionable title of an
under-secretary of state. Mr. Waldershare was going
to make a collection of portraits of Under-Secretaries
for Foreign Affairs whose chiefs had been in the
House of Lords. It would be a collection of the most
eminent statesmen that England had ever produced.
For the rest, during his Italian tour, Waldershare
seemed to have conducted himself with distinguished
discretion, and had been careful not to solicit an
audience of the Duke of Modena in order to renew
his oath of allegiance.

When Lady Montfort successfully tempted Lady
Roehampton to be her travelling companion to Paris,
the contemplated visit was to have been a short one
— 'a week, perhaps ten days at the outside.' The
outside had been not inconsiderably passed, and yet
the beautiful Berengaria showed no disposition of returning to England. Myra was uneasy at her own protracted absence from her lord, and having made a last,
but fruitless effort to induce Lady Montfort to accompany her, she said one day to Endymion, 'I think I
must ask you to take me back. And indeed you

ought to be with my lord some little time before the meeting of Parliament.'

Endymion was really of the same opinion, though he was conscious of the social difficulty which he should have to encounter in order to effect his purpose. Occasionally a statesman in opposition is assisted by the same private secretary who was his confidant when in office; but this is not always the case—perhaps not even generally. In the present instance, the principal of Lord Roehampton's several secretaries had been selected from the permanent clerks in the Foreign Office itself, and therefore when his chief retired from his official duties, the private secretary resumed his previous post, an act which necessarily terminated all relations between himself and the late minister, save those of private, though often still intimate, acquaintance.

Now, one of the great objects of Lady Roehampton for a long time had been, that her brother should occupy a confidential position near her husband. The desire had originally been shared, and even warmly, by Lady Montfort; but the unexpected entrance of Endymion into the House of Commons had raised a technical difficulty in this respect which seemed to terminate the cherished prospect. Myra, however, was resolved not to regard these technical difficulties, and was determined to establish at once the intimate relations she desired between her husband and her brother. This purpose had been one of the principal causes which induced her to accompany Lady Montfort to Paris. She wanted to see Endymion, to see what he was about, and to prepare him for the future which she contemplated.

The view which Lady Montfort took of these matters was very different from that of Lady Roehampton. Lady Montfort was in her riding habit, leaning back in an easy chair, with her whip in one hand and the *Charivari* in the other, and she said, 'Are you not going to ride to-day, Endymion?'

'I think not. I wanted to talk to you a little about my plans, Lady Montfort.'

'Your plans? Why should you have any plans?'

'Well, Lady Roehampton is about to return to England, and she proposes I should go with her.'

'Why?'

And then Endymion entered into the whole case, the desirableness of being with Lord Roehampton before the meeting of Parliament, of assisting him, working with him, acting for him, and all the other expedient circumstances of the situation.

Lady Montfort said nothing. Being of an eager nature, it was rather her habit to interrupt those who addressed her, especially on matters she deemed disagreeable. Her husband used to say, 'Berengaria is a charming companion, but if she would only listen a little more, she would have so much more to tell me.' On the present occasion, Endymion had no reason to complain that he had not a fair opportunity of stating his views and wishes. She was quite silent, changed colour occasionally, bit her beautiful lip, and gently but constantly lashed her beautiful riding habit. When he paused, she inquired if he had done, and he assenting, she said, 'I think the whole thing preposterous. What can Lord Roehampton have to do before the meeting of Parliament? He has not got to write the Queen's speech. The only use of being in opposition is that we may enjoy ourselves. The best thing that Lord Roehampton and all his friends can do is to travel for a couple of years. Ask the Count of Ferroll what he thinks of the situation. He will tell you that he never knew one more hopeless. Taxes and tariffs — that's the future of England, and, so far as I can see, it may go on for ever. The government here desires nothing better than what they call Peace. What they mean by peace is agiotage, shares at a premium, and bubble companies. The whole thing is corrupt, as it ever must be when government is in the hands of a mere middle class, and that, too, a limited one; but it may last hopelessly long, and in the meantime, *Vive la bagatelle!* '

'These are very different views from those which, I had understood, were to guide us in opposition,' said Endymion, amazed.

'There is no opposition,' rejoined Lady Montfort, somewhat tartly. 'For a real opposition there must be a great policy. If your friend, Lord Roehampton, when he was settling the Levant, had only seized upon Egypt, we should have been somewhere. Now we are the party who wanted to give, not even cheap bread to the people, but only cheaper bread. Faugh!'

'Well, I do not think the occupation of Egypt in the present state of our finances' ——

'Do not talk to me about "the present state of our finances." You are worse than Mr. Sidney Wilton. The Count of Ferroll says that a ministry which is upset by its finances must be essentially imbecile. And that, too, in England — the richest country in the world!'

'Well, I think the state of the finances had something to do with the French Revolution,' observed Endymion quietly.

'The French Revolution! You might as well talk of the fall of the Roman Empire. The French Revolution was founded on nonsense — on the rights of man; when all sensible people in every country are now agreed that man has no rights whatever.'

'But, dearest Lady Montfort,' said Endymion, in a somewhat deprecating tone, 'about my returning; for that is the real subject on which I wish to trouble you.'

'You have made up your mind to return,' she replied. 'What is the use of consulting me with a foregone conclusion? I suppose you think it a compliment.'

'I should be very sorry to do anything without consulting you,' said Endymion.

'The worst person in the world to consult,' said Lady Montfort, impatiently. 'If you want advice, you had better go to your sister. Men who are guided by their sisters seldom make very great mistakes. They are generally so prudent; and, I must say, I think a prudent man quite detestable.'

Endymion turned pale, his lips quivered. What might have been the winged words they would have sent forth it is impossible to say, for at that moment the door opened, and the servant announced that her ladyship's horse was at the door. Lady Montfort jumped up quickly, and saying, 'Well, I suppose I shall see you before you go,' disappeared.

CHAPTER LXXV.

A Sisterly Hint.

N THE meantime, Lady Roehampton was paying her farewell visit to her former pupil. They were alone, and Adriana was hanging on her neck and weeping.

'We were so happy,' she murmured.

'And are so happy, and will be,' said Myra.

'I feel I shall never be happy again,' sighed Adriana.

'You deserve to be the happiest of human beings, and you will be.'

'Never, never!'

Lady Roehampton could say no more; she pressed her friend to her heart, and left the room in silence.

When she arrived at her hotel, her brother was leaving the house. His countenance was disquieted; he did not greet her with that mantling sunniness of aspect which was natural to him when they met.

'I have made all my farewells,' she said; 'and how have you been getting on?' And she invited him to re-enter the hotel.

'I am ready to depart at this moment,' he said somewhat fiercely, 'and was only thinking how I could extricate myself from that horrible dinner to-day at the Count of Ferroll's.'

'Well, that is not difficult,' said Myra; 'you can write a note here if you like, at once. I think you must have seen quite enough of the Count of Ferroll and his friends.'

Endymion sat down at the table, and announced his intended non-appearance at the Count's dinner, for it could not be called an excuse. When he had finished, his sister said —

'Do you know, we were near having a travelling companion to-morrow?'

He looked up with a blush, for he fancied she was alluding to some previous scheme of Lady Montfort. 'Indeed!' he said, 'and who?'

'Adriana.'

'Adriana!' he repeated, somewhat relieved; 'would she leave her family?'

'She had a fancy, and I am sure I do not know any companion I could prefer to her. She is the only person of whom I could truly say, that every time I see her, I love her more.'

'She seemed to like Paris very much,' said Endymion a little embarrassed.

'The first part of her visit,' said Lady Roehampton, 'she liked it amazingly. But my arrival and Lady Montfort's, I fear, broke up their little parties. You were a great deal with the Neuchatels before we came?'

'They are such a good family,' said Endymion; 'so kind, so hospitable, such true friends. And Mr. Neuchatel himself is one of the shrewdest men that probably ever lived. I like talking with him, or rather, I like to hear him talk.'

'Oh, Endymion!' said Lady Roehampton, 'if you were to marry Adriana, my happiness would be complete.'

'Adriana will never marry,' said Endymion; 'she is afraid of being married for her money. I know twenty men who would marry her, if they thought there was a chance of being accepted; and the best man, Eusford, did make her an offer—that I know. And where could she find a match more suitable?—high rank, and large estate, and a man that everybody speaks well of.'

'Adriana will never marry except for the affections; there you are right, Endymion; she must love and she must be loved; but that is not very unreasonable in a person who is young, pretty, accomplished, and intelligent.'

'She is all that,' said Endymion moodily.

'And she loves you,' said Lady Roehampton.

Endymion rather started, looked up for a moment at his sister, and then withdrew as hastily an agitated glance, and then with his eyes on the ground said, in a voice half murmuring, and yet scoffingly: 'I should like to see Mr. Neuchatel's face were I to ask permission to marry his daughter. I suppose he would not kick me downstairs; that is out of fashion; but he certainly would never ask me to dinner again, and that would be a sacrifice.'

'You jest, Endymion; I am not jesting.'

'There are some matters that can only be treated as a jest; and my marriage with Miss Neuchatel is one.'

'It would make you one of the most powerful men in England,' said his sister.

'Other impossible events would do the same.'

'It is not impossible; it is very possible,' said his sister, 'believe me, trust in me. The happiness of their daughter is more precious to the Neuchatels than even their fortune.'

'I do not see why, at my age, I should be in such a hurry to marry,' said Endymion.

'You cannot marry too soon, if by so doing you obtain the great object of life. Early marriages are to be deprecated, especially for men, because they are too frequently imprudent; but when a man can marry while he is young, and at once realise, by so doing, all the results which successful time may bring to him, he should not hesitate.'

'I hesitate very much,' said Endymion. 'I should hesitate very much, even if affairs were as promising as I think you may erroneously assume.'

'But you must not hesitate, Endymion. We must never forget the great object for which we two live, for which, I believe, we were born twins — to rebuild our house; to raise it from poverty, and ignominy, and misery and squalid shame, to the rank and position which we demand, and which we believe we deserve. Did I hesitate when an offer of marriage was made to me, and the most unexpected that could have occurred? True it is, I married the best and greatest of men, but I did not know that when I accepted his hand. I married him for your sake, I married him for my own sake, for the sake of the house of Ferrars, which I wished to release and raise from its pit of desolation. I married him to secure for us both that opportunity for our qualities which they had lost, and which, I believed, if enjoyed, would render us powerful and great.'

Endymion rose from his seat and kissed his sister.

'So long as you live,' he said, 'we shall never be ignominious.'

'Yes, but I am nothing; I am not a man, I am not a Ferrars. The best of me is that I may be a transient help to you. It is you who must do the deed. I am wearied of hearing you described as Lady Roehampton's brother, or Lord Roehampton's brother-in-law. I shall never be content till you are greater than we are, and there is but one and only one immediate way of accomplishing it — it is by this marriage, and a marriage with whom? with an angelic being!'

'You take me somewhat by surprise, Myra. My thoughts have not been upon this matter. I cannot fairly describe myself at this moment as a marrying man.'

'I know what you mean. You have female friendships, and I approve of them. They are invaluable to youth, and you have been greatly favoured in this respect. They have been a great assistance to you; beware lest they become a hindrance. A few years of such feelings in a woman's life are a blazoned page, and when it is turned she has many other chapters, though they may not be as brilliant or adorned. But these few years in a man's life may be, and in your case certainly would be, the very marrow of his destiny. During the last five or six years, ever since our emancipation, there has been a gradual but continuous development in your life. All has been preparatory for a position which you have acquired. That position may lead to anything — in your case, I will still believe, to everything — but there must be no faltering. Having crossed the Alps, you must not find a Capua. I speak to you as I have not spoken to you of late, because it was not necessary. But here is an opportunity which must not be lost. I feel half inspired, as when we parted in our misery at Hurstley, and I bade you, poor and obscure, go forth and conquer the world.'

Late on the night of the day, their last day at Paris, on which this conversation took place, Endymion received a note in a well-known handwriting, and it ran thus:

'If it be any satisfaction to you to know that you made me very unhappy by not dining here to-day, you may be gratified. I am very unhappy. I know that I was unkind this morning, and rude, but as my anger was occasioned by your leaving me, my conduct might annoy but surely could not mortify you. I shall see you to-morrow, however early you may depart, as I cannot let your dear sister leave Paris without my embracing her.

'Your faithful friend,

'BERENGARIA.'

CHAPTER LXXVI.

DWELLERS ON 'THE MOUNTAIN.'

IN OLD days, it was the habit to think and say that the House of Commons was an essentially 'queer place,' which no one could understand until he was a member of it. It may, perhaps, be doubted whether that somewhat mysterious quality still altogether attaches to that assembly. 'Our own Reporter,' has invaded it in all its purlieus. No longer content with giving an account of the speeches of its members, he is not satisfied unless he describes their persons, their dress, and their characteristic mannerisms. He tells us how they dine, even the wines and dishes which they favour, and follows them into the very mysteries of their smoking-room. And yet there is perhaps a certain fine sense of the feelings, and opinions, and humours of this assembly, which cannot be acquired by hasty notions and necessarily superficial remarks, but must be the result of long and patient observation, and of that quick sympathy with human sentiment, in all its classes, which is involved in the possession of that inestimable quality styled tact.

When Endymion Ferrars first took his seat in the House of Commons, it still fully possessed its character of enigmatic tradition. It had been thought that this, in a great degree, would have been dissipated by the Reform Act of 1832, which suddenly introduced into the hallowed precinct a number of individuals whose education, manners, modes of thought, were different from those of the previous inhabitants, and in some instances, and in some respects, quite contrary to them. But this was not so. After a short time it was observed that the old material, though at first much less in quantity, had leavened the new mass; that the tone of the former House was imitated and adopted, and that at the end of five years, about the time Endymion was returned to Parliament, much of its serene, and refined, and even classical character had been recovered.

For himself, he entered the chamber with a certain degree of awe, which, with use, diminished, but never entirely disappeared. The scene was one over which even his boyhood had long mused, and it was associated with all those traditions of genius, eloquence, and power that charm and inspire youth. His practical acquaintance with the forms and habits of the House from his customary attendance on their debates as private secretary to a cabinet minister, was of great advantage to him, and restrained that excitement which dangerously accompanies us when we enter into a new life, and especially a life of such deep and thrilling interests and such large proportions. This result was also assisted by his knowledge, at least by sight, of a large proportion of the old members, and by his personal and sometimes intimate acquaintance with those of his own party. There was much in his position, therefore, to soften that awkward feeling of being a freshman, which is always embarrassing.

He took his place on the second bench of the opposition side of the House, and nearly behind Lord Roehampton. Mr. Bertie Tremaine, whom Endymion encountered in the lobby as he was escaping to dinner, highly disapproved of this step. He had greeted Endymion with affable condescension. 'You made your first mistake to-night, my dear Ferrars. You should have taken your seat below the gangway and near me, on the Mountain. You, like myself, are a man of the future.'

'I am a member of the opposition. I do not suppose it signifies much where I sit.'

'On the contrary, it signifies everything. After this great Tory reaction there is nothing to be done now by speeches, and, in all probability, very little that can be effectually opposed. Much, therefore, depends upon where you sit. If you sit on the Mountain, the public imagination will be attracted to you, and when they are aggrieved, which they will be in good time, the public passion, which is called opinion, will look to you for representation. My advice to my friends now is to sit together and say nothing, but to profess through the press the most advanced opinions. We sit on the back bench of the gangway, and we call ourselves the Mountain.'

Notwithstanding Mr. Bertie Tremaine's oracular revelations, Endymion was very glad to find his old friend Trenchard generally his neighbour. He had a high opinion both of Trenchard's judgment and acquirements, and he liked the man. In time they always managed to sit together. Job Thornberry took his seat below the gangway, on the opposition side, and on the floor of the House. Mr. Bertie Tremaine had sent his brother, Mr. Tremaine Bertie, to look after this new star, who he was anxious should ascend the Mountain; but Job Thornberry wishing to know whether the Mountain were going for 'total and immediate,' and not obtaining a sufficiently distinct reply, declined the proffered intimation. Mr. Bertie Tremaine, being a landed proprietor as well as leader of the Mountain, was too much devoted to the rights of labour to sanction such middle-class madness.

'Peel will have to do it,' said Job. 'You will see.'

'Peel now occupies the position of Necker,' said Mr. Bertie Tremaine, 'and will make the same *fiasco*. Then you will at last have a popular government.'

'And the rights of labour?' asked Job. 'All I hope is, I may have got safe to the States before that day.'

'There will be no danger,' said Mr. Bertie Tremaine. 'There is this difference between the English Mountain and the French. The English Mountain has its government prepared. And my brother spoke to you because, when the hour arrives, I wished to see you a member of it.'

'My dear Endymion,' said Waldershare, 'let us dine together before we meet in mortal conflict, which I suppose will be soon. I really think your Mr. Bertie Tremaine the most absurd being out of Colney Hatch.'

'Well, he has a purpose,' said Endymion; 'and they say that a man with a purpose generally sees it realised.'

'What I do like in him,' said Waldershare, 'is this revival of the Pythagorean system, and leading a party of silence. That is rich.'

One of the most interesting members of the House of Commons was Sir Fraunceys Scrope. He was the father of the House, though it was difficult to believe that from his appearance. He was tall, and had kept

his distinguished figure; a handsome man, with a
musical voice, and a countenance now benignant,
though very bright, and once haughty. He still retained the same fashion of costume in which he had
ridden up to Westminster more than half a century
ago, from his seat in Derbyshire, to support his dear
friend Charles Fox; real top-boots, and a blue coat
and buff waistcoat. He was a great friend of Lord
Roehampton, had a large estate in the same county,
and had refused an earldom. Knowing Endymion, he
came and sat by him one day in the House, and
asked him, good-naturedly, how he liked his new life.

'It is very different from what it was when I was
your age. Up to Easter we rarely had a regular debate, never a party division; very few people came
up indeed. But there was a good deal of speaking
on all subjects before dinner. We had the privilege
then of speaking on the presentation of petitions at
any length, and we seldom spoke on any other occasion. After Easter there was always at least one great
party fight. This was a mighty affair, talked of for
weeks before it came off, and then rarely an adjourned
debate. We were gentlemen, used to sit up late,
and should have been sitting up somewhere else had
we not been in the House of Commons. After this
party fight, the House for the rest of the session was
a mere club.'

'There was not much business doing then,' said
Endymion.

'There was not much business in the country then.
The House of Commons was very much like what the
House of Lords is now. You went home to dine,
and now and then came back for an important division.'

'But you must always have had the estimates here,' said Endymion.

'Yes, but they ran through very easily. Hume was the first man who attacked the estimates. What are you going to do with yourself to-day? Will you take your mutton with me? You must come in boots, for it is now dinner-time, and you must return, I fancy. Twenty years ago, no man would think of coming down to the House except in evening dress. I remember so late as Mr. Canning, the minister always came down in silk stockings and pantaloons, or knee breeches. All things change, and quoting Virgil, as that young gentleman has just done, will be the next thing to disappear. In the last Parliament we often had Latin quotations, but never from a member with a new constituency. I have heard Greek quoted here, but that was long ago, and a great mistake. The House was quite alarmed. Charles Fox used to say as to quotation — "No Greek; as much Latin as you like; and never French under any circumstances. No English poet unless he had completed his century." These were like some other good rules, the unwritten orders of the House of Commons.'

CHAPTER LXXVII.

St. Barbe Is Asked to Dinner.

WHILE parliaments were dissolving and ministries forming, the disappointed seeking consolation and the successful enjoying their triumph, Simon, Earl of Montfort, who just missed being a great philosopher, was reading *Topsy-Turvy,* which infinitely amused him; the style so picturesque and lambent! the tone so divertingly cynical! And if the knowledge of society in its pages was not so distinguished as that of human nature generally, this was a deficiency obvious only to a comparatively limited circle of its readers.

Lord Montfort had reminded Endymion of his promise to introduce the distinguished author to him, and accordingly, after due researches as to his dwelling-place, Mr. Ferrars called in Jermyn Street and sent up his card, to know whether Mr. St. Barbe would receive him. This was evidently not a matter-of-course affair, and some little time had elapsed when the maid-servant reappeared, and beckoned to Endymion to follow her upstairs.

In the front drawing-room of the first floor, robed in a flaming dressing-gown, and standing with his

(93)

back to the fire and to the looking-glass, the frame
of which was encrusted with cards of invitation, the
former colleague of Endymion received his visitor
with a somewhat haughty and reserved air.

'Well, I am delighted to see you again,' said
Endymion.

No reply but a ceremonious bow.

'And to congratulate you,' Endymion added after
a moment's pause. 'I hear of nothing but of your
book; I suppose one of the most successful that have
appeared for a long time.'

'Its success is not owing to your friends,' said
Mr. St. Barbe tartly.

'My friends!' said Endymion; 'what could they
have done to prevent it?'

'They need not have dissolved Parliament,' said
Mr. St. Barbe with irritation. 'It was nearly fatal to
me; it would have been to anybody else. I was selling forty thousand a month; I believe more than
Gushy ever reached; and so they dissolved Parliament.
The sale went down half at once—and now you expect me to support your party!'

'Well, it was unfortunate, but the dissolution
could hardly have done you any permanent injury,
and you could scarcely expect that such an event
could be postponed even for the advantage of an
individual so distinguished as yourself.'

'Perhaps not,' said St. Barbe, apparently a little
mollified, 'but they might have done something to
show their regret at it.'

'Something!' said Endymion, 'what sort of
thing?'

'The Prime Minister might have called on me, or
at least have written to me a letter. I want none of

their honours; I have scores of letters every day, suggesting that some high distinction should be conferred on me. I believe the nation expects me to be made a baronet. By-the-bye, I heard the other day you had got into Parliament. I know nothing of these matters; they do not interest me. Is it the fact?'

'Well, I was so fortunate, and there are others of your old friends, Trenchard, for example.'

'You do not mean to say that Trenchard is in Parliament!' said St. Barbe, throwing off all his affected reserve. 'Well, it is too disgusting! Trenchard in Parliament, and I obliged to think it a great favour if a man gives me a frank! Well, representative institutions have seen their day. That is something.'

'I have come here on a social mission,' said Endymion in a soothing tone. 'There is a great admirer of yours who much wishes to make your acquaintance. Trusting to our old intimacy, of which of course I am very proud, it was even hoped that you might waive ceremony, and come and dine.'

'Quite impossible!' exclaimed St. Barbe, and turning round, he pointed to the legion of invitations before him. 'You see, the world is at my feet. I remember that fellow Seymour Hicks taking me to his room to show me a card he had from a countess. What would he say to this?'

'Well, but you cannot be engaged to dinner every day,' said Endymion; 'and you really may choose any day you like.'

'Well, there are not many dinners among them, to be sure,' said St. Barbe. 'Small and earlies. How I hate a "small and early"! Shown into a room where you meet a select few who have been asked to dinner, and who are chewing the cud like a herd of kine, and you are expected to tumble before them to assist their digestion! Faugh! No, sir; we only dine out now, and we think twice, I can tell you, before we accept even an invitation to dinner. Who's your friend?'

'Well, my friend is Lord Montfort.'

'You do not mean to say that! And he is an admirer of mine?'

'An enthusiastic admirer.'

'I will dine with Lord Montfort. There is no one who appreciates so completely and so highly the old nobility of England as myself. They are a real aristocracy. None of the pinchbeck pedigrees and ormolu titles of the continent. Lord Montfort is, I think, an earl. A splendid title, earl! an English earl; count goes for nothing. The Earl of Montfort! An enthusiastic admirer of mine! The aristocracy of England, especially the old aristocracy, are highly cultivated. Sympathy from such a class is to be valued. I care for no other—I have always despised the million of vulgar. They have come to me, not I to them, and I have always told them the truth about themselves, that they are a race of snobs, and they rather like being told so. And now for your day?'

'Why not this day, if you be free? I will call for you about eight, and take you in my brougham to Montfort House.'

'You have got a brougham! Well, I suppose so, being a member of Parliament, though I know a good many members of Parliament who have not got broughams. But your family, I remember, married into the swells. I do not grudge it you. You were always a good comrade to me. I never knew a man more free from envy than you, Ferrars, and envy is an odious vice. There are people I know who when they hear I have dined with the Earl of Montfort, will invent all sorts of stories against me, and send them to what they call the journals of society.'

'Well, then, it shall be to-day,' said Endymion, rising.

'It shall be to-day, and to tell you the truth, I was thinking this morning where I should dine to-day. What I miss here are the cafés. Now in Paris you can dine every day exactly as it suits your means and mood. You may dine for a couple of francs in a quiet, unknown street, and very well; or you may dine for a couple of napoleons in a flaming saloon, with windows opening on a crowded boulevard. London is deficient in dining capability.'

'You should belong to a club. Do you not?'

'So I was told by a friend of mine the other day, —one of your great swells. He said I ought to belong to the Athenæum, and he would propose me, and the committee would elect me as a matter of course. They rejected me and selected a bishop. And then people are surprised that the Church is in danger!'

CHAPTER LXXVIII.

A GREAT FINANCIAL AWAKENING.

THE condition of England at the meeting of Parliament in 1842 was not satisfactory. The depression of trade in the manufacturing districts seemed overwhelming, and continued increasing during the whole of the year. A memorial from Stockport to the Queen in the spring represented that more than half the master spinners had failed, and that no less than three thousand dwelling-houses were untenanted. One-fifth of the population of Leeds were dependent on the poor-rates. The state of Sheffield was not less severe — and the blast furnaces of Wolverhampton were extinguished. There were almost daily meetings, at Liverpool, Manchester, and Leeds, to consider the great and increasing distress of the country, and to induce ministers to bring forward remedial measures; but as these were impossible, violence was soon substituted for passionate appeals to the fears or the humanity of the government. Vast bodies of the population assembled in Staleybridge, and Ashton, and Oldham, and marched into Manchester.

For a week the rioting was unchecked, but the government despatched a strong military force to that city, and order was restored.

The state of affairs in Scotland was not more favourable. There were food riots in several of the Scotch towns, and in Glasgow the multitude assembled, and then commenced what they called a begging tour, but which was really a progress of not disguised intimidation. The economic crisis in Ireland was yet to come, but the whole of that country was absorbed in a harassing and dangerous agitation for the repeal of the union between the two countries.

During all this time, the Anti-Corn-Law League was holding regular and frequent meetings at Manchester, at which statements were made distinguished by great eloquence and little scruple. But the able leaders of this confederacy never succeeded in enlisting the sympathies of the great body of the population. Between the masters and the workmen there was an alienation of feeling, which apparently never could be removed. This reserve, however, did not enlist the working-classes on the side of the government; they had their own object, and one which they themselves enthusiastically cherished. And this was the Charter, a political settlement which was to restore the golden age, and which the master manufacturers and the middle classes generally looked upon with even more apprehension than Her Majesty's advisers. It is hardly necessary to add, that in a state of affairs like that which is here faintly but still faithfully sketched, the rapid diminution of the revenue was inevitable, and of course that decline mainly occurred in the two all-important branches of the customs and excise.

There was another great misfortune also which at this trying time hung over England. The country was dejected. The humiliating disasters of Afghanistan, dark narratives of which were periodically arriving, had produced a more depressing effect on the spirit of the country than all the victories and menaces of Napoleon in the heyday of his wild career. At home and abroad, there seemed nothing to sustain the national spirit; financial embarrassment, commercial and manufacturing distress, social and political agitation on the one hand, and on the other, the loss of armies, of reputation, perhaps of empire. It was true that these external misfortunes could hardly be attributed to the new ministry—but when a nation is thoroughly perplexed and dispirited, it soon ceases to make distinctions between political parties. The country is out of sorts, and the 'government' is held answerable for the disorder.

Thus it will be seen that, though the new ministry were supported by a commanding majority in Parliament, and that, too, after a recent appeal to the country, they were not popular; it may be truly said they were even the reverse. The opposition, on the contrary, notwithstanding their discomfiture, and, on some subjects, their disgrace, were by no means disheartened, and believed that there were economical causes at work, which must soon restore them to power.

The minister brought forward his revision of the tariff, which was denounced by the League as futile, and in which anathema the opposition soon found it convenient to agree. Had the minister included in his measure that 'total and immediate repeal' of the existing Corn Laws which was preached by many as a panacea, the effect would have been probably much the same. No doubt a tariff may aggravate, or may mitigate, such a condition of commercial depression as periodically visits a state of society like that of England, but it does not produce it. It was produced in 1842, as it had been produced at the present time, by an abuse of capital and credit, and by a degree of production which the wants of the world have not warranted.

And yet all this time, there were certain influences at work in the great body of the nation, neither foreseen, nor for some time recognised, by statesmen and those great capitalists on whose opinion statesmen much depend, which were stirring, as it were, like the unconscious power of the forces of nature, and which were destined to baffle all the calculations of persons in authority and the leading spirits of all parties, strengthen a perplexed administration, confound a sanguine opposition, render all the rhetoric, statistics, and subscriptions of the Anti-Corn-Law League fruitless, and absolutely make the Chartists forget the Charter.

'My friends will not assist themselves by resisting the government measures,' said Mr. Neuchatel, with his usual calm smile, half sceptical, half sympathetic. 'The measures will do no good, but they will do no harm. There are no measures that will do any good at this moment. We do not want measures; what we want is a new channel.'

That is exactly what was wanted. There was abundant capital in the country and a mass of unemployed labour. But the markets on which they had of late depended, the American especially, were overworked and overstocked, and in some instances were not only overstocked, but disturbed by war, as the Chinese, for example — and capital and labour wanted 'a new channel.'

The new channel came, and all the persons of authority, alike political and commercial, seemed quite surprised that it had arrived; but when a thing or a man is wanted, they generally appear. One or two lines of railway, which had been long sleepily in formation, about this time were finished, and one or two lines of railway, which had been finished for some time and were unnoticed, announced dividends, and not contemptible ones. Suddenly there was a general feeling in the country that its capital should be invested in railways; that the whole surface of the land should be transformed, and covered, as by a network, with these mighty means of communication. When the passions of the English, naturally an enthusiastic people, are excited on a subject of finance, their will, their determination, and resource, are irresistible. This was signally proved in the present instance, for they never ceased subscribing their capital until the sum entrusted to this new form of investment reached an amount almost equal to the national debt; and this too in a very few years. The immediate effect on the condition of the country was absolutely prodigious. The value of land rose, all the blast furnaces were relit, a stimulant was given to every branch of the home trade, the amount suddenly paid in wages exceeded that ever known in this country, and wages too at a high rate. Large portions of the labouring classes not only enjoyed comfort, but commanded luxury. All this of course soon acted on the revenue, and customs, especially excise, soon furnished an ample surplus.

It cannot be pretended that all this energy and enterprise were free in their operation from those evils which, it seems, must inevitably attend any extensive public speculation, however well founded. Many of the scenes and circumstances recalled the days of the South Sea Scheme. The gambling in shares of companies which were formed only in name was without limit. The principal towns of the north established for that purpose stock exchanges of their own, and Leeds especially, one-fifth of whose population had been authoritatively described in the first session of the new Parliament as dependent on the poor-rates, now boasted of a stock exchange which in the extent of its transactions rivalled that of the metropolis. And the gambling was universal, from the noble to the mechanic. It was confined to no class and to neither sex. The scene occurring at the Board of Trade on the last day on which plans could be lodged, and when midnight had arrived while crowds from the country were still filling the hall, and pressing at the doors, deserved and required for its adequate representation the genius of a Hogarth. This was the day on which it was announced that the total number of railway projects, on which deposits had been paid, had reached nearly to eight hundred.

What is remarkable in this vast movement in which so many millions were produced, and so many more promised, is, that the great leaders of the financial world took no part in it. The mighty loanmongers, on whose fiat the fate of kings and empires sometimes depended, seemed like men who, witnessing some eccentricity of nature, watch it with mixed feelings of curiosity and alarm. Even Lombard

Street, which never was more wanted, was inactive, and it was only by the irresistible pressure of circumstances that a banking firm which had an extensive country connection was ultimately forced to take the leading part that was required, and almost unconsciously lay the foundation of the vast fortunes which it has realised, and organise the various connection which it now commands. All seemed to come from the provinces, and from unknown people in the provinces.

But in all affairs there must be a leader, and a leader appeared. He was more remarkable than the movement itself. He was a London tradesman, though a member of Parliament returned for the first time to this House of Commons. This leader was Mr. Vigo.

Mr. Vigo had foreseen what was coming, and had prepared for it. He agreed with Mr. Neuchatel, what was wanted was 'a new channel.' That channel he thought he had discovered, and he awaited it. He himself could command no inconsiderable amount of capital, and he had a following of obscure rich friends who believed in him, and did what he liked. His daily visits to the city, except when he was travelling over England, and especially the north and midland counties, had their purpose and bore fruit. He was a director, and soon the chairman and leading spirit, of a railway which was destined to be perhaps our most important one. He was master of all the details of the business; he had arrived at conclusions on the question of the gauges, which then was a *pons asinorum* for the multitude, and understood all about rolling stock and permanent ways, and sleepers and branch lines, which were then cabalistic terms to the general. In his first session in Parliament he had passed quietly and almost unnoticed several bills on these matters, and began to be recognised by the Committee of Selection as a member who ought to be 'put on' for questions of this kind.

The great occasion had arrived, and Mr. Vigo was equal to it. He was one of those few men who awake one day and find themselves famous. Suddenly it would seem that the name of Mr. Vigo was in everybody's mouth. There was only one subject which interested the country, and he was recognised as the man who best understood it. He was an oracle, and, naturally, soon became an idol. The tariff of the ministers was forgotten, the invectives of the League were disregarded, their motions for the repeal of the Corn Laws were invariably defeated by large and contemptuous majorities. The House of Commons did nothing but pass railway bills, measures which were welcomed with unanimity by the House of Lords, whose estates were in consequence daily increasing in value. People went to the gallery to see Mr. Vigo introduce bills, and could scarcely restrain their enthusiasm at the spectacle of so much patriotic energy, which secured for them premiums for shares, which they held in undertakings of which the first sod was not yet cut. On one morning, the Great Cloudland Company, of which he was chairman, gave their approval of twenty-six bills, which he immediately introduced into Parliament. Next day, the Ebor and North Cloudland sanctioned six bills under his advice, and affirmed deeds and agreements which affected all the principal railway projects in Lancashire and Yorkshire. A quarter of an hour later, just time to hurry from one meeting to another, where he was always received with rampant enthusiasm, Newcastle and the extreme north accepted his dictatorship. During a portion of two days, he obtained the consent of shareholders to forty bills, involving an expenditure of ten millions; and the engagements for one session alone amounted to one hundred and thirty millions sterling.

Mr. Neuchatel shrugged his shoulders, but no one would listen even to Mr. Neuchatel, when the Prime Minister himself, supposed to be the most wary of men, and especially on financial subjects, in the very white heat of all this speculation, himself raised the first sod on his own estate in a project of extent and importance.

Throughout these extraordinary scenes, Mr. Vigo, though not free from excitement, exhibited, on the whole, much self-control. He was faithful to his old friends, and no one profited more in this respect than Mr. Rodney. That gentleman became the director of several lines, and vice-chairman of one over which Mr. Vigo himself presided. No one was surprised that Mr. Rodney therefore should enter Parliament. He came in by virtue of one of those petitions that Tadpole was always cooking or baffling. Mr. Rodney was a supporter of the ministry, and Mr. Vigo was a Liberal, but Mr. Vigo returned Mr. Rodney to Parliament all the same, and no one seemed astonished or complained. Political connection, political consistency, political principle, all vanished before the fascination of premiums.

As for Endymion, the great man made him friendly and earnest overtures, and offered, if he would give his time to business, which, as he was in opposition, would be no great sacrifice, to promote and secure

his fortune. But Endymion, after due reflection, declined, though with gratitude, these tempting pro-
posals. Ferrars was an ambitious man, but not too
imaginative a one. He had a main object in life, and
that was to regain the position which had been for-
feited, not by his own fault. His grandfather and
his father had both been privy councillors and ministers of state. There had, indeed, been more than
the prospect of his father filling a very prominent
position. All had been lost, but the secret purpose
of the life of Endymion was that, from being a clerk
in a public office, he should arrive by his own energies at the station to which he seemed, as it were,
born. To accomplish this he felt that the entire devotion of his labour and thought was requisite. His
character was assentially tenacious, and he had already realised no inconsiderable amount of political
knowledge and official experience. His object seemed
difficult and distant, but there was nothing wild or
visionary in its pursuit. He had achieved some of
the first steps, and he was yet very young. There
were friends about him, however, who were not
content with what they deemed his moderate ambition, and thought they discerned in him qualities
which might enable him to mount to a higher stage.
However this might be, his judgment was that he
must resist the offers of Mr. Vigo, though they were
sincerely kind, and so he felt them.

In the meantime, he frequently met that gentleman, and not merely in the House of Commons.
Mr. St. Barbe would have been frantically envious
could he have witnessed and perused the social invitations that fell like a continuous snow-storm on the
favoured roof of Mr. Vigo. Mr. Vigo was not a party

question. He dined with high patricians who forgot
their political differences, while they agreed in court-
ing the presence of this great benefactor of his country. The fine ladies were as eager in their homage
to this real patriot, and he might be seen between
rival countesses, who emulated each other in their appreciation of his public services. These were Mr.
Vigo's dangerous suitors. He confessed to Endymion one
day that he could not manage the great ladies. 'Male
swells,' he would say laughingly, 'I have measured
physically and intellectually.' The golden youth of
the country seemed indeed fascinated by his society,
repeated his sententious bons-mots, and applied for
shares in every company which he launched into
prosperous existence.

Mr. Vigo purchased a splendid mansion in St.
James' Square, where invitations to his banquets were
looked upon almost as commands. His chief cook
was one of the celebrities of Europe, and though he
had served emperors, the salary he received from Mr.
Vigo exceeded any one he had hitherto condescended
to pocket. Mr. Vigo bought estates, hired moors,
lavished his money, not only with profusion, but
with generosity. Everything was placed at his command, and it appeared that there was nothing that he
refused. 'When this excitement is over,' said Mr.
Bertie Tremaine, 'I hope to induce him to take
India.'

In the midst of this commanding effulgence, the
calmer beam of Mr. Rodney might naturally pass unnoticed, yet its brightness was clear and sustained.
The Rodneys engaged a dwelling of no mean proportion in that favoured district of South Kensington
which was then beginning to assume the high char-

acter it has since obtained. Their equipages were distinguished, and when Mrs. Rodney entered the Park, driving her matchless ponies, and attended by outriders, and herself bright as Diana, the world leaning over its palings witnessed her appearance with equal delight and admiration.

CHAPTER LXXIX.

ENDYMION'S MAIDEN SPEECH.

E HAVE rather anticipated, for the sake of the subject, in our last chapter, and we must now recur to the time when, after his return from Paris, Endymion entered into what was virtually his first session in the House of Commons. Though in opposition, and with all the delights of the most charming society at his command, he was an habitual and constant attendant. One might have been tempted to believe that he would turn out to be, though a working, only a silent member, but his silence was only prudence. He was deeply interested and amused in watching the proceedings, especially when those took part in them with whom he was acquainted.

Job Thornberry took a leading position in the debates. He addressed the House very shortly after he took his seat, and having a purpose and a most earnest one, and being what is styled a representative man of his subject, the House listened to him at once, and his place in debate was immediately recognised. The times favoured him, especially during the first and second sessions, while the commercial de-

pression lasted; afterwards, he was always listened
to, because he had great oratorical gifts, a persuasive
style that was winning, and, though he had no inconsiderable powers of sarcasm, his extreme tact
wisely guided him to restrain for the present that
dangerous, though most effective, weapon.

The Pythagorean school, as Waldershare styled
Mr. Bertie Tremaine and his following, very much
amused Endymion. The heaven-born minister air of
the great leader was striking. He never smiled, or
at any rate contemptuously. Notice of a question
was sometimes publicly given from this bench, but so
abstruse in its nature and so quaint in its expression,
that the House never comprehended it, and the unfortunate minister who had to answer, even with
twenty-four hours' study, was obliged to commence
his reply by a conjectural interpretation of the query
formally addressed to him. But though they were silent
in the House, their views were otherwise powerfully
represented. The weekly journal devoted to their
principles was sedulously circulated among members
of the House. It was called the *Precursor,* and systematically attacked not only every institution, but, it
might be said, every law, and all the manners and
customs, of the country. Its style was remarkable,
never excited or impassioned, but frigid, logical, and
incisive, and suggesting appalling revolutions with
the calmness with which one would narrate the ordinary incidents of life. The editor of the *Precursor* was Mr. Jawett, selected by that great master of
human nature, Mr. Bertie Tremaine. When it got
about that the editor of this fearful journal was a
clerk in a public office, the indignation of the government, or at least of their supporters, was extreme,

and there was no end to the punishments and disgrace to which he was to be subjected; but Waldershare, who lived a good deal in Bohemia, was
essentially cosmopolitan, and dabbled in letters, persuaded his colleagues not to make the editor of the
Precursor a martyr, and undertook with their authority to counteract his evil purposes by literary means
alone.

Being fully empowered to take all necessary steps
for this object, Waldershare thought that there was
no better mode of arresting public attention to his
enterprise than by engaging for its manager the most
renowned pen of the hour, and he opened himself on
the subject in the most sacred confidence to Mr. St.
Barbe. That gentlemen, invited to call upon a minister, sworn to secrecy, and brimful of state secrets,
could not long restrain himself, and with admirable
discretion consulted on his views and prospects Mr.
Endymion Ferrars.

'But I thought you were one of us,' said Endymion; 'you asked me to put you in the way of
getting into Brooks's!'

'What of that?' said Mr. St. Barbe; 'and when
you remember what the Whigs owe to literary men,
they ought to have elected me into Brooks's without
my asking for it.'

'Still, if you be on the other side?

'It is nothing to do with sides,' said Mr. St.
Barbe; 'this affair goes far beyond sides. The *Precursor* wants to put down the Crown; I shall put
down the *Precursor*. It is an affair of the closet,
not of sides — an affair of the royal closet, sir. I am
acting for the Crown, sir; the Crown has appealed
to me. I save the Crown, and there must be per-

sonal relations with the highest,' and he looked quite fierce.

'Well, you have not written your first article yet,' said Endymion. 'I shall look forward to it with much interest.'

After Easter, Lord Roehampton said to Endymion that a question ought to be put on a subject of foreign policy of importance, and on which he thought the ministry were in difficulties; 'and I think you might as well ask it, Endymion. I will draw up the question, and you will give notice of it. It will be a reconnaissance.'

The notice of this question was the first time Endymion opened his mouth in the House of Commons. It was an humble and not a very hazardous office, but when he got on his legs his head swam, his heart beat so violently that it was like a convulsion preceding death, and though he was only on his legs for a few seconds, all the sorrows of his life seemed to pass before him. When he sat down, he was quite surprised that the business of the House proceeded as usual, and it was only after some time that he became convinced that no one but himself was conscious of his sufferings, or that he had performed a routine duty otherwise than in a routine manner.

The crafty question, however, led to some important consequences. When asked, to the surprise of every one the minister himself replied to it. Waldershare, with whom Endymion dined at Bellamy's that day, was in no good humour in consequence.

When Lord Roehampton had considered the ministerial reply, he said to Endymion, 'This must be followed up. You must move for papers. It will be a good opportunity for you, for the House is up to

something being in the wind, and they will listen.
It will be curious to see whether the minister follows
you. If so, he will give me an opening.'

Endymion felt that this was the crisis of his life.
He knew the subject well, and he had all the tact
and experience of Lord Roehampton to guide him in his
statement and his arguments. He had also the great
feeling that, if necessary, a powerful arm would support
him. It was about a week before the day arrived, and
Endymion slept very little that week, and the night
before his motion not a wink. He almost wished he
was dead as he walked down to the House in the
hope that the exercise might remedy, or improve,
his languid circulation; but in vain, and when his
name was called and he had to rise, his hands and
feet were like ice.

Lady Roehampton and Lady Montfort were both
in the ventilator, and he knew it.

It might be said that he was sustained by his utter
despair. He felt so feeble and generally imbecile that
he had not vitality enough to be sensible of failure.

He had a kind audience, and an interested one.
When he opened his mouth, he forgot his first sentence, which he had long prepared. In trying to recall it and failing, he was for a moment confused.
But it was only for a moment; the unpremeditated
came to his aid, and his voice, at first tremulous, was
recognised as distinct and rich. There was a murmur
of sympathy, and not merely from his own side.
Suddenly, both physically and intellectually, he was
quite himself. His arrested circulation flowed, and fed
his stagnant brain. His statement was lucid, his arguments were difficult to encounter, and his manner
was modest. He sat down amid general applause,

and though he was then conscious that he had omitted more than one point on which he had relied, he was on the whole satisfied, and recollected that he might use them in reply, a privilege to which he now looked forward with feelings of comfort and confidence.

The minister again followed him, and in an elaborate speech. The subject evidently, in the opinion of the minister, was of too delicate and difficult a character to trust to a subordinate. Overwhelmed as he was with the labours of his own department, the general conduct of affairs, and the leadership of the House, he still would undertake the representation of an office with whose business he was not familiar. Wary and accurate he always was, but in discussions on foreign affairs, he never exhibited the unrivalled facility with which he ever treated a commercial or financial question, or that plausible promptness with which, at a moment's notice, he could encounter any difficulty connected with domestic administration.

All these were qualities which Lord Roehampton possessed with reference to the affairs over which he had long presided, and in the present instance, following the minister, he was particularly happy. He had a good case, and he was gratified by the success of Endymion. He complimented him and confuted his opponent, and, not satisfied with demolishing his arguments, Lord Roehampton indulged in a little raillery which the House enjoyed, but which was never pleasing to the more solemn organisation of his rival.

No language can describe the fury of Waldershare as to the events of this evening. He looked upon the conduct of the minister, in not permitting him to represent his department, as a decree of the incapacity of his subordinate, and of the virtual termination of the official career of the Under-Secretary of State. He would have resigned the next day had it not been for the influence of Lady Beaumaris, who soothed him by suggesting that it would be better to take an early opportunity of changing his present post for another.

The minister was wrong. He was not fond of trusting youth, but it is a confidence which should be exercised, particularly in the conduct of a popular assembly. If the Under-Secretary had not satisfactorily answered Endymion, which no one had a right to assume, for Waldershare was a brilliant man, the minister could have always advanced to the rescue at the fitting time. As it was, he made a personal enemy of one who naturally might have ripened into a devoted follower, and who from his social influence, as well as from his political talents, was no despicable foe.

CHAPTER LXXX.

Rumours from Rome.

NOTWITHSTANDING the great political, and consequently social, changes that had taken place, no very considerable alteration occurred in the general life of those chief personages in whose existence we have attempted to interest the reader. However vast may appear to be the world in which we move, we all of us live in a limited circle. It is the result of circumstances; of our convenience and our taste. Lady Beaumaris became the acknowledged leader of Tory society, and her husband was so pleased with her position, and so proud of it, that he in a considerable degree sacrificed his own pursuits and pleasures for its maintenance. He even refused the mastership of a celebrated hunt, which had once been an object of his highest ambition, that he might be early and always in London to support his wife in her receptions. Imogene herself was universally popular. Her gentle and natural manners, blended with a due degree of self-respect, her charming appearance, and her ready but unaffected sympathy, won every heart. Lady Roehampton was her frequent guest.

Myra continued her duties as a leader of society, as her lord was anxious that the diplomatic world should not forget him. These were the two principal and rival houses. The efforts of Lady Montfort were more fitful, for they were to a certain degree dependent on the moods of her husband. It was observed that Lady Beaumaris never omitted attending the receptions of Lady Roehampton, and the tone of almost reverential affection with which she ever approached Myra was touching to those who were in the secret, but they were few.

No great change occurred in the position of Prince Florestan, except that in addition to the sports to which he was apparently devoted, he gradually began to interest himself in the turf. He had bred several horses of repute, and one, which he had named Lady Roehampton, was the favourite for a celebrated race. His highness was anxious that Myra should honour him by being his guest. This had never occurred before, because Lord Roehampton felt that so avowed an intimacy with a personage in the peculiar position of Prince Florestan was hardly becoming a Secretary of State for Foreign Affairs; but that he was no longer, and being the most good-natured man that ever lived, and easily managed in little things, he could not refuse Myra when she consulted him, as they call it, on the subject, and it was settled that Lord and Lady Roehampton were to dine with Prince Florestan. The prince was most anxious that Mr. Sidney Wilton should take this occasion of consenting to a reconciliation with him, and Lady Roehampton exerted herself much for this end. Mr. Sidney Wilton was in love with Lady Roehampton, and yet on this point he was inexorable. Lord and Lady Beaumaris went, and Lady

Montfort, to whom the prince had addressed a private note of his own that quite captivated her, and Mr. and Mrs. Neuchatel and Adriana. Waldershare, Endymion, and Baron Sergius completed the guests, who were received by the Duke of St. Angelo and a couple of aides-de-camp. When the prince entered all rose, and the ladies curtseyed very low. Lord Roehampton resumed his seat immediately, saying to his neighbour, 'I rose to show my respect to my host; I sit down to show that I look upon him as a subject like myself.'

'A subject of whom?' inquired Lady Montfort.

'There is something in that,' said Lord Roehampton, smiling.

The Duke of St. Angelo was much disturbed by the conduct of Lord Roehampton, which had disappointed his calculations, and he went about lamenting that Lord Roehampton had a little gout.

They had assembled in the library and dined on the same floor. The prince was seated between Lady Montfort, whom he accompanied to dinner, and Lady Roehampton. Adriana fell to Endymion's lot. She looked very pretty, was beautifully dressed, and for her, was even gay. Her companion was in good spirits, and she seemed interested and amused. The prince never spoke much, but his remarks always told. He liked murmuring to women, but when requisite, he could throw a fly over the table with adroitness and effect. More than once during the dinner he whispered to Lady Roehampton: 'This is too kind — your coming here. But you have always been my best friend.' The dinner would have been lively and successful even if Waldershare had not been there, but he to-day was exuberant and irresistible.

His chief topic was abuse of the government of which
he was a member, and he lavished all his powers of
invective and ridicule alike on the imbecility of their
policy and their individual absurdities.   All this much
amused Lady Montfort, and gave Lord Roehampton
an opportunity to fool the Under-Secretary of State to
the top of his bent.

'If you do not take care,' said Mr. Neuchatel,
'they will turn you out.'

'I wish they would,' said Waldershare.   'That is
what I am longing for.   I should go then all over the
country and address public meetings.   It would be the
greatest thing since Sacheverell.'

'Our people have not behaved well to Mr. Waldershare,' whispered Imogene to Lord Roehampton, 'but
I think we shall put it all right.'

'Do you believe it?' inquired Lady Montfort of
Lord Roehampton.   He had been speaking to her for
some little time in a hushed tone, and rather earnestly.

'Indeed I do; I cannot well see what there is to
doubt about it.   We know the father very well—an
excellent man; he was the parish priest of Lady Roehampton before her marriage, when she lived in the
country.   And we know from him that more than a
year ago something was contemplated.   The son gave
up his living then; he has remained at Rome ever
since.   And now I am told he returns to us, the Pope's
legate and an archbishop *in partibus!*'

'It is most interesting,' said Lady Montfort. 'I was
always his great admirer.'

'I know that; you and Lady Roehampton made
me go and hear him.   The father will be terribly distressed.'

'I do not care at all about the father,' said Lady Montfort; 'but the son had such a fine voice and was so very good-looking. I hope I shall see him.'

They were speaking of Nigel Penruddock, whose movements had been a matter of much mystery during the last two years. Rumours of his having been received into the Roman Church had been often rife; sometimes flatly, and in time faintly, contradicted. Now the facts seemed admitted, and it would appear that he was about to return to England not only as a Roman Catholic, but as a distinguished priest of the Church, and, it was said, even the representative of the Papacy.

All the guests rose at the same time — a pleasant habit — and went upstairs to the brilliantly lighted saloons. Lord Roehampton seated himself by Baron Sergius, with whom he was always glad to converse. 'We seem here quiet and content?' said the ex-minister inquiringly.

'I hope so, and I think so,' said Sergius. 'He believes in his star, and will leave everything to its influence. There are to be no more adventures.'

'It must be a great relief to Lord Roehampton to have got quit of office,' said Mrs. Neuchatel to Lady Roehampton. 'I always pitied him so much. I never can understand why people voluntarily incur such labours and anxiety.'

'You should join us,' said Mr. Neuchatel to Waldershare. 'They would be very glad to see you at Brooks's.'

'Brooks's may join the October Club, which I am going to revive,' said Waldershare.

'I never heard of that club,' said Mr. Neuchatel.

'It was a much more important thing than the Bill of Rights or the Act of Settlement,' said Waldershare, 'all the same.'

'I want to see his mother's portrait in the farther saloon,' said Lady Montfort to Myra.

'Let us go together.' And Lady Roehampton rose, and they went.

It was a portrait of Queen Agrippina by a master hand, and admirably illumined by reflected light, so that it seemed to live.

'She must have been very beautiful,' said Lady Montfort.

'Mr. Sidney Wilton was devotedly attached to her, my lord has told me,' said Lady Roehampton.

'So many were devotedly attached to her,' said Lady Montfort.

'Yes; she was like Mary of Scotland, whom some men are in love with even to this day. Her spell was irresistible. There are no such women now.'

'Yes; there is one,' said Lady Montfort, suddenly turning round and embracing Lady Roehampton; 'and I know she hates me, because she thinks I prevent her brother from marrying.'

'Dear Lady Montfort, how can you use such strong expressions? I am sure there can be only one feeling of Endymion's friends to you, and that is gratitude for your kindness to him.'

'I have done nothing for him; I can do nothing for him. I felt that when we were trying to get him into Parliament. If he could marry, and be independent, and powerful, and rich, it would be better, perhaps, for all of us.'

'I wish he were independent, and powerful, and rich,' said Myra musingly. 'That would be a fairy tale. At present, he must be content that he has some of the kindest friends in the world.'

'He interests me very much; no one so much. I am sincerely, even deeply, attached to him; but it is like your love, it is a sister's love. There is only one person I really love in the world, and alas! he does not love me!' And her voice was tremulous.

'Do not say such things, dear Lady Montfort. I never can believe what you sometimes intimate on that subject. Do you know, I think it a little hallucination.'

Lady Montfort shook her head with a truly mournful expression, and then suddenly, her beautiful face wreathed with smiles, she said in a gay voice, 'We will not think of such sorrows. I wish them to be entombed in my heart, but the spectres will rise sometimes. Now about your brother. I do not mean to say that it would not be a great loss to me if he married, but I wish him to marry if you do. For myself, I must have a male friend, and he must be very clever, and thoroughly understand politics. You know you deprived me of Lord Roehampton,' she continued smilingly, 'who was everything I could desire; and the Count of Ferroll would have suited me excellently, but then he ran away. Now Endymion could not easily run away, and he is so agreeable and so intelligent, that at last I thought I had found a companion worth helping—and I meant, and still mean, to work hard—until he is Prime Minister.'

'I have my dreams too about that,' said Lady Roehampton, 'but we are all about the same age, and can wait a little.'

'He cannot be minister too soon,' said Lady Montfort. 'It was not being minister soon that ruined Charles Fox.'

The party broke up. The prince made a sign to Waldershare, which meant a confidential cigar, and in a few minutes they were alone together.

'What women!' exclaimed the prince. 'Not to be rivalled in this city, and yet quite unlike each other.'

'And which do you admire most, sir?' said Waldershare.

The prince trimmed his cigar, and then he said, 'I will tell you this day five years.'

CHAPTER LXXXI.

THE POPE'S LEGATE.

THE ecclesiastical incident mentioned at the dinner described in our last chapter, produced a considerable effect in what is called society. Nigel Penruddock had obtained great celebrity as a preacher, while his extreme doctrines and practices had alike amazed, fascinated, and alarmed a large portion of the public. For some time he had withdrawn from the popular gaze, but his individuality was too strong to be easily forgotten, even if occasional paragraphs as to his views and conduct, published, contradicted, and reiterated, were not sufficient to sustain, and even stimulate, curiosity. That he was about to return to his native land, as the Legate of His Holiness, was an event which made many men look grave, and some female hearts flutter.

The memory of Lady Roehampton could not escape from the past, and she could not recall it and all the scenes at Hurstley without emotion; and Lady Montfort remembered with some pride and excitement, that the Legate of the Pope had once been one of her heroes. It was evident that he had no wish to avoid his old acquaintances, for shortly after his arrival, and after he had assembled his suffragans, and instructed the clergy of his district, for dioceses did not then exist, Archbishop Penruddock, for so the Metropolitan of Tyre simply styled himself, called upon both these ladies.

His first visit was to Myra, and notwithstanding her disciplined self-control, her intense pride, and the deep and daring spirit which always secretly sustained her, she was nervous and agitated, but only in her boudoir. When she entered the saloon to welcome him, she seemed as calm as if she were going to an evening assembly.

Nigel was changed. Instead of that anxious and moody look which formerly marred the refined beauty of his countenance, his glance was calm and yet radiant. He was thinner, it might almost be said emaciated, which seemed to add height to his tall figure.

Lady Roehampton need not have been nervous about the interview, and the pain of its inevitable associations. Except one allusion at the end of his visit, when his Grace mentioned some petty grievance, of which he wished to relieve his clergy, and said, 'I think I will consult your brother; being in the opposition, he will be less embarrassed than some of my friends in the government, or their supporters,' he never referred to the past. All he spoke of was the magnitude of his task, the immense but inspiring labours which awaited him, and his deep sense of his responsibility. Nothing but the Divine principle of the Church could sustain him. He was at one time hopeful that His Holiness might have thought the time ripe for the restoration of the national hierarchy, but it was decreed otherwise. Had it been accorded, no doubt it would have assisted him. A prelate *in par-*

tibus is, in a certain sense, a stranger, whatever his
duties, and the world is more willing when it is appealed to by one who has 'a local habitation and a
name;' he is identified with the people among whom
he lives. There was much to do. The state of the
Catholic poor in his own district was heartrending.
He never could have conceived such misery, and that
too under the shadow of the Abbey. The few schools
which existed were wretched, and his first attention
must be given to this capital deficiency. He trusted
much to female aid. He meant to invite the great
Catholic ladies to unite with him in a common labour
of love. In this great centre of civilisation, and wealth,
and power, there was need of the spirit of a St. Ur-
sula.

No one seemed more pleased by the return of
Archbishop Penruddock than Lord Montfort. He appeared to be so deeply interested in his Grace's mission, sought his society so often, treated him with
such profound respect, almost ceremony, asked so
many questions about what was happening at Rome,
and what was going to be done here — that Nigel
might have been pardoned if he did not despair of
ultimately inducing Lord Montfort to return to the
faith of his illustrious ancestors. And yet, all this time,
Lord Montfort was only amusing himself; a new character was to him a new toy, and when he could not
find one, he would dip into the *Memoirs of St. Simon.*

Instead of avoiding society, as was his wont in
old days, the Archbishop sought it. And there was
nothing exclusive in his social habits; all classes and
all creeds, all conditions and orders of men, were
alike interesting to him; they were part of the mighty
community, with all whose pursuits, and passions,

and interests, and occupations he seemed to sympathise, but respecting which he had only one object —
to bring them back once more to that imperial fold
from which, in an hour of darkness and distraction,
they had miserably wandered. The conversion of
England was deeply engraven on the heart of Penruddock; it was his constant purpose, and his daily
and nightly prayer.

So the Archbishop was seen everywhere, even at
fashionable assemblies. He was a frequent guest at
banquets which he never tasted, for he was a smiling
ascetic, and though he seemed to be preaching or
celebrating high mass in every part of the metropolis,
organising schools, establishing convents, and building cathedrals, he could find time to move philan-
thropic resolutions at middle-class meetings, attend
learned associations, and even occasionally send a
paper to the Royal Society.

The person who fell most under the influence of
the Archbishop was Waldershare. He was fairly captivated by him. Nothing would satisfy Waldershare
till he had brought the Archbishop and Prince Florestan together. 'You are a Roman Catholic prince,
sir,' he would say. 'It is absolute folly to forego
such a source of influence and power as the Roman
Catholic Church. Here is your man; a man made
for the occasion, a man who may be pope. Come
to an understanding with him, and I believe you will
regain your throne in a year.'

'My dear Waldershare, it is very true that I am
a Roman Catholic, but I am also the head of the
Liberal party in my country, and perhaps also on
the continent of Europe, and they are not particularly
affected to archbishops and popes.'

'Old-fashioned twaddle of the Liberal party,' exclaimed Waldershare. 'There is more true democracy in the Roman Catholic Church than in all the secret societies of Europe.'

'There is something in that,' said the prince musingly, 'and my friends are Roman Catholics, nominally Roman Catholics. If I were quite sure your man and the priests generally were nominally Roman Catholics, something might be done.'

'As for that,' said Waldershare, 'sensible men are all of the same religion.'

'And pray what is that?' inquired the prince.

'Sensible men never tell.'

Perhaps there was no family which suited him more, and where the archbishop became more intimate, than the Neuchatels. He very much valued a visit to Hainault, and the miscellaneous and influential circles he met there—merchant princes, and great powers of Lombard Street and the Stock Exchange. The Governor of the Bank happened to be a high churchman, and listened to the Archbishop with evident relish. Mrs. Neuchatel also acknowledged the spell of his society, and he quite agreed with her that people should be neither so poor nor so rich. She had long mused over plans of social amelioration, and her new ally was to teach her how to carry them into practice. As for Mr. Neuchatel, he was pleased that his wife was amused, and liked the Archbishop as he liked all clever men. ' You know,' he would say, ' I am in favour of all churches, provided, my lord Archbishop, they do not do anything very foolish. Eh? So I shall subscribe to your schools with great pleasure. We cannot have too many schools, even if they only keep young people from doing mischief.'

CHAPTER LXXXII.

THE POTATO FAMINE.

HE prosperity of the country was so signal, while Mr. Vigo was unceasingly directing millions of our accumulated capital, and promises of still more, into the 'new channel,' that it seemed beyond belief that any change of administration could ever occur, at least in the experience of the existing generation. The minister to whose happy destiny it had fallen to gratify the large appetites and reckless consuming powers of a class now first known in our social hierarchy as 'Navvies,' was hailed as a second Pitt. The countenance of the opposition was habitually dejected, with the exception of those members of it on whom Mr. Vigo graciously conferred shares, and Lady Montfort taunted Mr. Sidney Wilton with inquiries, why he and his friends had not made railroads, instead of inventing nonsense about cheap bread. Job Thornberry made wonderful speeches in favour of total and immediate repeal of the Corn Laws, and the Liberal party, while they cheered him, privately expressed their regret that such a capital speaker, who might be anything, was not a practical man. Low prices, abundant harvests, and a thriving commerce had rendered all appeals, varied even by the persuasive ingenuity of Thornberry, a wearisome iteration; and, though the League had transplanted itself from Manchester to the metropolis, and hired theatres for their rhetoric, the close of 1845 found them nearly reduced to silence.

Mr. Bertie Tremaine, who was always studying the spirit of the age, announced to the initiated that Mr. Vigo had something of the character and structure of Napoleon, and that he himself began to believe, that an insular nation, with such an enormous appetite, was not adapted to cosmopolitan principles, which were naturally of a character more spiritual and abstract. Mr. Bertie Tremaine asked Mr. Vigo to dinner, and introduced him to several distinguished youths of extreme opinions, who were dining off gold plate. Mr. Vigo was much flattered by his visit; his host made much of him; and he heard many things on the principles of government, and even of society, in the largest sense of the expression, which astonished and amused him. In the course of the evening he varied the conversation — one which became the classic library and the busts of the surrounding statesmen — by promising to most of the guests allotments of shares in a new company, not yet launched, but whose securities were already at a high premium.

Endymion, in the meantime, pursued the even tenor of his way. Guided by the experience, unrivalled knowledge, and consummate tact of Lord Roehampton, he habitually made inquiries, or brought forward motions, which were evidently inconvenient or embarrassing to the ministry; and the very circumstance that he was almost always replied to by the

Prime Minister, elevated him in the estimation of the
House as much as the pertinence of his questions, and
the accurate information on which he founded his
motions. He had not taken the House with a rush
like Job Thornberry, but, at the end of three sessions,
he was a personage universally looked upon as one
who was 'certain to have office.'

There was another new member who had also
made way, though slowly, and that was Mr. Trenchard; he had distinguished himself on a difficult
committee, on which he had guided a perplexed minister, who was chairman, through many intricacies.
Mr. Trenchard watched the operations of Mr. Vigo
with a calm, cold scrutiny, and ventured one day to
impart his conviction to Endymion that there were
breakers ahead. 'Vigo is exhausting the floating capital of the country,' he said, and he offered to Endymion to give him all the necessary details, if he would
call the attention of the House to the matter. Endymion declined to do this, chiefly because he wished to
devote himself to foreign affairs and thought the
House would hardly brook his interference also in
finance. So he strongly advised Trenchard himself to
undertake the task. Trenchard was modest, and a
little timid about speaking; so it was settled that he
should consult the leaders on the question, and particularly the gentleman who it was supposed would
be their Chancellor of the Exchequer, if ever they were
again called upon to form a ministry. This right
honourable individual listened to Trenchard with the
impatience which became a man of great experience
addressed by a novice, and concluded the interview
by saying, that he thought 'there was nothing in it;'
at the same time, he would turn it in his mind, and

consult some practical men. Accordingly the ex- and future minister consulted Mr. Vigo, who assured him that he was quite right; that 'there was nothing in it,' and that the floating capital of the country was inexhaustible.

In the midst of all this physical prosperity, one fine day in August, Parliament having just been prorogued, an unknown dealer in potatoes wrote to the Secretary of State, and informed him that he had reason to think that a murrain had fallen over the whole of the potato crops in England, and that, if it extended to Ireland, the most serious consequences must ensue.

This mysterious but universal sickness of a single root changed the history of the world.

'There is no gambling like politics,' said Lord Roehampton, as he glanced at the *Times,* at Princedown; 'four cabinets in one week; the government must be more sick than the potatoes.'

'Berengaria always says,' said Lord Montfort, 'that you should see Princedown in summer. I, on the contrary, maintain it is essentially a winter residence, for, if there ever be a sunbeam in England, Princedown always catches it. Now to-day, one might fancy one's self at Cannes.'

Lord Montfort was quite right, but even the most wilful and selfish of men was generally obliged to pass his Christmas at his northern castle. Montforts had passed their Christmas in that grim and mighty dwelling-place for centuries. Even he was not strong enough to contend against such tradition. Besides, every one loves power, even if they do not know what to do with it. There are such things as memberships for counties, which, if public feeling be not outraged, are hereditary, and adjacent boroughs, which, with a little management and much expense, become reasonable and loyal. If the flag were rarely to wave on the proud keep of Montfort, all these satisfactory circumstances would be greatly disturbed and baffled; and if the ancient ensign did not promise welcome and hospitality at Christmas, some of the principal uses even of Earls of Montfort might be questioned.

There was another reason, besides the distance and the clime, why Lord Montfort disliked the glorious pile which every Englishman envied him for possessing. The mighty domain of Montfort was an estate in strict settlement. Its lord could do nothing but enjoy its convenience and its beauty, and expend its revenues. Nothing could be sold or bought, not the slightest alteration — according to Lord Montfort — be made, without applying to trustees for their sanction. Lord Montfort spoke of this pitiable state of affairs as if he were describing the serfdom of the Middle Ages. 'If I were to pull this bell-rope, and it came down,' he would say, 'I should have to apply to the trustees before it could be arranged.'

Such a humiliating state of affairs had induced his lordship, on the very first occasion, to expend half a million of accumulations, which were at his own disposal, in the purchase of Princedown, which certainly was a very different residence from Montfort Castle, alike in its clime and character.

Princedown was situate in a southern county, hardly on a southern coast, for it was ten miles from the sea, though enchanting views of the Channel were frequent and exquisite. It was a palace built in old days upon the Downs, but sheltered and screened from every hostile wind. The full warmth of the south fell upon the vast but fantastic pile of the Renaissance style, said to have been built by that gifted but mysterious individual, John of Padua. The gardens were wonderful, terrace upon terrace, and on each terrace a tall fountain. But the most peculiar feature was the park, which was undulating and extensive, but its timber entirely ilex: single trees of an age and size not common in that tree, and groups and clumps of ilex, but always ilex. Beyond the park, and extending far into the horizon, was Princedown forest, the dominion of the red deer.

The Roehamptons and Endymion were the only permanent visitors at Princedown at this moment, but every day brought guests who stayed eight-and-forty hours, and then flitted. Lady Montfort, like the manager of a theatre, took care that there should be a succession of novelties to please or to surprise the wayward audience for whom she had to cater. On the whole, Lord Montfort was, for him, in an extremely good humour; never very ill; Princedown was the only place where he never was very ill; he was a little excited, too, by the state of politics, though he did not exactly know why; 'though, I suppose,' he would say to Lord Roehampton, 'if you do come in again, there will be no more nonsense about O'Connell and all that sort of thing. If you are prudent on that head, and carry a moderate fixed duty, not too high, say ten shillings — that would satisfy everybody — I do not see why the thing might not go on as long as you liked.'

Mr. Waldershare came down, exuberant with endless combinations of persons and parties. He foresaw in all these changes that most providential consummation, the end of the middle class.

Mr. Waldershare had become quite a favourite with Lord Montfort, who delighted to talk with him about the Duke of Modena, and imbibe his original views of English History. 'Only,' Lord Montfort would observe, 'the Montforts have so much Church property, and I fancy the Duke of Modena would want us to disgorge.'

St. Barbe had been invited, and made his appearance. There had been a degree of estrangement between him and his patron. St. Barbe was very jealous; he was indeed jealous of everybody and everything, and of late there was a certain Doctor Comeley, an Oxford don of the new school, who had been introduced to Lord Montfort, and was initiating him in all the mysteries of Neology. This celebrated divine, who, in a sweet silky voice, quoted Socrates instead of St. Paul, and was opposed to all symbols and formulas as essentially unphilosophical, had become the hero of 'the little dinners' at Montfort House, where St. Barbe had been so long wont to shine, and who in consequence himself had become every day more severely orthodox.

'Perhaps we may meet to-day,' said Endymion one morning to St. Barbe in Pall Mall as they were separating. 'There is a little dinner at Montfort House.'

'Confound your little dinners!' exclaimed the indignant St. Barbe; 'I hope never to go to another little dinner, and especially at Montfort House. I do not want to be asked to dinner to tumble and play tricks to amuse my host. I want to be amused myself. One cannot be silent at these little dinners, and the consequence is, you say all the good things which are in your next number, and when it comes out, people say they have heard them before. No, sir, if

Lord Montfort, or any other lord, wishes me to dine with him, let him ask me to a banquet of his own order, and where I may hold my tongue like the rest of his aristocratic guests.'

Mr. Trenchard had come down and brought the news that the ministry had resigned, and that the Queen had sent for the leader of the opposition, who was in Scotland.

'I suppose we shall have to go to town,' said Lady Roehampton to her brother, in a room busy and full. 'It is so difficult to be alone here,' she continued in a whisper; 'let us get into the gardens.' And they escaped. And then, when they were out of hearing and of sight of any one, she said, 'This is a most critical time in your life, Endymion; it makes me very anxious. I look upon it as certain that you will be in office, and in all probability under my lord. He has said nothing to me about it, but I feel quite assured it will happen. It will be a great event. Poor papa began by being an Under-Secretary of State!' she continued in a moody tone, half speaking to herself, 'and all seemed so fair then, but he had no root. What I want, Endymion, is that you should have a root. There is too much chance and favour in your lot. They will fail you some day, some day too when I may not be by you. Even this great opening, which is at hand, would never have been at your command, but for a mysterious gift on which you never could have counted.'

'It is very true, Myra, but what then?'

'Why, then, I think we should guard against such contingencies. You know what is in my mind; we have spoken of it before, and not once only. I want you to marry, and you know whom.'

'Marriage is a serious affair!' said Endymion, with a distressed look.

'The most serious. It is the principal event for good or for evil in all lives. Had I not married, and married as I did, we should not have been here — and where, I dare not think.'

'Yes; but you made a happy marriage; one of the happiest that was ever known, I think.'

'And I wish you, Endymion, to make the same. I did not marry for love, though love came, and I brought happiness to one who made me happy. But had it been otherwise, if there had been no sympathy, or prospect of sympathy, I still should have married, for it was the only chance of saving you.'

'Dearest sister! Everything I have, I owe to you.'

'It is not much,' said Myra, 'but I wish to make it much. Power in every form, and in excess, is at your disposal if you be wise. There is a woman, I think with every charm, who loves you; her fortune may have no limit; she is a member of one of the most powerful families in England — a noble family I may say, for my lord told me last night that Mr. Neuchatel would be instantly raised to the peerage, and you hesitate! By all the misery of the past — which never can be forgotten — for Heaven's sake, be wise; do not palter with such a chance.'

'If all be as you say, Myra, and I have no reason but your word to believe it so — if, for example, of which I never saw any evidence, Mr. Neuchatel would approve, or even tolerate, this alliance — I have too deep and sincere a regard for his daughter, founded on much kindness to both of us, to mock her with an offer of a heart which she has not gained.'

'You say you have a deep and sincere regard for Adriana,' said his sister. 'Why, what better basis for enduring happiness can there be? You are not a man to marry for romantic sentiment, and pass your life in writing sonnets to your wife till you find her charms and your inspiration alike exhausted; you are already wedded to the State, you have been nurtured in the thoughts of great affairs from your very child-hood, and even in the darkest hour of our horrible adversity. You are a man born for power and high condition, whose name in time ought to rank with those of the great statesmen of the continent, the true lords of Europe. Power, and power alone, should be your absorbing object, and all the accidents and inci-dents of life should only be considered with reference to that main result.'

'Well, I am only five-and-twenty, after all. There is time yet to consider this.'

'Great men should think of opportunity, and not of time. Time is the excuse of feeble and puzzled spirits. They make time the sleeping partner of their lives to accomplish what ought to be achieved by their own will. In this case, there certainly is no time like the present. The opportunity is unrivalled. All your friends would, without an exception, be de-lighted if you now were wise.'

'I hardly think my friends have given it a thought,' said Endymion, a little flushed.

'There is nothing that would please Lady Mont-fort more.'

He turned pale. 'How do you know that?' he inquired.

'She told me so, and offered to help me in bring-ing about the result.'

'Very kind of her! Well, dearest Myra, you and Lord Roehampton have much to think of at this anxious moment. Let this matter drop. We have discussed it before, and we have discussed it enough. It is more than pain for me to differ from you on any point, but I cannot offer to Adriana a heart which belongs to another.'

CHAPTER LXXXIII.

THE HOUR OF RETRIBUTION.

ALL the high expectations of December at Princedown were doomed to disappointment; they were a further illustration of Lord Roehampton's saying, that there was no gambling like politics. The leader of the opposition came up to town, but he found nothing but difficulties, and a few days before Christmas he had resigned the proffered trust. The protectionist ministry were to remain in office, and to repeal the Corn Laws. The individual who was most baulked by this unexpected result was perhaps Lord Roehampton. He was a man who really cared for nothing but office and affairs, and being advanced in life, he naturally regretted a lost opportunity. But he never showed his annoyance. Always playful, and even taking refuge in a bantering spirit, the world seemed to go light with him when everything was dark and everybody despondent.

The discontent or indignation which the contemplated revolution in policy was calculated to excite in the Conservative party generally were to a certain degree neutralised for the moment by mysterious and confidential communications, circulated by Mr. Tadpole and the managers of the party, that the change was to be accompanied by 'immense compensations.' As Parliament was to meet as soon as convenient after Christmas, and the statement of the regenerated ministry was then to be made immediately, every one held his hand, as they all felt the blow must be more efficient when the scheme of the government was known.

The Montforts were obliged to go to their castle, a visit the sad necessity of which the formation of a new government, at one time, they had hoped might have prevented. The Roehamptons passed their Christmas with Mr. Sidney Wilton at Gaydene, where Endymion also and many of the opposition were guests. Waldershare took refuge with his friends the Beaumaris', full of revenge and unceasing combinations. He took down St. Barbe with him, whose services in the session might be useful. There had been a little misunderstanding between these two eminent personages during the late season. St. Barbe was not satisfied with his position in the new journal which Waldershare had established. He affected to have been ill-treated and deceived, and this with a mysterious shake of the head which seemed to intimate state secrets that might hereafter be revealed.

The fact is, St. Barbe's political articles were so absurd it was impossible to print them; but as his name stood high as a clever writer on matters with which he was acquainted, they permitted him, particularly as they were bound to pay him a high salary, to contribute essays on the social habits and opinions of the day, which he treated in a happy and taking manner. St. Barbe himself had such a quick perception of peculiarities, so fine a power of observation,

and so keen a sense of the absurd, that when he revealed in confidence the causes of his discontent, it was
almost impossible to believe that he was entirely
serious. It seems that he expected this connection
with the journal in question to have been, to use his
own phrase, 'a closet affair,' and that he was habitually to have been introduced by the backstairs of the
palace to the presence of Royalty to receive encour-
agement and inspiration. 'I do not complain of the
pay,' he added, 'though I could get more by writing
for Shuffle and Screw, but I expected a decoration.
However, I shall probably stand for next Parliament
on the principles of the Mountain, so perhaps it is
just as well.'

Parliament soon met, and that session began which
will long be memorable. The 'immense compensations' were nowhere. Waldershare, who had only
waited for this, resigned his office as Under-Secretary
of State. This was a bad example and a blow, but
nothing compared to the resignation of his great office
in the Household by the Earl of Beaumaris. This involved unhappily the withdrawal of Lady Beaumaris,
under whose bright, inspiring roof the Tory party had
long assembled, sanguine and bold. Other considerable peers followed the precedent of Lord Beaumaris,
and withdrew their support from the ministry. Waldershare moved the amendment to the first reading
of the obnoxious bill; but although defeated by a considerable majority, the majority was mainly formed of
members of the opposition. Among these was Mr.
Ferrars, who it was observed never opened his lips
during the whole session.

This was not the case with Mr. Bertie Tremaine
and the school of Pythagoras. The opportunity long

waited for had at length arrived. There was a great parliamentary connection deserted by their leaders. This distinguished rank and file required officers. The cabinet of Mr. Bertie Tremaine was ready, and at their service. Mr. Bertie Tremaine seconded the amendment of Waldershare, and took the occasion of expounding the new philosophy, which seemed to combine the principles of Bentham with the practice of Lord Liverpool. 'I offered to you this,' he said reproachfully to Endymion; 'you might have been my secretary of state. Mr. Tremaine Bertie will now take it. He would rather have had an embassy, but he must make the sacrifice.'

The debates during the session were much carried on by the Pythagoreans, who never ceased chattering. They had men ready for every branch of the subject, and the debate was often closed by their chief in mystical sentences, which they cheered like awestruck zealots.

The bill was carried, but the dark hour of retribution at length arrived. The ministry, though sanguine of success to the last, and not without cause, were completely and ignominiously defeated. The new government, long prepared, was at once formed. Lord Roehampton again became Secretary of State, and he appointed Endymion to the post under him. 'I shall not press you unfairly,' said Mr. Bertie Tremaine to Endymion, with encouraging condescension. 'I wish my men for a season to comprehend what is a responsible opposition. I am sorry Hortensius is your solicitor-general, for I had intended him always for my chancellor.'

CHAPTER LXXXIV.

A Terrible Loss.

ERY shortly after the prorogation of parliament, an incident occurred which materially affected the position of Endymion. Lord Roehampton had a serious illness. Having a fine constitution, he apparently completely rallied from the attack, and little was known of it by the public. The world also, at that moment, was as usual much dispersed and distracted; dispersed in many climes, and distracted by the fatigue and hardships they annually endure, and which they call relaxation. Even the colleagues of the great statesman were scattered, and before they had realised that he had been seriously ill, they read of him in the fulfilment of official duties. But there was no mistake as to his state under his own roof.

Lord Roehampton had, during the later period of his life, been in the habit of working at night. It was only at night that he could command that abstraction necessary for the consideration of great affairs. He was also a real worker. He wrote his own despatches, whenever they referred to matters of moment. He left to the permanent staff of his office little but the fulfilment of duties which, though heavy and multi-farious, were duties of routine. The composition of these despatches was a source to Lord Roehampton of much gratification and excitement. They were of European fame, and their terse argument, their clear determination, and often their happy irony, were acknowledged in all the cabinets, and duly apprehended.

The physicians impressed upon Lady Roehampton that this night-work must absolutely cease. A neglect of their advice must lead to serious consequences; following it, there was no reason why her husband should not live for years, and continue to serve the State. Lord Roehampton must leave the House of Commons; he must altogether change the order of his life; he must seek more amusement in society, and yet keep early hours; and then he would find himself fresh and vigorous in the morning, and his work would rather benefit than distress him. It was all an affair of habit.

Lady Roehampton threw all her energies into this matter. She entertained for her lord a reverential affection, and his life to her seemed a precious deposit, of which she was the trustee. She succeeded where the physicians would probably have failed. Towards the end of the year Lord Roehampton was called up to the House of Lords for one of his baronies, and Endymion was informed that when Parliament met, he would have to represent the Foreign Office in the House of Commons.

Waldershare heartily congratulated him. 'You have got what I most wished to have in the world; but I will not envy you, for envy is a vile passion. You have the good fortune to serve a genial chief. I had to deal with a Harley,— cold, suspicious, ambiguous, pretending to be profound, and always in a state of perplexity.'

It was not a very agreeable session. The potato famine did something more than repeal the Corn Laws. It proved that there was no floating capital left in the country; and when the Barings and Rothschilds combined, almost as much from public spirit as from private speculation, to raise a loan of a few millions for the minister, they absolutely found the public purse was exhausted, and had to supply the greater portion of the amount from their own resources. In one of many financial debates that consequently occurred, Trenchard established himself by a clear and comprehensive view of the position of affairs, and by modestly reminding the House, that a year ago he had predicted the present condition of things, and indicated its inevitable cause.

This was the great speech on a great night, and Mr. Bertie Tremaine walked home with Trenchard. It was observed that Mr. Bertie Tremaine always walked home with the member who had made the speech of the evening.

'Your friends did not behave well to you,' he said in a hollow voice to Trenchard. 'They ought to have made you Secretary of the Treasury. Think of this. It is an important post, and may lead to anything; and, so far as I am concerned, it would give me real pleasure to see it.'

But besides the disquietude of domestic affairs, famine and failures competing in horrible catastrophe, and the Bank Act suspended, as the year advanced matters on the Continent became not less dark and troubled. Italy was mysteriously agitated; the Pope announced himself a reformer; there were disturbances in Milan, Ancona, and Ferrara; the Austrians threatened the occupation of several States, and Sardinia offered to defend His Holiness from the Austrians. In addition to all this, there were reform banquets in France, a civil war in Switzerland, and the King of Prussia thought it prudent to present his subjects with a Constitution.

The Count of Ferroll about this time made a visit to England. He was always a welcome guest there, and had received the greatest distinction which England could bestow upon a foreigner; he had been elected an honorary member of White's. 'You may have troubles here,' he said to Lady Montfort, 'but they will pass; you will have mealy potatoes again and plenty of bank notes, but we shall not get off so cheaply. Everything is quite rotten throughout the Continent. This year is tranquillity to what the next will be. There is not a throne in Europe worth a year's purchase. My worthy master wants me to return home and be minister; I am to fashion for him a new constitution. I will never have anything to do with new constitutions; their inventors are always the first victims. Instead of making a constitution, he should make a country, and convert his heterogeneous domains into a patriotic dominion.'

'But how is that to be done?'

'There is only one way; by blood and iron.'

'My dear count, you shock me!'

'I shall have to shock you a great deal more before the inevitable is brought about.'

'Well, I am glad that there is something,' said Lady Montfort, 'which is inevitable. I hope it will come soon. I am sure this country is ruined. What with cheap bread at famine prices and these railroads,

we seem quite finished. I thought one operation
was to counteract the other; but they appear both to
turn out equally fatal.'

Endymion had now one of those rare opportuni-
ties which, if men be equal to them, greatly affect
their future career. As the session advanced, debates
on foreign affairs became frequent and deeply interesting. So far as the ministry was concerned, the
burthen of these fell on the Under-Secretary of State.
He was never wanting. The House felt that he had
not only the adequate knowledge, but that it was
knowledge perfectly digested; that his remarks and
conduct were those of a man who had given constant thought to his duties, and was master of his subject. His oratorical gifts also began to be recognised.
The power and melody of his voice had been before remarked, and that is a gift which much contributes to
success in a popular assembly. He was ready without being too fluent. There were light and shade in
his delivery. He repressed his power of sarcasm;
but if unjustly and inaccurately attacked, he could be
keen. Over his temper he had a complete control; if,
indeed, his entire insensibility to violent language on
the part of an opponent was not organic. All acknowledged his courtesy, and both sides sympathised
with a young man who proved himself equal to no
ordinary difficulties. In a word, Endymion was popular, and that popularity was not diminished by the
fact of his being the brother of Lady Roehampton,
who exercised great influence in society, and who
was much beloved.

As the year advanced external affairs became
daily more serious, and the country congratulated
itself that its interests were entrusted to a minister of

the experience and capacity of Lord Roehampton. That statesman seemed never better than when the gale ran high. Affairs of France began to assume the complexion that the Count of Ferroll had prophetically announced. If a crash occurred in that quarter, Lord Roehampton felt that all Europe might be in a blaze. Affairs were never more serious than at the turn of the year. Lord Roehampton told his wife that their holidays must be spent in St. James' Square, for he could not leave London; but he wished her to go to Gaydene, where they had been invited by Mr. Sidney Wilton to pass their Christmas as usual. Nothing, however, would induce her to quit his side. He seemed quite well, but the pressure of affairs was extreme; and sometimes, against all her remonstrances, he was again working at night. Such remonstrances on other subjects would probably have been successful, for her influence over him was extreme. But to a minister responsible for the interests of a great country they are vain, futile, impossible. One might as well remonstrate with an officer on the field of battle on the danger he was incurring. She said to him one night in his library, where she paid him a little visit before she retired, 'My heart, I know it is no use my saying anything, and yet — remember your promise. This night-work makes me very unhappy.'

'I remember my promise, and I will try not to work at night again in a hurry, but I must finish this despatch. If I did not, I could not sleep, and you know sleep is what I require.'

'Good night, then.'

He looked up with his winning smile, and held out his lips. 'Kiss me,' he said; 'I never felt better.'

Lady Roehampton after a time slumbered; how long she knew not, but when she woke, her lord was not at her side. She struck a light and looked at her watch. It was past three o'clock; she jumped out of bed, and, merely in her slippers and her *robe de chambre,* descended to the library. It was a large, long room, and Lord Roehampton worked at the extreme end of it. The candles were nearly burnt out. As she approached him, she perceived that he was leaning back in his chair. When she reached him, she observed he was awake, but he did not seem to recognise her. A dreadful feeling came over her. She took his hand. It was quite cold. Her intellect for an instant seemed to desert her. She looked round her with an air void almost of intelligence, and then rushing to the bell she continued ringing it till some of the household appeared. A medical man was near at hand, and in a few minutes arrived, but it was a bootless visit. All was over, and all had been over, he said, 'for some time.'

CHAPTER LXXXV.

FLORESTAN'S FAREWELL.

'WELL, have you made up your government?' asked Lady Montfort of the Prime Minister as he entered her boudoir. He shook his head.

'Have you seen her?' he inquired.

'No, not yet; I suppose she will see me as soon as any one.'

'I am told she is utterly overwhelmed.'

'She was devoted to him; it was the happiest union I ever knew; but Lady Roehampton is not the woman to be utterly overwhelmed. She has too imperial a spirit for that.'

'It is a great misfortune,' said the Prime Minister. 'We have not been lucky since we took the reins.'

'Well, there is no use in deploring. There is nobody else to take the reins, so you may defy misfortunes. The question now is, what are you going to do?'

'Well, there seems to me only one thing to do. We must put Rawchester there.'

'Rawchester!' exclaimed Lady Montfort, 'what, "Niminy-Piminy"?'

'Well, he is conciliatory,' said the Premier, 'and if you are not very clever, you should be conciliatory.'

'He never knows his own mind for a week together.'

'We will take care of his mind,' said the Prime Minister, 'but he has travelled a good deal, and knows the public men.'

'Yes,' said Lady Montfort, 'and the public men, I fear, know him.'

'Then he can make a good House of Lords' speech, and we have a firstrate man in the Commons; so it will do.'

'I do not think your firstrate man in the House of Commons will remain,' said Lady Montfort drily.

'You do not mean that?' said the Prime Minister, evidently alarmed.

'His health is delicate,' said Lady Montfort; 'had it not been for his devotion to Lord Roehampton, I know he thought of travelling for a couple of years.'

'Ferrars' health delicate?' said the Premier; 'I thought he was the picture of health and youthful vigour. Health is one of the elements to be considered in calculating the career of a public man, and I have always predicted an eminent career for Ferrars, because, in addition to his remarkable talents, he had apparently such a fine constitution.'

'No health could stand working under Lord Rawchester.'

'Well, but what am I to do? I cannot make Mr. Ferrars Secretary of State.'

'Why not?'

The Prime Minister looked considerably perplexed. Such a promotion could not possibly have occurred

to him. Though a man of many gifts, and a statesman, he had been educated in high Whig routine,
and the proposition of Lady Montfort was like recom-
mending him to make a curate a bishop.

'Well,' he said, 'Ferrars is a very clever fellow.
He is our rising young man, and there is no doubt
that, if his health is not so delicate as you fear, he
will mount high; but though our rising young man,
he is a young man, much too young to be a Secretary of State. He wants age, larger acquaintance
with affairs, greater position, and more root in the
country.'

'What was Mr. Canning's age, who held Mr.
Ferrars' office when he was made Secretary of State?
and what root in the country had he?'

When the Prime Minister got back to Downing
Street, he sent immediately for his head whip. 'Look
after Ferrars,' he said; 'they are trying to induce him
to resign office. If he does, our embarrassments will
be extreme. Lord Rawchester will be Secretary of
State; send a paragraph at once to the papers announcing it. But look after Ferrars, and immediately,
and report to me.'

Lord Roehampton had a large entailed estate,
though his affairs were always in a state of confusion.
That seems almost the inevitable result of being absorbed in the great business of governing mankind.
If there be exceptions among statesmen of the highest
class, they will generally be found among those who
have been chiefly in opposition, and so have had
leisure and freedom of mind sufficient to manage
their estates. Lord Roehampton had, however, extensive powers of charging his estate in lieu of dower,
and he had employed them to their utmost extent;

so his widow was well provided for. The executors were Mr. Sidney Wilton and Endymion.

After a short period, Lady Roehampton saw Adriana, and not very long after, Lady Montfort. They both of them, from that time, were her frequent, if not constant, companions, but she saw no one else. Once only, since the terrible event, was she seen by the world, and that was when a tall figure, shrouded in the darkest attire, attended as chief mourner at the burial of her lord in Westminster Abbey. She remained permanently in London, not only because she had no country house, but because she wished to be with her brother. As time advanced she frequently saw Mr. Sidney Wilton, who, being chief executor of the will, and charged with all her affairs, had necessarily much on which to consult her.

One of the difficulties was to find for her a suitable residence, for of course, she was not to remain in the family mansion in St. James' Square. That difficulty was ultimately overcome in a manner highly interesting to her feelings. Her father's mansion in Hill Street, where she had passed her prosperous and gorgeous childhood, was in the market, and she was most desirous to occupy it. 'It will seem like a great step towards the restoration,' she said to Endymion. 'My plans are, that you should give up the Albany, and that we should live together. I should like to live together in Hill Street; I should like to see our nursery once more. The past then will be a dream, or at least all the past that is disagreeable. My fortune is yours; as we are twins, it is likely that I may live as long as you do. But I wish you to be the master of the house, and in time receive your friends in a manner becoming your position. I do

not think that I shall ever much care to go out again,
but I may help you at home, and then you can invite women; a mere bachelor's house is always dull.'

There was one difficulty still in this arrangement.
The mansion in Hill Street was not to be let, it
was for sale, and the price naturally for such a mansion, in such a situation, was considerable; quite beyond the means of Lady Roehampton, who had a
very ample income, but no capital. This difficulty
however, vanished in a moment. Mr. Sidney Wilton
purchased the house; he wanted an investment, and
this was an excellent one; so Lady Roehampton became his tenant.

The change was great in the life of Myra, and she
felt it. She loved her lord, and had cut off her beautiful hair, which reached almost to her feet, and had
tied it round his neck in his coffin. But Myra, notwithstanding she was a woman, and a woman of
transcendent beauty, had never had a romance of the
heart. Until she married, her pride and her love for
her brother, which was part of her pride, had absorbed her being. When she married, and particularly as time advanced, she felt all the misery of her
existence had been removed, and nothing could exceed the tenderness and affectionate gratitude, and
truly unceasing devotion, which she extended to the
gifted being to whom she owed this deliverance.
But it was not in the nature of things that she could
experience those feelings which still echo in the
heights of Meilleraie, and compared with which all
the glittering accidents of fortune sink into insignifi-
cance.

The year rolled on, an agitated year of general
revolution. Endymion himself was rarely in society,

for all the time which the House of Commons spared to him he wished chiefly to dedicate to his sister. His brougham was always ready to take him up to Hill Street for one of those somewhat hurried, but amusing little dinners, which break the monotony of parliamentary life. And sometimes he brought a companion, generally Mr. Wilton, and sometimes they met Lady Montfort or Adriana, now ennobled as the daughter of Lord Hainault. There was much to talk about, even if they did not talk about themselves and their friends, for every day brought great events, fresh insurrections, new constitutions, changes of dynasties, assassinations of ministers, states of siege, evanescent empires, and premature republics.

On one occasion, having previously prepared his sister, who seemed not uninterested by the suggestion, Endymion brought Thornberry to dine in Hill Street. There was no one else present except Adriana. Job was a great admirer of Lady Roehampton, but was a little awestruck by her. He remembered her in her childhood, a beautiful being who never smiled. She received him very graciously, and after dinner, inviting him to sit by her on the sofa, referred with delicacy to old times.

'Your ladyship,' said Thornberry, 'would not know that I live myself now at Hurstley.'

'Indeed!' said Myra unaffectedly surprised.

'Well, it happened in this way; my father now is in years, and can no longer visit us as he occasionally did in Lancashire; so wishing to see us all, at least once more, we agreed to pay him a visit. I do not know how it exactly came about, but my wife took a violent fancy to the place. They all received us very kindly. The good rector and his dear kind wife made it very pleasant, and the Archbishop was there— whom we used to call Mr. Nigel—only think! That is a wonderful affair. He is not at all high and mighty, but talked with us, and walked with us, just the same as in old days. He took a great fancy to my boy, John Hampden, and, after all, my boy is to go to Oxford, and not to Owens College, as I had first intended.'

'That is a great change.'

'Well, I wanted him to go to Owens College, I confess, but I did not care so much about Mill Hill. That was his mother's fancy; she was very strong about that. It is a Nonconformist school, but I am not a Nonconformist. I do not much admire dogmas, but I am a Churchman, as my fathers were. However, John Hampden is not to go to Mill Hill. He has gone to a sort of college near Oxford, which the Archbishop recommended to us; the principal, and all the tutors are clergymen—of course of our Church. My wife is quite delighted with it all.'

'Well, that is a good thing.'

'And so,' continued Thornberry, 'she got it into her head she should like to live at Hurstley, and I took the place. I am afraid I have been foolish enough to lay out a great deal of money there—for a place not my own. Your ladyship would not know the old hall. I have, what they call, restored it, and upon my word, except the new hall of the Clothworkers' Company, where I dined the other day, I do not know anything of the kind that is prettier.'

'The dear old hall!' murmured Lady Roehampton.

In time, though no one mentioned it, everybody thought that if an alliance ultimately took place between Lady Roehampton and Mr. Sidney Wilton, it would be the most natural thing in the world, and everybody would approve it. True, he was her father's friend, and much her senior, but then he was still good-looking, very clever, very much considered, and lord of a large estate, and at any rate he was a younger man than her late husband.

When these thoughts became more rife in society, and began to take the form of speech, the year was getting old, and this reminds us of a little incident which took place many months previously, at the beginning of the year, and which we ought to record.

Shortly after the death of Lord Roehampton, Prince Florestan called one morning in St. James' Square. He said he would not ask Lady Roehampton to see him, but he was obliged suddenly to leave England, and he did not like to depart without personally inquiring after her. He left a letter and a little packet. And the letter ran thus:—

'I am obliged, madam, to leave England suddenly, and it is probable that we shall never meet again. I should be happy if I had your prayers! This little jewel enclosed belonged to my mother, the Queen Agrippina. She told me that I was never to part with it, except to somebody I loved as much as herself. There is only one person in the world to whom I owe affection. It is to her who from the first was always kind to me, and who, through dreary years of danger and anxiety, has been the charm and consolation of the life of

'FLORESTAN.'

CHAPTER LXXXVI.

FLORESTAN PROCLAIMS HIMSELF
A SOVEREIGN.

ON THE evening of the day on which Prince Florestan personally left the letter with Lady Roehampton, he quitted London with the Duke of St. Angelo and his aides-de-camp, and, embarking in his steam yacht, which was lying at Southampton, quitted England. They pursued a prosperous course for about a week, when they passed through the Straits of Gibraltar, and, not long afterwards, cast anchor in a small and solitary bay. There the prince and his companions, and half-a-dozen servants, well armed and in military attire, left the yacht, and proceeded on foot into the country for a short distance, when they arrived at a large farmhouse. Here, it was evident, they were expected. Men came forward with many horses, and mounted, and accompanied the party which had arrived. They advanced about ten miles, and halted as they were approaching a small but fortified town.

The prince sent the Duke of St. Angelo forward to announce his arrival to the governor, and to require him to surrender. The governor, however, refused, and ordered the garrison to fire on the invaders. This they declined to do; the governor, with many ejaculations, and stamping with rage, broke his sword, and the prince entered the town. He was warmly received, and the troops, amounting to about twelve hundred men, placed themselves at his disposal. The prince remained at this town only a couple of hours, and at the head of his forces advanced into the country. At a range of hills he halted, sent out reconnoitring parties, and pitched his camp. In the morning, the Marquis of Vallombrosa, with a large party of gentlemen well mounted, arrived, and were warmly greeted. The prince learnt from them that the news of his invasion had reached the governor of the province, who was at one of the most considerable cities of the kingdom, with a population exceeding two hundred thousand, and with a military division for its garrison. 'They will not wait for our arrival,' said Vallombrosa, 'but, trusting to their numbers, will come out and attack us.'

The news of the scouts being that the mountain passes were quite unoccupied by the enemy, the prince determined instantly to continue his advance, and take up a strong position on the other side of the range, and await his fate. The passage was well effected, and on the fourth day of the invasion the advanced guard of the enemy was in sight. The prince commanded that no one should attend him, but alone and tying a white handkerchief round his sword, he galloped up to the hostile lines, and said in a clear, loud voice, 'My men, this is the sword of my father!'

'Florestan for ever!' was the only and universal reply. The cheers of the advanced guard reached and were re-echoed by the main body. The commander-in-chief, bareheaded, came up to give in his allegiance and receive His Majesty's orders. They were for immediate progress, and at the head of the army which had been sent out to destroy him, Florestan in due course entered the enthusiastic city, which recognised him as its sovereign. The city was illuminated, and he went to the opera in the evening. The singing was not confined to the theatre. During the whole night the city itself was one song of joy and triumph, and that night no one slept.

After this there was no trouble and no delay. It was a triumphal march. Every town opened its gates, and devoted municipalities proffered golden keys. Every village sent forth its troop of beautiful maidens, scattering roses, and singing the national anthem, which had been composed by Queen Agrippina. On the tenth day of the invasion King Florestan, utterly unopposed, entered the magnificent capital of his realm, and slept in the purple bed which had witnessed his princely birth.

Among all the strange revolutions of this year, this adventure of Florestan was not the least interesting to the English people. Although society had not smiled on him, he had always been rather a favourite with the bulk of the population. His fine countenance, his capital horsemanship, his graceful bow that always won a heart, his youth, and love of sport, his English education, and the belief that he was sincere in his regard for the country where he had been so long a guest, were elements of popularity that, particularly now he was successful, were unmistakable. And certainly Lady Roehampton, in her solitude, did not disregard his career or conduct. They were naturally often in her thoughts, for there was scarcely a day in which his name did not figure in the newspapers, and always in connection with matters of general interest and concern. The government he established was liberal, but it was discreet, and, though conciliatory, firm. 'If he declares for the English alliance,' said Waldershare, 'he is safe;' and he did declare for the English alliance, and the English people were very pleased by his declaration, which in their apprehension meant national progress, the amelioration of society, and increased exports.

The main point, however, which interested his subjects was his marriage. That was both a difficult and a delicate matter to decide. The great continental dynasties looked with some jealousy and suspicion on him, and the small reigning houses, who were all allied with the great continental dynasties, thought it prudent to copy their example. All these reigning families, whether large or small, were themselves in a perplexed and alarmed position at this period, very disturbed about their present, and very doubtful about their future. At last it was understood that a Princess of Saxe-Babel, though allied with royal and imperial houses, might share the diadem of a successful adventurer, and then in time, and when it had been sufficiently reiterated, paragraphs appeared unequivocally contradicting the statement, followed with agreeable assurances that it was unlikely that a Princess of Saxe-Babel, allied with royal and imperial houses, should unite herself to a parvenu monarch, however powerful. Then in turn these articles were stigmatised as libels, and entirely unauthorised, and no less a personage than a princess of the House of Saxe-Genesis was talked of as the future queen; but on referring to the 'Almanach de Gotha,' it was discovered that family had been extinct since the first French Revolution. So it seemed at last that nothing was certain except that his subjects were very anxious that King Florestan should present them with a queen.

CHAPTER LXXXVII.

AS TIME flew on, the friends of Lady Roehampton thought, and spoke, with anxiety about her re-entrance into society. Mr. Sidney Wilton had lent Gaydene to her for the autumn, when he always visited Scotland, and the winter had passed away uninterruptedly, at a charming and almost unknown watering-place, where she seemed the only visitant, and where she wandered about in silence on the sands. The time was fast approaching when the inevitable year of seclusion would expire, and Lady Roehampton gave no indication of any change in her life and habits. At length, after many appeals, and expostulations, and entreaties, and little scenes, the second year of the widowhood having advanced some months, it was decided that Lady Roehampton should re-enter society, and the occasion on which this was to take place was no mean one.

Lady Montfort was to give a ball early in June, and royalty itself was, to be her guests. The entertainments at Montfort House were always magnificent, but this was to exceed accustomed splendour. All the world were to be there, and all the world who were not invited were in as much despair as if they had lost their fortune or their character.

Lady Roehampton had a passion for light, provided the light was not supplied by gas or oil. Her saloons, even when alone were always brilliantly illuminated. She held that the moral effect of such a circumstance on her temperament was beneficial, and not slight. It is a rare, but by no means a singular, belief. When she descended into her drawing-room on the critical night, its resplendence was some preparation for the scene which awaited her. She stood for a moment before the tall mirror which reflected her whole person. What were her thoughts? What was the impression that the fair vision conveyed?

Her countenance was grave, but it was not sad. Myra had now completed, or was on the point of completing, her thirtieth year. She was a woman of transcendent beauty; perhaps she might justly be described as the most beautiful woman then alive. Time had even improved her commanding mien, the graceful sweep of her figure and the voluptuous undulation of her shoulders; but time also had spared those charms which are more incidental to early youth, the splendour of her complexion, the whiteness of her teeth, and the lustre of her violet eyes. She had cut off in her grief the profusion of her dark chestnut locks, that once reached to her feet, and she wore her hair in, what was then and perhaps is now called, a crop, but it was luxuriant in natural quantity and rich in colour, and most effectively set off her arched brow, and the oval of her fresh and beauteous cheek. The crop was crowned to-night by a coronet of brilliants.

Copyright 1904 by M. Walter Dunne.

AFTER AN ORIGINAL DRAWING BY GEORGE ALFRED
WILLIAMS.

'Your carriage is ready, my lady,' said a servant,
*'but there is a gentleman below who has brought
a letter for your ladyship.'*

'Your carriage is ready, my lady,' said a servant; 'but there is a gentleman below who has brought a letter for your ladyship, and which, he says, he must personally deliver to you, madam. I told him your ladyship was going out and could not see him, but he put his card in this envelope, and requested that I would hand it to you, madam. He says he will only deliver the letter to your ladyship, and not detain you a moment.'

Lady Roehampton opened the envelope, and read the card, 'THE DUKE OF ST. ANGELO.'

'The Duke of St. Angelo!' she murmured to herself, and looked for a moment abstracted. Then turning to the servant, she said, 'He must be shown up.'

'Madam,' said the duke as he entered, and bowed with much ceremony, 'I am ashamed of appearing to be an intruder, but my commands were to deliver this letter to your ladyship immediately on my arrival, whatever the hour. I have only this instant arrived. We had a bad passage. I know your ladyship's carriage is at the door. I will redeem my pledge and not trespass on your time for one instant. If your ladyship requires me, I am ever at your command.'

'At Carlton Gardens?'

'No; at our embassy.'

'His Majesty, I hope, is well?'

'In every sense, my lady,' and bowing to the ground the duke withdrew.

She broke the seal of the letter while still standing, and held it to a sconce that was on the mantelpiece, and then she read:—

'You were the only person I called upon when I suddenly left England. I had no hope of seeing you, but it was the homage of gratitude and adoration. Great events have happened since we last met. I have realised my dreams, dreams which I sometimes fancied you, and you alone, did not depreciate or discredit, and, in the sweetness of your charity, would not have been sorry were they accomplished.

'I have established what I believe to be a strong and just government in a great kingdom. I have not been uninfluenced by the lessons of wisdom I gained in your illustrious land. I have done some things which it was a solace for me to believe you would not altogether disapprove.

' My subjects are anxious that the dynasty I have re-established should not be evanescent. Is it too bold to hope that I may find a companion in you to charm and to counsel me? I can offer you nothing equal to your transcendent merit, but I can offer you the heart and the throne of   FLORESTAN.'

Still holding the letter in one hand, she looked around as if some one might be present. Her cheek was scarlet, and there was for a moment an expression of wildness in her glance. Then she paced the saloon with an agitated step, and then she read the letter again and again, and still she paced the saloon. The whole history of her life revolved before her; every scene, every character, every thought, and sentiment, and passion. The brightness of her nursery days, and Hurstley with all its miseries, and Hainault with its gardens, and the critical hour, which had opened to her a future of such unexpected lustre and happiness.

The clock had struck more than once during this long and terrible soliloquy, wherein she had to search and penetrate her inmost heart, and now it struck two. She started, and hurriedly rang the bell.

'I shall not want the carriage to-night,' she said, and when again alone, she sat down and, burying her face in her alabaster arms, for a long time remained motionless.

CHAPTER LXXXVIII.

Mr. Wilton Is Disappointed.

AD he been a youth about to make a *début* in the great world, Sidney Wilton could not have been more agitated than he felt at the prospect of the fête at Montfort House. Lady Roehampton, after nearly two years of retirement, was about to re-enter society. During this interval she had not been estranged from him. On the contrary, he had been her frequent and customary companion. Except Adriana, and Lady Montfort, and her brother, it might almost be said, her only one. Why, then, was he agitated? He had been living in a dream for two years, cherishing wild thoughts of exquisite happiness. He would have been content had the dream never been disturbed; but this return to hard and practical life of her whose unconscious witchery had thrown a spell over his existence, roused him to the reality of his position, and it was one of terrible emotion.

During the life of her husband, Sidney Wilton had been the silent adorer of Myra. With every accomplishment and every advantage that are supposed to make life delightful — a fine countenance, a noble mien, a manner natural and attractive, an ancient lineage, and a vast estate — he was the favourite of society, who did more than justice to his talents, which, though not brilliant, were considerable, and who could not too much appreciate the high tone of his mind; his generosity and courage, and true patrician spirit which inspired all his conduct, and guided him ever to do that which was liberal and gracious and just.

There was only one fault which society found in Sidney Wilton; he would not marry. This was provoking, because he was the man of all others who ought to marry, and make a heroine happy. Society did not give it up till he was forty, about the time he became acquainted with Lady Roehampton; and that incident threw no light on his purposes or motives, for he was as discreet as he was devoted, and Myra herself was unconscious of his being anything to her save the dearest friend of her father, and the most cherished companion of her husband.

When one feels deeply, one is apt to act suddenly, perhaps rashly. There are moments in life when suspense can be borne no longer. And Sidney Wilton, who had been a silent votary for more than ten years, now felt that the slightest delay in his fate would be intolerable. It was the ball at Montfort House that should be the scene of this decision of destiny.

She was about to re-enter society, radiant as the morn, amid flowers and music, and all the accidents of social splendour. His sympathetic heart had been some solace to her in her sorrow and her solitude. Now, in the joyous blaze of life, he was resolved to ask her whether it were impossible that they should never again separate, and in the crowd, as well as when alone, feel their mutual devotion.

Mr. Wilton was among those who went early to Montfort House, which was not his wont; but he was restless and disquieted. She could hardly have arrived; but there would be some there who would speak of her. That was a great thing. Sidney Wilton had arrived at that state when conversation can only interest on one subject. When a man is really in love, he is disposed to believe that, like himself, everybody is thinking of the person who engrosses his brain and heart.

The magnificent saloons, which in half an hour would be almost impassable, were only sprinkled with guests, who, however, were constantly arriving. Mr. Wilton looked about him in vain for the person who, he was quite sure, could not then be present. He lingered by the side of Lady Montfort, who bowed to those who came, but who could spare few consecutive words, even to Mr. Wilton, for her watchful eye expected every moment a summons to descend her marble staircase and receive her royal guests.

The royal guests arrived; there was a grand stir, and many gracious bows, and some cordial, but dignified, shake-hands. The rooms were crowded; yet space in the ball-room was well preserved, so that the royal vision might range with facility from its golden chairs to the beauteous beings, and still more beautiful costumes, displaying with fervent loyalty their fascinating charms.

There was a new band to-night, that had come from some distant but celebrated capital; musicians known by fame to everybody, but whom nobody had ever heard. They played wonderfully on instruments of new invention, and divinely upon old ones. It was impossible that anything could be more gay and inspiriting than their silver bugles, and their carillons of tinkling bells.

They found an echo in the heart of Sidney Wilton, who, seated near the entrance of the ball-room, watched every arrival with anxious expectation. But the anxiety vanished for a moment under the influence of the fantastic and frolic strain. It seemed a harbinger of happiness and joy. He fell into a reverie, and wandered with a delightful companion in castles of perpetual sunshine, and green retreats, and pleasant terraces.

But the lady never came.

Then the strain changed. There happened to be about this time a truly diabolic opera much in vogue, with unearthly choruses, and dances of fiendish revelry. These had been skilfully adapted and introduced by the musicians, converting a dark and tragic theme into wild and grotesque merriment. But they could not succeed in diverting the mind of one of their audience from the character of the original composition. Dark thoughts and images fell upon the spirit of Sidney Wilton; his hope and courage left him. He almost felt he could not execute to-night the bold purpose he had brooded over. He did not feel in good fortune. There seemed some demon gibbering near him, and he was infinitely relieved, like a man released from some mesmeric trance, when the music ceased, the dance broke up, and he found himself surrounded, not by demons, but the usual companions of his daily life.

But the lady never came.

'Where can your sister be?' said Lady Montfort to Endymion. 'She promised me to come early; something must have happened. Is she ill?'

'Quite well; I saw her before I left Hill Street. She wished me to come alone, as she would not be here early.'

'I hope she will be in time for the royal supper table; I quite count on her.'

'She is sure to be here.'

Lord Hainault was in earnest conversation with Baron Sergius, now the minister of King Florestan at the Court of St. James'. It was a wise appointment, for Sergius knew intimately all the English statesmen of eminence, and had known them for many years. They did not look upon him as the mere representative of a revolutionary and parvenu sovereign; he was quite one of themselves, had graduated at the Congress of Vienna, and, it was believed, had softened many subsequent difficulties by his sagacity. He had always been a cherished guest at Apsley House, and it was known the great duke often consulted him. 'As long as Sergius sways his councils, he will indulge in no adventures,' said Europe. 'As long as Sergius remains here, the English alliance is safe,' said England. After Europe and England, the most important confidence to obtain was that of Lord Hainault, and Baron Sergius had been not unsuccessful in that respect.

'Your master has only to be liberal and steady,' said Lord Hainault, with his accustomed genial yet half-sarcastic smile, 'and he may have anything he likes. But we do not want any wars; they are not liked in the city.'

'Our policy is peace,' said Sergius.

'I think we ought to congratulate Sir Peter,' said Mr. Waldershare to Adriana, with whom he had been dancing, and whom he was leading back to Lady Hainault. 'Sir Peter, here is a lady who wishes to congratulate you on your deserved elevation.'

'Well, I do not know what to say about it,' said the former Mr. Vigo, highly gratified, but a little confused; 'my friends would have it.'

'Ay, ay,' said Waldershare, '"at the request of friends;" the excuse I gave for publishing my sonnets.' And then, advancing, he delivered his charge to her *chaperone,* who looked dreamy, abstracted, and uninterested.

'We have just been congratulating the new baronet, Sir Peter Vigo,' said Waldershare.

'Ah!' said Lady Hainault with a contemptuous sigh, 'he is, at any rate, not obliged to change his name. The desire to change one's name does indeed appear to me to be a singular folly. If your name had been disgraced, I could understand it, as I could understand a man then going about in a mask. But the odd thing is, the persons who always want to change their names are those whose names are the most honoured.'

'Oh, you are here!' said Mr. St. Barbe acidly to Mr. Seymour Hicks. 'I think you are everywhere. I suppose they will make you a baronet next. Have you seen the batch? I could not believe my eyes when I read it. I believe the government is demented. Not a single literary man among them. Not that I wanted their baronetcy. Nothing would have tempted me to accept one. But there is Gushy; he, I know, would have liked it. I must say I feel for Gushy; his works only selling half what they did, and then thrown over in this insolent manner!'

'Gushy is not in society,' said Mr. Seymour Hicks in a solemn tone of contemptuous pity.

'That is society,' said St. Barbe, as he received a bow of haughty grace from Mrs. Rodney, who, fascinating and fascinated, was listening to the enamoured murmurs of an individual with a very bright star and a very red ribbon.

'I dined with the Rodneys yesterday,' said Mr. Seymour Hicks; 'they do the thing well.'

'You dined there!' exclaimed St. Barbe. 'It is very odd, they have never asked me. Not that I would have accepted their invitation. I avoid parvenus. They are too fidgety for my taste. I require repose, and only dine with the old nobility.'

CHAPTER LXXXIX.

Job Thornberry at Hurstley.

THE Right Honourable Job Thornberry and Mrs. Thornberry had received an invitation to the Montfort ball. Job took up the card, and turned it over more than once, and looked at it as if it were some strange animal, with an air of pleased and yet cynical perplexity; then he shrugged his shoulders and murmured to himself, 'No; I don't think that will do. Besides, I must be at Hurstley by that time.'

Going to Hurstley now was not so formidable an affair as it was in Endymion's boyhood. Then the journey occupied a whole and wearisome day. Little Hurstley had become a busy station of the great Slap-Bang railway, and a despatch train landed you at the bustling and flourishing hostelry, our old and humble friend, the Horse Shoe, within the two hours. It was a rate that satisfied even Thornberry, and almost reconciled him to the too frequent presence of his wife and family at Hurstley, a place to which Mrs. Thornberry had, it would seem, become passionately attached.

'There is a charm about the place, I must say,' said Job to himself, as he reached his picturesque home on a rich summer evening; 'and yet I hated it as a boy. To be sure, I was then discontented and unhappy, and now I have every reason to be much the reverse. Our feelings affect even scenery. It certainly is a pretty place; I really think one of the prettiest places in England.'

Job was cordially welcomed. His wife embraced him, and the younger children clung to him with an affection which was not diminished by the remembrance that their father never visited them with empty hands. His eldest son, a good-looking and well-grown stripling, just home for the holidays, stood apart, determined to show he was a man of the world, and superior to the weakness of domestic sensibility. When the hubbub was a little over, he advanced and shook hands with his father with a certain dignity.

'And when did you arrive, my boy? I was looking up your train at Bradshaw as I came along. I made out you should get the branch at Culvers Gate.'

'I drove over,' replied the son; 'I and a friend of mine drove tandem, and I'll bet we got here sooner than we should have done by the branch.'

'Hem!' said Job Thornberry.

'Job,' said Mrs. Thornberry, 'I have made two engagements for you this evening. First, we will go and see your father, and then we are to drink tea at the rectory.'

'Hem!' said Job Thornberry; 'well, I would rather the first evening should have been a quiet one; but let it be so.'

The visit to the father was kind, dutiful, and wearisome. There was not a single subject on which the father and son had thoughts in common. The con-

versation of the father took various forms of expressing his wonder that his son had become what he
was, and the son could only smile, and turn the
subject, by asking after the produce of some particular field that had been prolific or obstinate in old
days. Mrs. Thornberry looked absent, and was think-
ing·of the rectory; the grandson who had accompanied
them was silent and supercilious; and everybody felt
relieved when Mrs. Thornberry, veiling her impatience
by her fear of keeping her father-in-law up late,
made a determined move and concluded the domestic
ceremony.

The rectory afforded a lively contrast to the late
scene. Mr. and Mrs. Penruddock were full of intelligence and animation. Their welcome of Mr. Thornberry was exactly what it ought to have been; re-
spectful, even somewhat deferential, but cordial and
unaffected. They conversed on all subjects, public
and private, and on both seemed equally well informed,
for they not only read more than one newspaper, but
Mrs. Penruddock had an extensive correspondence,
the conduct of which was one of the chief pleasures
and excitements of her life. Their tea-equipage, too,
was a picture of abundance and refinement. Such
pretty china, and such various and delicious cates!
White bread, and brown bread, and plum cakes, and
seed cakes, and no end of cracknels, and toasts, dry
or buttered. Mrs. Thornberry seemed enchanted and
gushing with affection,— everybody was dear or dearest. Even the face of John Hampden beamed with
condescending delight as he devoured a pyramid of
dainties.

Just before the tea-equipage was introduced Mrs.
Penruddock rose from her seat and whispered some-

thing to Mrs. Thornberry, who seemed pleased and agitated and a little blushing, and then their hostess addressed Job and said, 'I was mentioning to your wife that the Archbishop is here, and that I hoped you would not dislike meeting him.'

And very shortly after this, the Archbishop, who had been taking a village walk, entered the room. It was evident that he was intimate with the occupiers of Hurstley Hall. He addressed Mrs. Thornberry with the ease of habitual acquaintance, while John Hampden seemed almost to rush into his arms. Job himself had seen his Grace in London, though he had never had the opportunity of speaking to him, but yielded to his cordiality, when the Archbishop, on his being named, said, 'It is a pleasure to meet an old friend, and in times past a kind one.'

It was a most agreeable evening. The Archbishop talked to every one, but never seemed to engross the conversation. He talked to the ladies of gardens, and cottages, and a little of books, seemed deeply interested in the studies and progress of the grandson Thornberry, who evidently idolised him; and in due course his Grace was engaged in economical speculations with Job himself, who was quite pleased to find a priest as liberal and enlightened as he was able and thoroughly informed. An hour before midnight they separated, though the Archbishop attended them to the hall.

Mrs. Thornberry's birthday was near at hand, which Job always commemorated with a gift. It had commenced with some severe offering, like 'Paradise Lost,' then it fell into the gentler form of Tennyson, and, of late, unconsciously under the influence of his wife, it had taken the shape of a bracelet or a shawl.

This evening, as he was rather feeling his way as to what might please her most, Mrs. Thornberry embracing him, and hiding her face on his breast, murmured, 'Do not give me any jewel, dear Job. What I should like would be that you should restore the chapel here.'

'Restore the chapel here! oh, oh!' said Job Thornberry.

CHAPTER XC.

HE Archbishop called at Hurstley House the next day. It was a visit to Mr. Thornberry, but all the family were soon present, and clustered round the visitor. Then they walked together in the gardens, which had become radiant under the taste and un-limited expenditure of Mrs. Thornberry; beds glow-ing with colour or rivalling mosaics, choice conifers with their green or purple fruit, and rare roses with their fanciful and beauteous names; one, by-the-bye, named 'Mrs. Penruddock,' and a very gorgeous one, 'The Archbishop.'

As they swept along the terraces, restored to their pristine comeliness, and down the green avenues bounded by copper beeches and ancient yews, where men were sweeping away every leaf and twig that had fallen in the night and marred the consummate order, it must have been difficult for the Archbishop of Tyre not to recall the days gone by, when this brilliant and finished scene, then desolate and neglected, the abode of beauty and genius, yet almost of penury, had been to him a world of deep and familiar inter-

est. Yes, he was walking in the same glade where
he had once pleaded his own cause with an eloquence
which none of his most celebrated sermons had ex-
celled. Did he think of this? If he did, it was only
to wrench the thought from his memory. Archbishops
who are yet young, who are resolved to be cardinals,
and who may be popes, are superior to all human
weakness.

'I should like to look at your chapel,' said his
Grace to Mr. Thornberry; 'I remember it a lumber
room, and used to mourn over its desecration.'

'I never was in it,' said Job, 'and cannot understand why my wife is so anxious about it as she
seems to be. When we first went to London, she
always sat under the Reverend Socinus Frost, and
seemed very satisfied. I have heard him; a sensible
man—but sermons are not much in my way, and I
do not belong to his sect, or indeed any other.'

However, they went to the chapel all the same,
for Mrs. Thornberry was resolved on the visit. It
was a small chamber, but beautifully proportioned,
like the mansion itself—of a blended Italian and
Gothic style. The roof was flat, but had been richly
gilt and painted, and was sustained by corbels of
angels, divinely carved. There had been some pews
in the building; some had fallen to pieces, and some
remained, but these were not in the original design.
The sacred table had disappeared, but two saintly
statues, sculptured in black oak, seemed still to guard
the spot which it had consecrated.

'I wonder what became of the communion table?'
said Job.

'Oh! my dear father, do not call it a communion
table,' exclaimed John Hampden pettishly.

'Why, what should I call it, my boy?'

'The altar.'

'Why, what does it signify what we call it? The thing is the same.'

'Ah!' exclaimed the young gentleman, in a tone of contemptuous enthusiasm, 'it is all the difference in the world. There should be a stone altar and a reredos. We have put up a reredos in our chapel at Bradley. All the fellows subscribed; I gave a sovereign.'

'Well, I must say,' said the Archbishop, who had been standing in advance with Mrs. Thornberry and the children, while this brief and becoming conversation was taking place between father and son, 'I think you could hardly do a better thing than restore this chapel, Mr. Thornberry, but there must be no mistake about it. It must be restored to the letter, and it is a style that is not commonly understood. I have a friend, however, who is master of it, the most rising man in his profession, as far as church architecture is concerned, and I will get him just to run down and look at this, and if, as I hope, you resolve to restore it, rest assured he will do you justice, and you will be proud of your place of worship.'

'I do not care how much we spend on our gardens,' said Job, 'for they are transitory pleasures, and we enjoy what we produce; but why I should restore a chapel in a house which does not belong to myself is not so clear to me.'

'But it should belong to yourself,' rejoined the Archbishop. 'Hurstley is not in the market, but it is to be purchased. Take it altogether, I have always thought it one of the most enviable possessions in the world. The house, when put in order, would be one of the ornaments of the kingdom. The acreage, though considerable, is not overwhelming, and there is a range of wild country of endless charm. I wandered about it in my childhood and my youth, and I have never known anything equal to it. Then as to the soil and all that, you know it. You are a son of the soil. You left it for great objects, and you have attained those objects. They have given you fame as well as fortune. There would be something wonderfully dignified and graceful in returning to the land after you have taken the principal part in solving the difficulties which pertained to it, and emancipating it from many perils.'

'I am sure it would be the happiest day of my life, if Job would purchase Hurstley,' said Mrs. Thornberry.

'I should like to go to Oxford, and my father purchase Hurstley,' said the young gentleman. 'If we have not landed property, I would sooner have none. If we have not land, I should like to go into the Church, and if I may not go to Oxford, I would go to Cuddesdon at once. I know it can be done, for I know a fellow who has done it.'

Poor Job Thornberry! He had ruled multitudes, and had conquered and commanded senates. His Sovereign had made him one of her privy councillors, and half a million of people had returned him their representative to Parliament. And here he stood silent, and a little confused; sapped by his wife, bullied by his son, and after having passed a great part of his life in denouncing sacerdotalism, finding his whole future career chalked out, without himself being consulted, by a priest who was so polite, sensible, and so truly friendly, that his manner seemed to deprive its victims of every faculty of retort or repartee. Still, he was going to say something when the door opened, and Mrs. Penruddock appeared, exclaiming in a cheerful voice, 'I thought I should find you here. I would not have troubled your Grace, but this letter marked "Private, immediate, and to be forwarded," has been wandering about for some time, and I thought it was better to bring it to you at once.'

The Archbishop of Tyre took the letter, and seemed to start as he read the direction. Then he stood aside, opened it, and read its contents. The letter was from Lady Roehampton, desiring to see him as soon as possible on a matter of the utmost gravity, and entreating him not to delay his departure, wherever he might be.

'I am sorry to quit you all,' said his Grace; 'but I must go up to town immediately. The business is urgent.'

CHAPTER XCI.

A 'STAG' DINNER.

ENDYMION arrived at home very late from the Montfort ball, and rose in consequence at an unusually late hour. He had taken means to become sufficiently acquainted with the cause of his sister's absence the night before, so he had no anxiety on that head. Lady Roehampton had really intended to have been present, was indeed dressed for the occasion; but when the moment of trial arrived, she was absolutely unequal to the effort. All this was amplified in a little note from his sister, which his valet brought him in the morning. What, however, considerably surprised him in this communication was her announcement that her feelings last night had proved to her that she ought not to remain in London, and that she intended to find solitude and repose in the little watering-place where she had passed a tranquil autumn during the first year of her widowhood. What completed his astonishment, however, was the closing intimation that, in all probability, she would have left town before he rose. The moment she had got a little settled she would write to him, and when business permitted, he must come and pay her a little visit.

'She was always capricious,' exclaimed Lady Montfort, who had not forgotten the disturbance of her royal supper-table.

'Hardly that, I think,' said Endymion. 'I have always looked on Myra as a singularly consistent character.'

'I know, you never admit your sister has a fault.'

'You said the other day yourself that she was the only perfect character you knew.'

'Did I say that? I think her capricious.'

'I do not think you are capricious,' said Endymion, 'and yet the world sometimes says you are.'

'I change my opinion of persons when my taste is offended,' said Lady Montfort. 'What I admired in your sister, though I confess I sometimes wished not to admire her, was that she never offended my taste.'

'I hope satisfied it,' said Endymion.

'Yes, satisfied it, always satisfied it. I wonder what will be her lot, for, considering her youth, her destiny has hardly begun. Somehow or other, I do not think she will marry Sidney Wilton.'

'I have sometimes thought that would be,' said Endymion.

'Well, it would be, I think, a happy match. All the circumstances would be collected that form what is supposed to be happiness. But tastes differ about destinies as well as about manners. For my part, I think to have a husband who loved you, and he clever, accomplished, charming, ambitious, would be happiness; but I doubt whether your sister cares so much about these things. She may, of course does, talk to you more freely; but with others, in her most open hours, there seems a secret fund of reserve in her character which I never could penetrate, except, I think, it is a reserve which does not originate in a love of tranquillity, but quite the reverse. She is a strong character.'

'Then, hardly a capricious one.'

'No, not capricious; I only said that to tease you. I am capricious; I know it. I disregard people sometimes that I have patronised and flattered. It is not merely that I have changed my opinion of them, but I positively hate them.'

'I hope you will never hate me,' said Endymion.

'You have never offended my taste yet,' said Lady Montfort with a smile.

Endymion was engaged to dine to-day with Mr. Bertie Tremaine. Although now in hostile political camps, that great leader of men never permitted their acquaintance to cease. 'He is young,' reasoned Mr. Bertie Tremaine; 'every political party changes its principles on an average once in ten years. Those who are young must often then form new connections, and Ferrars will then come to me. He will be ripe and experienced, and I could give him a good deal. I do not want numbers. I want men. In opposition, numbers often only embarrass. The power of the future is ministerial capacity. The leader with a cabinet formed will be the minister of England. He is not to trouble himself about numbers; that is an affair of the constituencies.'

Male dinners are in general not amusing. When they are formed, as they usually are, of men who are supposed to possess a strong and common sympathy — political, sporting, literary, military, social — there is necessarily a monotony of thought and feeling, and of the materials which induce thought and feeling. In a male dinner of party politicians, conversation soon degenerates into what is termed 'shop;' ancedotes about divisions, criticism of speeches, conjectures about office, speculations on impending elections, and above all, that heinous subject on which enormous fibs are ever told, the registration. There are, however, occasional glimpses in their talk which would seem to intimate that they have another life outside the Houses of Parliament. But that extenuating circumstance does not apply to the sporting dinner. There they begin with odds and handicaps, and end with handicaps and odds, and it is doubtful whether it ever occurs to any one present, that there is any other existing combination of atoms than odds and handicaps.

A dinner of wits is proverbially a gathering of silence; and the envy and hatred which all literary men really feel for each other, especially when they are exchanging dedications of mutual affection, always ensure, in such assemblies, the agreeable presence of a general feeling of painful constraint. If a good thing occurs to a guest, he will not express it, lest his neighbour, who is publishing a novel in numbers, shall appropriate it next month, or he himself, who has the same responsibility of production, be deprived of its legitimate appearance. Those who desire to learn something of the manœuvres at the Russian and Prussian reviews, or the last rumour at Aldershot or the military clubs, will know where to find this feast of reason. The flow of soul in these male festivals is perhaps, on the whole, more genial when found in a society of young gentlemen, graduates of the Turf and the Marlborough, and guided in their benignant studies by the gentle experience and the mild wisdom of White's. The startling scandal, the rattling anecdote, the astounding leaps, and the amazing shots, afford for the moment a somewhat pleasing distraction, but when it is discovered that all these habitual flim-flams are, in general, the airy creatures of inaccuracy and exaggeration—that the scandal is not true, the anecdote has no foundation, and that the feats of skill and strength are invested with the organic weakness of tradition, the vagaries lose something of the charm of novelty, and are almost as insipid as claret from which the bouquet has evaporated.

The male dinners of Mr. Bertie Tremaine were an exception to the general reputation of such meetings. They were never dull. In the first place, though to be known at least by reputation was an indispensable condition of being present, he brought different classes together, and this, at least for once, stimulates and gratifies curiosity. His house too was open to foreigners of celebrity, without reference to their political parties or opinions. Every one was welcome except absolute assassins. The host had studied the art of developing character and conversation, and if sometimes he was not so successful in this respect as he deserved, there was no lack of amusing entertainment, for in these social encounters Mr. Bertie Tremaine was a reserve in himself, and if nobody else would talk, he would avail himself of the opportunity of pouring forth the treasures of his own teeming intelligence. His various knowledge, his power of speech, his eccentric paradoxes, his pompous rhetoric, relieved by some happy sarcasm, and the obvious sense, in all he said and did, of innate superiority to all his guests, made these exhibitions extremely amusing.

'What Bertie Tremaine will end in,' Endymion would sometimes say, 'perplexes me. Had there been no revolution in 1832, and he had entered Parliament for his family borough, I think he must by this time have been a minister. Such tenacity of purpose could scarcely fail. But he has had to say and do so many odd things, first to get into Parliament, and secondly to keep there, that his future now is not so clear. When I first knew him, he was a Benthamite; at present, I sometimes seem to foresee that he will end by being the leader of the Protectionists and the Protestants.'

'And a good strong party too,' said Trenchard, 'but query whether strong enough?'

'That is exactly what Bertie Tremaine is trying to find out.'

Mr. Bertie Tremaine's manner in receiving his guests was courtly and ceremonious; a contrast to the free and easy style of the time. But it was adopted after due reflection. 'No man can tell what will be the position he may be called upon to fill. But he has a right to assume he will always be ascending. I, for example, may be destined to be the president of a republic, the regent of a monarchy, or a sovereign myself. It would be painful and disagreeable to have to change one's manner at a perhaps advanced period of life, and become liable to the unpopular imputation that you had grown arrogant and overbearing. On the contrary, in my case, whatever my elevation, there will be no change. My brother, Mr. Tremaine Bertie, acts on a different principle. He is a Sybarite, and has a general contempt for mankind, certainly for the mob and the middle class, but he is "Hail fellow, well met!" with them all. He says it answers at elections; I doubt it. I myself represent a popular constituency, but I believe I owe my success in no slight measure to the manner in which I gave my hand when I permitted it to be touched. As I say sometimes to Mr. Tremaine Bertie, "You will find this habit of social familiarity embarrassing when I send you to St. Petersburg or Vienna."'

Waldershare dined there, now a peer, though, as he rejoiced to say, not a peer of Parliament. An Irish peer, with an English constituency, filled, according to Waldershare, the most enviable of positions. His rank gave him social influence, and his seat in the House of Commons that power which all aspire to obtain. The cynosure of the banquet, however, was a gentleman who had, about a year before, been the president of a republic for nearly six weeks, and who, being master of a species of rhapsodical rhetoric, highly useful in troubled times, when there is no real business to transact, and where there is nobody to transact it, had disappeared when the treasury was quite empty, and there were no further funds to reward the enthusiastic citizens who had hitherto patriotically maintained order at wages about double in amount to what they had previously received in their handicrafts. This great reputation had been brought over by Mr. Tremaine Bertie, now introducing him into English political society. Mr. Tremaine Bertie hung upon the accents of the oracle, every word of which was intended to be picturesque or profound, and then surveyed his friends with a glance of appreciating wonder. Sensible Englishmen, like Endymion and Trenchard, looked upon the whole exhibition as fustian, and received the revelations with a smile of frigid courtesy.

The presence, however, of this celebrity of six weeks gave occasionally a tone of foreign politics to the conversation, and the association of ideas, which, in due course, rules all talk, brought them, among other incidents and instances, to the remarkable career of King Florestan.

'And yet he has his mortifications,' said a sensible man. 'He wants a wife, and the princesses of the world will not furnish him with one.'

'What authority have you for saying so?' exclaimed the fiery Waldershare. 'The princesses of the world would be great fools if they refused such a man, but I know of no authentic instance of such denial.'

'Well, it is the common rumour.'

'And, therefore, probably a common falsehood.'

'Were he wise,' said Mr. Tremaine Bertie, 'King Florestan would not marry. Dynasties are unpopular; especially new ones. The present age is monarchical, but not dynastic. The King, who is a man of reach, and who has been pondering such circumstances all his life, is probably well aware of this, and will not be such a fool as to marry.'

'How is the monarchy to go on, if there is to be no successor?' inquired Trenchard. 'You would not renew the Polish constitution?'

'The Polish constitution, by-the-bye, was not so bad a thing,' said Mr. Bertie Tremaine. 'Under it a distinguished Englishman might have mixed with the crowned heads of Europe, as Sir Philip Sidney nearly did. But I was looking to something superior to the Polish constitution, or perhaps any other; I was contemplating a monarchy with the principle of adoption. That would give you all the excellence of the Polish constitution, and the order and constancy in which it failed. It would realise the want of the age; monarchical, not dynastical, institutions, and it would act independent of the passions and intrigues of the multitude. The principle of adoption was the secret of the strength and endurance of Rome. It gave Rome alike the Scipios and the Antonines.'

'A court would be rather dull without a woman at its head.'

'On the contrary,' said Mr. Bertie Tremaine. 'It was Louis Quatorze who made the court; not his queen.'

'Well,' said Waldershare, 'all the same, I fear King Florestan will adopt no one in this room, though he has several friends here, and I am one; and I believe that he will marry, and I cannot help fancying the partner of his throne will not be as insignificant as Louis the Fourteenth's wife, or Catherine of Braganza.'

Jawett dined this day with Mr. Bertie Tremaine. He was a frequent guest there, and still was the editor of the *Precursor,* though it sometimes baffled all that lucidity of style for which he was celebrated to reconcile the conduct of the party, of which the *Precursor* was alike the oracle and organ, with the opinions with which that now well-established journal first attempted to direct and illuminate the public mind. It seemed to the editor that the *Precursor* dwelt more on the past than became a harbinger of the future. Not that Mr. Bertie Tremaine ever for a moment admitted that there was any difficulty in any case. He never permitted any dogmas that he had ever enunciated to be surrendered, however contrary at their first aspect.

'All are but parts of one stupendous whole,'

and few things were more interesting than the conferences in which Mr. Bertie Tremaine had to impart his views and instructions to the master of that lucid style, which had the merit of making everything so very clear when the master himself was, as at present, extremely perplexed and confused. Jawett lingered after the other guests, that he might have the advantage of consulting the great leader on the course which he ought to take in advocating a measure which seemed completely at variance with all the principles they had ever upheld.

'I do not see your difficulty,' wound up the host. 'Your case is clear. You have a principle which will carry you through everything. That is the charm of a principle. You have always an answer ready.'

'But in this case,' somewhat timidly inquired Mr. Jawett, 'what would be the principle on which I should rest?'

'You must show,' said Mr. Bertie Tremaine, 'that democracy is aristocracy in disguise; and that aristocracy is democracy in disguise. It will carry you through everything.'

Even Jawett looked a little amazed.

'But'—he was beginning, when Mr. Bertie Tremaine arose. 'Think of what I have said, and if on reflection any doubt or difficulty remain in your mind, call on me to-morrow before I go to the House. At present, I must pay my respects to Lady Beaumaris. She is the only woman the Tories can boast of; but she is a firstrate woman, and is a power which I must secure.'

CHAPTER XCII.

MYRA'S NEWS.

A MONTH had nearly elapsed since the Montfort ball; the season was over and the session was nearly finished. The pressure of parliamentary life for those in office is extreme during this last month, yet Endymion would have contrived, were it only for a day, to have visited his sister, had Lady Roehampton much encouraged his appearance. Strange as it seemed to him, she did not, but, on the contrary, always assumed that the prorogation of Parliament would alone bring them together again. When he proposed on one occasion to come down for four-and-twenty hours, she absolutely, though with much affection, adjourned the fulfilment of the offer. It seemed that she was not yet quite settled.

Lady Montfort lingered in London even after Goodwood. She was rather embarrassed, as she told Endymion, about her future plans. Lord Montfort was at Princedown, where she wished to join him, but he did not respond to her wishes; on the contrary, while announcing that he was indisposed, and meant to remain at Princedown for the summer, he suggested that she should avail herself of the opportunity, and pay a long visit to her family in the north.

'I know what he means,' she observed; 'he wants the world to believe that we are separated. He cannot repudiate me — he is too great a gentleman to do anything coarsely unjust; but he thinks, by tact and indirect means, he may attain our virtual separation. He has had this purpose for years, I believe now ever since our marriage, but hitherto I have baffled him. I ought to be with him; I really believe he is indisposed, his face has become so pale of late; but were I to persist in going to Princedown I should only drive him away. He would go off in the night without leaving his address, and something would happen — dreadful or absurd. What I had best do, I think, is this. You are going at last to pay your visit to your sister; I will write to my lord and tell him that as he does not wish me to go to Princedown, I propose to go to Montfort Castle. When the flag is flying at Montfort, I can pay a visit of any length to my family. It will only be a neighbouring visit from Montfort to them; perhaps, too, they might return it. At any rate, then they cannot say my lord and I are separated. We need not live under the same roof, but so long as I live under his roof the world considers us united. It is a pity to have to scheme in this manner, and rather degrading, particularly when one might be so happy with him. But you know, my dear Endymion, all about our affairs. Your friend is not a very happy woman, and if not a very unhappy one, it is owing much to your dear friendship, and a little to my own spirit which keeps me up under what is frequent and sometimes bitter mortification. And now adieu! I suppose you cannot be away less than a week. Probably on your return you will find me here. I cannot go to Montfort without his permission. But he will give it. I observe that he will always do anything to gain his immediate object. His immediate object is, that I shall not go to Princedown, and so he will agree that I shall go to Montfort.'

For the first time in his life, Endymion felt some constraint in the presence of Myra. There was something changed in her manner. No diminution of affection, for she threw her arms around him and pressed him to her heart; and then she looked at him anxiously, even sadly, and kissed both his eyes, and then she remained for some moments in silence with her face hid on his shoulder. Never since the loss of Lord Roehampton had she seemed so subdued.

'It is a long separation,' she at length said, with a voice and smile equally faint, 'and you must be a little wearied with your travelling. Come and refresh yourself, and then I will show you my boudoir I have made here, rather pretty, out of nothing. And then we will sit down and have a long talk together, for I have much to tell you, and I want your advice.'

'She is going to marry Sidney Wilton,' thought Endymion; 'that is clear.'

The boudoir was really pretty, 'made out of nothing,' a gay chintz, some shelves of beautiful books, some fanciful chairs, and a portrait of Lord Roehampton.

It was a long interview, very long, and if one could judge by the countenance of Endymion, when he quitted the boudoir and hastened to his room, of

grave import. Sometimes his face was pale, sometimes scarlet; the changes were rapid, but the expression was agitated rather than one of gratification.

He sent instantly for his servant, and then penned
this telegram to Lady Montfort: ' My visit here will
be short. I am to see you immediately. Nothing
must prevent your being at home when I call to-
morrow, about four o'clock. Most, most important.'

CHAPTER XCIII.

SOCIETY IS STARTLED.

ELL, something has happened at last,' said Lady Montfort with a wondering countenance; 'it is too marvellous!'

'She goes to Osborne to-day,' continued Endymion, 'and I suppose after that, in due course, it will be generally known. I should think the formal announcement would be made abroad. It has been kept wonderfully close. She wished you to know it first, at least from her. I do not think she ever hesitated about accepting him. There was delay from various causes; whether there should be a marriage by proxy first in this country, and other points; about religion, for example.'

'Well?'

'She enters the Catholic Church; the Archbishop of Tyre has received her. There is no difficulty and no great ceremonies in such matters. She was rebaptized, but only by way of precaution. It was not necessary, for our baptism, you know, is recognised by Rome.'

'And that was all!'

'All, with a first communion and confession. It is all consummated now; as you say, "It is too wonderful." A first confession, and to Nigel Penruddock, who says life is flat and insipid!'

'I shall write to her: I must write to her. I wonder if I shall see her before she departs.'

'That is certain if you wish it; she wishes it.'

'And when does she go? And who goes with her?'

'She will be under my charge,' said Endymion. 'It is fortunate that it should happen at a time when I am free. I am personally to deliver her to the King. The Duke of St. Angelo, Baron Sergius, and the Archbishop accompany her, and Waldershare, at the particular request of His Majesty.'

'And no lady?'

'She takes Adriana with her.'

'Adriana!' repeated Lady Montfort, and a cloud passed over her brow. There was a momentary pause, and then Lady Montfort said, 'I wish she would take me.'

'That would be delightful,' said Endymion, 'and most becoming — to have for a companion the greatest lady of our court.'

'She will not take me with her,' said Lady Montfort, sorrowfully but decisively, and shaking her head. 'Dear woman! I loved her always, often most when I seemed least affectionate — but there was between us something'— and she hesitated. 'Heigho! I may be the greatest lady of our court, but I am a very unhappy woman, Endymion, and what annoys and dispirits me most, sometimes quite breaks me down, is that I cannot see that I deserve my lot.'

It happened as Endymion foresaw; the first announcement came from abroad. King Florestan suddenly sent a message to his parliament, that His Majesty was about to present them with a queen. She was not the daughter of a reigning house, but she came from the land of freedom and political wisdom, and from the purest and most powerful court in Europe. His subjects soon learnt that she was the most beautiful of women, for the portrait of the Countess of Roehampton, as it were by magic, seemed suddenly to fill every window in every shop in the teeming and brilliant capital where she was about to reign.

It was convenient that these great events should occur when everybody was out of town. Lady Montfort alone remained, the frequent, if not constant, companion of the new sovereign. Berengaria soon recovered her high spirits. There was much to do and prepare in which her hints and advice were invaluable. Though she was not to have the honour of attending Myra to her new home, which, considering her high place in the English court, was perhaps hardly consistent with etiquette, for so she now cleverly put it, she was to pay Her Majesty a visit in due time. The momentary despondency that had clouded her brilliant countenance had not only disappeared, but she had quite forgotten, and certainly would not admit, that she was anything but the most sanguine and energetic of beings, and rallied Endymion unmercifully for his careworn countenance and too frequent air of depression. The truth is, the great change that was impending was one which might well make him serious, and sometimes sad.

The withdrawal of a female influence so potent on his life as that of his sister, was itself a great event. There had been between them from the cradle, which, it may be said, they had shared, a strong and perfect sympathy. They had experienced together vast and strange vicissitudes of life. Though much separated in their early youth, there had still been a constant interchange of thought and feeling between them. For the last twelve years or so, ever since Myra had become acquainted with the Neuchatel family, they may be said never to have separated — at least they had maintained a constant communication, and generally a personal one. She had in a great degree moulded his life. Her unfaltering, though often unseen, influence had created his advancement. Her will was more powerful than his. He was more prudent and plastic. He felt this keenly. He was conscious that, left to himself, he would probably have achieved much less. He remembered her words, when they parted for the first time at Hurtsley, 'Women will be your best friends in life.' And that brought his thoughts to the only subject on which they had ever differed — her wished-for union between himself and Adriana. He felt he had crossed her there — that he had prevented the fulfilment of her deeply-matured plans. Perhaps, had that marriage taken place, she would never have quitted England. Perhaps; but was that desirable? Was it not fitter that so lofty a spirit should find a seat as exalted as her capacity?

Myra was actually a sovereign! In this age of strange events, not the least strange. No petty cares and griefs must obtrude themselves in such majestic associations. And yet the days at Hainault were very happy, and the bright visits to Gaydene, and her own pleasant though stately home. His heart was agitated, and his eyes were often moistened with emotion.

He seemed to think that all the thrones of Christendom could be no compensation for the loss of this beloved genius of his life, whom he might never see again. Sometimes, when he paid his daily visit to Berengaria, she who knew him by heart, who studied every expression of his countenance and every tone of his voice, would say to him, after a few minutes of desultory and feeble conversation, 'You are thinking of your sister, Endymion?'

He did not reply, but gave a sort of faint mournful smile.

'This separation is a trial, a severe one, and I knew you would feel it,' said Lady Montfort. 'I feel it; I loved your sister, but she did not love me. Nobody that I love ever does love me.'

'Oh! do not say that, Lady Montfort.'

'It is what I feel. I cannot console you. There is nothing I can do for you. My friendship, if you value it, which I will not doubt you do, you fully possessed before your sister was a queen. So that goes for nothing.'

'I must say, I feel sometimes most miserable.'

'Nonsense, Endymion; if anything could annoy your sister more than another, it would be to hear of such feelings on your part. I must say she has courage. She has found her fitting place. Her brother ought to do the same. You have a great object in life, at least you had, but I have no faith in sentimentalists. If I had been sentimental, I should have gone into a convent long ago.'

'If to feel is to be sentimental, I cannot help it.'

'All feeling which has no object to attain is morbid and maudlin,' said Lady Montfort. 'You say you are very miserable, and at the same time you do not

know what you want. Would you have your sister
dethroned ? And if you would, could you accomplish
your purpose ? Well, then, what nonsense to think
about her except to feel proud of her elevation, and
prouder still that she is equal to it!'

'You always have the best of every argument,'
said Endymion.

'Of course,' said Lady Montfort. 'What I want
you to do is to exert yourself. You have now a
strong social position, for Sidney Wilton tells me the
Queen has relinquished to you her mansion and the
whole of her income, which is no mean one. You
must collect your friends about you. Our government
is not too strong, I can tell you. We must brush up
in the recess. What with Mr. Bertie Tremaine and
his friends joining the Protectionists, and the ultra-
Radicals wanting, as they always do, something impossible, I see seeds of discomfiture unless they are
met with energy. You stand high, and are well
spoken of even by our opponents. Whether we stand
or fall, it is a moment for you to increase your personal influence. That is the element now to encourage in your career, because you are not like the old
fogies in the cabinet, who, if they go out, will never
enter another again. You have a future, and though
you may not be an emperor, you may be what I esteem more, Prime Minister of this country.'

'You are always so sanguine.'

'Not more sanguine than your sister. Often we
have talked of this. I wish she were here to help us,
but I will do my part. At present let us go to
luncheon.'

CHAPTER XCIV.

THE BRIDE OF A KING.

HERE was a splendid royal yacht, though not one belonging to our gracious Sovereign, lying in one of Her Majesty's southern ports, and the yacht was convoyed by a smart frigate. The crews' were much ashore, and were very popular, for they spent a great deal of money. Everybody knew what was the purpose of their bright craft, and every one was interested in it. A beautiful Englishwoman had been selected to fill a foreign and brilliant throne occupied by a prince, who had been educated in our own country, who ever avowed his sympathies with 'the inviolate island of the sage and free.' So in fact there was some basis for the enthusiasm which was felt on this occasion by the inhabitants of Nethampton. What every one wanted to know was when she would sail. Ah! that was a secret, still a secret that could hardly be kept for the eight-and-forty hours preceding her departure, and therefore, one day, with no formal notice, all the inhabitants of Nethampton were in gala; streets and ships dressed out with the flags of all nations; the church bells ringing; and busy little girls running about with huge bouquets.

At the very instant expected, the special train was signalled, and drove into the crimson station amid the thunder of artillery, the blare of trumpets, the beating of drums, and cheers from thousands even louder and longer than the voices of the cannon. Leaning on the arm of her brother, and attended by the Princess of Montserrat, and the Honourable Adriana Neuchatel, Baron Sergius, the Duke of St. Angelo, the Archbishop of Tyre, and Lord Waldershare, the daughter of William Ferrars, gracious, yet looking as if she were born to empire, received the congratulatory address of the mayor and corporation and citizens of Nethampton, and permitted her hand to be kissed, not only by his worship, but by at least two aldermen.

They were on the waters, and the shores of Albion, fast fading away, had diminished to a speck. It is a melancholy and tender moment, and Myra was in her ample and splendid cabin and alone. 'It is a trial,' she felt, 'but all that I love and value in this world are in this vessel,' and she thought of Endymion and Adriana. The gentlemen were on deck, chiefly smoking or reconnoitring their convoy through their telescopes.

'I must say,' said Waldershare, 'it was a grand idea of our kings making themselves sovereigns of the sea. The greater portion of this planet is water; so we at once became a firstrate power. We owe our navy entirely to the Stuarts. King James the Second was the true founder and hero of the British navy. He was the worthy son of his admirable father, that blessed martyr, the restorer at least, if not the inventor, of ship money; the most patriotic and popular tax that ever was devised by man. The Nonconformists thought themselves so wise in resisting it, and they have got the naval estimates instead!'

The voyage was propitious, the weather delightful, and when they had entered the southern waters Waldershare confessed that he felt the deliciousness of life. If the scene and the impending events, and their own fair thoughts, had not been adequate to interest them, there were ample resources at their command; all the ladies were skilled musicians, their concerts commenced at sunset, and the sweetness of their voices long lingered over the moonlit waters.

Adriana, one evening, bending over the bulwarks of the yacht, was watching the track of phosphoric light, struck into brilliancy from the dark blue waters by the prow of their rapid vessel. 'It is a fascinating sight, Miss Neuchatel, and it seems one might gaze on it for ever.'

'Ah! Lord Waldershare, you caught me in a reverie.'

'What more sweet?'

'Well, that depends on its subject. To tell the truth, I was thinking that these lights resembled a little your conversation; all the wondrous things you are always saying or telling us.'

The Archbishop was a man who never recurred to the past. One never could suppose that Endymion and himself had been companions in their early youth, or, so far as their intercourse was concerned, that there was such a place in the world as Hurstley. One night, however, as they were pacing the deck together, he took the arm of Endymion, and said, 'I trace the hand of Providence in every incident of your sister's life. What we deemed misfortunes, sor-

rows, even calamities, were forming a character originally endowed with supreme will, and destined for
the highest purposes. There was a moment at Hurstley when I myself was crushed to the earth, and
cared not to live; vain, short-sighted mortal! Our
great Master was at that moment shaping everything
to His ends, and preparing for the entrance into His
Church of a woman who may be, who will be, I believe, another St. Helena.'

'We have not spoken of this subject before,' said
Endymion, 'and I should not have cared had our silence continued, but I must now tell you frankly, the
secession of my sister from the Church of her fathers
was to me by no means a matter of unmixed satisfaction.'

'The time will come when you will recognise it
as the consummation of a Divine plan,' said the Archbishop.

'I feel great confidence that my sister will never
be the slave of superstition,' said Endymion. 'Her
mind is too masculine for that; she will remember
that the throne she fills has been already once lost by
the fatal influence of the Jesuits.'

'The influence of the Jesuits is the influence of
Divine truth,' said his companion. 'And how is it
possible for such influence not to prevail? What you
treat as defeats, discomfitures, are events which you
do not comprehend. They are incidents all leading
to one great end — the triumph of the Church — that
is, the triumph of God.'

'I will not decide what are great ends; I am content to ascertain what is wise conduct. And it would
not be wise conduct, in my opinion, for the King to
rest upon the Jesuits.'

'The Jesuits never fell except from conspiracy against them. It is never the public voice that demands their expulsion or the public effort that accomplishes it. It is always the affair of sovereigns and statesmen, of politicians, of men, in short, who feel that there is a power at work, and that power one not favourable to their schemes or objects of government.'

'Well, we shall see,' said Endymion; 'I candidly tell you, I hope the Jesuits will have as little influence in my brother-in-law's kingdom as in my own country.'

'As little!' said Nigel, somewhat sarcastically; 'I should be almost content if the holy order in every country had as much influence as it now has in England.'

'I think your Grace exaggerates.'

'Before two years are past,' said the Archbishop, speaking very slowly, 'I foresee that the Jesuits will be privileged in England, and the hierarchy of our Church recognised.'

It was a delicious afternoon; it had been sultry, but the sun had now greatly declined, when the captain of the yacht came down to announce to the Queen that they were in sight of her new country, and she hastened on deck to behold the rapidly nearing shore. A squadron of ships of war had stood out to meet her, and in due time the towers and spires of a beautiful city appeared, which was the port of the capital, and itself almost worthy of being one. A royal barge, propelled by four-and-twenty rowers, and bearing the lord chamberlain, awaited the Queen, and the moment her Majesty and the Princess of Montserrat had taken their seats, salutes thundered from every ship of war, responded to by fort and battery ashore.

When they landed, they were conducted by chief officers of the court to a pavilion which faced the western sky, now glowing like an opal with every shade of the iris, and then becoming of a light green colour, varied only by some slight clouds burnished with gold. A troop of maidens brought flowers as bright as themselves, and then a company of pages advanced, and kneeling, offered to the Queen chocolate in a crystal cup.

According to the programme drawn up by the heralds, and every tittle of it founded on precedents, the King and the royal carriages were to have met the travellers on their arrival at the metropolis; but there are feelings which heralds do not comprehend, and which defy precedents. Suddenly there was a shout, a loud cheer, a louder salute. Some one had arrived unexpectedly. A young man, stately but pale, moved through the swiftly receding crowd, alone and unattended, entered the pavilion, advanced to the Queen, kissed her hand, and then both her cheeks, just murmuring, 'My best beloved, this, this indeed is joy.'

The capital was fortified, and the station was without the walls; here the royal carriages awaited them. The crowd was immense; the ramparts on this occasion were covered with people. It was an almost sultry night, with every star visible and clear, and warm and sweet. As the royal carriage crossed the drawbridge and entered the chief gates, the whole city was in an instant suddenly illuminated — in a flash. The architectural lines of the city walls, and of every street, were indicated, and along the ramparts at not distant intervals were tripods, each crowned with a silver flame, which cast around the radiance of day.

He held and pressed her hand as in silence she beheld the wondrous scene. They had to make a progress of some miles; the way was kept throughout by soldiery and civic guards, while beyond them was an infinite population, all cheering and many of them waving torches. They passed through many streets, and squares with marvellous fountains, until they arrived at the chief and royal street, which has no equal in the world. It is more than a mile long, never swerving from a straight line, broad, yet the houses so elevated that they generally furnish the shade this ardent clime requires. The architecture of this street is so varied that it never becomes monotonous, some beautiful church, or palace, or ministerial hotel perpetually varying the effect. All the windows were full on this occasion, and even the roofs were crowded. Every house was covered with tapestry, and the line of every building was marked out by artificial light. The moon rose, but she was not wanted; it was as light as day.

They were considerate enough not to move too rapidly through this heart of the metropolis, and even halted at some stations, where bands of music and choirs of singers welcomed and celebrated them. They moved on more quickly afterwards, made their way through a pretty suburb, and then entered a park. At the termination of a long avenue was the illumined and beautiful palace of the Prince of Montserrat, where Myra was to reside and repose until the momentous morrow, when King Florestan was publicly to place on the brow of his affianced bride the crown which to his joy she had consented to share.

CHAPTER XCV.

The Nuptials.

THERE are very few temperaments that can resist an universal and unceasing festival in a vast and beautiful metropolis. It is inebriating, and the most wonderful of all its accidents is how the population can ever calm and recur to the monotony of ordinary life. When all this happens, too, in a capital blessed with purple skies, where the moonlight is equal to our sunshine, and where half the population sleep in the open air and wish for no roof but the heavens, existence is a dream of phantasy and perpetual loveliness, and one is at last forced to believe that there is some miraculous and supernatural agency that provides the ever-enduring excitement and ceaseless incidents of grace and beauty.

After the great ceremony of the morrow in the cathedral, and when Myra, kneeling at the altar with her husband, received, under a canopy of silver brocade, the blessings of a cardinal and her people, day followed day with court balls and municipal banquets, state visits to operas, and reviews of sumptuous troops. At length the end of all this pageantry and enthusiasm approached, and amid a blaze of fire-works, the picturesque population of this fascinating city tried to return to ordinary feeling and to common sense.

If amid this graceful hubbub and this glittering riot any one could have found time to remark the carriage and conduct of an individual, one might have observed, and perhaps been surprised at, the change in those of Miss Neuchatel. That air of pensive resignation which distinguished her seemed to have vanished. She never wore that doleful look for which she was too remarkable in London saloons, and which marred a countenance favoured by nature and a form intended for gaiety and grace. Perhaps it was the influence of the climate, perhaps the excitement of the scene, perhaps some rapture with the wondrous fortunes of the friend whom she adored, but Adriana seemed suddenly to sympathise with everybody and to appreciate everything; her face was radiant, she was in every dance, and visited churches and museums, and palaces and galleries, with keen delight. With many charms, the intimate friend of their sovereign, and herself known to be noble and immensely rich, Adriana became the fashion, and a crowd of princes were ever watching her smiles, and sometimes offering her their sighs.

'I think you enjoy our visit more than any one of us,' said Endymion to her one day, with some feeling of surprise.

'Well, one cannot mope for ever,' said Miss Neuchatel; 'I have passed my life in thinking of one subject, and I feel now it made me very stupid.'

Endymion felt embarrassed, and, though generally ready, had no repartee at command. Lord Waldershare, however, came to his relief, and claimed Adriana for the impending dance.

This wondrous marriage was a grand subject for 'our own correspondents,' and they abounded. Among them were Jawett and St. Barbe. St. Barbe hated Jawett, as indeed he did all his brethren, but his appointment in this instance he denounced as an infamous job. 'Merely to allow him to travel in foreign parts, which he has never done, without a single qualification for the office! However, it will ruin his paper, that is some consolation. Fancy sending here a man who has never used his pen except about those dismal statistics, and what he calls first principles! I hate his style, so neat and frigid. No colour, sir. I hate his short sentences, like a dog barking; we want a word-painter here, sir. My description of the wedding sold one hundred and fifty thousand, and it is selling now. If the proprietors were gentlemen, they would have sent me an unlimited credit, instead of their paltry fifty pounds a day and my expenses; but you never meet a liberal man now, — no such animal known. What I want you to do for me, Lord Waldershare, is to get me invited to the Villa Aurea when the court moves there. It will be private life there, and that is the article the British public want now. They are satiated with ceremonies and festivals. They want to know what the royal pair have for dinner when they are alone, how they pass their evenings, and whether the Queen drives ponies.'

'So far as I am concerned,' said Waldershare, 'they shall remain state secrets.'

'I have received no special favours here,' rejoined St. Barbe, 'though with my claims, I might have counted on the uttermost. However, it is always so.

I must depend on my own resources. I have a retainer, I can tell you, my lord, from the *Rigdum Funidos,* in my pocket, and it is in my power to keep up such a crackling of jokes and sarcasms that a very different view would soon be entertained in Europe of what is going on here than is now the fashion. The *Rigdum Funidos* is on the breakfast-table of all England, and sells thousands in every capital of the world. You do not appreciate its power; you will now feel it.'

'I also am a subscriber to the *Rigdum Funidos,*' said Waldershare, 'and tell you frankly, Mr. St. Barbe, that if I see in its columns the slightest allusion to any person or incident in this country, I will take care that you be instantly consigned to the galleys; and, this being a liberal government, I can do that without even the ceremony of a primary inquiry.'

'You do not mean that?' said St. Barbe; 'of course, I was only jesting. It is not likely that I should say or do anything disagreeable to those whom I look upon as my patrons—I may say friends—through life. It makes me almost weep when I remember my early connection with Mr. Ferrars, now an Under-Secretary of State, and who will mount higher. I never had a chance of being a minister, though I suppose I am not more incapable than others who get the silver spoon into their mouths. And then his divine sister! Quite an heroic character! I never had a sister, and so I never had even the chance of being nearly related to royalty. But so it has been throughout my life. No luck, my lord; no luck. And then they say one is misanthropical. Hang it! who can help being misanthropical when he finds everybody getting on in life except himself?'

The court moved to their favourite summer residence, a Palladian palace on a blue lake, its banks clothed with forests abounding with every species of game, and beyond them loftier mountains. The King was devoted to sport, and Endymion was always among his companions. Waldershare rather attached himself to the ladies, who made gay parties floating in gondolas, and refreshed themselves with picnics in sylvan retreats. It was supposed Lord Waldershare was a great admirer of the Princess of Montserrat, who in return referred to him as that 'lovable eccentricity.' As the autumn advanced, parties of guests of high distinction, carefully arranged, periodically arrived. Now there was more ceremony, and every evening the circle was formed, while the King and Queen exchanged words, and sometimes ideas, with those who were so fortunate as to be under their roof. Frequently there were dramatic performances, and sometimes a dance. The Princess of Montserrat was invaluable in these scenes; vivacious, imaginative, a consummate mimic, her countenance, though not beautiful, was full of charm. What was strange, Adriana took a great fancy to her Highness, and they were seldom separated. The only cloud for Endymion in this happy life was, that every day the necessity of his return to England was more urgent, and every day the days vanished more quickly. That return to England, once counted by weeks, would soon be counted by hours. He had conferred once or twice with Waldershare on the subject, who always turned the conversation; at last Endymion reminded him that the time of his departure was at hand, and that, originally, it had been agreed they should return together.

'Yes, my dear Ferrars, we did so agree, but the agreement was permissive, not compulsory. My views are changed. Perhaps I shall never return to England again; I think of being naturalised here.'

The Queen was depressed at the prospect of being separated from her brother. Sometimes she remonstrated with him for his devotion to sport which deprived her of his society; frequently in a morning she sent for him to her boudoir, that they might talk together as in old times. 'The King has invited Lord and Lady Beaumaris to pay us a visit, and they are coming at once. I had hoped the dear Hainaults might have visited us here. I think she would have liked it. However, they will certainly pass the winter with us. It is some consolation to me not to lose Adriana.'

'The greatest,' said Endymion, 'and she seems so happy here. She seems quite changed.'

'I hope she is happier,' said the Queen, 'but I trust she is not changed. I think her nearly perfection. So pure, even so exalted a mind, joined with so sweet a temper, I have never met. And she is very much admired too, I can tell you. The Prince of Arragon would be on his knees to her to-morrow, if she would only give a single smile. But she smiles enough with the Princess of Montserrat. I heard her the other day absolutely in uncontrollable laughter. That is a strange friendship; it amuses me.'

'The princess has immense resource.'

The Queen suddenly rose from her seat; her countenance was disturbed.

'Why do we talk of her, or of any other trifler of the court, when there hangs over us so great a

sorrow, Endymion, as our separation? Endymion, my
best beloved,' and she threw her arms round his neck,
' my heart! my life! Is it possible that you can leave
me, and so miserable as I am?'

' Miserable!'

'Yes! miserable when I think of your position—
and even my own. Mine own has risen like a palace in a dream, and may vanish like one. But that
would not be a calamity if you were safe. If I
quitted this world to-morrow, where would you be?
It gives me sleepless nights and anxious days. If
you really loved me as you say, you would save
me this. I am haunted with the perpetual thought
that all this glittering prosperity will vanish as it did
with our father. God forbid that, under any circumstances, it should lead to such an end—but who
knows? Fate is terribly stern; ironically just. O
Endymion! if you really love me, your twin, half of
your blood and life, who have laboured for you so
much, and thought for you so much, and prayed for
you so much—and yet I sometimes feel have done
so little—O Endymion! my adored, my own Endymion, if you wish to preserve my life—if you
wish me not only to live, but really to be happy
as I ought to be and could be, but for one dark
thought, help me, aid me, save me—you can, and
by one single act.'

' One single act!'

'Yes! marry Adriana.'

'Ah!' and he sighed.

'Yes, Adriana, to whom we both of us owe
everything. Were it not for Adriana, you would not
be here, you would be nothing,' and she whispered

some words which made him start, and alternately blush and look pale.

'Is it possible?' he exclaimed. 'My sister, my beloved sister, I have tried to keep my brain cool in many trials. But I feel, as it were, as if life were too much for me. You counsel me to that which we should all repent.'

'Yes, I know it; you may for a moment think it a sacrifice, but believe me, that is all phantasy. I know you think your heart belongs to another. I will grant everything, willingly grant everything you could say of her. Yes, I admit, she is beautiful, she has many charms, has been to you a faithful friend, you delight in her society; such things have happened before to many men, to every man they say they happen, but that has not prevented them from being wise and very happy too. Your present position, if you persist in it, is one most perilous. You have no root in the country; but for an accident you could not maintain the public position you have nobly gained. As for the great crowning consummation of your life, which we dreamed over at unhappy Hurstley, which I have sometimes dared to prophesy, that must be surrendered. The country at the best will look upon you only as a reputable adventurer to be endured, even trusted and supported, in some secondary post but nothing more. I touch on this, for I see it is useless to speak of myself and my own fate and feelings; only remember, Endymion, I have never deceived you. I cannot endure any longer this state of affairs. When in a few days we part, we shall never meet again. And all the devotion of Myra will end in your destroying her.'

'My own, my beloved Myra, do with me what you like. If——'

At this moment there was a gentle tap at the door, and the King entered.

'My angel,' he said, 'and you too, my dear Endymion. I have some news from England which I fear may distress you. Lord Montfort is dead.'

CHAPTER XCVI

THE INFLUENCE OF DEATH.

HERE was ever, when separated, an uninterrupted correspondence between Berengaria and Endymion. They wrote to each other every day, so that when they met again there was no void in their lives and mutual experience, and each was acquainted with almost every feeling and incident that had been proved, or had occurred, since they parted. The startling news, however, communicated by the King had not previously reached Endymion, because he was on the eve of his return to England, and his correspondents had been requested to direct their future letters to his residence in London.

His voyage home was an agitated one, and not sanguine or inspiriting. There was a terrible uncertainty in the future. What were the feelings of Lady Montfort towards himself? Friendly, kind, affectionate, in a certain sense, even devoted, no doubt; but all consistent with a deep and determined friendship which sought and wished for no return more ardent. But now she was free. Yes, but would she again forfeit her freedom? And if she did, would it not be to

attain some great end, probably the great end of her
life? Lady Montfort was a woman of far-reaching
ambition. In a certain degree, she had married to
secure her lofty aims; and yet it was only by her
singular energy, and the playfulness and high spirit
of her temperament, that the sacrifice had not proved
a failure; her success, however, was limited, for the
ally on whom she had counted rarely assisted and
never sympathised with her. It was true she admired and even loved her husband; her vanity,
which was not slight, was gratified by her conquest
of one whom it had seemed no one could subdue,
and who apparently placed at her feet all the power
and magnificence which she appreciated.

Poor Endymion, who loved her passionately, over
whom she exercised the influence of a divinity, who
would do nothing without consulting her, and who
was moulded, and who wished to be moulded, in all
his thoughts and feelings, and acts, and conduct, by
her inspiring will, was also a shrewd man of the
world, and did not permit his sentiment to cloud his
perception of life and its doings. He felt that Lady
Montfort had fallen from a lofty position, and she
was not of a temperament that would quietly brook
her fate. Instead of being the mistress of castles and
palaces, with princely means, and all the splendid accidents of life at her command, she was now a dow-
ager with a jointure! Still young, with her charms
unimpaired, heightened even by the maturity of her fascinating qualities, would she endure this? She might
retain her friendship for one who, as his sister ever
impressed upon him, had no root in the land, and
even that friendship, he felt conscious, must yield
much of its entireness and intimacy to the influence

of new ties; but for their lives ever being joined together, as had sometimes been his wild dream, his cheek, though alone, burned with the consciousness of his folly and self-deception.

'He is one of our rising statesmen,' whispered the captain of the vessel to a passenger, as Endymion, silent, lonely, and absorbed, walked, as was his daily custom, the quarterdeck. 'I daresay he has a good load on his mind. Do you know, I would sooner be a captain of a ship than a minister of state?'

Poor Endymion! Yes, he bore his burthen, but it was not secrets of state that overwhelmed him. If his mind for a moment quitted the contemplation of Lady Montfort, it was only to encounter the recollection of a heart-rending separation from his sister, and his strange and now perplexing relations with Adriana.

Lord Montfort had passed the summer, as he had announced, at Princedown, and alone; that is to say, without Lady Montfort. She wrote to him frequently, and if she omitted doing so for a longer interval than usual, he would indite to her a little note, always courteous, sometimes even almost kind, reminding her that her letters amused him, and that of late they had been rarer than he wished. Lady Montfort herself made Montfort Castle her home, paying sometimes a visit to her family in the neighbourhood, and sometimes receiving them and other guests. Lord Montfort himself did not live in absolute solitude. He had society always at command. He always had a court about him; equerries, and secretaries, and doctors, and odd and amusing men whom they found out for him, and who were well pleased to find themselves in his beautiful and magnificent Princedown, wandering in woods and parks and pleasaunces, devouring his choice *entrées,* and quaffing his curious wines. Sometimes he dined with them, sometimes a few dined with him, sometimes he was not seen for weeks; but whether he were visible or not, he was the subject of constant thought and conversation by all under his roof.

Lord Montfort, it may be remembered, was a great fisherman. It was the only sport which retained a hold upon him. The solitude, the charming scenery, and the requisite skill, combined to please him. He had a love for nature, and he gratified it in this pursuit. His domain abounded in those bright chalky streams which the trout love. He liked to watch the moor-hens, too, and especially a kingfisher.

Lord Montfort came home late one day after much wading. It had been a fine day for anglers, soft and not too bright, and he had been tempted to remain long in the water. He drove home rapidly, but it was in an open carriage, and when the sun set there was a cold autumnal breeze. He complained at night, and said he had been chilled. There was always a doctor under the roof, who felt his patient's pulse, ordered the usual remedies, and encouraged him. Lord Montfort passed a bad night, and his physician in the morning found fever, and feared there were symptoms of pleurisy. He prescribed accordingly, but summoned from town two great authorities. The great authorities did not arrive until the next day. They approved of everything that had been done, but shook their heads. ' No immediate danger, but serious.'

Four-and-twenty hours afterwards they inquired of Lord Montfort whether they should send for his wife.

'On no account whatever,' he replied. 'My orders on this head are absolute.' Nevertheless, they did send for Lady Montfort, and as there was even then a telegraph to the north, Berengaria, who departed from her castle instantly, and travelled all night, arrived in eight-and-forty hours at Princedown. The state of Lord Montfort then was critical.

It was broken to Lord Montfort that his wife had arrived.

'I perceive, then,' he replied, 'that I am going to die, because I am disobeyed.'

These were the last words he uttered. He turned in his bed, as it were to conceal his countenance, and expired without a sigh or sound.

There was not a single person at Princedown in whom Lady Montfort could confide. She had summoned the family solicitor, but he could not arrive until the next day, and until he came she insisted that none of her late lord's papers should be touched. She at first thought he had made a will, because otherwise all his property would go to his cousin, whom he particularly hated, and yet on reflection she could hardly fancy his making a will. It was a trouble to him—a disagreeable trouble; and there was nobody she knew whom he would care to benefit. He was not a man who would leave anything to hospitals and charities. Therefore, on the whole, she arrived at the conclusion he had not made a will, though all the guests at Princedown were of a different opinion, and each was calculating the amount of his own legacy.

At last the lawyer arrived, and he brought the will with him. It was very short, and not very recent. Everything he had in the world except the settled estates, Montfort Castle and Montfort House, he bequeathed to his wife. It was a vast inheritance; not only Princedown, but great accumulations of personal property, for Lord Montfort was fond of amassing, and admired the sweet simplicity of the three per cents.

CHAPTER XCVII.

LADY MONTFORT.

HEN Endymion arrived in London he found among his letters two brief notes from Lady Montfort; one hurriedly written at Montfort Castle at the moment of her departure, and another from Princedown, with these words only, 'All is over.' More than a week had elapsed since the last was written, and he had already learnt from the newspapers that the funeral had taken place. It was a painful but still necessary duty to fulfil, to write to her, which he did, but he received no answer to his letter of sympathy, and to a certain degree, of condolence. Time flew on, but he could not venture to write again, and without any absolute cause for his discomfort, he felt harassed and unhappy. He had been so accustomed all his life to exist under the genial influence of women that his present days seemed lone and dark. His sister and Berengaria, two of the most gifted and charming beings in the world, had seemed to agree that their first duty had ever been to sympathise with his fortunes and to aid them. Even his correspondence with Myra was changed. There was a tone of constraint in their communications; perhaps it was the great alteration in her position that occasioned it? His heart assured him that such was not the case. He felt deeply and acutely what was the cause. The subject most interesting to both of them could not be touched on. And then he thought of Adriana, and contrasted his dull and solitary home in Hill Street with what it might have been, graced by her presence, animated by her devotion, and softened by the sweetness of her temper.

Endymion began to feel that the run of his good fortune was dried. His sister, when he had a trouble, would never hear of this; she always held that the misery and calamities of their early years had exhausted the influence of their evil stars, and apparently she had been right, and perhaps she would have always been right had he not been perverse, and thwarted her in the most important circumstances of his life.

In this state of mind, there was nothing for him to do but to plunge into business; and affairs of state are a cure for many cares and sorrows. What are our petty annoyances and griefs when we have to guard the fortunes and the honour of a nation?

The November cabinets had commenced, and this brought all the chiefs to town, Sidney Wilton among them; and his society was always a great pleasure to Endymion; the only social pleasure now left to him was a little dinner at Mr. Wilton's, and little dinners there abounded. Mr. Wilton knew all the persons that he was always thinking about, but whom, it might be noticed, they seemed to agree now rarely to mention. As for the rest, there was nobody to call upon in the delightful hours between official duties and dinner. No Lady Roehampton now, no brilliant Berengaria, not even the gentle Imogene with her welcome smile. He looked in at the Coventry Club, a club of fashion, and also much frequented by diplomatists. There were a good many persons there, and a foreign minister immediately buttonholed the Under-Secretary of State.

'I called at the Foreign Office to-day,' said the foreign minister. 'I assure you it is very pressing.'

'I had the American with me,' said Endymion, 'and he is lengthy. However, as to your business, I think we might talk it over here, and perhaps settle it.' And so they left the room together.

'I wonder what is going to happen to that gentleman,' said Mr. Ormsby, glancing at Endymion, and speaking to Mr. Cassilis.

'Why?' replied Mr. Cassilis, 'is anything up?'

'Will he marry Lady Montfort?'

'Poh!' said Mr. Cassilis.

'You may poh!' said Mr. Ormsby, 'but he was a great favourite.'

'Lady Montfort will never marry. She had always a poodle, and always will have. She was never so liée with Ferrars as with the Count of Ferroll, and half a dozen others. She must have a slave.'

'A very good mistress with thirty thousand a year.'

'She has not that,' said Mr. Cassilis doubtingly.

'What do you put Princedown at?' said Mr. Ormsby.

'That I can tell you to a T,' replied Mr. Cassilis, 'for it was offered to me when old Rambrooke died. You will never get twelve thousand a year out of it.'

'Well, I will answer for half a million consols,' said Ormsby, 'for my lawyer, when he made a little

investment for me the other day, saw the entry himself in the bank-books; our names are very near, you
know — M, and O. Then there is her jointure, something like ten thousand a year.'

'No, no; not seven.'

'Well, that would do.'

'And what is the amount of your little investment
in consols altogether, Ormsby?'

'Well, I believe I top Montfort,' said Mr. Ormsby
with a complacent smile, 'but then you know, I am
not a swell like you; I have no land.'

'Lady Montfort, thirty thousand a year,' said Mr.
Cassilis musingly. 'She is only thirty. She is a woman
who will set the Thames on fire, but she will never
marry. Do you dine to-day, by any chance, with
Sidney Wilton?'

When Endymion returned home this evening, he
found a letter from Lady Montfort. It was a month
since he had written to her. He was so nervous that
he absolutely for a moment could not break the seal,
and the palpitation of his heart was almost overpow-
ering.

Lady Montfort thanked him for his kind letter,
which she ought to have acknowledged before, but
she had been very busy — indeed, quite overwhelmed
with affairs. She wished to see him, but was sorry
she could not ask him down to Princedown, as she
was living in complete retirement, only her aunt with
her, Lady Gertrude, whom, she believed, he knew.
He was aware, probably, how good Lord Montfort
had been to her. Sincerely she could say, nothing
could have been more unexpected. If she could have
seen her husband before the fatal moment, it would
have been a consolation to her. He had always been

kind to Endymion; she really believed sometimes that
Lord Montfort was even a little attached to him. She
should like Endymion to have some souvenir of her
late husband. Would he choose something, or would
he leave it to her?

One would rather agree, from the tone of this letter, that Mr. Cassilis knew what he was talking about.
It fell rather cold on Endymion's heart, and he passed
a night of some disquietude; not one of those nights,
exactly, when we feel that the end of the world has
at length arrived, and that we are the first victim,
but a night when you slumber rather than sleep, and
wake with the consciousness of some indefinable chagrin.

This was a dull Christmas for Endymion Ferrars.
He passed it, as he had passed others, at Gaydene,
but what a contrast to the old assemblies there! Every
source of excitement that could make existence absolutely fascinating seemed then to unite in his happy
fate. Entrancing love and the very romance of domestic affection, and friendships of honour and happiness, and all the charms of an accomplished society,
and the feeling of a noble future, and the present and
urgent interest in national affairs — all gone, except
some ambition which might tend to consequences not
more successful than those that had ultimately visited
his house with irreparable calamity.

The meeting of Parliament was a great relief to
Endymion. Besides his office, he had now the House
of Commons to occupy him. He was never absent
from his place; no little runnings up to Montfort
House or Hill Street just to tell them the authentic
news, or snatch a hasty repast with furtive delight,
with persons still more delightful, and flattering one's

self all the time that, so far as absence was concerned, the fleetness of one's gifted brougham horse really made it no difference between Mayfair and Bellamy's.

Endymion had replied, but not very quickly, to Lady Montfort's letter, and he had heard from her again, but her letter requiring no reply, the correspondence had dropped. It was the beginning of March when she wrote to him to say that she was obliged to come to town to see her lawyer and transact some business; that she would be 'at papa's in Grosvenor Square,' though the house was shut up, on a certain day, that she much wished to see Endymion, and begged him to call on her.

It was a trying moment when about noon he lifted the knocker in Grosvenor Square. The door was not opened rapidly, and the delay made him more nervous. He almost wished the door would never open. He was shown into a small back room on the ground floor in which was a bookcase, and which chamber, in the language of Grosvenor Square, is called a library.

'Her ladyship will see you presently,' said the servant, who had come up from Princedown.

Endymion was standing before the fire, and as nervous as a man could well be. He sighed, and he sighed more than once. His breathing was oppressed; he felt that life was too short to permit us to experience such scenes and situations. He heard the lock of the door move, and it required all his manliness to endure it.

She entered; she was in weeds, but they became her admirably; her countenance was grave and apparently with an effort to command it. She did not move hurriedly, but held out both her hands to Endymion and retained his, and all without speaking.

Her lips then seemed to move, when, rather suddenly, withdrawing her right hand, and placing it on his shoulder and burying her face in her arm, she wept.

He led her soothingly to a seat, and took a chair by her side. Not a word had yet been spoken by either of them; only a murmur of sympathy on the part of Endymion. Lady Montfort spoke first.

'I am weaker than I thought, but it is a great trial.' And then she said how sorry she was, that she could not receive him at Princedown; but she thought it best that he should not go there. 'I have a great deal of business to transact — you would not believe how much. I do not dislike it, it occupies me, it employs my mind. I have led so active a life, that solitude is rather too much for me. Among other business, I must buy a town house, and that is the most difficult of affairs. There never was so great a city with such small houses. I shall feel the loss of Montfort House, though I never used it half so much as I wished. I want a mansion; I should think you could help me in this. When I return to society, I mean to receive. There must be therefore good reception rooms; if possible, more than good. And now let us talk about our friends. Tell me all about your royal sister, and this new marriage; it rather surprised me, but I think it excellent. Ah! you can keep a secret, but you see it is no use having a secret with me. Even in solitude everything reaches me.'

'I assure you most seriously, that I can annex no meaning to what you are saying.'

'Then I can hardly think it true; and yet it came from high authority, and it was not told me as a real secret.'

'A marriage, and whose?'

'Miss Neuchatel's,— Adriana.'

'And to whom?' inquired Endymion, changing colour.

'To Lord Waldershare.'

'To Lord Waldershare!'

'And has not your sister mentioned it to you?'

'Not a word; it cannot be true.'

'I will give to you my authority,' said Lady Montfort. 'Though I came here in the twilight in a hired brougham, and with a veil, I was caught before I could enter the house by, of all people in the world, Mrs. Rodney. And she told me this in what she called "real confidence," and it was announced to her in a letter from her sister, Lady Beaumaris. They seem all delighted with the match.'

CHAPTER XCVIII.

ADRIANA'S MARRIAGE.

THIS marriage of Adriana was not an event calculated to calm the uneasy and dissatisfied temperament of Endymion. The past rendered it impossible that this announcement should not in some degree affect him. Then the silence of his sister on such a subject was too significant; the silence even of Waldershare. Somehow or other, it seemed that all these once dear and devoted friends stood in different relations to him and to each other from what they once filled. They had become more near and intimate together, but he seemed without the pale; he, that Endymion, who once seemed the prime object, if not the centre, of all their thoughts and sentiment. And why was this? What was the influence that had swayed him to a line contrary to what was once their hopes and affections? Had he an evil genius? And was it she? Horrible thought!

The interview with Lady Montfort had been deeply interesting — had for a moment restored him to himself. Had it not been for this news, he might have returned home, soothed, gratified, even again indulging in dreams. But this news had made him ponder;

had made him feel what he had lost, and forced him to ask himself what he had gained.

There was one thing he had gained, and that was the privilege of calling on Lady Montfort the next day. That was a fact that sometimes dissipated all the shadows. Under the immediate influence of her presence, he became spell-bound as of yore, and in the intoxication of her beauty, the brightness of her mind, and her ineffable attraction, he felt he would be content with any lot, provided he might retain her kind thoughts and pass much of his life in her society.

She was only staying three or four days in town, and was much engaged in the mornings; but Endymion called on her every afternoon, and sat talking with her till dinner-time, and they both dined very late. As he really on personal and domestic affairs never could have any reserve with her, he told her, in that complete confidence in which they always indulged, of the extraordinary revelation which his sister had made to him about the parliamentary qualification. Lady Montfort was deeply interested in this; she was even agitated, and looked very grave.

'I am sorry,' she said, 'we know this. Things cannot remain now as they are. You cannot return the money, that would be churlish; besides, you cannot return all the advantages which it gained for you, and they must certainly be considered part of the gift, and the most precious; and then, too, it would betray what your sister rightly called a "sacred confidence." And yet something must be done—you must let me think. Do not mention it again.' And then they talked a little of public affairs. Lady Montfort saw no one, and heard from no one now; but judging from the journals, she thought the position of the government feeble. 'There cannot be a Protectionist government,' she said; 'and yet that is the only parliamentary party of importance. Things will go on till some blow, and perhaps a slight one, will upset you all. And then who is to succeed? I think some queer *mélange* got up perhaps by Mr. Bertie Tremaine.'

The last day came. She parted from Endymion with kindness, but not with tenderness. He was choking with emotion, and tried to imitate her calmness.

'Am I to write to you?' he asked in a faltering voice.

'Of course you are,' she said, 'every day, and tell me all the news.'

The Hainaults, and the Beaumaris, and Waldershare, did not return to England until some time after Easter. The marriage was to take place in June — Endymion was to be Waldershare's best man. There were many festivities, and he was looked upon as an indispensable guest in all. Adriana received his congratulations with animation, but with affection. She thanked him for a bracelet which he had presented to her; 'I value it more,' she said, 'than all my other presents together, except what dear Waldershare has given to me.' Even with that exception, the estimate was high, for never a bride in any land ever received the number of splendid offerings which crowded the tables of Lord Hainault's new palace, which he had just built in Park Lane. There was not a Neuchatel in existence, and they flourished in every community, who did not send her, at least, a rivière of brilliants. King Florestan and his Queen sent offerings worthy

of their resplendent throne and their invaluable friendship. But nothing surpassed, nothing approached, the
contents of a casket, which, a day before the wedding, arrived at Hainault House. It came from a foreign land, and Waldershare superintended the opening
of the case, and the appearance of a casket of crimson velvet, with genuine excitement. But when it
was opened! There was a coronet of brilliants; a
necklace of brilliants and emeralds, and one of sapphires and brilliants; and dazzling bracelets, and all
the stones more than precious; gems of Golconda no
longer obtainable, and lustrous companions which
only could have been created in the hot earth of Asia.
From whom? Not a glimpse of meaning. All that
was written, in a foreign handwriting on a sheet of
notepaper, was, 'For the Lady Viscountess Waldershare.'

'When the revolution comes,' said Lord Hainault,
'Lord Waldershare and my daughter must turn jewel-
lers. Their stock in trade is ready.'

The correspondence between Lady Montfort and
Endymion had resumed its ancient habit. They wrote
to each other every day, and one day she told him
that she had purchased a house and that she must
come up to town to examine and to furnish it. She
probably should be a month in London, and remain-
ing there until the end of the season, in whose amuse-
ments and business, of course, she could not share.
She should 'be at papa's,' though he and his family
were in town; but that was no reason why Endymion should not call on her. And he came, and called
every day. Lady Montfort was full of her new house;
it was in Carlton Gardens, the house she always
wished, always intended to have. There is nothing

like will; everybody can do exactly what they like in this world, provided they really like it. Sometimes they think they do, but in general, it is a mistake. Lady Montfort, it seemed, was a woman who always could do what she liked. She could do what she liked with Endymion Ferrars; that was quite certain. Supposed by men to have a strong will and a calm judgment, he was a nose of wax with this woman. He was fascinated by her, and he had been fascinated now for nearly ten years. What would be the result of this irresistible influence upon him? Would it make or mar those fortunes that once seemed so promising? The philosophers of White's and the Coventry were generally of opinion that he had no chance.

Lady Montfort was busy every morning with her new house, but she never asked Endymion to accompany her, though it seemed natural to do so. But he saw her every day, and 'papa,' who was a most kind and courtly gentleman, would often ask him, 'if he had nothing better to do,' to dine there, and he dined there frequently; and if he were engaged, he was always of opinion that he had nothing better to do.

At last, however, the season was over; the world had gone to Goodwood, and Lady Montfort was about to depart to Princedown. It was a dreary prospect for Endymion, and he could not conceal his feelings. He could not help saying one day, 'Do you know, now that you are going I almost wish to die.'

Alas! she only laughed. But he looked grave. 'I am very unhappy,' he sighed rather than uttered.

She looked at him with seriousness. 'I do not think our separation need be very long. Papa and all my family are coming to me in September to pay me a very long visit. I really do not see why you should not come too.'

Endymion's countenance mantled with rapture. 'If I might come, I think I should be the happiest of men!'

The month that was to elapse before his visit, Endymion was really, as he said, the happiest of men; at least, the world thought him so. He seemed to walk upon tip-toe. Parliament was prorogued, office was consigned to permanent secretaries, and our youthful statesman seemed only to live to enjoy, and add to, the revelry of existence. Now at Cowes, now stalking in the Highlands, dancing at balls in the wilderness, and running races of fantastic feats, full of health, and frolic, and charm; he was the delight of society, while, the whole time, he had only one thought, and that was the sacred day when he should again see the being whom he adored, and that in her beautiful home, which her presence made more lovely.

Yes! he was again at Princedown, in the bosom of her family; none others there; treated like one of themselves. The courtly father pressed his hand; the amiable and refined mother smiled upon him; the daughters, pretty, and natural as the air, treated him as if they were sisters, and even the eldest son, who generally hates you, after a little stiffness, announced in a tone never questioned under the family roof, that Ferrars was a firstrate shot.

And so a month rolled on; immensely happy, as any man who has loved, and loved in a beautiful scene, alone can understand. One morning Lady Montfort said to him, 'I must go up to London about my house. I want to go and return the same day.

Do you know, I think you had better come with me ?
You shall give me a luncheon in Hill Street, and we
shall be back by the last train. It will be late, but
we shall wake in the morning in the country, and
that I always think a great thing.'

And so it happened; they rose early and arrived
in town in time to give them a tolerably long morning. She took him to her house in Carlton Gardens,
and showed to him exactly how it was all she
wanted; accommodation for a firstrate establishment;
and then the reception rooms, few houses in London
could compare with them; a gallery and three saloons.
Then they descended to the dining-room. 'It is a
dining-room, not a banqueting hall,' she said, ' which
we had at Montfort House, but still it is much larger
than most dining-rooms in London. But, I think this
room, at least I hope you do, quite charming,' and
she took him to a room almost as large as the dining-room, and looking into the garden. It was fitted
up with exquisite taste; calm subdued colouring,
with choice marble busts of statesmen, ancient and
of our times, but the shelves were empty.

'They are empty,' she said, 'but the volumes to
fill them are already collected. Yes,' she added in a
tremulous voice, and slightly pressing the arm on
which she leant. 'If you will deign to accept it,
this is the chamber I have prepared for you.'

'Dearest of women!' and he took her hand.

'Yes,' she murmured, 'help me to realise the
dream of my life;' and she touched his forehead with
her lips.

CHAPTER XCIX.

ENDYMION'S BRIDE.

THE marriage of Mr. Ferrars with Lady Montfort surprised some, but, on the whole, pleased everybody. They were both highly popular, and no one seemed to envy them their happiness and prosperity. The union took place at a season of the year when there was no London world to observe and to criticise. It was a quiet ceremony; they went down to Northumberland to Lady Montfort's father, and they were married in his private chapel. After that they went off immediately to pay a visit to King Florestan and his Queen; Myra had sent her a loving letter.

'Perhaps it will be the first time that your sister ever saw me with satisfaction,' remarked Lady Montfort, 'but I think she will love me now! I always loved her; perhaps because she is so like you.'

It was a happy meeting and a delightful visit. They did not talk much of the past. The enormous change in the position of their host and hostess since the first days of their acquaintance, and, on their own part, some indefinite feeling of delicate reserve, combined to make them rather dwell on a present which was full of novelty so attractive and so absorbing. In his manner, the King was unchanged; he was never a demonstrative person, but simple, un-affected, rather silent; with a sweet temper and a tender manner, he seemed to be gratified that he had the power of conferring happiness on those around him. His feeling to his Queen was one of idolatry, and she received Berengaria as a sister and a much-loved one. Their presence and the season of the year made their life a festival, and when they parted, there were entreaties and promises that the visit should be often repeated.

'Adieu! my Endymion,' said Myra at the last moment they were alone. 'All has happened for you beyond my hopes; all now is safe. I might wish we were in the same land, but not if I lost my husband, whom I adore.'

The reason that forced them to curtail their royal visit was the state of politics at home, which had suddenly become critical. There were symptoms, and considerable ones, of disturbance and danger when they departed for their wedding tour, but they could not prevail on themselves to sacrifice a visit on which they had counted so much, and which could not be fulfilled on another occasion under the same interesting circumstances. Besides, the position of Mr. Ferrars, though an important, was a subordinate one, and though cabinet ministers were not justified in leaving the country, an Under-Secretary of State and a bridegroom might, it would seem, depart on his irresponsible holiday. Mr. Sidney Wilton, how-ever, shook his head; 'I do not like the state of affairs,' he said, 'I think you will have to come back sooner than you imagine.'

'You are not going to be so foolish as to have an early session?' inquired Lady Montfort.

He only shrugged his shoulders, and said, 'We are in a mess.'

What mess? and what was the state of affairs?

This had happened. At the end of the autumn, his Holiness the Pope had made half a dozen new cardinals, and to the surprise of the world, and the murmurs of the Italians, there appeared among them the name of an Englishman, Nigel Penruddock, Archbishop *in partibus*. Shortly after this, a papal bull, 'given at St. Peter's, Rome, under the seal of the fisherman,' was issued, establishing a Romish hierarchy in England. This was soon followed by a pastoral letter by the new cardinal, 'given out of the Appian Gate,' announcing that 'Catholic England had been restored to its orbit in the ecclesiastical firmament.'

The country at first was more stupefied than alarmed. It was conscious that something extraordinary had happened, and some great action taken by an ecclesiastical power, which from tradition it was ever inclined to view with suspicion and some fear. But it held its breath for a while. It so happened that the Prime Minister was a member of a great house which had become illustrious by its profession of Protestant principles, and even by its sufferings in a cause which England had once looked on as sacred. The prime minister, a man of distinguished ability, not devoid even of genius, was also a wily politician, and of almost unrivalled experience in the management of political parties. The ministry was weak and nearly worn out, and its chief, influenced partly by noble and historical sentiments, partly by a conviction that he had a fine occasion to rally the confidence of the country round himself and his friends, and to restore the repute of his political connection, thought fit, without consulting his colleagues, to publish a manifesto denouncing the aggression of the Pope upon our Protestantism as insolent and insidious, and as expressing a pretension of supremacy over the realm of England which made the minister indignant.

A confused public wanted to be led, and now they were led. They sprang to their feet like an armed man. The corporation of London, the universities of Oxford and Cambridge had audiences of the Queen; the counties met, the municipalities memorialised; before the first of January there had been held nearly seven thousand public meetings, asserting the supremacy of the Queen and calling on Her Majesty's Government to vindicate it by stringent measures.

Unfortunately, it was soon discovered by the minister that there had been nothing illegal in the conduct of the Pope or the Cardinal, and a considerable portion of the Liberal party began to express the inconvenient opinion that the manifesto of their chief was opposed to those principles of civil and religious liberty of which he was the hereditary champion. Some influential members of his own cabinet did not conceal their disapprobation of a step on which they had not been consulted.

Immediately after Christmas, Endymion and Lady Montfort settled in London. She was anxious to open her new mansion as soon as Parliament met, and to organise continuous receptions. She looked upon the ministry as in a critical state, and thought it was an occasion when social influences might not inconsiderably assist them.

But though she exhibited for this object her wonted energy and high spirit, a fine observer — Mr. Sidney Wilton for example — might have detected a change in the manner of Berengaria. Though the strength of her character was unaltered, there was an absence of that restlessness, it might be said, that somewhat feverish excitement, from which formerly she was not always free. The truth is, her heart was satisfied, and that brought repose. Feelings of affection, long mortified and pent up, were now lavished and concentrated on a husband of her heart and adoration, and she was proud that his success and greatness might be avowed as the objects of her life.

The campaign, however, for which such preparations were made, ended almost before it began. The ministry, on the meeting of Parliament, found themselves with a discontented House of Commons, and discordant counsels among themselves. The anti-papal manifesto was the secret cause of this evil state, but the Prime Minister, to avoid such a mortifying admission, took advantage of two unfavourable divisions on other matters and resigned.

Here was a crisis — another crisis! Could the untried Protectionists, without men, form an administration? It was whispered that Lord Derby had been sent for, and declined the attempt. Then there was another rumour, that he was going to try. Mr. Bertie Tremaine looked mysterious. The time for the third party had clearly arrived. It was known that he had the list of the next ministry in his breast-pocket, but it was only shown to Mr. Tremaine Bertie, who con-

fided in secrecy to the initiated that it was the
strongest government since 'All the Talents.'

Notwithstanding this great opportunity, 'All the
Talents' were not summoned. The leader of the
Protectionists renounced the attempt in despair, and
the author of the anti-papal manifesto was again sent
for, and obliged to introduce the measure which had
already destroyed a government and disorganised a
party.

'Sidney Wilton,' said Lady Montfort to her husband, 'says that they are in the mud, and he for
one will not go back — but he will go. I know him.
He is too soft-hearted to stand an appeal from colleagues in distress. But were I you, Endymion, I
would not return. I think you want a little rest, or
you have got a great deal of private business to attend
to, or something of that kind. Nobody notices the
withdrawal of an under-secretary except those in office.
There is no necessity why you should be in the mud.
I will continue to receive, and do everything that is
possible for our friends, but I think my husband has
been an under-secretary long enough.'

Endymion quite agreed with his wife. The minister offered him preferment and the Privy Council,
but Lady Montfort said it was really not so important
as the office he had resigned. She was resolved that
he should not return to them, and she had her way.
Ferrars himself now occupied a rather peculiar position, being the master of a great fortune and of an
establishment which was the headquarters of the party
of which he was now only a private member; but,
calm and collected, he did not lose his head; always
said and did the right thing, and never forgot his

early acquaintances.   Trenchard was his bosom political friend.   Seymour Hicks, who, through Endymion's
kindness, had now got into the Treasury, and was quite
fashionable, had the run of the House, and made
himself marvellously useful, while St. Barbe, who had
become by mistake a member of the Conservative
Club, drank his frequent claret cup every Saturday
evening at Lady Montfort's receptions, with many
pledges to the welfare of the Liberal administration.

The flag of the Tory party waved over the magnificent mansion of which Imogene Beaumaris was
the graceful life.   As parties were nearly equal, and
the ministry was supposed to be in decay, the
rival reception was as well attended as that of Berengaria.   The two great leaders were friends, intimate,
but not perhaps quite so intimate as a few years
before.   'Lady Montfort is very kind to me,' Imogene
would say, 'but I do not think she now quite remem-
bers we are cousins.'   Both Lord and Lady Waldershare seemed equally devoted to Lady Beaumaris.   'I
do not think,' he would say, 'that I shall ever get
Adriana to receive.   It is an organic gift, and very
rare.   What I mean to do is to have a firstrate villa
and give the party strawberries.   I always say Adriana is like Nell Gwyn, and she shall go about with
a pottle.   One never sees a pottle of strawberries now.
I believe they went out, like all good things, with
the Stuarts.'

And so, after all these considerable events, the
season rolled on and closed tranquilly.   Lord and Lady
Hainault continued to give banquets, over which the
hostess sighed; Sir Peter Vigo had the wisdom to
retain his millions, which few manage to do, as it is

admitted that it is easier to make a fortune than to keep one. Mrs. Rodney, supremely habited, still drove her ponies, looking younger and prettier than ever, and getting more fashionable every day, and Mr. Ferrars and Berengaria, Countess of Montfort, retired in the summer to their beautiful and beloved Princedown.

CHAPTER C.

The Consummation of Early Hopes.

ALTHOUGH the past life of Endymion had, on the whole, been a happy life, and although he was destined also to a happy future, perhaps the four years which elapsed from the time he quitted office, certainly in his experience had never been exceeded, and it was difficult to imagine could be exceeded, in felicity. He had a great interest, and even growing influence in public life without any of its cares; he was united to a woman whom he had long passionately loved, and who had every quality and accomplishment to make existence delightful; he was master of a fortune which secured him all those advantages which are appreciated by men of taste and generosity. He became a father, and a family name which had been originally borne by a courtier of the elder Stuarts was now bestowed on the future lord of Princedown.

Lady Montfort herself had no thought but her husband. His happiness, his enjoyment of existence, his success and power in life, entirely absorbed her. The anxiety which she felt that in everything he should

be master was touching. Once looked upon as the
most imperious of women, she would not give a
direction on any matter without his opinion and sanction. One would have supposed from what might
be observed under their roof, that she was some
beautiful but portionless maiden whom Endymion
had raised to wealth and power.

All this time, however, Lady Montfort sedulously
maintained that commanding position in social politics for which she was singularly fitted. Indeed, in
that respect, she had no rival. She received the world
with the same constancy and splendour, as if she were
the wife of a minister. Animated by Waldershare,
Lady Beaumaris maintained in this respect a certain
degree of rivalry. She was the only hope and refuge
of the Tories, and rich, attractive, and popular, her
competition could not be disregarded. But Lord Beaumaris was a little freakish. Sometimes he would sail
in his yacht to odd places, and was at Algiers or in
Egypt when, according to Tadpole, he ought to have
been at Piccadilly Terrace. Then he occasionally got
crusty about his hunting. He would hunt, whatever
were the political consequences, but whether he were
in Africa or Leicestershire, Imogene must be with
him. He could not exist without her constant presence. There was something in her gentleness, combined with her quick and ready sympathy and playfulness of mind and manner, which alike pleased and
soothed his life.

The Whigs tottered on for a year after the rude
assault of Cardinal Penruddock, but they were doomed,
and the Protectionists were called upon to form an
administration. As they had no one in their ranks
who had ever been in office except their chief, who

was in the House of Lords, the affair seemed impossible. The attempt, however, could not be avoided. A dozen men, without the slightest experience of official life, had to be sworn in as privy councillors, before even they could receive the seals and insignia of their intended offices. On their knees, according to the constitutional custom, a dozen men, all in the act of genuflexion at the same moment, and headed, too, by one of the most powerful peers in the country, the Lord of Alnwick Castle himself, humbled themselves before a female Sovereign, who looked serene and imperturbable before a spectacle never seen before, and which, in all probability, will never be seen again.

One of this band, a gentleman without any official experience whatever, was not only placed in the cabinet, but was absolutely required to become the leader of the House of Commons, which had never occurred before, except in the instance of Mr. Pitt in 1782. It has been said that it was unwise in the Protectionists assuming office when, on this occasion and on subsequent ones, they were far from being certain of a majority in the House of Commons. It should, however, be remembered, that unless they had dared these ventures, they never could have formed a body of men competent, from their official experience and their practice in debate, to form a ministry. The result has rather proved that they were right. Had they continued to refrain from incurring responsibility, they must have broken up and merged in different connections, which, for a party numerically so strong as the Protectionists, would have been a sorry business, and probably have led to disastrous results.

Mr. Bertie Tremaine having been requested to call on the Protectionist Prime Minister, accordingly repaired to headquarters with the list of his colleagues in his pocket. He was offered for himself a post of little real importance, but which secured to him the dignity of the privy council. Mr. Tremaine Bertie and several of his friends had assembled at his house, awaiting with anxiety his return. He had to communicate to them that he had been offered a privy councillor's post, and to break to them that it was not proposed to provide for any other member of his party. Their indignation was extreme; but they naturally supposed that he had rejected the offer to himself with becoming scorn. Their leader, however, informed them that he had not felt it his duty to be so peremptory. They should remember that the recognition of their political status by such an offer to their chief was a considerable event. For his part, he had for some time been painfully aware that the influence of the House of Commons in the constitutional scheme was fast waning, and that the plan of Sir William Temple for the reorganisation of the privy council, and depositing in it the real authority of the State, was that to which we should be obliged to have recourse. This offer to him of a seat in the council was, perhaps, the beginning of the end. It was a crisis; they must look to seats in the privy council, which, under Sir William Temple's plan, would be accompanied with ministerial duties and salaries. What they had all, at one time, wished, had not exactly been accomplished, but he had felt it his duty to his friends not to shrink from responsibility. So he had accepted the minister's offer.

Mr. Bertie Tremaine was not long in the busy enjoyment of his easy post. Then the country was governed for two years by all its ablest men, who, by the end of that term, had succeeded, by their coalesced genius, in reducing that country to a state of desolation and despair. 'I did not think it would have lasted even so long,' said Lady Montfort; 'but then I was acquainted with their mutual hatreds and their characteristic weaknesses. What is to happen now? Somebody must be found of commanding private character and position, and with as little damaged a public one as in this wreck of reputations is possible. I see nobody but Sidney Wilton. Everybody likes him, and he is the only man who could bring people together.'

And everybody seemed to be saying the same thing at the same time. The name of Sidney Wilton was in everybody's mouth. It was unfortunate that he had been a member of the defunct ministry, but then it had always been understood that he had always disapproved of all their measures. There was not the slightest evidence of this, but everybody chose to believe it.

Sidney Wilton was chagrined with life, and had become a martyr to the gout, which that chagrin had aggravated; but he was a great gentleman, and too chivalric to refuse a royal command when the Sovereign was in distress. Sidney Wilton became Premier, and the first colleague he recommended to fill the most important post after his own, the Secretaryship of State for Foreign Affairs, was Mr. Ferrars.

'It ought to last ten years,' said Lady Montfort. 'I see no danger except his health. I never knew a man so changed. At his time of life five years ought to make no difference in a man. I cannot believe he is the person who used to give us those charming parties at Gaydene. Whatever you may say, Endymion, I feel convinced that something must have passed between your sister and him. Neither of them ever gave me a hint of such a matter, or of the possibility of its ever happening, but feminine instinct assures me that something took place. He always had the gout, and his ancestors have had the gout for a couple of centuries; and all prime ministers have the gout. I dare say you will not escape, darling, but I hope it will never make you look as if you had just lost paradise, or, what would be worst, become the last man.'

Lady Montfort was right. The ministry was strong and it was popular. There were no jealousies in it; every member was devoted to his chief, and felt that he was rightly the chief, whereas, as Lady Montfort said, the Whigs never had a ministry before in which there were not at least a couple of men who had been prime ministers, and as many more who thought they ought to be.

There were years of war, and of vast and critical negotiations. Ferrars was equal to the duties, for he had much experience, and more thought, and he was greatly aided by the knowledge of affairs, and the clear and tranquil judgment of the chief minister. There was only one subject on which there was not between them that complete and cordial unanimity which was so agreeable and satisfactory. And even in this case, there was no difference of opinion, but rather of sentiment and feeling. It was when Prince Florestan expressed his desire to join the grand alliance, and become our active military ally. It was perhaps impossible, under any circumstances, for the Powers to refuse such an offer, but Endymion was strongly in favour of accepting it. It consolidated our interests in a part of Europe where we required sympathy and support, and it secured for us the aid and influence of the great Liberal party of the continent as distinguished from the secret societies and the socialist republicans. The Count of Ferroll, also, whose opinion weighed much with Her Majesty's Government, was decidedly in favour of the combination. The English Prime Minister listened to their representations frigidly; it was difficult to refute the arguments which were adverse to his own feelings, and to resist the unanimous opinion not only of his colleagues, but of our allies. But he was cold and silent, or made discouraging remarks.

'Can you trust him?' he would say. 'Remember he himself has been, and still is, a member of the very secret societies whose baneful influence we are now told he will neutralise or subdue. Whatever the cabinet decides, and I fear that with this strong expression of opinion on the part of our allies we have little option left, remember I gave you my warning. I know the gentleman, and I do not trust him.'

After this, the Prime Minister had a most severe attack of the gout, remained for weeks at Gaydene, and saw no one on business except Endymion and Baron Sergius.

While the time is elapsing which can alone decide whether the distrust of Mr. Wilton were well-founded or the reverse, let us see how the world is treating the rest of our friends.

Lord Waldershare did not make such a pattern husband as Endymion, but he made a much better one than the world ever supposed he would. Had he married Berengaria, the failure would have been great; but he was united to a being capable of deep affection and very sensitive, yet grateful for kindness from a husband to a degree not easily imaginable. And Waldershare had really a good heart, though a bad temper, and he was a gentleman. Besides, he had a great admiration and some awe of his father-in-law, and Lord Hainault, with his good-natured irony, and consummate knowledge of men and things, quite controlled him. With Lady Hainault he was a favourite. He invented plausible theories and brilliant paradoxes for her, which left her always in a state of charmed wonder, and when she met him again, and adopted or refuted them, for her intellectual power was considerable, he furnished her with fresh dogmas and tenets, which immediately interested her intelligence, though she generally forgot to observe that they were contrary to the views and principles of the last visit.

Between Adriana and Imogene there was a very close alliance, and Lady Beaumaris did everything in her power to develop Lady Waldershare advantageously before her husband; and so, not forgetting that Waldershare, with his romance, and imagination, and fancy, and taste, and caprice, had a considerable element of worldliness in his character, and that he liked to feel that, from living in lodgings, he had become a Monte Cristo, his union with Adriana may be said to be a happy and successful one.

The friendship between Sir Peter Vigo and his brother M.P., Mr. Rodney, never diminished, and Mr. Rodney became richer every year. He experienced considerable remorse at sitting in opposition to the

son of his right honourable friend, the late William
Pitt Ferrars, and frequently consulted Sir Peter on his
embarrassment and difficulty. Sir Peter, who never
declined arranging any difficulty, told his friend to be
easy, and that he, Sir Peter, saw his way. It became
gradually understood, that if ever the government
was in difficulties, Mr. Rodney's vote might be
counted on. He was peculiarly situated, for, in a
certain sense, his friend the Right Honourable William
Pitt Ferrars had entrusted the guardianship of his child
to his care. But whenever the ministry was not in
danger, the ministry must not depend upon his vote.

Trenchard had become Secretary of the Treasury
in the Wilton administration, had established his reputation, and was looked upon as a future minister.
Jawett, without forfeiting his post and promotion at
Somerset House, had become the editor of a new
periodical magazine, called the *Privy Council*. It was
established and maintained by Mr. Bertie Tremaine,
and was chiefly written by that gentleman himself.
It was full of Greek quotations, to show that it was
not Grub Street, and written in a style as like that of
Sir William Temple, as a paper in 'Rejected Addresses' might resemble the classic lucubrations of
the statesman-sage who, it is hoped, will be always
remembered by a grateful country for having introduced into these islands the Moor Park apricot.
What the pages of the *Privy Council* meant no human being had the slightest conception except Mr.
Tremaine Bertie.

Mr. Thornberry remained a respected member of
the cabinet. It was thought his presence there secured the sympathies of advanced Liberalism throughout the country; but that was a tradition rather than

a fact. Statesmen in high places are not always so well acquainted with the changes and gradations of opinion in political parties at home as they are with those abroad. We hardly mark the growth of the tree we see every day. Mr. Thornberry had long ceased to be popular with his former friends, and the fact that he had become a minister was one of the causes of this change of feeling. That was unreasonable, but in politics unreasonable circumstances are elements of the problem to be solved. It was generally understood that, on the next election, Mr. Thornberry would have to look out for another seat; his chief constituents, those who are locally styled the leaders of the party, were still faithful to him, for they were proud of having a cabinet minister for their member, to be presented by him at court, and occasionally to dine with him; but the 'masses,' who do not go to court, and are never asked to dinner, require a member who would represent their whims, and it was quite understood that, on the very first occasion, this enlightened community had resolved to send up to Westminster — Mr. Enoch Craggs.

It was difficult to say, whether in his private life Job found affairs altogether more satisfactory than in his public. His wife had joined the Roman Communion. An ingrained perverseness which prevented his son from ever willingly following the advice or example of his parents, had preserved John Hampden to the Anglican faith, but he had portraits of Laud and Strafford over his mantelpiece, and embossed in golden letters on a purple ground the magical word 'THOROUGH.' His library chiefly consisted of the *Tracts for the Times,* and a colossal edition of the 'Fathers' gorgeously bound. He was a very clever fellow, this young Thornberry, a natural orator, and was leader of the High Church party in the Oxford Union. He brought home his friends occasionally to Hurstley, and Job had the opportunity of becoming acquainted with a class and school of humanity with which, notwithstanding his considerable experience of life, he had no previous knowledge — young gentlemen, apparently half-starved and dressed like priests, and sometimes an enthusiastic young noble, in much better physical condition, and in costume becoming a cavalier, ready to raise the royal standard at Edgehill.

What a little annoyed Job was that his son addressed him as 'Squire,' a habit even pedantically followed by his companions. He was, however, justly entitled to this ancient and reputable honour, for Job had been persuaded to purchase Hurstley, was a lord of several thousand acres, and had the boar's head carried in procession at Christmas in his ancient hall. It is strange, but he was rather perplexed than annoyed by all these marvellous metamorphoses in his life and family. His intelligence was as clear as ever, and his views on all subjects unchanged; but he was, like many other men, governed at home by his affections. He preferred the new arrangement, if his wife and family were happy and contented, to a domestic system founded on his own principles, accompanied by a sullen or shrewish partner of his life and rebellious offspring.

What really vexed him, among comparatively lesser matters, was the extraordinary passion which in time his son imbibed for game-preserving. He did at last interfere on this matter, but in vain. John Hampden announced that he did not value land if he was only to look at it, and that sport was the patriotic pastime of an English gentleman. 'You used in old days never to be satisfied with what I got out of the land,' said the old grandfather to Job, with a little amiable malice; 'there is enough at any rate now for the hares and rabbits, but I doubt for anybody else.'

We must not forget our old friend St. Barbe. Whether he had written himself out or had become lazy in the luxurious life in which he now indulged, he rarely appealed to the literary public, which still admired him. He was given to intimating that he was engaged in a great work, which, though written in his taking prose, was to be really the epopee of social life in this country. Dining out every day, and ever arriving, however late, at those 'small and earlies,' which he once despised, he gave to his friends frequent intimations that he was not there for pleasure, but rather following his profession; he was in his studio, observing and reflecting on all the passions and manners of mankind, and gathering materials for the great work which was eventually to enchant and instruct society, and immortalise his name.

'The fact is, I wrote too early,' he would say. 'I blush when I read my own books, though compared with those of the brethren, they might still be looked on as classics. They say no artist can draw a camel, and I say no author ever drew a gentleman. How can they, with no opportunity of ever seeing one? And so with a little caricature of manners, which they catch second-hand, they are obliged to have recourse to outrageous nonsense, as if polished life consisted only of bigamists, and that ladies of fashion were in the habit of paying blackmail to returned convicts. However, I shall put an end to all this. I have now got the materials, or am accumulating them daily.

You hint that I give myself up too much to society. You are talking of things you do not understand. A dinner party is a chapter. I catch the Cynthia of the minute, sir, at a *soirée*. If I only served a grateful country, I should be in the proudest position of any of its sons; if I had been born in any country but this, I should have been decorated, and perhaps made secretary of state like Addison, who did not write as well as I do, though his style somewhat resembles mine.'

Notwithstanding these great plans, it came in time to Endymion's ear, that poor St. Barbe was in terrible straits. Endymion delicately helped him and then obtained for him a pension, and not an inconsiderable one. Relieved from anxiety, St. Barbe resumed his ancient and natural vein. He passed his days in decrying his friend and patron, and comparing his miserable pension with the salary of a secretary of state, who, so far as his experience went, was generally a second-rate man. Endymion, though he knew St. Barbe was always decrying him, only smiled, and looked upon it all as the necessary consequence of his organisation, which involved a singular combination of vanity and envy in the highest degree. St. Barbe was not less a guest in Carlton Terrace than heretofore, and was even kindly invited to Princedown to profit by the distant sea-breeze. Lady Montfort, whose ears some of his pranks had reached, was not so tolerant as her husband. She gave him one day her views of his conduct. St. Barbe was always a little afraid of her, and on this occasion entirely lost himself; vented the most solemn affirmations that there was not a grain of truth in these charges; that he was the victim, as he had been all

his life, of slander and calumny—the sheer creatures
of envy, and then began to fawn upon his hostess,
and declared that he had ever thought there was
something godlike in the character of her husband.

'And what is there in yours, Mr. St. Barbe?'
asked Lady Montfort.

The ministry had lasted several years; its foreign
policy had been successful; it had triumphed in war
and secured peace. The military conduct of the
troops of King Florestan had contributed to these results, and the popularity of that sovereign in England
was for a foreigner unexampled. During this agitated
interval, Endymion and Myra had met more than
once through the providential medium of those favoured spots of nature—German baths.

There had arisen a public feeling that the ally
who had served us so well should be invited to visit
again a country wherein he had so long sojourned,
and where he was so much appreciated. The only
evidence that the Prime Minister gave that he was
conscious of this feeling was an attack of gout.
Endymion himself, though in a difficult and rather
painful position in this matter, did everything to
shield and protect his chief, but the general sentiment
became so strong, sanctioned too, as it was understood, in the highest quarter, that it could no longer
be passed by unnoticed; and, in due time, to the
great delight and satisfaction of the nation, an impending visit from our faithful ally, King Florestan,
and his beautiful wife, Queen Myra, was authoritatively announced.

Every preparation was made to show them honour.
They were the guests of our Sovereign; but from the
palace which they were to inhabit, to the humblest

tenement in the meanest back street, there was only one feeling of gratitude, and regard, and admiration. The English people are the most enthusiastic people in the world; there are other populations which are more excitable, but there is no nation, when it feels, where the sentiment is so profound and irresistible.

The hour arrived. The season and the weather were favourable. From the port where they landed to their arrival at the metropolis, the whole country seemed poured out into the open air; triumphal arches, a way of flags and banners, and bits of bunting on every hovel. The King and Queen were received at the metropolitan station by Princes of the blood, and accompanied to the palace, where the great officers of state and the assembled ministry were gathered together to do them honour. A great strain was thrown upon Endymion throughout these proceedings, as the Prime Minister, who had been suffering the whole season, and rarely present in his seat in Parliament, was, at this moment, in his worst paroxysm. He could not therefore be present at the series of balls and banquets, and brilliant public functions, which greeted the royal guests. Their visit to the city, when they dined with the Lord Mayor, and to which they drove in royal carriages through a sea of population tumultuous with devotion, was the most gratifying of all these splendid receptions, partly from the associations of mysterious power and magnificence connected with the title and character of Lord Mayor. The Duke of St. Angelo, the Marquis of Vallombrosa, and the Prince of Montserrat, quite lost their presence of mind. Even the Princess of Montserrat, with more quarterings on her own side than any house in Europe, confessed that she trembled when Her Serene Highness courtesied before the Lady Mayoress.

Perhaps, by far, however, the most brilliant, fanciful, and the most costly entertainment that was given on this memorable occasion, was the festival at Hainault. The whole route from town to the forest was lined with thousands, perhaps hundreds of thousands, of spectators; a thousand guests were received at the banquet, and twelve palaces were raised by that true magician, Mr. Benjamin Edgington, in the park, for the countless visitors in the evening. At night the forest was illuminated. Everybody was glad except Lady Hainault, who sighed, and said, 'I have no doubt the Queen would have preferred her own room, and that we should have had a quiet dinner, as in old days, in the little Venetian parlour.'

When Endymion returned home at night, he found a summons to Gaydene; the Prime Minister being, it was feared, in a dangerous state.

The next day, late in the afternoon, there was a rumour that the Prime Minister had resigned. Then it was authoritatively contradicted, and then at night another rumour rose that the minister had resigned, but that the resignation would not be accepted until after the termination of the royal visit. The King and Queen had yet to remain a short week.

The fact is, the resignation had taken place, but it was known only to those who then could not have imparted the intelligence. The public often conjectures the truth, though it clothes its impression or information in the vague shape of a rumour. In four-and-twenty hours the great fact was authoritatively announced in all the journals, with leading articles speculating on the successor to the able and accomplished minister of whose services the Sovereign and the country were so unhappily deprived. Would his successor be found in his own cabinet? And then several names were mentioned; Rawchester, to Lady Montfort's disgust. Rawchester was a safe man, and had had much experience, which, as with most safe men, probably left him as wise and able as before he imbibed it. Would there be altogether a change of parties? Would the Protectionists try again? They were very strong, but always in a minority, like some great continental powers, who have the finest army in the world, and yet always get beaten. Would that band of self-admiring geniuses, who had upset every cabinet with whom they were ever connected, return on the shoulders of the people, as they always dreamed, though they were always the persons of whom the people never seemed to think?

Lady Montfort was in a state of passive excitement. She was quite pale, and she remained quite pale for hours. She would see no one. She sat in Endymion's room, and never spoke, while he continued writing and transacting his affairs. She thought she was reading the *Morning Post,* but really could not distinguish the advertisements from leading articles.

There was a knock at the library door, and the groom of the chambers brought in a note for Endymion. He glanced at the handwriting of the address, and then opened it, as pale as his wife. Then he read it again, and then he gave it to her. She threw her eyes over it, and then her arms around his neck.

'Order my brougham at three o'clock.'

CHAPTER CI.

THE SCENES OF CHILDHOOD.

NDYMION was with his sister.

'How dear of you to come to me,' she said, 'when you cannot have a moment to yourself.'

'Well, you know,' he replied, 'it is not like forming a government. That is an affair. I have reason to think all my colleagues will remain with me. I shall summon them for this afternoon, and if we agree, affairs will go on as before. I should like to get down to Gaydene to-night.'

'To-night!' said the Queen musingly. 'We have only one day left, and I wanted you to do something for me.'

'It shall be done, if possible; I need not say that.'

'It is not difficult to do, if we have time — if we have to-morrow morning, and early. But if you go to Gaydene you will hardly return to-night, and I shall lose my chance, — and yet it is to me a business most precious.'

'It shall be managed; tell me then.'

'I learnt that Hill Street is not occupied at this moment. I want to visit the old house with you,

before I leave England, probably for ever. I have
only got the early morn to-morrow, but with a veil
and your brougham, I think we might depart unob-
served, before the crowd begins to assemble. Do
you think you could be here at nine o'clock?'

So it was settled, and being hurried, he departed.

And next morning he was at the palace before
nine o'clock; and the Queen, veiled, entered his
brougham. There were already some loiterers, but
the brother and sister passed through the gates un-
observed.

They reached Hill Street. The Queen visited all
the principal rooms, and made many remarks appropriate to many memories. 'But,' she said, 'it was
not to see these rooms I came, though I was glad to
do so, and the corridor on the second story whence
I called out to you when you returned, and for ever,
from Eton, and told you there was bad news. What
I came for was to see our old nursery, where we
lived so long together, and so fondly! Here it is;
here we are. All I have desired, all I have dreamed,
have come to pass. Darling, beloved of my soul, by
all our sorrows, by all our joys, in this scene of our
childhood and bygone days, let me give you my last
embrace.'

MISCELLANEA

ON THE LIFE AND WRITINGS

OF

ISAAC D'ISRAELI

———

HE traditionary notion that the life of a man of letters is necessarily deficient in incident appears to have originated in a misconception of the essential nature of human action. The life of every man is full of incidents, but the incidents are insignificant, because they do not affect his species; and in general the importance of every occurrence is to be measured by the degree with which it is recognised by mankind. An author may influence the fortunes of the world to as great an extent as a statesman or a warrior; and the deeds and performances by which this influence is created and exercised, may rank in their interest and importance with the decisions of great Congresses, or the skilful valour of a memorable field. M. de Voltaire was certainly a greater Frenchman than Cardinal Fleury, the Prime Minister of France in his time. His actions were more important; and it is certainly not too much to maintain, that the exploits

of Homer, Aristotle, Dante, or my Lord Bacon, were
as considerable events as anything that occurred at
Actium, Lepanto, or Blenheim. A book may be as
great a thing as a battle, and there are systems of
philosophy that have produced as great revolutions as
any that have disturbed even the social and political
existence of our centuries.

The life of the author whose character and career
we are venturing to review, extended far beyond the
allotted term of man: and, perhaps, no existence of
equal duration ever exhibited an uniformity more sustained. The strong bent of his infancy was pursued
through youth, matured in manhood, and maintained
without decay to an advanced old age. In the bio-
graphic spell, no ingredient is more magical than predisposition. How pure, and native, and indigenous it
was in the character of this writer, can only be properly appreciated by an acquaintance with the circumstances amid which he was born, and by being able
to estimate how far they could have directed or developed his earliest inclinations.

My grandfather, who became an English denizen
in 1748, was an Italian descendant from one of those
Hebrew families whom the Inquisition forced to emi-
grate from the Spanish Peninsula at the end of the
fifteenth century, and who found a refuge in the more
tolerant territories of the Venetian Republic. His ancestors had dropped their Gothic surname on their
settlement in the Terra Firma, and grateful to the God
of Jacob who had sustained them through unprecedented trials and guarded them through unheard-of
perils, they assumed the name of DISRAELI, a name
never borne before, or since, by any other family, in
order that their race might be for ever recognised.

Undisturbed and unmolested, they flourished as merchants for more than two centuries under the protection of the lion of St. Mark, which was but just, as the patron saint of the Republic was himself a child of Israel. But towards the middle of the eighteenth century, the altered circumstances of England, favourable, as it was then supposed, to commerce and religious liberty, attracted the attention of my great-grandfather to this island, and he resolved that the youngest of his two sons, Benjamin, the 'son of his right hand,' should settle in a country where the dynasty seemed at length established through the recent failure of Prince Charles Edward, and where public opinion appeared definitely adverse to persecution on matters of creed and conscience.

The Jewish families, who were then settled in England, were few, though from their wealth, and other circumstances, they were far from unimportant. They were all of them Sephardim, that is to say, children of Israel, who had never quitted the shores of the Midland Ocean, until Torquemada had driven them from their pleasant residences and rich estates in Arragon, and Andalusia, and Portugal, to seek greater blessings even than a clear atmosphere and a glowing sun, amid the marshes of Holland and the fogs of Britain. Most of these families who held themselves aloof from the Hebrews of Northern Europe, then only occasionally stealing into England, as from an inferior caste, and whose synagogue was reserved only for Sephardim, are now extinct; while the branch of the great family, which, notwithstanding their own sufferings from prejudice, they had the hardihood to look down upon, has achieved an amount of wealth and consideration which the Sephardim, even with the patronage of Mr. Pelham, never could have contemplated. Nevertheless, at the time when my grandfather settled in England, and when Mr. Pelham, who was very favourable to the Jews, was Prime Minister, there might be found, among other Jewish families flourishing in this country, the Villa Reals, who brought wealth to these shores almost as great as their name, though that is the second in Portugal, and who have twice allied themselves with the English aristocracy, the Medinas — the Laras, who were our kinsmen — and the Mendez da Costas, who, I believe, still exist.

Whether it were that my grandfather, on his arrival, was not encouraged by those to whom he had a right to look up, — which is often our hard case in the outset of life, — or whether he was alarmed at the unexpected consequences of Mr. Pelham's favourable disposition to his countrymen in the disgraceful repeal of the Jew Bill, which occurred a very few years after his arrival in this country, I know not; but certainly he appears never to have cordially or intimately mixed with his community. This tendency to alienation was no doubt subsequently encouraged by his marriage, which took place in 1765. My grandmother, the beautiful daughter of a family who had suffered much from persecution, had imbibed that dislike for her race which the vain are too apt to adopt when they find that they are born to public contempt. The indignant feeling that should be reserved for the persecutor, in the mortification of their disturbed sensibility, is too often visited on the victim; and the cause of annoyance is recognised not in the ignorant malevolence of the powerful, but in the conscientious conviction of the innocent sufferer.

But seventeen years elapsed before my grandfather entered into this union, and during that interval he had not been idle. He was only eighteen when he commenced his career, and when a great responsibility devolved upon him, he was not unequal to it. He was a man of ardent character; sanguine, courageous, speculative, and fortunate; with a temper which no disappointment could disturb, and a brain, amid reverses, full of resource. He made his fortune in the midway of life, and settled near Enfield, where he formed an Italian garden, entertained his friends, played whist with Sir Horace Mann, who was his great acquaintance, and who had known his brother at Venice as a banker, ate macaroni which was dressed by the Venetian Consul, sang canzonettas, and notwithstanding a wife who never pardoned him for his name, and a son who disappointed all his plans, and who to the last hour of his life was an enigma to him, lived till he was nearly ninety, and then died in 1817, in the full enjoyment of prolonged existence.

My grandfather retired from active business on the eve of that great financial epoch, to grapple with which his talents were well adapted; and when the wars and loans of the Revolution were about to create those families of millionaires, in which he might probably have enrolled his own. That, however, was not our destiny. My grandfather had only one child, and nature had disqualified him, from his cradle, for the busy pursuits of men.

A pale, pensive child, with large dark brown eyes, and flowing hair, had grown up beneath this roof of worldly energy and enjoyment, indicating even in his infancy, by the whole carriage of his life, that he was

of a different order from those among whom he lived.
Timid, susceptible, lost in reverie, fond of solitude,
or seeking no better company than a book, the years
had stolen on, till he had arrived at that mournful
period of boyhood when eccentricities excite attention
and command no sympathy.   In the chapter on Predisposition, in the most delightful of his works,* my
father has drawn from his own, though his unacknowledged feelings, immortal truths. Then commenced the age of domestic criticism. His mother,
not incapable of deep affections, but so mortified by
her social position that she lived until eighty without
indulging in a tender expression, did not recognise in
her only offspring a being qualified to control or van-
quish his impending fate. His existence only served
to swell the aggregate of many humiliating par-
ticulars. It was not to her a source of joy, or sympathy, or solace. She foresaw for her child only a
future of degradation. Having a strong clear mind,
without any imagination, she believed that she beheld
an inevitable doom. The tart remark and the contemptuous comment on her part, elicited, on the other,
all the irritability of the poetic idiosyncrasy. After
frantic ebullitions for which, when the circumstances
were analysed by an ordinary mind, there seemed no
sufficient cause, my grandfather always interfered to
soothe with good-tempered commonplaces, and promote peace. He was a man who thought that the
only way to make people happy was to make them
a present. He took it for granted that a boy in a
passion wanted a toy or a guinea. At a later date,
when my father ran away from home, and after some

---

* *Essay on the Literary Character*, Vol. I. chap. v.

wanderings was brought back, found lying on a tombstone in Hackney churchyard, he embraced him and gave him a pony.

In this state of affairs, being sent to school in the neighbourhood was a rather agreeable incident. The school was kept by a Scotchman, one Morison, a good man, and not untinctured with scholarship, and it is possible that my father might have reaped some advantage from this change; but the school was too near home, and his mother, though she tormented his existence, was never content if he were out of her sight. His delicate health was an excuse for converting him, after a short interval, into a day scholar; then many days of attendance were omitted, finally, the solitary walk home through Mr. Mellish's park was dangerous to the sensibilities that too often exploded when they encountered on the arrival at the domestic hearth a scene which did not harmonise with the fairyland of reverie.

The crisis arrived when, after months of unusual abstraction and irritability, my father produced a poem. For the first time, my grandfather was seriously alarmed. The loss of one of his argosies, uninsured, could not have filled him with more blank dismay. His idea of a poet was formed from one of the prints of Hogarth hanging in his room, where an unfortunate wight in a garret was inditing an ode to riches, while dunned for his milk-score. Decisive measures were required to eradicate this evil, and to prevent future disgrace — so, as seems the custom when a person is in a scrape, it was resolved that my father should be sent abroad, where a new scene and a new language might divert his mind from the ignominious pursuit which so fatally attracted him. The unhappy

poet was consigned like a bale of goods to my grandfather's correspondent at Amsterdam, who had instructions to place him at some collegium of repute
in that city.

Here were passed several years not without profit,
though his tutor was a great impostor, very neglect-
ful of his pupils, and both unable and disinclined to
guide them in severe studies. This preceptor was a
man of letters, though a wretched writer, with a good
library, and a spirit inflamed with all the philosophy
of the eighteenth century, then (1780–81) about to bring
forth and bear its long matured fruits. The intelligence
and disposition of my father attracted his attention, and
rather interested him. He taught his charge little, for
he was himself generally occupied in writing bad odes,
but he gave him free warren in his library, and before his pupil was fifteen, he had read the works of
Voltaire and had dipped into Bayle. Strange that the
characteristics of a writer so born and brought up
should have been so essentially English; not merely
from his mastery over our language, but from his
keen and profound sympathy with all that concerned
the literary and political history of our country at its
most important epoch.

When he was eighteen he returned to England a
disciple of Rousseau. He had exercised his imagination during the voyage in idealising the interview
with his mother, which was to be conducted on both
sides with sublime pathos. His other parent had frequently visited him during his absence. He was prepared to throw himself on his mother's bosom, to
bedew her hand with his tears, and to stop her lips
with his own; but, when he entered, his strange appearance, his gaunt figure, his excited manners, his

long hair, and his unfashionable costume, only filled her with a sentiment of tender aversion; she broke into derisive laughter, and noticing his intolerable garments, she reluctantly lent him her cheek. Whereupon Emile, of course, went into heroics, wept, sobbed, and finally, shut up in his chamber, composed an impassioned epistle. My grandfather, to soothe him, dwelt on the united solicitude of his parents for his welfare, and broke to him their intention, if it were agreeable to him, to place him in the establishment of a great merchant of Bordeaux. My father replied that he had written a poem of considerable length, which he wished to publish, against Commerce, which was the corruptor of man. In eight-and-forty hours confusion again reigned in this household, and all from a want of psychological perception in its master and mistress.

My father, who had lost the timidity of his childhood, who, by nature, was very impulsive, and indeed endowed with a degree of volatility which is only witnessed in the south of France, and which never deserted him to his last hour, was no longer to be controlled. His conduct was decisive. He enclosed his poem to Dr. Johnson, with an impassioned statement of his case, complaining, which he ever did, that he had never found a counsellor or literary friend. He left his packet himself at Bolt Court, where he was received by Mr. Francis Barber, the doctor's well-known black servant, and told to call again in a week. Be sure that he was very punctual; but the packet was returned to him unopened, with a message that the illustrious doctor was too ill to read anything. The unhappy and obscure aspirant, who received this disheartening message, accepted it, in his utter despondency, as a mechanical excuse. But, alas! the cause was too true; and, a few weeks after, on that bed beside which the voice of Mr. Burke faltered, and the tender spirit of Bennett Langton was ever vigilant, the great soul of Johnson quitted earth.

But the spirit of self-confidence, the resolution to struggle against his fate, the paramount desire to find some sympathising sage — some guide, philosopher, and friend — was so strong and rooted in my father, that I observed, a few weeks ago, in a magazine, an original letter, written by him about this time to Dr. Vicesimus Knox, full of high-flown sentiments, reading indeed like a romance of Scudéry, and entreating the learned critic to receive him in his family, and give him the advantage of his wisdom, his taste, and his erudition.

With a home that ought to have been happy, surrounded with more than comfort, with the most good-natured father in the world, and an agreeable man, and with a mother whose strong intellect, under ordinary circumstances, might have been of great importance to him, my father, though himself of a very sweet disposition, was most unhappy. His parents looked upon him as moonstruck, while he himself, whatever his aspirations, was conscious that he had done nothing to justify the eccentricity of his course, or the violation of all prudential considerations in which he daily indulged. In these perplexities, the usual alternative was again had recourse to — absence; he was sent abroad, to travel in France, which the peace then permitted, visit some friends, see Paris, and then proceed to Bordeaux if he felt inclined. My father travelled in France and then proceeded to Paris, where he remained till the eve of great events in that capital. This was a visit recollected with satisfaction. He lived with learned men and moved in vast libraries, and returned in the earlier part of 1788, with some little knowledge of life, and with a considerable quantity of books.

At this time Peter Pindar flourished in all the wantonness of literary riot. He was at the height of his flagrant notoriety. The novelty and the boldness of his style carried the million with him. The most exalted station was not exempt from his audacious criticism, and learned institutions trembled at the sallies whose ribaldry often cloaked taste, intelligence, and good sense. His 'Odes to the Academicians,' which first secured him the ear of the town, were written by one who could himself guide the pencil with skill and feeling, and who, in the form of a mechanic's son, had even the felicity to discover the vigorous genius of Opie. The mock-heroic which invaded with success the sacred recesses of the palace, and which was fruitlessly menaced by Secretaries of State, proved a reckless intrepidity, which is apt to be popular with 'the general.' The powerful and the learned quailed beneath the lash with an affected contempt which scarcely veiled their tremor. In the meantime, as in the latter days of the empire, the barbarian ravaged the country, while the pale-faced patricians were inactive within the walls. No one offered resistance.

There appeared about this time a satire 'On the Abuse of Satire.' The verses were polished and pointed; a happy echo of that style of Mr. Pope which still lingered in the spell-bound ear of the public. Peculiarly they offered a contrast to the irregular

effusions of the popular assailant whom they in turn
assailed, for the object of their indignant invective was
the bard of the 'Lousiad.' The poem was anonymous, and was addressed to Dr. Wharton in lines of
even classic grace. Its publication was appropriate.
There are moments when every one is inclined to
praise, especially when the praise of a new pen may
at the same time revenge the insults of an old one.

But if there could be any doubt of the success of
this new hand, it was quickly removed by the conduct of Peter Pindar himself. As is not unusual with
persons of his habits, Wolcot was extremely sensitive,
and, brandishing a tomahawk, always himself shrank
from a scratch. This was shown some years afterwards by his violent assault on Mr. Gifford, with a
bludgeon, in a bookseller's shop, because the author
of the 'Baviad and Mæviad' had presumed to casti-
gate the great lampooner of the age. In the present
instance, the furious Wolcot leapt to the rash conclusion that the author of the satire was no less a personage than Mr. Hayley, and he assailed the elegant
author of the 'Triumphs of Temper' in a virulent
pasquinade. This ill-considered movement of his ad-
versary of course achieved the complete success of the
anonymous writer.

My father, who came up to town to read the
newspapers at the St. James' Coffee-house, found
their columns filled with extracts from the fortunate
effusion of the hour, conjectures as to its writer, and
much gossip respecting Wolcot and Hayley. He returned to Enfield laden with the journals, and, presenting them to his parents, broke to them the
intelligence that at length he was not only an author,
but a successful one.

He was indebted to this slight effort for something almost as agreeable as the public recognition of his ability, and that was the acquaintance, and almost immediately the warm personal friendship, of Mr. Pye. Mr. Pye was the head of an ancient English family that figured in the Parliaments and struggles of the Stuarts; he was member for the County of Berkshire, where his ancestral seat of Farringdon was situate, and at a later period (1790) became Poet Laureate. In those days, when literary clubs did not exist, and when even political ones were extremely limited and exclusive in their character, the booksellers' shops were social rendezvous. Debrett's was the chief haunt of the Whigs; Hatchard's, I believe, of the Tories. It was at the latter house that my father made the acquaintance of Mr. Pye, then publishing his translation of Aristotle's Poetics, and so strong was party feeling at that period, that one day, walking together down Piccadilly, Mr. Pye, stopping at the door of Debrett, requested his companion to go in and purchase a particular pamphlet for him, adding that if he had the audacity to enter, more than one person would tread upon his toes.

My father at last had a friend. Mr. Pye, though double his age, was still a young man, and the literary sympathy between them was complete. Unfortunately, the member for Berkshire was a man rather of an elegant turn of mind, than one of that energy and vigour which a youth required for a companion at that moment. Their tastes and pursuits were perhaps a little too similar. They addressed poetical epistles to each other, and were reciprocally, too gentle critics. But Mr. Pye was a most amiable and accomplished man, a fine classical scholar, and a master of correct versification. He paid a visit to Enfield, and by his influence hastened a conclusion at which my grandfather was just arriving, to wit, that he would no longer persist in the fruitless effort of converting a poet into a merchant, and that, content with the independence he had realised, he would abandon his dreams of founding a dynasty of financiers. From this moment all disquietude ceased beneath this always well-meaning, though often perplexed, roof, while my father, enabled amply to gratify his darling passion of book-collecting, passed his days in tranquil study, and in the society of congenial spirits.

His new friend introduced him almost immediately to Mr. James Pettit Andrews, a Berkshire gentleman of literary pursuits, and whose hospitable table at Brompton was the resort of the best literary society of the day. Here my father was a frequent guest, and walking home one night together from this house, where they had both dined, he made the acquaintance of a young poet, which soon ripened into intimacy, and which throughout sixty years, notwithstanding many changes of life, never died away. This youthful poet had already gained laurels, though he was only three or four years older than my father, but I am not at this moment quite aware whether his brow was yet encircled with the amaranthine wreath of the 'Pleasures of Memory.'

Some years after this, great vicissitudes unhappily occurred in the family of Mr. Pye. He was obliged to retire from Parliament, and to sell his family estate of Farringdon. His Majesty had already, on the death of Thomas Wharton, nominated him Poet Laureate, and after his retirement from Parliament, the government which he had supported appointed him a Commissioner of Police. It was in these days, that his friend, Mr. Penn of Stoke Park, in Buckinghamshire, presented him with a cottage worthy of a poet on his beautiful estate; and it was thus my father became acquainted with the amiable descendant of the most successful of colonisers, and with that classic domain which the genius of Gray, as it were, now haunts, and has for ever hallowed, and from which he beheld with fond and musing eye, those

'Distant spires and antique towers,'

that no one can now look upon without remembering him. It was amid these rambles in Stoke Park, amid the scenes of Gray's genius, the elegiac churchyard, and the picturesque fragments of the Long Story, talking over the deeds of the 'Great Rebellion' with the descendants of Cavaliers and Parliament-men, that my father first imbibed that feeling for the county of Buckingham, which induced him occasionally to be a dweller in its limits, and ultimately, more than a quarter of a century afterwards, to establish his household gods in its heart. And here, perhaps, I may be permitted to mention a circumstance which is indeed trifling, and yet, as a coincidence, not, I think, without interest. Mr. Pye was the great-grandson of Sir Robert Pye of Bradenham, who married Anne, the eldest daughter of Mr. Hampden. How little could my father dream, sixty years ago, that he would pass the last quarter of his life in the mansion-house of Bradenham; that his name would become intimately connected with the county of Buckingham; and that his own remains would be interred in the vault of the chancel of Bradenham Church, among the coffins of the descendants of the Hampdens and the Pyes.

All which should teach us that, whatever may be our natural bent, there is a power in the disposal of events greater than human will.

It was about two years after his first acquaintance with Mr. Pye, that my father, being then in his twenty-fifth year, influenced by the circle in which he then lived, gave an anonymous volume to the press, the fate of which he could little have foreseen. The taste for literary history was then of recent date in England. It was developed by Dr. Johnson and the Whartons, who were the true founders of that elegant literature in which France had so richly preceded us. The fashion for literary anecdote prevailed at the end of the last century. Mr. Pettit Andrews, assisted by Mr. Pye and Captain Grose, and shortly afterwards, his friend, Mr. Seward, in his *Anecdotes of Distinguished Persons,* had both of them produced ingenious works, which had experienced public favour. But these volumes were rather entertaining than substantial, and their interest in many instances was necessarily fleeting; all which made Mr. Rogers observe, that the world was far gone in its anecdotage.

While Mr. Andrews and his friend were hunting for personal details in the recollections of their contemporaries, my father maintained one day that the most interesting of miscellanies might be drawn up by a well-read man from the library in which he lived. It was objected, on the other hand, that such a work would be a mere compilation, and could not succeed with its dead matter in interesting the public. To test the truth of this assertion, my father occupied himself in the preparation of an octavo volume, the principal materials of which were found in the

diversified collections of the French Ana; but he enriched his subjects with as much of our own literature as his reading afforded, and he conveyed the
result in that lively and entertaining style which he
from the first commanded. This collection of *Anecdotes, Characters, Sketches, and Observations; Literary, Critical, and Historical,*—as the title-page of the
first edition figures, he invested with the happy baptism of *Curiosities of Literature.*

He sought by this publication neither reputation
nor a coarser reward, for he published his work
anonymously, and avowedly as a compilation; and he
not only published the work at his own expense, but
in his heedlessness made a present of the copyright
to the bookseller, which three or four years afterwards, he was fortunate enough to purchase at a
public sale. The volume was an experiment whether
a taste for literature could not be infused into the
multitude. Its success was so decided that its pro-
jector was tempted to add a second volume two
years afterwards, with a slight attempt at more original research; I observe that there was a second edition of both volumes in 1794. For twenty years the
brother volumes remained favourites of the public;
when after that long interval their writer, taking advantage of a popular title, poured forth all the riches
of his matured intellect, his refined taste, and accumulated knowledge into their pages, and produced
what may be fairly described as the most celebrated
Miscellany of Modern Literature.

The moment that the name of the youthful author
of the 'Abuse of Satire' had transpired, Peter Pindar,
faithful to the instinct of his nature, wrote a letter of
congratulation and compliment to his assailant, and

desired to make his acquaintance. The invitation was responded to, and until the death of Wolcot, they were intimate. My father always described Wolcot as a warm-hearted man, coarse in his manners, and rather rough, but eager to serve those whom he liked, of which, indeed, I might appropriately mention an instance.

It so happened, that about the year 1795, when he was in his twenty-ninth year, there came over my father that mysterious illness to which the youth of men of sensibility, and especially literary men, is frequently subject — a failing of nervous energy, occasioned by study and too sedentary habits, early and habitual reverie, restless and indefinite purpose. The symptoms, physical and moral, are most distressing: lassitude and despondency. And it usually happens, as in the present instance, that the cause of suffering is not recognised; and that medical men, misled by the superficial symptoms, and not seeking to acquaint themselves with the psychology of their patients, arrive at erroneous, often fatal, conclusions. In this case, the most eminent of the faculty gave it as their opinion that the disease was consumption. Dr. Turton, if I recollect right, was then the most considered physician of the day. An immediate visit to a warmer climate was his specific; and as the Continent was then disturbed and foreign residence out of the question, Dr. Turton recommended that his patient should establish himself without delay in Devonshire.

When my father communicated this impending change in his life to Wolcot, the modern Skelton shook his head. He did not believe that his friend was in consumption, but being a Devonshire man, and loving very much his native province, he highly approved of the remedy. He gave my father several letters of introduction to persons of consideration at Exeter; among others, one whom he justly described as a poet and a physician, and the best of men, the late Dr. Hugh Downman. Provincial cities very often enjoy a transient term of intellectual distinction. An eminent man often collects around him congenial spirits, and the power of association sometimes produces distant effects which even an individual, however gifted, could scarcely have anticipated. A combination of circumstances had made at this time Exeter a literary metropolis. A number of distinguished men flourished there at the same moment: some of their names are even now remembered. Jackson of Exeter still survives as a native composer of original genius. He was also an author of high æsthetical speculation. The heroic poems of Hole are forgotten, but his essay on the Arabian Nights is still a cherished volume of elegant and learned criticism. Hayter was the classic antiquary who first discovered the art of unrolling the MSS. of Herculaneum. There were many others, noisier and and more bustling, who are now forgotten, though they in some degree influenced the literary opinion of their time. It was said, and I believe truly, that the two principal, if not sole, organs of periodical criticism at that time, I think the *Critical Review* and the *Monthly Review*, were principally supported by Exeter contributions. No doubt this circumstance may account for a great deal of mutual praise and sympathetic opinion on literary subjects, which, by a convenient arrangement, appeared in the pages of publications otherwise professing contrary opinions on all others. Exeter had then even a learned society which published its Transactions.

With such companions, by whom he was received with a kindness and hospitality which to the last he often dwelt on, it may easily be supposed that the banishment of my father from the delights of literary London was not as productive a source of gloom as the exile of Ovid to the savage Pontus, even if it had not been his happy fortune to have been received on terms of intimate friendship by the accomplished family of Mr. Baring, who was then member for Exeter, and beneath whose roof he passed a great portion of the period of nearly three years, during which he remained in Devonshire.

The illness of my father was relieved, but not removed, by this change of life. Dr. Downman was his physician, whose only remedies were port wine, horse-exercise, rowing on the neighbouring river, and the distraction of agreeable society. This wise physician recognised the temperament of his patient, and perceived that his physical derangement was an effect instead of a cause. My father instead of being in a consumption was endowed with a frame of almost superhuman strength, and which was destined for half a century of continuous labour and sedentary life. The vital principle in him, indeed, was so strong that when he left us at eighty-two, it was only as the victim of a violent epidemic, against whose virulence he struggled with so much power that it was clear, but for this casualty, he might have been spared to this world even for several years.

I should think that this illness of his youth, and which, though of a fitful character, was of many years' duration, arose from his inability to direct to a satisfactory end the intellectual power which he was conscious of possessing. He would mention the ten years of his life, from twenty-five to thirty-five years of age, as a period very deficient in self-contentedness. The fact is, with a poetic temperament, he had been born in an age when the poetic faith of which he was a votary had fallen into decrepitude, and had become only a form with the public, not yet gifted with sufficient fervour to discover a new creed. He was a pupil of Pope and Boileau, yet both from his native impulse and from the glowing influence of Rousseau, he felt the necessity and desire of infusing into the verse of the day more passion than might resound from the frigid lyre of Mr. Hayley.

My father had fancy, sensibility, and exquisite taste, but he had not that rare creative power which the blended and simultaneous influence of the individual organisation and the spirit of the age, reciprocally acting upon each other, can alone, perhaps, perfectly develop; the absence of which, at periods of transition, is so universally recognised and deplored, and yet which always, when it does arrive, captivates us, as it were, by surprise. How much there was of freshness, and fancy, and natural pathos in his mind, may be discerned in his Persian romance of *The Loves of Mejnoon and Leila*. We who have been accustomed to the great poets of the nineteenth century seeking their best inspiration in the climate and manners of the East; who are familiar with the land of the sun from the isles of Ionia to the vales of Cashmere, can scarcely appreciate the literary originality of a writer who, fifty years ago, dared to devise a real Eastern story, and seeking inspiration in the pages of Oriental literature, compose it with reference to the Eastern mind, and customs, and landscape. One must have been familiar with the Almoran and

Hamets, the visions of Mirza and the kings of Ethiopia, and the other dull and monstrous masquerades of Orientalism then prevalent, to estimate such an enterprise, in which, however, one should not forget the author had the advantage of the guiding friendship of that distinguished Orientalist, Sir William Ouseley.

The reception given to this work by the public, and to other works of fiction which its author gave to them anonymously, was in every respect encouraging, and their success may impartially be registered as fairly proportionate to their merits; but it was not a success, or a proof of power, which, in my father's opinion, compensated for that life of literary research and study which their composition disturbed and enfeebled. It was at the ripe age of five-and-thirty that he renounced his dreams of being an author, and resolved to devote himself for the rest of his life to the acquisition of knowledge.

When my father, many years afterwards, made the acquaintance of Sir Walter Scott, the great poet saluted him by reciting a poem of half-a-dozen stanzas which my father had written in his early youth. Not altogether without agitation, surprise was expressed that these lines should have been known, still more that they should have been remembered. 'Ah!' said Sir Walter, 'if the writer of these lines had gone on, he would have been an English poet.' *

It is possible, it is even probable, that if my father had devoted himself to the art, he might have become the author of some elegant and popular didactic poem,

---

*Sir Walter was sincere, for he inserted the poem in the *English Minstrelsy*.

on some ordinary subject, which his fancy would have adorned with grace, and his sensibility invested with sentiment; some small volume which might have reposed with a classic title upon our library shelves, and served as a prize volume at Ladies' Schools. This celebrity was not reserved for him; instead of this he was destined to give to his country a series of works illustrative of its literary and political history, full of new information and new views, which time and opinion have ratified as just. But the poetical temperament was not thrown away upon him; it never is on any one; it was this great gift which prevented his being a mere literary antiquary; it was this which animated his page with picture and his narrative with interesting vivacity; above all, it was this temperament, which invested him with that sympathy with his subject which made him the most delightful biographer in our language. In a word, it was because he was a poet that he was a popular writer, and made *belles-lettres* charming to the multitude.

It was during the ten years that now followed that he mainly acquired that store of facts which were the foundation of his future speculations. His pen was never idle, but it was to note and to register, not to compose. His researches were prosecuted every morning among the MSS. of the British Museum, while his own ample collections permitted him to pursue his investigation in his own library into the night. The materials which he accumulated during this period are only partially exhausted. At the end of ten years, during which, with the exception of one anonymous work, he never indulged in composition, the irresistible desire of communicating his conclusions to the world came over him, and after all his almost childish aspirations, his youth of reverie and hesitating and imperfect effort, he arrived at the mature age of forty-five before his career as a great author, influencing opinion, really commenced.

The next ten years passed entirely in production: from 1812 to 1822 the press abounded with his works. His *Calamities of Authors,* his *Memoirs of Literary Controversy,* in the manner of Bayle; his *Essay on the Literary Character,* the most perfect of his compositions, were all chapters in that History of English Literature which he then commenced to meditate, and which it was fated should never be completed.

It was during this period also that he published his *Inquiry into the Literary and Political Character of James the First,* in which he first opened those views respecting the times and the conduct of the Stuarts, which were opposed to the long prevalent opinions of this country, but which with him were at least the result of unprejudiced research, and their promulgation, as he himself expressed it, 'an affair of literary conscience.' *

But what retarded his project of a History of our Literature at this time was the almost embarrassing success of his juvenile production, *The Curiosities of Literature.* These two volumes had already reached

---

* 'The present inquiry originates in an affair of literary conscience. Many years ago I set off with the popular notions of the character of James the First; but in the course of study, and with a more enlarged comprehension of the age, I was frequently struck by the contrast between his real and his apparent character. . . . It would be a cowardly silence to shrink from encountering all that popular prejudice and party feeling may oppose; this would be incompatible with that constant search after truth, which at least may be expected from the retired student.'— *Preface to the Inquiry.*

five editions, and their author found himself, by the public demand, again called upon to sanction their reappearance. Recognising in this circumstance some proof of their utility, he resolved to make the work more worthy of the favour which it enjoyed, and more calculated to produce the benefit which he desired. Without attempting materially to alter the character of the first two volumes, he revised and enriched them, while at the same time he added a third volume of a vein far more critical, and conveying the results of much original research. The success of this publication was so great that its author, after much hesitation, resolved, as he was wont to say, to take advantage of a popular title and pour forth the treasures of his mind in three additional volumes, which unlike continuations in general, were at once greeted with the highest degree of popular delight and esteem. And, indeed, whether we consider the choice of variety of the subjects, the critical and philosophical speculation which pervades them, the amount of new and interesting information brought to bear, and the animated style in which all is conveyed, it is difficult to conceive miscellaneous literature in a garb more stimulating and attractive. These six volumes after many editions are now condensed into the form at present given to the public, and in which the development of their writer's mind for a quarter of a century may be completely traced.

Although my father had on the whole little cause to complain of unfair criticism, especially considering how isolated he always remained, it is not to be supposed that a success so eminent should have been exempt in so long a course from some captious comment. It has been alleged of late years by some crit-

ics, that he was in the habit of exaggerating the
importance of his researches; that he was too fond of
styling every accession to our knowledge, however
slight, a discovery; that there were some inaccuracies
in his early volumes (not very wonderful in so multifarious a work), and that the foundation of his
'secret history' was often only a single letter, or
a passage in a solitary diary.

The sources of secret history at the present day
are so rich and various; there is such an eagerness
among their possessors to publish family papers, even
sometimes in shapes, and at dates so recent, as
scarcely to justify their appearance, that modern critics in their embarrassment of manuscript wealth, are
apt to view with too depreciating an eye the more
limited resources of men of letters at the commence-
ment of the century. Not five-and-twenty years ago,
when preparing his work on King Charles the First,
the application of my father to make some researches
in the State Paper Office was refused by the Secretary of State of the day. Now, foreign potentates and
ministers of State, and public corporations and the
heads of great houses, feel honoured by such appeals,
and respond to them with cordiality. It is not only
the State Paper Office of England, but the Archives of
France, that are open to the historical investigator.
But what has produced this general and expanding
taste for literary research in the world, and especially
in England? The labours of our elder authors, whose
taste and acuteness taught us the value of the materials which we in our ignorance neglected.

When my father first frequented the library of the
British Museum at the end of the last century, his
companions never numbered half a dozen: among

them, if I remember rightly, were Mr. Pinkerton and Mr. Douce. Now these daily pilgrims of research may be counted by as many hundreds. Few writers have more contributed to form and diffuse this delightful and profitable taste for research, than the author of the *Curiosities of Literature;* few writers have been more successful in inducing us to pause before we accepted without a scruple the traditionary opinion that has distorted a fact or calumniated a character; and independently of every other claim which he possesses to public respect, his literary discoveries, viewed in relation to the age and the means, were considerable. But he had other claims: a vital spirit in his page, kindred to the souls of a Bayle and a Montaigne. His innumerable imitators and their inevitable failure for half a century alone prove this, and might have made them suspect that there were some ingredients in the spell besides the accumulation of facts and a happy title. Many of their publications, perpetually appearing and constantly forgotten, were drawn up by persons of considerable acquirements, and were ludicrously mimetic of their prototype, even as to the size of the volume and the form of the page. What has become of these *Varieties of Literature,* and *Delights of Literature,* and *Delicacies of Literature,* and *Relics of Literature,*— and the other protean forms of uninspired compilation? Dead, as they deserve to be: while the work, the idea of which occurred to its writer in his early youth, and which he lived virtually to execute in all the ripeness of his studious manhood, remains as fresh and popular as ever,— the Literary Miscellany of the English people.

I have ventured to enter into some details as to the earlier and obscurer years of my father's life, because I thought that they threw light upon human character, and that without them, indeed, a just appreciation of his career could hardly be formed. I am mistaken if we do not recognise in his instance two very interesting qualities of life; predisposition and self-formation. There was a third, which I think is to be honoured, and that was his sympathy with his order. No one has written so much about authors, and so well. Indeed, before his time the literary character had never been fairly placed before the world. He comprehended its idiosyncrasy: all its strength and all its weakness. He could soften, because he could explain, its infirmities; in the analysis and record of its power, he vindicated the right position of authors in the social scale. They stand between the governors and the governed, he impresses on us in the closing pages of his greatest work.* Though he shared none of the calamities, and scarcely any of the controversies, of literature, no one has sympathised so intimately with the sorrows, or so zealously and impartially registered the instructive disputes, of literary men. He loved to celebrate the exploits of great writers, and to show that, in these ages, the pen is a weapon as puissant as the sword. He was also the first writer who vindicated the position of the great artist in the history of genius. His pages are studded with pregnant instances and graceful details, borrowed from the life of Art and its votaries, and which his intimate and curious acquaintance with Italian letters readily and happily supplied. Above all writers, he has maintained the greatness of intellect, and the immortality of thought.

---

* *Essay on the Literary Character*, vol. ii., chap. xxv.

He was himself a complete literary character, a man who really passed his life in his library. Even marriage produced no change in these habits; he rose to enter the chamber where he lived alone with his books, and at night his lamp was ever lit within the same walls. Nothing, indeed, was more remarkable than the isolation of this prolonged existence; and it could only be accounted for by the united influence of three causes: his birth, which brought him no relations or family acquaintance, the bent of his disposition, and the circumstance of his inheriting an independent fortune, which rendered unnecessary those exertions that would have broken up his self-reliance. He disliked business, and he never required relaxation; he was absorbed in his pursuits. In London his only amusement was to ramble among booksellers; if he entered a club, it was only to go into the library.

In the country, he seldom left his room but to saunter in abstraction upon a terrace, muse over a chapter, or coin a sentence. He had not a single passion or prejudice: all his convictions were the result of his own studies, and were often opposed to the impressions which he had early imbibed. He not only never entered into the politics of the day, but he could never understand them. He never was connected with any particular body or set of men; comrades of school or college, or confederates in that public life which in England, is, perhaps, the only foundation of real friendship. In the consideration of a question, his mind was quite undisturbed by traditionary preconceptions; and it was this exemption from passion and prejudice which, although his intelligence was naturally somewhat too ingenious and fanciful for the conduct of close argument, enabled him, in investigation, often to show many of the highest attributes of the judicial mind, and particularly to sum up evidence with singular happiness and ability.

Although in private life he was of a timid nature, his moral courage as a writer was unimpeachable. Most certainly, throughout his long career, he never wrote a sentence which he did not believe was true. He will generally be found to be the advocate of the discomfited and the oppressed. So his conclusions are often opposed to popular impressions. This was from no love of paradox, to which he was quite superior; but because in the conduct of his researches, he too often found that the unfortunate are calumniated.

His famous vindication of King James the First he has himself described as 'an affair of literary conscience:' his great work on the life and times of the son of the first Stuart arose from the same impulse. He had deeply studied our history during the first moiety of the seventeenth century; he looked upon it as a famous age; he was familiar with the works of its great writers, and there was scarcely one of its almost innumerable pamphlets with which he was not acquainted. During the thoughtful investigations of many years, he had arrived at results which were not adapted to please the passing multitude, but which, because he held them to be authentic, he was uneasy lest he should die without recording. Yet, strong as were his convictions, although, notwithstanding his education in the revolutionary philosophy of the eighteenth century, his nature and his studies had made him a votary of loyalty and reverence, his pen was always prompt to do justice to those who might be looked upon as the adversaries of his own cause: and this was because his cause was really truth. If he has upheld Laud under unjust aspersions, the last labour of his literary life was to vindicate the character of Hugh Peters.

If, from remembering the sufferings of his race, and from profound reflection on the principles of the Institution, he was hostile to the Papacy, no writer in our literature has done more complete justice to the conduct of the English Romanists. Who can read his history of Chidiock Titchbourne unmoved? Or can refuse to sympathise with his account of the painful difficulties of the English Monarchs with their loyal subjects of the old faith? If in a parliamentary country he has dared to criticise the conduct of Parliaments, it was only because an impartial judgment had taught him, as he himself expresses it, that 'Parliaments have their passions as well as individuals.'

He was five years in the composition of his work on the *Life and Reign of Charles the First,* and the five volumes appeared at intervals between 1828 and 1831. It was feared by his publishers that the distracted epoch at which this work was issued, and the tendency of the times, apparently so adverse to his own views, might prove very injurious to its reception. But the effect of these circumstances was the reverse. The minds of men were inclined to the grave and national considerations that were involved in these investigations. The principles of political institutions, the rival claims of the two Houses of Parliament, the authority of the Established Church, the demands of religious sects, were, after a long lapse of years, anew the theme of public discussion. Men were attracted to a writer who traced the origin of the anti-monarchical principle in modern

Europe: treated of the arts of insurgency; gave them, at the same time, a critical history of the Puritans, and a treatise on the genius of the Papacy; scrutinised the conduct of triumphant patriots, and vindicated a decapitated monarch. The success of this work was eminent; and its author appeared for the first, and only time, of his life in public, when amidst the cheers of the under-graduates, and the applause of graver men, the solitary student received an honorary degree from the University of Oxford, a fitting homage, in the language of the great University, ' OPTIMI REGIS OPTIMO VINDICI. '

I cannot but recall a trait that happened on this occasion. After my father returned to his hotel from the theatre, a stranger requested an interview with him. A Swiss gentleman, travelling in England at the time, who had witnessed the scene just closed, begged to express the reason why he presumed thus personally and cordially to congratulate the new Doctor of Civil Law. He was the son of my grandfather's chief clerk, and remembered his parent's employer, whom he regretted did not survive to be aware of this honourable day. Thus, amid all the strange vicissitudes of life, we are ever, as it were, moving in a circle.

Notwithstanding he was now approaching his seventieth year, his health being unbroken and his constitution very robust, my father resolved vigorously to devote himself to the composition of the history of our vernacular literature. He hesitated for a moment, whether he should at once address himself to this great task, or whether he should first complete a Life of Pope, for which he had made great preparations, and which had long occupied his thoughts. His review of 'Spence's Anecdotes' in the *Quarterly,* so

far back as 1820, which gave rise to the celebrated
Pope Controversy, in which Mr. Campbell, Lord
Byron, Mr. Bowles, Mr. Roscoe, and others less eminent, broke lances, would prove how well qualified,
even at that distant date, the critic was to become
the biographer of the great writer whose literary ex-
cellency and moral conduct he, on that occasion, alike
vindicated.

But, unfortunately as matters turned out, my father
was persuaded to address himself to the weightier
task. Hitherto, in his publications, he had always
felt an extreme reluctance to travel over ground which
others had previously visited. He liked to give new
matter, and devote himself to detached points, on
which he entertained different opinions from those
prevalent. Thus his works are generally of a supple-
mentary character, and assume in their readers a certain degree of preliminary knowledge. In the present
instance, he was induced to frame his undertaking on
a different scale, and to prepare a history which would
be complete in itself, and supply the reader with a
perfect view of the gradual formation of our language
and literature. He proposed to effect this in six volumes; though, I apprehend, he would not have succeeded in fulfilling his intentions within that limit.
His treatment of the period of Queen Anne would
have been very ample, and he would also have accomplished in this general work a purpose which he
had also long contemplated, and for which he had
made curious and extensive collections, namely, a
History of the English Freethinkers.

But all these great plans were destined to a terrible defeat. Towards the end of the year 1839, still
in the full vigour of his health and intellect, he suf-

fered a paralysis of the optic nerve; and that eye, which for so long a term had kindled with critical interest over the volumes of so many literatures and so many languages, was doomed to pursue its animated course no more. Considering the bitterness of such a calamity to one whose powers were otherwise not in the least impaired, he bore, on the whole, his fate with magnanimity, even with cheerfulness. Unhappily, his previous habits of study and composition rendered the habit of dictation intolerable, even impossible to him. But with the assistance of his daughter, whose intelligent solicitude he has commemorated in more than one grateful passage, he selected from his manuscripts three volumes, which he wished to have published under the becoming title of *A Fragment of the History of English Literature,* but which was eventually given to the public under that of *Amenities of Literature.*

He was also enabled during these last years of physical though not of moral gloom, to prepare a new edition of his work on the *Life and Times of Charles the First* which had been for some time out of print. He contrived, though slowly, and with great labour, very carefully to revise, and improve, and enrich these volumes, which will now be condensed into three. His miscellaneous works, all illustrative of the political and literary history of this country, will form three more. He was wont to say that the best monument to an author was a good edition of his works: it is my purpose that he should possess this memorial. He has been described by a great authority as a writer *sui generis;* and indeed had he never written, it appears to me that there would have been a gap in our libraries which it would have been difficult to supply. Of him it might be added that, for an author, his end was an euthanasia, for on the day before he was seized by that fatal epidemic, of the danger of which, to the last moment, he was unconscious, he was apprised by his publishers that all his works were out of print and that their re-publication could no longer be delayed.

In this notice of the career of my father, I have ventured to draw attention to three circumstances which I thought would be esteemed interesting, namely, predisposition, self-formation, and sympathy with his order. There is yet another which completes and crowns the character,— constancy of purpose; and it is only in considering his course as a whole that we see how harmonious and consistent has been that life and its labours, which, in a partial and brief view, might be supposed to have been somewhat desultory and fragmentary.

On his moral character I shall scarcely presume to dwell. The philosophic sweetness of his disposition, the serenity of his lot, and the elevating nature of his pursuits, combined to enable him to pass through life without an evil act, almost without an evil thought.

As the world has always sought personal details respecting men who have been celebrated, I will mention that he was fair, with a Bourbon nose, and brown eyes of extraordinary beauty and lustre. He wore a small black velvet cap, but his white hair latterly touched his shoulders in curls almost as flowing as in his boyhood. His extremities were delicate and well-formed, and his leg, at his last hour, as shapely as in his youth, which showed the vigour of his frame. Latterly he had become corpulent. He did not excel in conversation, though in his domestic circle he was garrulous. Everything interested him; and blind, and eighty-two, he was still as susceptible as a child. One of his last acts was to compose some verses of gay gratitude to his daughter-in-law, who was his London correspondent, and to whose lively pen his last years were indebted for constant amusement.

He had by nature a remarkable volatility which never deserted him. His feelings, though always amiable, were not painfully deep, and amid joy or sorrow, the philosophic vein was ever evident. He more resembled Goldsmith than any man that I can compare him to: in his conversation, his apparent confusion of ideas ending with some felicitous phrase of genius, his naïveté, his simplicity not untouched with a dash of sarcasm affecting innocence — one was often reminded of the gifted and interesting friend of Burke and Johnson. There was, however, one trait in which my father did not resemble Goldsmith: he had no vanity. Indeed, one of his few infirmities was rather a deficiency of self-esteem.

On the whole, I hope — nay, I believe — that taking all into consideration — the integrity and completeness of his existence, the fact that, for sixty years he largely contributed to form the taste, charm the leisure, and direct the studious dispositions of the great body of the public, and that his works have extensively and curiously illustrated the literary and political history of our country, it will be conceded that in his life and labours he repaid England for the protection and the hospitality which this country accorded to his father a century ago.   D.

HUGHENDEN MANOR,
    Christmas, 1848.

THE SPEAKING HARLEQUIN

THE TWO LOSSES; IN ONE ACT.

SCENE I.

*A Room in a Hotel; Harlequin in an easy chair, and
Colombine in attitudes before a
pier-glass.*

ARLEQUIN. What an astonishing
city! and what an easy chair! We
shall find Bergamo very dull after it.
Colombine. Pray, my love, leave
off mentioning that vulgar place.
He certainly has dressed my hair
charmingly. Nobody here ever heard of Bergamo.
These people only know Rome, Florence, and Naples;
and if you would only hold that stupid tongue of yours,
we really might pass off as Italians who had moved
in our own country in the best English society.

Harlequin. Every one calls upon us. What a
number of visiting tickets! All the diplomatic body!
I like this London very much.

Colombine. My dear Harlequin, for Heaven's sake
never appear astonished that people pay you attention: you are always exposing us; treat everything as

matter of course. Have I not told you a thousand times that there is no city in the world where we strangers, if discreet, can get on so well as London?

Harlequin. Well, my love, what harm is there in speaking to you? I am sure I always hold my tongue when I am in society.

Colombine. You should practise silence when we are alone, and rehearse in private your public performance.

Harlequin. Ah! that silence, it is very dull work: I love gaiety.

Colombine. My dear Harlequin, gaiety is very vulgar. If you want to be gay, take a ride by yourself into the country. Always be gay in solitude.

Harlequin. It is a little difficult. When I am alone, do you know, I always feel very stupid.

Colombine. 'Tis a pity; but really, my dearest Harlequin, you must control yourself. London is not Bergamo. You must not be frisking about here like a monkey, and twirling your head like a mandarin; and, above all, no practical jests, I entreat,—no smacking people on their backs, or drawing their seats from under them, or cutting them over their heads with that old-fashioned wand of yours.

Harlequin. Ah, my dear Colombine, what should we be without the wand?

Colombine. 'Tis a truth, though; whom do you ever see with a wand except yourself? And further, my dear Harlequin, let me tell you once for all, pray have the kindness not to be so attentive to me. Nothing can be more unfashionable than to be always looking after your wife. Lady Pantaloon told me, only yesterday, that you were really just like my shadow; and last night, when I was on the very point of taking Count Scaramouch's arm to my carriage, what must you do but thrust your great hand between us! 'Twas absolutely disgusting. If you had only seen the Count's stare.

Harlequin. Well, my love, I thought it was only civil.

Colombine. Civil! What a word! Never be civil.

Harlequin. How droll! What should I be?

Colombine. Be! Be kind, be courteous, be cutting, be sarcastic, be careless, be desperate, be in love, be in a rage, be anything, but never be *civil.*

Harlequin. Well, I have been trying to be civil all my life. What a blunder!

Enter Scaramouch.

Scaramouch. A pleasant morning, fairest Colombine. I hope you are not wearied by last night's dissipation. I have brought you a bouquet. My dear Harlequin, how do you do?

Harlequin (*aside*). Here, at least, is a civil gentleman. I never spoke to him in my life, and he addresses me in terms even of affection. I hope you are very well, sir? He turns his back upon me, and talks to my wife!

Scaramouch. What are you going to do? Will you ride? 'Tis a charming day. Not inclined? Well, then, a promenade. Let me drive you to the gardens.

Colombine. You are so kind. And, now I think again, I am for riding. A canter is so exhilarating. And where did you gather this bouquet? It is too beautiful.

Scaramouch. Sweets to the sweet.

Colombine. Did you stay long after us last night?

Scaramouch. I had no inducement.

Harlequin. He has not yet answered my question.

Scaramouch. There have been so many inquiries made after that beautiful dress you wore.

Harlequin. I am glad they all liked it. It came, sir, from——

Colombine. It is a national costume. You have been in Italy, no doubt?

Scaramouch. Divine land! What sort of opera have you now at San Carlo?

Harlequin. The south of Italy is a part which——

Colombine. Is generally preferred by your nation. You are riding yourself?

Scaramouch. I have, in fact, brought with me a a horse which I would induce you to try.

Harlequin. Civil again. Colombine is evidently wrong: civility must be the fashion.

Scaramouch. Where do you go to-night?

Colombine. We have several invitations.

Harlequin. Our friends are really too kind.

Colombine. Lady Brazilia Forrester has sent us a card.

Harlequin. And wishes us very much to go.

Scaramouch. Oh! by no means. You cannot possibly venture. 'Tis a place where you will meet nothing but tigers.

Harlequin. How horrible! Tigers!

Colombine. 'Tis quite frightful. I cannot think of going. What say you to Mrs. Bluebell's?

Scaramouch. Why, sometimes one does meet something there that, for once, one wishes to look at; but, for myself, I abhor assemblies which consist only of lions.

Harlequin. Tigers and lions! How ferocious!

Colombine (*aside*). I suppose these menageries are fashionable, but I am so nervous I think I had better keep away, and Harlequin is so simple that he is sure to get scratched at least. Well, then, what think you, Count, of Sir Tusky de Grunt?

Scaramouch. Impossible! Nothing but bores.

Harlequin. Tigers, lions, and boars! Did any one ever hear of anything so dreadful? What next?

Colombine (*aside*). Hush! Harlequin, do not expose yourself. You know very well you once kept a monkey yourself.

Harlequin. And never shall forget it. If one monkey did so much mischief, what must be expected from a whole roomful of wild beasts?

Scaramouch. I propose a plan. It is not yet five o'clock. We will ride down quietly to Richmond; we shall get there by sunset, and just be in time for the Queen of Diamonds' breakfast.

Harlequin. Breakfast at sunset! Why, at Berg——

Colombine. Hush! Your plan, Count, is delightful. I shall be prepared in a moment.   [*Exit Colombine.*

Harlequin. I am not very fond of riding, I confess. It is so awkward in these slippers. What shall I do with my wand? I had better leave it at home.

Scaramouch. Take it instead of a cane. It is quite the mode! And your cap will make a capital dress hat. Put it under your arm. So. Why, well done! You have quite the air *degagé*.

Harlequin. The air *degagé!* My cap will make a capital dress hat! And my wand will do for a cane! It is quite the mode! Parties of tigers and lions and boars! Breakfast at sunset! Oh, my! What would they say at——

Colombine. Harlequin! Harlequin! Are you ready?

Scene II.

Scaramouch solus.

I like the simplicity of her affectation. She amuses me. A new manner is even more interesting than a new face, and she has both. He is a good-humoured booby, and Brillanta has a design upon his wand, which, really, it is quite ridiculous that such a *bête* should wave. So we have entered to-day into a little conspiracy, and are mutually to assist each other in our several objects. A female friend is invaluable. I have never succeeded without such aid.

Scene III.

The Gardens of the Queen of Diamonds. Guests in groups: some dancing in a Pavilion in the background.

Enter Scaramouch, Harlequin, and Colombine.

Colombine. Oh, how beautiful!
Scaramouch. 'Tis pretty.
Harlequin. How I should like to have a dance!
Scaramouch. Let me introduce you, Signor Harlequin, to my friend the Knave of Clubs. You will find him of use. He will put you down as an honorary member of the Travellers'. See! here comes our hostess. Brillanta, I have the pleasure of presenting to you our interesting friends.

Brillanta. Dearest Lady Colombine, this is a gratification I have long desired. And you, too, signor, of whom we have heard so much, how shall I express the delight I experience at finding you my guest?

Harlequin. Madam——

Colombine. Your Majesty does us great honour.

Harlequin. It is a droll custom this breakfasting at sunset, but it pleases me much.

Colombine. I assure your Majesty that Harlequin was always an admirer of late breakfasts.

Harlequin. Though I was ever an early riser. When we were at Ber——

Colombine. I think you had better go and breakfast now. (*Aside.*) Anything to stop his *mal apropos.*

Brillanta. I elect you my cavalier, signor (*takes Harlequin's arm*). Count, you are charged with the care of our fair friend. Do you find us strangers endurable, signor?

Harlequin. Not near so bad as I expected, I assure you.

Brillanta. Charming naïveté! I am pleased, however, to hear you give us so good a character. I fear, though, you must find society here on the whole somewhat insipid? Your admirers here must enter into a very unequal rivalry with the Italian dames?

Harlequin. It is true. She is nothing like my countrywomen. Watch Colombine a moment. She is dancing with the Count. Mark that turn. Did you ever see anything so graceful in your life?

Brillanta. I missed it. I was looking in the lake.

Harlequin. Ah! the beautiful lake. I see you are smiling, although I am not looking at you. I see you smile in the water. Oh! how pretty it is!

Brillanta. But not so pretty as Colombine?

Harlequin. It is very pretty. I like very much a pretty woman when she smiles.

Brillanta. I should fancy you were a very light-hearted personage.

Harlequin. Without doubt, and do you know, that is the reason why Colombine says I can never be interesting. It is not my fault that I am always in such good spirits. I often try to be gloomy, but, some-how or other, with all my exertions, I never succeed.

Brillanta. How provoking!

Harlequin. Very. Because I like to please Colombine in every possible manner. Often, when I see her approach, I look as unhappy as possible, because I know she likes poetry, and then she inquires what ails me in so touching a tone, that I always lose my presence of mind, and make her quite miserable, by telling her that I never was happier in my life.

Brillanta. You amuse me.

Harlequin. I am very glad I do. I generally am considered by my friends as rather entertaining company.

Brillanta. I fear my arm wearies you?

Harlequin. Not at all.

Brillanta. You must find your wand very heavy. Let me carry it for you.

Harlequin. Don't mention it. It is extremely light.

Brillanta. Will you dance?

Harlequin. I should like to dance with you.

Brillanta. I anticipate that pleasure.

SCENE IV.

Another part of the Gardens: an illuminated Kiosk.

Enter Scaramouch and Colombine.

Scaramouch. That galop was exhausting.   Let us rest ourselves here.

Colombine. I wonder where Harlequin is?

Scaramouch. In very amusing company.   Here is a pretty summer-house.   Let us enter.   (*They go in.*) A guitar!   Touch it.

Colombine. Nay, I have, indeed, no voice.

Scaramouch. No one ever has.   Yet an air would be delightful.

Colombine. You are too kind.   Now, really I feel persuaded I cannot sing, and yet to please you, if it must be so, there is a Ritornella which I will try to remember, and which was once thought pretty.

COLOMBINE'S RITORNELLA.

I.

Now is the hour
To leave thy bower,
And wander in these gardens bright;
All that is fairest
On earth, and rarest,
Meet in these starry halls to-night.
Now is the hour
To leave thy bower,
And wander in these gardens bright.

2.

But oh! the fairest,
And oh! the rarest,
Will seem but dull without thy light;—
Then hasten, sweetest,
For time is fleetest,
And give thy beauty to our sight.
Now is the hour
To leave thy bower,
And wander in these gardens bright.

Scaramouch. A sweet song, and sweeter singer.

Colombine. Nay, a truce to compliments.

Scaramouch. Indeed I am sincere. Can you play piquet?

Colombine. Dominoes is the only game I know.

Scaramouch. So much the better! I will teach you piquet. Nothing is more amusing than teaching when you have a docile pupil. See now, I shall deal first. So and so. [*The door of the Kiosk closes.*

Enter Harlequin.

Harlequin. After all, what an astonishingly little affair the great world is! I observe I always begin to moralise when I get tired; I have danced myself to death. I wonder where her Majesty is? she vanished as I entered this walk, which seems to have no end, and winds about like a boa constrictor. I am afraid I have got into a maze; it is very awkward. What is all this? a summer-house? illuminated too; in all probability containing something to eat. I am exceedingly hungry. The door locked! Mysterious! Perhaps a fancy wine-celler; a strange smell of Roman punch; no doubt some fun going on. I must be in it, and if I can open it in no other way I must have recourse to— oh, my wand, my wand! where is it? It was in my girdle this moment. Oh, Brillanta! false Brillanta!— Colombine! Colombine!— Hilliho! hilliho! Here is a pretty business! Stop thief! stop thief! Colombine! Colombine!

[*Colombine rushes out in great agitation.*

Colombine. What is the matter?

Harlequin. Stop thief! Where is Colombine? Lost my wand!— Colombine! Colombine!

Colombine. Why, you silly fellow, here I am! How you frightened me. What do you want?

Harlequin. Oh, this breakfasting at sunset! No good can ever come from setting the world upside downwards. Colombine, I have lost my wand.

Colombine. And, Harlequin, I have lost——

Scaramouch (*advancing*). A point at piquet. 'Tis no great affair; such light losses happen every day. Shall I see after your carriage?

POEMS

TO A BEAUTIFUL MUTE (THE ELDEST CHILD
OF MR. FAIRLIE).

ELL me the star from which she fell,
    Oh! name the flower
From out whose wild and perfumed bell
    At witching hour,
Sprang forth this fair and fairy maiden
Like a bee with honey laden.

They say that those sweet lips of thine
    Breathe not to speak:
Thy very ears that seem so fine
    No sound can seek,
And yet thy face beams with emotion,
Restless as the waves of ocean.

'Tis well. Thy face and form agree,
    And both are fair.
I would not that this child should be
    As others are:
I love to mark her indecision,
Smiling with seraphic vision

At our poor gifts of vulgar sense
   That cannot stain
Nor mar her mystic innocence,
   Nor cloud her brain
With all the dreams of worldly folly,
And its creature melancholy.

To thee I dedicate these lines,
   Yet read them not.
Cursed be the art that e'er refines
   Thy natural lot:
Read the bright stars and read the flowers,
And hold converse with the bowers.

TO A MAIDEN SLEEPING AFTER HER FIRST BALL.

DREAMS come from Jove, the poet says;
But as I watch the smile
That on thy lips now softly plays,
I can but deem the while,
Venus may also send a shade
To whisper to a slumbering maid.

What dark-eyed youth now culls the flower
That radiant brow to grace,
Or whispers in the starry hour
Words fairer than thy face?
Or singles thee from out the throng
To thee to breathe his minstrel song?

The ardent vow that ne'er can fail,
The sigh that is not sad,
The glance that tells a secret tale,
The spirit hushed yet glad:
These weave the dreams that maidens prove
The fluttering dream of virgin love.

Sleep on, sweet maid, nor sigh to break
The spell that binds thy brain,
Nor struggle from thy trance to wake
To life's impending pain.
Who wakes to love awake but knows
Love is a dream without repose.

ON THE PORTRAIT OF LADY MAHON.

FAIR lady! this the pencil of Vandyke
Might well have painted: thine the English air,
Graceful yet earnest, that his portraits bear,
In that far troubled time, when sword and pike
　　Gleamed round the ancient halls and castles fair
That shrouded Albion's beauty: though, when need,
　They too, though soft withal, would boldly dare,
Defend the leaguered breach, or charging steed,
　Mount in their trampled parks. Far different scene
　The bowers present before thee; yet serene
Though nowadays, if coming time impart
　Our ancient troubles, well I ween thy life
Would not reproach thy lot and what thou art,—
　A warrior's daughter and a statesman's wife.

Book of Beauty, 1839.

UPON THE DUKE OF WELLINGTON.

Not only that thy puissant arm could bind
　The Tyrant of a world and, conquering fate,
　Enfranchise Europe, so I deem thee great:
But that in all thy actions I do find
Exact propriety: no gusts of mind
　Fitful and wild, but that continuous state
　Of ordered impulse mariners await,
In some benignant and enriching wind,
　The break ordained of nature. Thy calm mien
Recalls old Rome as much as thy high deed;
　Duty thy only idol, and serene
When all are troubled; in the utmost need
　Prescient· thy country's servant ever seen,
Yet sovereign of thyself whate'er may speed.

WIT AND WISDOM

OF THE

EARL OF BEACONSFIELD

ABILITY.

PRIDE myself upon recognising and upholding ability in every party and wherever I meet it. —*Speech at Newport Pagnell (General Election), February* 5, 1874.

ABSENCE.

I believe absence is often a great element of charm. — ('Lord Roehampton') *Endymion.*

ABUSE.

It isn't calling your neighbours names that settles a question. — ('Widow Carey') *Sybil.*

ACTION.

Action may not always bring happiness; but there is no happiness without action.— ('The General') *Lothair.*

The standing committee of the Holy Alliance of Peoples all rose, although they were extreme Republicans, when the General entered. Such is the magical influence of a man of action over men of the pen and the tongue.— *Lothair*.

Action must be founded on knowledge.— *Contarini Fleming*.

ADOPTION.

The principle of adoption was the secret and endurance of Rome. It gave Rome alike the Scipios and the Antonines.— ('Bertie Tremaine') *Endymion*.

ADVANTAGE.

Next to knowing when to seize an opportunity, the most important thing in life is to know when to forego an advantage.— ('Tiresias') *The Infernal Marriage*.

ADVENTURE.

How full of adventure is life! It is monotonous only to the monotonous.— *Tancred*.

Adventure and contemplation share our being like day and night.— ('Sidonia') *Coningsby*.

The fruit of my tree of knowledge is plucked, and it is this, 'Adventures are to the adventurous.'— *Alroy*.

ADVERSITY.

There is no education like adversity.— ('Sidney Wilton') *Endymion*.

I suppose it is adversity that develops the kindly qualities of our nature. I believe the sense of common degradation has a tendency to make the degraded amiable—at least among themselves. I am told it is found so in the plantations in slave-gangs. —('St. Barbe') *Endymion.*

Adversity is necessarily not a sanguine season, and in this respect a political party is no exception to all other human combinations.— *Life of Lord George Bentinck.*

ADVICE.

Advice is not a popular thing to give.— ('Miss Arundel') *Lothair.*

I do not like giving advice, because it is an unnecessary responsibility under any circumstances.— *Speech at Aylesbury (Royal and Central Bucks Agricultural Association), September* 21, 1865.

Be patient: cherish hope. Read more: ponder less. Nature is more powerful than education: time will develop everything.— *Contarini Fleming.*

Advice to a Boy going to School.— You will find Eton a great change; you will experience many trials and temptations; but you will triumph over and withstand them all, if you will attend to these few directions. Fear God; morning and night let nothing induce you ever to omit your prayers to Him; you will find that praying will make you happy. Obey your superiors; always treat your masters with respect. Ever speak the truth. So long as you adhere to this rule, you never can be involved in any serious misfortune. A deviation from truth is, in general, the foundation of all misery. Be kind to your companions, but be firm. Do not be laughed into doing that which you know to be wrong. Be modest and humble, but ever respect yourself. Remember who you are, and also that it is your duty to excel.

Providence has given you a great lot. Think ever that you are born to perform great duties.— ('Lady Annabel') *Venetia*.

AGE.

Age was frequently beautiful, wisdom appeared like an aftermath, and the heart which seemed dry and deadened suddenly put forth shoots of sympathy. — ('Mr. Phœbus') *Lothair*.

The disappointment of manhood succeeds to the delusion of youth: let us hope that the heritage of age is not despair.— *Vivian Grey*.

'The spirit of the age is the very thing that a great man changes,' said Sidonia.

'Does he not rather avail himself of it?' asked Coningsby.

'Parvenus do, but not prophets, great legislators, great conquerors. They destroy and they create.'— *Coningsby*.

AGITATION.

Demagogues and agitators are very unpleasant, and leagues and registers may be very unpleasant, but they are incidents to a free and constitutional country, and you must put up with these inconveniences or do without many important advantages.— *Speech in House of Commons (Representation of the People Bill), April* 12, 1867.

ALHAMBRA.

Let us enter Alhambra!

See! here is the Court of Myrtles, and I gather you a sprig. Mark how exquisitely everything is proportioned; mark how slight, and small, and delicate! And now we are in the Court of Columns, the far-famed Court of Columns. Let us enter the chambers that open round this quadrangle. How beautiful are their deeply-carved and purple roofs, studded with gold, and the walls entirely covered with the most fanciful fret-work, relieved with that violet tint which must have been copied from their Andalusian skies. Here you may sit in the coolest shade, reclining on your divan, with your beads or pipe, and view the dazzling sunlight in the court, which assuredly must scorch the flowers, if the faithful lions ever ceased from pouring forth that element which you must travel in Spain or Africa to honour. How many chambers! the Hall of the Ambassadors ever the most sumptuous. How fanciful its mosaic ceiling of ivory and tortoiseshell, mother-of-pearl and gold! And then the Hall of Justice with its cedar roof, and the Harem, and the baths: all perfect. Not a single roof has yielded, thanks to those elegant horse-shoe arches and those crowds of marble columns, with their oriental capitals. What a scene! Is it beautiful? Oh! conceive it in the time of the Boabdils; conceive it with all its costly decorations, all the gilding, all the imperial purple, all the violet relief, all the scarlet borders, all the glittering inscriptions and precious mosaics, burnished, bright, and fresh. Conceive it full of still greater ornaments, the living groups, with their splendid and vivid and picturesque costume, and, above all, their rich and shining arms, some standing in conversing groups, some smoking in sedate silence, some telling their beads, some squatting round a storier. Then the bustle and the rush, and the coming horsemen, all in motion, and all glancing in the most brilliant sun.—*Contarini Fleming*.

ALLITERATION.

'Fancy franchises,'—alliteration tickles the ear, and is a very popular form of language among savages. It is, I believe, the characteristic of rude and barbarous poetry: but it is not an argument in legislation. — *Speech in House of Commons (Representation of the People Bill), March* 19, 1860.

AMBITION.

It was that noble ambition, the highest and the best, that must be born in the heart, and organised in the brain, which will not let a man be content unless his intellectual power is recognised by his race, and desires that it should contribute to their welfare. It is the heroic feeling; the feeling that in old days produced demi-gods; without which no State is safe; without which political institutions are meat without salt, the Crown a bauble, the Church an establishment, Parliaments debating clubs, and civilisation itself but a fitful and transient dream.— *Coningsby.*

AMERICA.

The enterprise of America generally precedes that of Europe, as the industry of England precedes that of the rest of Europe, and I look forward with confidence that the industry and enterprise of America will be productive of beneficial results upon this country. — *Speech in House of Commons (Address in answer to Her Majesty's most gracious Speech), December* 8, 1878.

AMERICANS.

American ladies — I can never make out what they believe, or what they disbelieve. It is a sort of con-

fusion between Mrs. Beecher Stowe and the Fifth
Avenue congregation and Barnum.— ('The Bishop')
Lothair.

I have not been influenced by that sort of rowdy
rhetoric which is expressed in public meetings and
public journals, from which, I fear, in this country, is
formed too rapidly our opinion of the character and
possible conduct of the American people. I look upon
such expressions as something like those strong and
fantastic drinks that we hear of as such favourites on
the other side of the Atlantic; and I should as soon
suppose that this rowdy rhetoric is a symbol of the
real character of the American people as that those
potations are symbols of the aliment and nutrition of
their bodies.— *Speech in House of Commons (Defences
of Canada), March* 13, 1865.

ANECDOTE.

An after-dinner anecdote ought to be as piquant
as anchovy toast.— ('Von Konigstein') *Vivian Grey.*

Mr. Pinto would sometimes remark that when a
man fell into his anecdotage, it was a sign for him
to retire from the world.— *Lothair.*

ANONYMOUS.

An anonymous writer should at least display
power. When Jupiter hurls a thunderbolt, it may be
mercy in the god to veil his glory with a cloud; but
we can only view with contemptuous lenity the mis-
chievous varlet who pelts us with mud as we are riding along, and then hides behind a dust-bin.— *Attack
on 'Globe,'* 1836.

Anonymous writing is not the exception, but it is
the rule of the literature of this country. Who wrote

Thomas à Kempis? Nobody knows. Who wrote *The Whole Duty of Man?* Now there is a book which every one of us ought to have studied — which for generations our predecessors have studied — which has had more editions than any book in the world, and which is not a scandalous book, a libellous book, or a political book, but an anonymous book. Who was the author of *Waverley?* An anonymous writer. Who was the author of *Robinson Crusoe?* An anonymous writer. Who was the author of *A Vindication of Natural Society?* Why — one who became afterwards one of the most brilliant ornaments of this House — Mr. Burke. What are the most brilliant performances of political literature? What are those works that were written by one who in this House occupied the highest post, whose name will ever be remembered, and whose oratory, though a tradition, lives in the memory of the nation? I mean Lord Bolingbroke. What are Lord Bolingbroke's works? All those works which we are continually quoting are anonymous.— *Speech in House of Commons (Newspaper Stamp Duties Bill), April 30, 1854.*

ANXIETY.

Nothing in life is more remarkable than the unnecessary anxiety which we endure and generally occasion ourselves.— *Lothair.*

Nobody should ever look anxious, except those who have no anxiety.— *Endymion.*

APOLOGIES.

Apologies only account for that which they do not alter.— *Speech in House of Commons (Order of Business), July 28, 1871.*

ARCHITECTURE.

What is wanted in architecture, as in so many things, is a man. One suggestion might be made — no profession in England has done its duty until it has furnished a victim; even our boasted navy never achieved a great victory until we shot an admiral. Suppose an architect were hanged. Terror has its inspiration, as well as competition.— *Tancred.*

ARISTOCRACY.

There is no longer, in fact, an aristocracy in England, for the superiority of the animal man is an essential quality of aristocracy.— *Sybil.*

ART.

Art is order, method, harmonious results, obtained by fine and powerful principles.— *Tancred.*

Greek Art.— In art the Greeks were the children of the Egyptians. The day may yet come when we shall do justice to the high powers of that mysterious and imaginative people.— *Contarini Fleming.*

In the study of the fine arts, they mutually assist each other.— *Contarini Fleming.*

ASSASSINATION.

Assassination has never changed the history of the world.— *Speech in House of Commons (Assassination of the President of the United States, May,* 1865).

ASSOCIATION.

The principle of association is the want of the age.— ('Stephen Morley') *Sybil.*

AUSTRIA.

Poor Austria! Two things made her a nation: she was German and she was Catholic, and now she is neither.— ('Monsignore Berwick') *Lothair*.

AUTHORS.

The creators of opinion.— *Speech in House of Commons (Copyright), April* 25, 1838.

I think the author who speaks about his own books is almost as bad as a mother who talks about her own children.— *Speech at Banquet to Lord Rector, Glasgow, November* 19, 1870.

The author is, as we must ever remember, of peculiar organisation. He is a being born with a predisposition which with him is irresistible, the bent of which he cannot in any way avoid, whether it directs him to the abstruse researches of erudition or induces him to mount into the fervid and turbulent atmosphere of imagination.— *Speech at Royal Literary Fund Dinner, May* 6, 1868.

BADINAGE.

Men destined to the highest places should beware of badinage. — ('Bertie Tremaine') *Endymion*.

BAR.

The Bar—pooh! Law and bad jokes till we are forty; and then, with the most brilliant success, the prospect of gout and a coronet.— *Vivian Grey*.

BARONETCY.

A baronetcy has become a distinction of the middle class: our physician, for example, is a baronet, and I dare say some of our tradesmen — brewers or people of that sort. — ('Lady Joan Fitz-Warene') *Sybil*.

BATHS.

Baths should only be used to drown the enemies of the people. I always was against washing, it takes the marrow out of a man. — ('The Liberator Hatton') *Sybil*.

BEAUTY.

Beauty can inspire miracles. — *Young Duke*.

BOOKS.

Bookworms do not make Chancellors of State. — ('Lady Montfort') *Endymion*.

Consols at a hundred were the origin of all book societies. — ('Cleveland') *Vivian Grey*.

Those that cannot themselves observe, can at least acquire the observation of others. — ('De Winter') *Contarini Fleming*.

It is difficult to decide which is the most valuable companion to a country eremite at his nightly studies, the volume that keeps him awake, or the one that sets him slumbering. — *Lothair*.

Books are fatal: they are the curse of the human race. Nine-tenths of existing books are nonsense, and the clever books are the refutation of that nonsense. The greatest misfortune that ever befel man was the invention of printing. — ('Mr. Phœbus') *Lothair*.

Book-making, a composition which requires no ordinary qualities of character and intelligence — method, judgment, self-restraint, not too much imagination, perception of character, and powers of calculation. — *Endymion*.

Brougham is a man who would say anything; and of one thing you may be quite certain, that there is no subject which Lord Brougham knows thoroughly. ('Mr. Ferrars') *Endymion*.

BYRON.

If one thing were more characteristic of Byron's mind than another, it was his strong, shrewd common sense; his pure, unalloyed sagacity. The loss of Byron can never be retrieved. He was indeed a real man; and when I say this, I award him the most splendid character which human nature need aspire to. Byron's mind was, like his own ocean, sublime in its yeasty madness, beautiful in its glittering summer brightness, mighty in the lone magnificence of its waste of waters, gazed upon from the magic of its own nature, yet capable of representing, but as in a glass darkly, the natures of all others. — ('Cleveland') *Vivian Grey*.

CAB.

A hansom cab — 'tis the gondola of London.— *Lothair*.

CALAMITIES.

What appear to be calamities are often the sources of fortune.— ('Mr. Ferrars') *Endymion*.

CALCULATION.

Everything in this world is calculation.— ('Lord Marney') *Sybil*.

CAPITAL.

In these days a great capitalist has deeper roots than a sovereign prince, unless he is very legitimate.— *Tancred*.

CARDS.

To a mind like that of Tiresias a pack of cards was full of human nature. A rubber was a microcosm.— *The Infernal Marriage.*

CASUALTIES.

Great things spring from casualties.— ('Gerard') *Sybil.*

CAUSE.

It is always when the game is played that we discover the cause of the result.— *Tancred.*

CELIBACY.

Melancholy, which, after a day of action, is the doom of energetic celibacy.— *Sybil.*

CHANCE.

If you mean by chance an absence of accountable cause, I do not believe such a quality as chance exists. Every incident that happens must be a link in a chain.— ('Herbert') *Venetia.*

CHANGE.

Change, in the abstract, is what is required by a people who are at the same time inquiring and wealthy.— *Tancred.*

CHARACTER.

In all lives there is a crisis in the formation of character. It comes from many causes, and from some which on the surface are apparently even trivial. But the result is the same; a sudden revelation to ourselves of our secret purpose, and a recognition of our perhaps long-shadowed, but now masterful convictions.— *Endymion*.

National Character.— A character is an assemblage of qualities; the character of England should be an assemblage of great qualities.— ('Sidonia') *Coningsby*.

CHRISTIANITY.

Christians may continue to persecute Jews, and Jews may persist in disbelieving Christianity, but who can deny that Jesus of Nazareth, the incarnate Son of the Most High God, is the eternal glory of the Jewish race?— *Life of Lord George Bentinck*.

Christianity is completed Judaism, or it is nothing. —('Egremont') *Sybil*.

CHURCH.

The Church has no fear of just reasoners.— ('Brother Anthony') *Contarini Fleming*.

The Church is cosmopolitan—the only practical means by which you can attain to identity of motive and action.— ('Nigel Penruddock') *Endymion*.

The doctrine of evolution affords no instance so striking as those of sacerdotal development.— *Lothair*.

What the soul is to the man, the Church is to the world.— ('Cardinal Grandison') *Lothair*.

The Church is a sacred corporation for the promulgation and maintenance in Europe of certain Asian principles which, although local in their birth, are of divine origin and eternal application.— *Coningsby*.

CIRCUMSTANCES.

Man is not the creature of circumstances, circumstances are the creatures of men. We are free agents, and man is more powerful than matter.— ('Becken-dorf') *Vivian Grey*.

Circumstances are beyond the control of man; but his conduct is in his own power.— *Contarini Fleming*.

> 'Tis circumstance makes conduct; life's a ship
> The sport of every wind.— ('Alarcos') *Count Alarcos*.

Circumstance has decided every crisis which I have experienced, and not the primitive facts on which we have consulted.— ('Baroni') *Tancred*.

Circumstance is the creature of cities, where the action of a multitude, influenced by different motives, produces innumerable and ever-changing combinations. — ('Tancred') *Tancred*.

CITY.

A great city, whose image dwells on the memory of man, is the type of some great idea. Rome represents conquest; faith hovers over Jerusalem; and Athens embodies the pre-eminent quality of the antique world-art.— *Coningsby*.

CIVILISATION.

The progressive development of the faculties of man.— ('Lord Henry Vavasour') *Tancred*.

Increased means and increased leisure are the two civilisers of man.— *Speech at Manchester, April 3, 1872.*

COERCION.

Men are apt to believe that crime and coercion are inevitably associated.— *Life of Lord George Bentinck*.

COLONIES.

Colonies do not cease to be colonies because they are independent.— *Speech in House of Commons (Address to Her Majesty on the Lords Commissioners' Speech), February* 5, 1863.

What is colonial necessarily lacks originality.— ('Lord Roehampton') *Endymion.*

COMBINATION.

There is a combination for every case.— ('Hatton') *Sybil.*

COMMISSION.

Nowadays public robbery is out of fashion, and takes the milder title of a commission of inquiry.— *Sybil.*

COMMITTEE.

Our statesmen never read, and are only converted by Parliamentary committees.— *Speech in House of Commons (Sugar Duties), July* 28, 1841.

CONCEIT.

Nothing depresses a man's spirits more completely than a self-conviction of self-conceit.— *Popanilla.*

CONCILIATION.

One should always conciliate.— ('Putney Giles') *Lothair.*

If you are not very clever, you should be conciliatory.— ('The Premier') *Endymion.*

CONDUCT.

The conduct of men depends upon the temperament, not upon a bunch of musty maxims.— *Henrietta Temple.*

CONSCIENCE.

A pure conscience may defy city gossips.— ('Eva') *Tancred.*

CONSOLS.

The sweet simplicity of the three per cents.— *Endymion.*

There is nothing like a fall in Consols to bring the blood of our good people of England into cool order.— ('Cleveland') *Vivian Grey.*

CONSTANCY.

Constancy is human nature.— ('Contarini') *Contarini Fleming*

CONSTITUENCIES.

I have always thought the ideal of the constituent body in England should be this — it should be numerous enough to be independent, and select enough to be responsible. — *Speech in House of Commons (Representation of the People), February* 28, 1859.

CONVERSATION.

Alfred Mountchesney hovered round Lady Joan Fitz-Warene; he uttered inconceivable nothings, and she replied to him in incomprehensible somethings.— *Sybil.*

The art of conversation is to be prompt without being stubborn, to refute without argument, and to clothe great matters in a motley garb.— ('Walder-share') *Endymion*.

A great thing is a great book; but a greater thing than all is the talk of a great man.— *Coningsby*.

There are men whose phrases are oracles; who condense in a sentence the secrets of a life; who blurt out an aphorism that forms a character or illustrates an existence.— *Coningsby*.

COUNTRY HOUSES.

A visit to a country-house, as Pinto says, is a series of meals mitigated by the new dresses of the ladies.— *Lothair*.

CREED.

A creed is imagination.— *Contarini Fleming*.

The Athanasian Creed is the most splendid ecclesiastical lyric ever poured forth by the genius of man.— ('Nigel Penruddock') *Endymion*.

CRITICS.

It is much easier to be critical than to be correct. — *Speech in House of Commons (Address in answer to Her Majesty's Speech), January 24, 1860.*

You know who critics are? The men who have failed in literature and art.— ('Mr. Phœbus') *Lothair*.

There are critics, who, abstractedly, do not approve of successful books, particularly if they have failed in the same style.— *Preface to Lothair*.

There is always, both in politics and literature, the race, the Dennises, the Oldmixons, and Curls, who flatter themselves that by systematically libelling some eminent person of their times, they have a chance of descending to posterity.— *Preface to Lothair.*

DAWN.

Eve has its spell of calmness and consolation, but dawn brings hope and joy.— *Lothair.*

It was just that single hour of the twenty-four, when crime ceases, debauchery is exhausted, and even desolation finds a shelter.— *Sybil.*

DAY.

Twilight makes us pensive: Aurora is the goddess of activity: despair curses at midnight: hope blesses at noon.— *The Young Duke.*

DEMOCRACY.

There is more true democracy in the Roman Catholic Church than in all the secret societies of Europe. — ('Waldershare') *Endymion.*

DEPARTURES.

Departures should be sudden.— ('Sidonia') *Coningsby.*

DERBY RACE (THE).

It is the blue ribbon of the turf.— *Life of Lord George Bentinck.*

DESPAIR.

Despair is the conclusion of fools.— ('Alroy') *Sybil.*

DESPERATION.

Desperation is sometimes as powerful an inspirer as genius.—*Endymion*.

DESTINY.

Destiny is our will, and our will is our nature.—*Contarini Fleming*.

Destiny bears us to our lot, and destiny is perhaps our own will.—*Contarini Fleming*.

Tastes differ about destinies, as about manners.—('Lady Montfort') *Endymion*.

Destiny for its fulfilment ordains action.—('Prince Florestan') *Endymion*.

If we cannot shape our destiny, there is no such thing as witchcraft.—('Lady Montfort') *Endymion*.

DEVELOPMENT.

Development is the discovery of utility.—*Popanilla*.

DIGESTION.

A good eater must be a good man; for a good eater must have a good digestion, and a good digestion depends upon a good conscience.—*The Young Duke*.

DINNER.

Turtle makes all men equal.—('Adriana Neuchatel') *Endymion*.

Tradesmen nowadays console themselves for not getting their bills paid by asking their customers to dinner.—*The Young Duke*.

Two things which are necessary to a perfect dinner are noiseless attendants and a precision in serving the various dishes of each course.—*Tancred*.

A dinner of wits is proverbially a palace of silence.—
Endymion.

DIPLOMACY.

All diplomacy since the Treaty of Utrecht seems
to me to be fiddle-faddle, and the country rewarded
the great man who made that treaty by an attainder.
—('Waldershare') *Endymion*.

Diplomacy is hospitable.—*Endymion*.

DIPLOMATISTS.

I always look upon diplomatists as the Hebrews
of politics.—('Sidonia') *Coningsby*.

DIVINITY.

Human wit ought to be exhausted before we presume to invoke Divine interposition.—('Eva') *Tancred*.

The Divine majesty has never thought fit to communicate except with human beings of the very highest powers.—*Tancred*.

There is but one God—is it Allah or Jehovah?
The palm-tree is sometimes called a date-tree, but
there is only one tree.—('Amalek') *Tancred*.

DIVORCE.

Lady Gaverstock was pure as snow; but, her
mother having been divorced, she ever fancied she
was paying a kind of homage to her parent by visiting those who might some day be in the same pre-
dicament.—*Coningsby*.

DYNASTIES.

Dynasties are unpopular, especially new ones; the present age is monarchical, but not dynastic. — ('Bertie Tremaine') *Endymion.*

EAST.

The East is a career. — ('Coningsby') *Tancred.*

ECONOMY.

Economy does not consist in the reckless reduction of estimates. On the contrary such a course almost necessarily tends to increased expenditure. There can be no economy where there is no efficiency. — *Letter to Constituents, October 3,* 1868.

EDUCATION.

The essence of education is the education of the body. Beauty and health are the chief sources of happiness. — ('Mr. Phœbus') *Lothair.*

ELOQUENCE.

(Knowledge is the foundation of eloquence.)— *Endymion.*

EMIGRATION.

When I observe year after year the vast emigration from Ireland, I feel that it is impossible to conceal the fact that we are experiencing a great social and political calamity. I acknowledge that under some conditions, and even under general conditions, emigration is the safety-valve of a people. But there is a difference between blood-letting and hæmorrhage. — *Election Speech on acceptance of office of Chancellor of Exchequer, July* 13, 1866.

EMPIRE.

It is not on our fleets and armies, however necessary they may be for the maintenance of our imperial strength, that I alone or mainly depend in that enterprise on which this country is about to enter. It is on what I most highly value—the consciousness that in the Eastern nations there is a confidence in this country, and that while they know we can enforce our policy, at the same time they know that our Empire is an Empire of liberty, of truth, and of justice. *Speech in House of Commons (Congress Correspondence and Protocols), July* 18, 1878.

ENGLAND.

England is a domestic country. Here the home is revered and the hearth sacred. The nation is represented by a family—the Royal family—and if that family is educated with a sense of responsibility and a sentiment of public duty, it is difficult to exaggerate the salutary influence it may exercise over a nation.— *Speech at Manchester, April* 3, 1872.

There is no sovereignty of any firstrate State which costs so little to the people as the sovereignty of England.— *Speech at Manchester, April* 3, 1872.

The people of England are the most enthusiastic in the world. There are others more excitable, but there are none so enthusiastic.— *Speech at Royal and Central Bucks Agricultural Association, September* 26, 1876.

The Continent will not suffer England to be the workshop of the world.— *Speech in House of Commons (Abolition of Corn Laws), March* 15, 1838.

The mind of England is the mind of the rising race.— ('Egremont') *Sybil.*

ENGLISH.

English is an expressive language, but not difficult to master. Its range is limited. It consists, as far as I can observe, of four words, 'nice,' 'jolly,' 'charming,' and 'bore,' and some grammarians add 'fond.' — ('Pinto') *Lothair.*

ENTERPRISE.

The enterprising are often fortunate.— *Tancred.*

ENTHUSIASM.

That youthful fervour which is sometimes called enthusiasm, but which is a heat of imagination subsequently discovered to be inconsistent with the experience of actual life.— *Endymion.*

EQUALITY.

Civil equality prevails in Britain, social equality prevails in France. The essence of civil equality is to abolish privilege; the essence of social equality is to destroy class.— *Speech at Glasgow University, November* 19, 1873.

The equality of man can only be accomplished by the sovereignty of God.— ('The Angel of Arabia') *Tancred.*

ESTATE.

If you want to understand the ups and downs of life, there is nothing like the parchments of an estate. — ('Gerard') *Sybil.*

ETERNITY.

The doom of eternity and the fortunes of life cannot be placed in competition.— ('Cardinal Grandison') *Lothair*.

EVENTS.

What wonderful things are events! The least are of greater importance than the most sublime and comprehensive speculations.— *Coningsby*.

Life is not dated merely by years. Events are sometimes the best calendar. There are epochs in our existence which cannot be ascertained by a formal appeal to the registry.— *Venetia*.

If you want to be a leader of the people, you must learn to watch events.— ('Devilsdust') *Sybil*.

EXAGGERATION.

There is no greater sin than to be *trop prononcé*.— *The Young Duke*.

EXPEDIENCY.

Expediency is the law of nature. The camel is a wonderful animal, but the desert made the camel.— ('Baroni') *Tancred*.

EXPERIENCE.

Experience is a thing that all men praise.— *The Young Duke*.

Great men never want experience.— ('Sidonia') *Coningsby*.

The sum of our experience is but a dim dream of the conduct of past generations — generations that lived in a total ignorance of their nature.— *Contarini Fleming*.

Experience, whose result is felt by all, whose nature is described by none.— *Vivian Grey*.

EXPLAIN.

He had lived long enough to know that it is unwise to wish everything explained.— *Coningsby*.

EXTREME.

Extreme views are never just; something always turns up which disturbs the calculations formed upon their data.— ('Baroni') *Tancred*.

FAITH.

To revive faith is more difficult than to create it.— *Lothair*.

Faith flourishes in solitude.— *Alroy*.

FAME.

Fame has eagle wings, and yet she mounts not so high as man's desires.— *The Young Duke*.

All we poor fellows can do is to wake the Hellenistic raptures of Mayfair; and that they call fame; as much like fame as a toadstool is like a truffle.— ('Cadurcis') *Venetia*.

To be famous when you are young is the fortune of the gods.— *Tancred*.

FAREWELL.

I never like to say farewell even for four-and-twenty hours: one should vanish like a spirit.— ('Theodora') *Lothair*.

FATE.

We make our fortunes, and we call them fate.— *Alroy*.

FEEBLENESS.

It may be that words are vain to save us, but feeble deeds are vainer than words.— *Sybil*.

FEELING.

Feeling without sufficient cause is weakness.— ('Lady Corisande') *Lothair*.

All feeling which has no object to attain is morbid and maudlin.— ('Lady Montfort') *Endymion*.

Never apologise for showing feeling. My friend, remember that when you do so, you apologise for truth.— ('Winter') *Contarini Fleming*.

FLIRTATION.

The soul-subduing sentiment, harshly called flirtation, which is the spell of a country house.— *Coningsby*.

FORMALITY.

Governments, like individuals, sometimes shrink from formality.— ('Prince Florestan') *Endymion*.

FORTUNE.

It is a great thing to make a fortune. There is only one thing greater, and that is to keep it when made.— ('Mr. Bond Sharpe') *Henrietta Temple*.

FRANKNESS.

Candour is a great virtue. There is a charm, a healthy charm, in frankness.— *Venetia*.

There is no wisdom like frankness.— *Sybil*.

Be frank and explicit. That is the right line to take, when you wish to conceal your own mind and to confuse the minds of others.—('The Gentleman in Downing Street.') *Sybil.*

FREEDOM.

Freedom, says the sage, will lead to prosperity, and despotism to destruction.—*Contarini Fleming.*

FRIENDSHIP.

Female friendships are of rapid growth.—*The Young Duke.*

Perhaps there is nothing more lovely than the love of two beautiful women, who are not jealous of each other's charms.—*The Young Duke.*

The friendships of the world are wind.—('Lord Cadurcis') *Venetia.*

Sidonia has no friends. No wise man has. What are friends? Traitors.—*Coningsby.*

I wear my old bonnets at Bath and use my new friends; but in town I have old friends and new dresses.—('Lady Bellair') *Henrietta Temple.*

It is seldom the lot of husbands, that their confidential friends gain the regards of their brides.—*Coningsby.*

There is magic in the memory of schoolboy friendships; it softens the heart, and even affects the nervous system of those who have no hearts.—*Endymion.*

FUTURE.

He was famous for discovering the future, when it has taken place.—*Contarini Fleming.*

The past is for wisdom, the present for action, but for joy the future.—*Alroy.*

GENIUS.

Nemesis favours genius.— *Sybil.*

He (Sievers) was one of those prudent geniuses who always leave off with a point.— *Vivian Grey.*

GENTLEMEN.

They say no artist can draw a camel, and I say no author ever drew a gentleman. How can they, with no opportunity of ever seeing one?— ('St. Barbe') *Endymion.*

GLADSTONE.

A sophistical rhetorician, inebriated with the exuberance of his own verbosity, and gifted with an egotistical imagination than can at all times command an interminable and inconsistent series of arguments to malign an opponent and to glorify himself.— *Banquet at Duke of Wellington's Riding School, July 28, 1878.*

GOVERNMENT.

The greatest of all evils is a weak government. They cannot carry good measures; they are forced to carry bad ones.— *Coningsby.*

Our domestic affections are the most salutary basis of all good government.— *Speech at Salthill (Royal South Buckinghamshire Agricultural Association), October 5, 1864.*

The divine right of kings may have been a plea for feeble tyrants, but the divine right of government is the key-stone of human progress, and without it government sinks into police, and a nation is degraded into a mob.— *Preface to 'Lothair.'*

GREATNESS.

Greatness no longer depends on rentals, the world is too rich; nor on pedigrees, the world is too knowing.— *Coningsby.*

All the great things have been done by little nations.— *Tancred.*

A great man is one who affects his generation.— *Coningsby.*

The age does not believe in great men, because it does not possess any.— ('Sidonia') *Coningsby.*

GRIEF.

Want of love, or want of money, lies at the bottom of all our griefs. — *Venetia.*

Those who have known grief seldom seem sad.— ('Agrippina') *Endymion.*

HANSARD.

Why, Hansard, instead of being the Delphi of Downing Street, is but the Dunciad of politics.— *Speech in House of Commons (Maynooth College), April 11, 1845.*

HAPPINESS.

The sense of existence is the greatest happiness.— *Contarini Fleming.*

Happiness is only to be found in a recurrence to the principles of human nature, and these will prompt very simple measures.— *Contarini Fleming.*

HEROES.

To believe in the heroic makes heroes.

— *Coningsby.*

The legacy of heroes—the memory of a great name and the inheritance of a great example.—*Speech in House of Commons (Address in answer to the Queen's Speech), February* 1, 1849.

HISTORY.

To study man from the past is to suppose that man is ever the same animal. Those who studied the career of Napoleon had ever a dog's-eared analyst to refer to.—*Contarini Fleming.*

HOLIDAYS.

I have a great confidence in the revelations which holidays bring forth.—*Speech in House of Commons, February* 29, 1864.

HOME.

> If kindness make a home,
> Believe it such.—*Alroy.*

The inn is a common home.—*Coningsby.*

Home is a barbarous idea; the method of a rude age: home is isolation, therefore antisocial—what we want is community.—('Stephen Morley') *Sybil.*

HOPE.

Hope and consolation are not the companions of solitude, which are of a darker nature.—('Lady Madeline Trevor') *Vivian Grey.*

The iris pencil of Hope.—*Venetia.*

The ministry only expresses 'a confident hope,' which is, at the best, but the language of amiable despair.—*Speech in House of Commons (Address in answer to Queen's Speech), February* 4, 1851.

Horse Exercise.

A canter is the cure for every evil.— *The Young Duke.*

House of Commons.

All the best speakers in the House of Commons are after-dinner speakers.— *Speech in House of Commons (Budget), April* 4, 1851.

House of Lords.

One thing is clear—a man may speak very well in the House of Commons and fail completely in the House of Lords. There are two distinct styles requisite. In the Lower House, *Don Juan* may perhaps be our model; in the Upper House, *Paradise Lost.* — *The Young Duke.*

The Lords do not encourage wit, and so are obliged to put up with pertness.— *The Young Duke.*

Divisions in the House of Lords are nowadays so thinly scattered, that, when one occurs, the peers cackle as if they had laid an egg.— *Tancred.*

Idea.

One should conquer the world, not to enthrone a man, but an idea, for ideas exist for ever.—*Tancred.*

Ignorance.

Ignorance never settles a question.— *Speech in House of Commons (Redistribution of Seats), May* 14, 1866.

Imprudence.

All men have their imprudent days.— ('Prince of Little Lilliput') *Vivian Grey.*

IMPUDENCE.

It is better to be impudent than servile.— ('Lady Bellair') *Henrietta Temple.*

IMPULSE.

It is not the fever of superficial impulse that can remove the deep fixed barriers of centuries of ignorance and crime.— ('Egremont') *Sybil.*

INHERITANCE.

To dream of inheritance is the most enervating of visions.— ('Sidonia') *Coningsby.*

INDIA.

The key of India is not at Candahar. The key of India is in London. The majesty and sovereignty, the spirit and vigour of your Parliament, the inexhaustible resources, the ingenuity and determination of your people, these are the keys of India.— *Speech in House of Lords, March* 5, 1881.

INSTITUTIONS.

Individuals may form communities, but it is institutions alone that can create a nation.— *Speech at Manchester,* 1866.

INVENTION.

A nation has a fixed quantity of invention, and it will make itself felt.— ('Prince Florestan') *Endymion.*

IRISH.

Their treason is a fairy tale, and their sedition a child talking in its sleep.— ('Captain Bruges') *Lothair.*

An Irish business is a thing to be turned over several times.— ('Captain Bruges') *Lothair*.

Whatever may be said, and however plausible things may look, in an Irish business there is always a priest at the bottom of it.— ('Captain Bruges') *Lothair*.

Irish Protestant Clergy.— Men who seldom stepped out of the sphere of their private virtues.— *Maiden Speech in House of Commons (Irish Election Petition), December 7, 1837.*

JERUSALEM.

The view of Jerusalem is the history of the world; it is more, it is the history of earth and of heaven.— *Tancred*.

Jerusalem at mid-day in midsummer is a city of stone in a land of iron with a sky of brass.— ('Baroni') *Tancred*.

JUSTICE.

A great writer has said that 'grace is beauty in action.' I say that Justice is truth in action. — *Speech in House of Commons (Agricultural Distress), February 11, 1851.*

KNOWLEDGE.

The tree of knowledge is the tree of death. — ('Egremont') *Sybil*.

She is calm, because she is the mistress of her subject; 'tis the secret of self-possession.— ('Sidonia') *Coningsby*.

A man can know nothing of mankind without knowing something of himself. Self knowledge is the property of that man whose passions have their full play, but who ponders over their results.— *The Young Duke.*

To be conscious that you are ignorant is a great step to knowledge.—*Vivian Grey.*

Eloquence is the child of knowledge. When a mind is full, like a wholesome river, it is also clear. Confusion and obscurity are much oftener the results of ignorance than of inefficiency.— *The Young Duke.*

Knowledge of mankind is a knowledge of their passions. Travel is not, as is imagined, the best school for that sort of science.— *The Young Duke.*

Knowledge must be gained by ourselves. Mankind may supply us with facts; but the results, even if they agree with previous ones, must be the work of our own minds.— *The Young Duke.*

Law.

When men are pure, laws are useless; when men are corrupt, laws are broken.— ('The Sheikh') *Contarini Fleming.*

Lawyers.

All lawyers are loose in their youth; but an insular country, subject to fogs and with a powerful middle class, requires grave statesmen.— ('Bertie Tremaine') *Endymion.*

Learning.

Learning is better than house and land.— ('Mrs. Carey') *Sybil.*

Legislators.

The most successful legislators are those who have consulted the genius of the people.—*Contarini Fleming.*

LIBERALISM.

My objection to Liberalism is this—that it is the introduction into the practical business of life of the highest kind—namely, politics—of philosophical ideas instead of political principles.— *Speech in House of Commons* (*Expulsion of British Ambassador from Madrid*), *June* 5, 1848.

An attempt to govern the country by the assertion of abstract principles, which it was now beginning to be the fashion to call Liberalism.— *Endymion.*

We know what Liberalism means on the Continent. It means the abolition of property and religion. — ('Great Personage') *Endymion.*

For my part I consider it a great homage to public opinion to find every scoundrel nowadays professing himself a Liberal.— ('Saturn') *Infernal Marriage.*

LIFE.

Life's a tumble-about thing of ups and downs.— ('Widow Carey') *Sybil.*

For life in general there is but one decree. Youth is a blunder, manhood a struggle, old age a regret.— ('Sidonia') *Coningsby.*

Be like me, live in the present, and when you dream, dream of the future.— ('Lady Montfort') *Endymion.*

LINEAGE.

What is the use of belonging to an old family unless to have the authority of an ancestor ready for any prejudice, religious or political, which your combinations may require?— ('Fakredeen') *Tancred.*

How those rooks bore! I hate staying with ancient families, you are always cawed to death.— *Vivian Grey.*

LITERATURE.

I may say of our literature that it has one characteristic which distinguishes it from almost all the other literatures of modern Europe, and that is its exuberant reproductiveness.— *Speech at Royal Literary Fund Dinner, May 6, 1868.*

LOCAL.

The local sentiment in man is the strongest passion in his nature. This local sentiment is the parent of most of our virtues.— *Speech at Royal South Buckinghamshire Agricultural Association Dinner at Salthill, November 5, 1864.*

LOCALITIES.

One should generally mention localities, because very often they indicate character.— *Tancred.*

LONDON.

A city of cities, an aggregation of humanity, that probably has never been equalled in any period of the history of the world, ancient or modern.— *Speech in House of Commons (Direct and Indirect Taxation), May 1, 1873.*

There never was such a great city with such small houses.— ('Lady Montfort') *Endymion.*

London is a roost for every bird.— ('Felix Drolin') *Lothair.*

Long-sight.

I look upon a long-sighted man as a brute, who, not being able to see with his mind, is obliged to see with his body.— *The Young Duke.*

Love.

Love is the May-day of the heart.— *Henrietta Temple.*

A simple story, and yet there are so many ways of telling it.— *Henrietta Temple.*

The principle of every motion — that is, of life — is desire or love.— *Venetia.*

There is no usury for love.— ('Herbert') *Venetia.*

The magic of first love is the ignorance that it can ever end.— *Henrietta Temple.*

To a man who is in love the thought of another woman is uninteresting if not repulsive.— *Contarini Fleming.*

The affections of the heart are property, and the sympathy of the right person is often worth a good estate.— *Endymion.*

Instead of love being the occasion of all the misery of this world, as is sung by fantastic bards, I believe that the misery of this world is occasioned by there not being love enough.— *Contarini Fleming.*

Experience is the best security for enduring love.— *Tancred.*

Love at first sight is often a genial and genuine sentiment, but first love at first sight is ever eventually branded as spurious.— *Tancred.*

There is no love but love at first sight. This is the transcendent and surpassing offspring of sheer and unpolluted sympathy. All other is the illegitimate result of observation, of reflection, of compromise, of comparison, of expediency.— *Henrietta Temple.*

When a man is really in love, he is disposed to believe that, like himself, every one is thinking of the person who engrosses his brain and heart.— *Endymion.*

The enamoured are always delighted with what is fanciful.— *The Young Duke.*

Restless are the dreams of the lover that is young. — *Henrietta Temple.*

I see no use of speaking to a man about love or religion: they are both stronger than friendship.— ('Bertram') *Lothair.*

Where we do not respect, we soon cease to love; where we cease to love, virtue weeps and flies.— *The Young Duke.*

If it be agonising to be deserted, there is at least consolation in being cherished.— *Henrietta Temple.*

He had not yet learned the bitter lesson that unless we despise a woman when we cease to love her, we are still a slave, without the consolation of intoxication.— *The Young Duke.*

MAJORITY.

A majority is always better than the best repartee. —('Coningsby') *Tancred.*

MAN.

When a man is not speaking, or writing, from his own mind, he is as insipid company as a looking-glass.— *The Young Duke.*

The man who anticipates his century is always persecuted when living, and is always pilfered when dead.— ('Sievers') *Vivian Grey.*

You cannot judge a man by only knowing what his debts are; you must be acquainted with his resources.— ('Fakredeen') *Tancred*.

A smile for a friend, and a sneer for the world, is the way to govern mankind.— *Vivian Grey*.

Man is only great when he acts from the passions; never irresistible but when he appeals to the imagination. Even Mormon counts more votaries than Bentham.— ('Sidonia') *Coningsby*.

Man is made to adore and obey; but if you do not command him, if you give him nothing to worship, he will fashion his own divinities and find a chieftain in his own passions.— ('Sidonia') *Coningsby*.

When a man at the same time believes in and sneers at his destiny, we may be sure that he considers his condition past redemption.— *Vivian Grey*.

Men never congregate together for any beneficial purpose.— ('Violet Fane') *Vivian Grey*.

Man is made to create, from the poet to the potter.— ('Winter') *Contarini Fleming*.

MANNERS.

Nowadays manners are easy and life is hard.— *Sybil*.

Manners change with time and circumstances; customs may be observed everywhere.— *Alroy*.

MARRIAGE.

Some experience of society before we settle is most desirable, and is one of the conditions, I cannot but believe, of that felicity which we seek.— ('The Duchess') —*Lothair*.

I respect the institution — I have always thought that every woman should marry, and no man. — ('Hugo Bohun') *Lothair*.

The day before marriage and the hour before death is when a man thinks least of his purse and most of his neighbour.— *Vivian Grey*.

It is very immoral and very unfair, that any man should marry for tin, who does not want it.— ('Lord Milford') *Tancred*.

It destroys one's nerves to be amiable every day to the same human being.— *The Young Duke*.

The character of a woman rapidly develops after marriage, and sometimes seems to change, when in fact it is only complete.— *Tancred*.

MEMORY.

We sometimes find that memory is as rare a quality as prediction.— *Tancred*.

What was most remarkable in him (Mr. Rodney) was the convenient and complete want of memory. — *Endymion*.

MINISTRY.

One of the greatest of Romans, when asked what were his politics, replied: *'Imperium et libertas.'* That would not make a bad programme for a British ministry.— *Speech in Guildhall, November* 9, 1879.

MISSION.

A special mission was at all times a delicate measure, and in general it was safest to make a special mission with some purpose really different from that which it was sent to fulfil.— *Speech in House of Commons* (*Distress of the Country*), *September* 14, 1843.

MONEY.

Money is power, and rare are the heads that can withstand the possession of great power.—('Bond Sharpe') *Henrietta Temple*.

As men advance in life, all passions resolve themselves into money. Love, ambition, even poetry, end in this.—*Henrietta Temple*.

MUSIC.

The greatest advantage that a writer can derive from music is, that it teaches most exquisitely the art of development.—*Contarini Fleming*.

MYSTERY.

Mystery too often presupposes the idea of guilt.—*Venetia*.

All is mystery; but he is a slave who will not struggle to penetrate the dark veil.—*Contarini Fleming*.

NATION.

The fate of a nation will ultimately depend upon the strength and health of the population.—('Mr. Phœbus') *Lothair*.

NATIONALITY.

There is a great difference between nationality and race. Nationality is the miracle of political independence. Race is the principle of physical analogy. —*Speech in House of Commons (Navy Estimates), August 9, 1848*.

NATURE.

Nature is stronger than education.—*Contarini Fleming*.

Nature has her laws, and this is one,—a fair day's wage for a fair day's work.— ('Nixon') *Sybil.*

Necessity.

The necessities of things are sterner stuff than the hopes of men.— ('Theodora') *Lothair.*

News.

News has been described by the initial letters of the four points of the compass. It is the initial letters of the four points of the compass that make the word N E W S, and it is to be understood that news is that which comes from the North, East, West, and South, and if it comes from only one point of the compass, then it is a class publication and not news.— *Speech in House of Commons (Newspaper Stamp Duties Bill), March 26, 1855.*

Night.

Night brings rest; night brings solace; rest to the weary, solace to the sad; and to the desperate night brings despair.— *Alroy.*

Nonsense.

Nonsense when earnest is impressive and sometimes takes you in. If you are in a hurry, you occasionally mistake it for sense.— *Contarini Fleming.*

Novel (Receipt for Writing a).

Take a pair of pistols and a pack of cards, a cookery-book and a set of new quadrilles; mix them up with half an intrigue and a whole marriage, and divide them into three equal portions.— *The Young Duke.*

NOVELTY.

Novelty is an essential attribute of the beautiful.— *Vivian Grey.*

OBLIVION.

It is the lot of man to suffer, it is also his fortune to forget. Oblivion and sorrow share our being, as darkness and light divide the course of time.— *Vivian Grey.*

OBSCURE.

The obscure is a principal ingredient of the sublime.— *Contarini Fleming.*

OFFER.

A good offer should never be refused, unless we have a better one at the same time.— ('Essper') *Vivian Grey.*

OPPORTUNITY.

Opportunity is more powerful even than conquerors and prophets.— *Tancred.*

Great men should think of opportunity and not of time. Time is the excuse of feeble and puzzled spirits.— ('Lady Roehampton') *Endymion.*

OPPOSITION.

In opposition numbers often embarrass.— ('Bertie Tremaine') *Endymion.*

Believe me, Opposition has its charms; indeed I sometimes think the principal reason why I have enjoyed our ministerial life so much is that it has been from the first a perpetual struggle for existence.— ('Lady Montfort') *Endymion.*

ORATORY.

His (Ferrars') Corinthian style, in which the Mœnad of Mr. Burke was habited in the last mode of Almack's.— *Endymion.*

ORIGINALITY.

The originality of a subject is in its treatment.— ('Mr. Phœbus') *Lothair.*

PALMERSTON (LORD).

A crimping lordship with a career as insignificant as his intellect.

He reminds one of a favourite footman on easy terms with his mistress.

He is the Sporus of politics, cajoling France with an airy compliment, and menacing Russia with a perfumed cane. — *Runnymede Letters,* 1836.

PARLIAMENT.

Parliament was never so great as when they debated with closed doors.— ('Tancred') *Tancred.*

A parliamentary career, that old superstition of the eighteenth century, was important when there was no other source of power and fame. — *Tancred.*

I go to a land that has never been blessed by that fatal drollery called a representative government, though omniscience once deigned to trace out the polity which should rule it.— *Tancred.*

Parliamentary speaking, like playing on the fiddle, requires practice.— *Speech in House of Commons (Elections Bill), July* 13, 1871.

PARTY.

Party is organised opinion.— *Speech at Meeting of Society for increasing Endowments of small Livings in Diocese of Oxford, November* 25, 1864.

PARVENUS.

There is little doubt that parvenus as often owe their advancement in society to their perseverance as to their pelf.— *The Young Duke.*

PAST.

There is so much to lament in the world in which we live that I can spare no pang for the past.— ('Stephen Morley') *Sybil.*

PATIENCE.

I think if one is patient and watches, all will come of which one is capable; but no one can be patient who is not independent.— *Endymion.*

Patience is a necessary ingredient of genius.— *Contarini Fleming.*

Everything comes if a man will only wait.— ('Fakredeen') *Tancred.*

They waited with that patience which insulted beings can alone endure.— *Vivian Grey.*

Greece has a future; and I would say, if I might be permitted, to Greece, what I would say to an individual who has a future—'Learn to be patient.'— *Speech in House of Commons (Congress: Correspondence and Protocols), July* 18, 1878.

PATRIOTISM.

Patriotism depends as much on mutual suffering as on mutual success, and it is by that experience of all fortunes and all feelings that a great national character is created.— *Speech in House of Commons (International Maritime Law), March* 18, 1862.

PEACE.

Lord Salisbury and myself have brought you back peace — but a peace I hope with honour, which may satisfy our Sovereign and tend to the welfare of the country.— *Speech on Return from Congress, July* 16, 1878.

The outcome has been a peace, which I believe will be enduring. And why do I believe that peace will be enduring? Because I see that every one of the Powers is benefited by that peace, and no one is humiliated.— *Banquet at Mansion House (Freedom of City), October* 8, 1878.

PEARLS.

Pearls are like girls, they require quite as much attention.— ('Mr. Ruby') *Lothair.*

PEEL (SIR ROBERT).

If, instead of having recourse to obloquy, he would only stick to quotation, he may rely upon it, it would be a safer weapon.

I look upon him as a man who has tamed the shrew of Liberalism by her own tactics. He is the political Petruchio who has outbid you all.— *Speech on the Opening of Letters, February* 28, 1845.

Sir Robert Peel had a peculiarity which is perhaps natural with men of great talents who have not the creative faculty: he had a dangerous sympathy with the creations of others.— *Biography of Lord George Bentinck.*

Peerage.

We owe the English peerage to three sources: the spoliation of the Church; the open and flagrant sale of its honours by the elder Stuarts; and the boroughmongering of our own times.— ('Mr. Millbank') *Coningsby.*

People.

Who should sympathise with the poor but the poor? When the people support the people, the divine blessing will not be wanting.— *Sybil.*

My sympathies and feelings have always been with the people, from whom I sprang; and when obliged to join a party, I joined that party with which I believed the people sympathised. — *Speech in House of Commons (Corn Importation Bill), May* 8, 1846.

The people do not want employment; it is the greatest mistake in the world—all this employment is a stimulus to population.— ('Lord Marney') *Sybil.*

Perseverance.

The determined and persevering need never despair of gaining their object in this world.— *Lothair.*

Personal.

Nothing is great but the personal.— *Coningsby.*

It is the personal that interests mankind, that frees their imagination, and wins their hearts. A cause is a great abstraction and fit only for students; embodied in a party it stirs men to action; but place at the head of a party a leader who can inspire enthusiasm, he commands the world.— *Coningsby.*

Piety.

One should never think of death, one should think of life. That is real piety.—('Waldershare') *Endymion*.

For the pious, Paradise exists everywhere.—('Lady Annabel') *Venetia*.

Pitt.

The Chatterton of politics—to understand Mr. Pitt one must understand one of the suppressed characters of English history, and that is Lord Shelburne. —*Sybil*.

Plato.

His spirit alternately bowed in trembling and in admiration, as he seemed to be listening to the secrets of the universe revealed in the glorious melodies of an immortal voice (Plato's).—*Vivian Grey*.

I look upon Plato as the wisest and the profoundest of men, and upon Epicurus as the most humane and gentle.—('Herbert') *Venetia*.

Pleasure.

His (Duke of St. James) life was an ocean of enjoyment, and each hour, like each wave, threw up its pearl.—*The Young Duke*.

Pleasure should follow business.—('Sidney Wilton') *Endymion*.

Poet.

Poets are the unacknowledged legislators of the world.—('Marmion Herbert') *Venetia*.

Is not a poet an artist, and is not writing an art equally with painting?—words are but chalk and colour.—('Winter') *Contarini Fleming*.

POLITICS.

Real politics are the possession and distribution of power.— ('Lady Montfort') *Endymion.*

Finality is not the language of politics.— *Speech in House of Commons (Representation of People Bill), February 28, 1859.*

In politics unreasonable circumstances are elements of the problem to be solved.— *Endymion.*

In politics nothing is contemptible.— ('Sievers') *Vivian Grey.*

There is no gambling like politics.— ('Lord Roehampton') *Endymion.*

The practice of politics in the East may be defined by one word — dissimulation.— *Contarini Fleming.*

A very famous monarch, King Louis Philippe, once said to me that he attributed the great success of the British nation in political life to their talking politics after dinner.— *Banquet to Lord Rector, Glasgow, November 19, 1873.*

It is not impossible that the political movements of our time, which seem on the surface to have a democratic tendency, may have in reality a monarchical bias.— *Coningsby.*

I will keep each faction in awe by the bugbear of the other's supremacy. Trust me, I am a profound politician.— ('Pluto') *Infernal Marriage.*

You must show that democracy is aristocracy in disguise, and that aristocracy is democracy in disguise. It will carry you through everything.— ('Bertie Tremaine') *Endymion.*

England should think more of the community and less of the Government.— ('Sidonia') *Coningsby.*

The power of the future is ministerial capacity.— ('Bertie Tremaine') *Endymion.*

PRACTICAL.

Everything is practical which we believe.— ('Nigel Penruddock') *Endymion.*

PRECEDENT.

A precedent embalms a principle.— *Speech in House of Commons (Expenditure of Country), February 22, 1848.*

The right honourable gentleman (Sir R. Peel) tells us to go back to precedents: with him a great measure is always founded on a small precedent. He traces the steam-engine always back to the tea-kettle.— *Speech in House of Commons (Maynooth), April 11, 1845.*

PRESS.

As for the press, I am myself a gentleman of the press, and bear no other scutcheon.— *Speech in House of Commons (Relations with France), February 18, 1853.*

PRETENDERS.

Ministers do not love pretenders.— *Endymion.*

PRIDE OF ANCESTRY.

There is no pride like the pride of ancestry, for it is a blending of all emotions. How immeasurably superior to the herd is the man whose father only is famous! Imagine then the feelings of one who can trace his line through a thousand years of heroes and of princes.— *The Young Duke.*

PRINCES.

Princes go for nothing, without a loan.— ('Fakredeen') *Tancred.*

The Crown Prince of all countries is only a puppet in the hands of the people to be played against his own father.— ('Sievers') *Vivian Grey*.

PROCESSIONS.

Every procession must end. It is a pity, for there is nothing so popular with mankind.— *Endymion*.

PROFOUND.

A profound thinker always suspects that he is superficial.— *Contarini Fleming*.

PROPERTY.

One of the elements of territorial property is that it is representative.— *Speech at Manchester, April 3,* 1872.

What is the first quality which is required in a second chamber? Without doubt, independence. What is the best foundation for independence? Without doubt, property.— *Speech at Manchester, April 3,* 1872.

PROPHECY (A).

I have begun several times many things, and I have often succeeded at last. I will sit down, but the time will come when you will hear me.— *Maiden Speech in House of Commons (Irish Election Petition), December* 7, 1837.

PROPHET.

Many a prophet is little honoured till the future proves his inspiration.— *Alroy*.

PROVERBS.

We cannot eat the fruit whilst the tree is in blossom.— *Alroy*.

One grape will not make a bunch, even though it be a great one.— *Tancred.*

When the infant begins to walk, it thinks it lives in strange times.— *Sybil.*

A frying egg will not wait for the King of Cordova.— *Count Alarcos.*

Who drinks, first chinks.

In a long journey and a small inn, one knows one's company.

An ass covered with gold has more respect than a horse with a pack saddle.

Courage is fire, and bullying is smoke.

The sheep should have his belly full who quarrels with his mate.

Who asks in God's name, asks for two.

There's no fishing for trout in dry breeches.

The fool wonders, the wise man asks.

An obedient wife commands her husband.

Business with a stranger is title enough.

The oldest pig must look for the knife.— *Count Alarcos.*

PRUDENCE.

We live in an age of prudence. The leaders of the people now generally follow.—*Coningsby.*

PUBLIC.

God made man in his own image; but the public is made by newspapers, members of Parliament, excise officers, and poor-law guardians. — (' Sidonia ') *Coningsby.*

Besides a free press, you must have a servile public.— *Tancred.*

Public Building.— Nothing more completely represents a nation than a public building.— *Tancred.*

Public Opinion.— Who will define public opinion? Any human conclusion that is arrived at with adequate knowledge and with sufficient thought is entitled to respect, and the public opinion of a great nation under such conditions is irresistible, and ought to be so. But what we call public opinion is generally public sentiment.— *Speech in House of Commons (Compensation for Disturbance Bill), August 3, 1880.*

The opinion of the reflecting majority.— ('Lord Henry Vavasour') *Tancred.*

Public opinion on the Continent has turned out to be the voice of secret societies; and public opinion in England is the clamour of organised clubs.— *Speech in House of Commons (Address in answer to Speech), February 1, 1849.*

The public passion which is called opinion. — *Endymion.*

His lordship found time to lead by the nose a most meek and milkwhite jackass that immediately followed him, and which, in spite of the remarkable length of its ears, seemed the object of great veneration. Among other characteristics, it was said at different seasons to be distinguished by different titles; for sometimes it was styled 'the public,' at others 'opinion,' and occasionally was saluted as 'the king's conscience.'— *The Infernal Marriage.*

PUBLICITY.

Without publicity there can be no public spirit, and without public spirit every nation must decay. — *August 8, 1871.*

PURPOSE.

The secret of success is constancy to purpose. — *Speech at Crystal Palace (Banquet of National Union of Conservative and Constitutional Associations), June 24, 1872.*

Duty scorns prudence, and criticism has few terrors for a man with a great purpose.—*Biography of Lord George Bentinck.*

I have brought myself by long meditation to the conviction that a human being with a settled purpose must accomplish it, and that nothing can resist a will that will stake even existence for its fulfilment. — ('Myra') *Endymion.*

He (Bertie Tremaine) had a purpose, and they say that a man with a purpose generally sees it realised.— *Endymion.*

QUEEN.

He who serves queens may expect backsheesh. — ('Darkush') *Tancred.*

QUESTION.

Questions are always easy.—('Morley') *Sybil.*

RACE.

The truth is, progress and reaction are but words to mystify the millions. They mean nothing, they are nothing, they are phrases and not facts. In the structure, the decay, and the development of the various families of man, the vicissitudes of history find their main solution — all is race.—*Biography of Lord George Bentinck.*

No one will treat with indifference the principle of race. It is the key of history.— ('Baron Sergius') *Endymion*.

Language and religion do not make a race. There is only one thing which makes a race, and that is blood.— ('Baron Sergius') *Endymion*.

The Semites are unquestionably a great race, for among the few things in this world which appear to be certain, nothing is more sure than that they invented the alphabet.— ('Baron Sergius') *Endymion*.

The decay of a race is an inevitable necessity unless it lives in deserts and never mixes its blood.— ('Sidonia') *Tancred*.

Saxon industry and Norman manners never will agree.— ('Mr. Millbank') *Coningsby*.

An unmixed race of a firstrate organisation is the aristocracy of nature.— *Coningsby*.

The difference of race is unfortunately one of the reasons why I fear war may always exist; because race implies difference, difference implies superiority, and superiority leads to predominance.— *Speech in House of Commons* (*Address in answer to Queen's Speech*), *February* 1, 1849.

RAILWAY MANIA.

Political connection, political consistency, political principle, all vanished before the fascination of premiums.— *Endymion*.

RANK.

You think as property has its duties as well as its rights, rank has its bores as well as its pleasures. — ('Lady Marney') *Sybil*.

REACTION.

Reaction is the law of life, and it is the characteristic of the House of Commons.— *Speech in House of Commons (Address on Queen's Speech), February* 6, 1867.

Reaction is the law of life.— ('Zenobia') *Endymion.*

Reaction is the ebb and flow of opinion incident to fallible beings; the consequence of hope deferred, of false representations, of expectations baulked. Reaction is the consequence of a nation waking from its illusions.— *Speech in House of Commons (Sugar Duties), February* 3, 1848.

RECIPROCITY.

The principle of reciprocity appears to rest on scientific grounds, and it is probable that experience may teach us that it has recklessly been disregarded by our legislators.— *Biography of Lord George Bentinck.*

RELIGION.

Religion should be the rule of life, not a casual incident of it.— ('Cardinal Grandison') *Lothair.*

What you call forms and ceremonies represent the devotional instincts of our nature.— ('Mr. St. Lys') *Sybil.*

'What is your religion?' asked Lothair.

'The true religion, I think. I worship in a church where I believe God dwells, and dwells for my guidance and my good: my conscience.'— ('Theodora') *Lothair.*

All things that are good and beautiful make us more religious. They tend to the development of the

religious principle in us, which is our divine nature.
— ('Cardinal Grandison') *Lothair*.

Religion is civilisation, the highest; it is a reclama-
tion of man from savageness by the Almighty.—
('Cardinal Grandison') *Lothair*.

The soul requires a sanctuary.— ('Cardinal Grandison') *Lothair*.

I was a Parliamentary Christian, till despondency
and study, and ceaseless thought and prayer, and the
divine will brought me to light and rest.— ('Cardinal
Grandison') *Lothair*.

REMORSE.

There is anguish in the recollection that we have
not adequately appreciated the affection of those
whom we have loved and lost.— *Endymion*.

RETIREMENT.

He (Ferrars senior) retired with the solace of a
sinecure, a pension, and a privy councillorship.—
Endymion.

RIDICULE.

A fear of becoming ridiculous is the best guide in
life, and will save a man from all sorts of scrapes.—
('Lord Monmouth') *Coningsby*.

RITUALISM.

What I do object to is the mass in masquerade.
— *Speech in House of Commons (Public Worship
Regulation Bill), May* 15, 1874.

ROUTINE.

It seems to me that the world is withering under
routine. 'Tis the inevitable lot of humanity; but in

old days it was a routine of great thoughts, and now it is a routine of little ones.— ('Sidonia') *Coningsby*.

RUMOUR.

A common rumour — and therefore probably a common falsehood.— ('Waldershare') *Endymion*.

RUSSIA.

It was the geographical position of the Russian Empire which rendered it necessary. Look at the map. Those two spots would be seen, the Dardanelles and the Sound, which if possessed by the same power must give that power universal empire.— *Speech in House of Commons (War with Afghanistan), June 23, 1842.*

RUSSIAN.

A Russian does not care much for rosaries unless they are made of diamonds.— ('Pasqualigo') *Tancred*.

SCIENCE.

What art was to the ancient world, science is to the modern.— *Coningsby*.

The pursuit of science leads only to the insoluble. — ('Cardinal Grandison') *Lothair*.

Scientific, like spiritual truth, has ever from the beginning been descending from heaven to man.— *Preface to 'Lothair.'*

Modern science has vindicated the natural equality of man.— ('Delegate from National Convention') *Sybil*.

SELF-RESPECT.

Self-respect is a superstition of past centuries, an affair of the Crusaders.— ('Fakredeen') *Tancred*.

All must respect those who respect themselves.—*Coningsby*.

SENTIMENTAL.

If to feel is to be sentimental, I cannot help it.—*Endymion*.

SERVILITY.

How singular it is that those who love servility are always the victims of impertinence!— *The Young Duke*.

RAIN.

Nature, like man, sometimes weeps for gladness. — *Coningsby*.

SILENCE.

Silence often expresses more powerfully than speech the verdict and judgment of society.— *Speech in House of Commons (Administration of Viscount Palmerston), August* 1, 1862.

SLEEP

Slavery's only service money, sweet sleep.—('Mrs. Lorraine') *Vivian Grey*.

SMILE.

There are few faces that can afford to smile: a smile is sometimes bewitching, in general vapid, often a contortion.— *Tancred*.

SOCIAL.

The darkest hour precedes the dawn, and a period of unusual stillness often, perhaps usually, heralds the social convulsion.— *Endymion*.

To throw over a host is the most heinous of social crimes.— *Lothair.*

He was an excellent host, which no one can be who does not combine a good heart with high breeding.— *Lothair.*

To be king of your company is a poor ambition; yet homage is homage, and smoke is smoke whether it comes out of the chimney of a palace or of a workhouse.— *The Young Duke.*

To be his uninvited guest proved at once that you had entered the highest circle of the social paradise. — *Endymion.*

My idea of an agreeable person is a person who agrees with me.— ('Hugo Bohun') *Lothair.*

There is not less treasure in the world because we use paper currency; and there is not less passion than of old, though it is thought *bon ton* to be tranquil.— ('Sidonia') *Coningsby.*

However vast may appear the world in which we move, we all of us live in a limited circle.— *Endymion.*

Society and politics have much to do with each other, but they are not identical.— ('Lady Roehampton') *Endymion.*

SOCIETY.

There is no doubt that that great pumice-stone, society, smooths down the edges of your thoughts and manners.— *The Young Duke.*

Some people have great knowledge of society, and little of mankind.— *Vivian Grey.*

Christianity teaches us to love our neighbour as ourself; modern society acknowledges no neighbour. — ('Stephen Morley') *Sybil.*

When we first enter society, we are everywhere; yet there are few, I imagine, who after a season do not subside into a coterie.—*The Infernal Marriage.*

It is a community of purpose that constitutes society. Without that men may be drawn into contiguity, but they still continue virtually isolated.— ('Stephen Morley') *Sybil.*

What necessity can there be in your troubling yourself to amuse people you meet every day in your life, and who, from the vulgar perversity of society, value you in exact proportion as you neglect them? — *Venetia.*

One cannot ask any person to meet another in one's own house, without going through a sum of moral arithmetic.— ('Neuchatel') *Endymion.*

There are no fits of caprice so hasty and so violent as those of society. Society indeed is all passion and no heart.—*Venetia.*

Lady St. Jerome received Lothair, as Pinto said, with extreme unction.— *Lothair.*

It often happens that worthless people are merely people who are worth knowing.— *Coningsby.*

What is crime amongst the multitude, is only vice among the few.— *Tancred.*

SORROW.

I am one of those who would rather cherish affection than indulge grief, but every one must follow his mood.— ('Adrian Neuchatel') *Endymion.*

His heart was so crushed, that hope could not find even one desolate chamber to smile in.— *The Young Duke.*

SOUTHEY.

The most philosophical of bigots and the most poetical of prose-writers.— ('Cleveland') *Vivian Grey*.

STATION.

Great duties could alone confer great station.— *Speech in House of Commons* (*National Petition*), *July* 12, 1839.

STRENGTH.

Human strength always seems to me the natural process of settling affairs. — ('Delegate to National Convention') *Sybil*.

SUBLIMITY.

We have long been induced to suspect that the seeds of true sublimity lurk in a life which, like this book, is half fashion and half passion.— *The Young Duke*.

SUCCESS.

Success is the child of audacity.— *Iskander*.

As a general rule the most successful man in life is the man who has the best information.— ('Baron Sergius') *Endymion*.

The impromptu is always successful in life.— ('Pinto') *Lothair*.

For my success in life, it may be principally ascribed to the observance of a simple rule—I never trust either God or man.— ('Tiresias') *Infernal Marriage*.

SUN.

The sun is not the light for study.— ('Sievers') *Vivian Grey*.

SUSPENSE.

Decision destroys suspense, and suspense is the charm of existence.— ('Mrs. Coningsby') *Tancred*.

SYMPATHY.

Sympathy is the solace of the poor; but for the rich there is compensation.— ('Simmons') *Sybil*.

There is a strange sympathy which whispers convictions that no evidence can authorise, and no arguments dispel.— *Venetia*.

Sympathy and antipathy share our being, as day and darkness share our lives.— *Lothair*.

SYSTEM.

A series of systems have mystified existence.— *Contarini Fleming*.

TACT.

Without tact you can learn nothing. Tact teaches you when to be silent. Inquirers who are always inquiring never learn anything.— ('Wilton') *Endymion*.

A want of tact is worse than a want of virtue. Some women, it is said, work on pretty well without the last: I never knew one who did not sink, who ever dared to sail without the other.— *The Young Duke*.

Perseverance and tact are the two great qualities most valuable for all men who would mount, but especially for those who have to step out of the crowd.— ('Sidney Wilton') *Endymion*.

Tact does not remove difficulties, but difficulties melt away under tact.— *Tancred*.

TAXATION.

Confiscation is a blunder that destroys public credit; taxation, on the contrary, improves it; and both come to the same thing.— *Tancred*.

THEOLOGY.

Theology requires an apprenticeship of some thousand years at least; to say nothing of clime or race. You cannot get on with theology as you do with chemistry and mechanics. Trust me, there is something deeper in it.— *Tancred*.

TIME.

He who gains time gains everything.— ('Baroni') *Tancred*.

TOIL.

Toil without glory is a menial's lot.—*Alroy*.
When toil ceases the people suffer.—*Sybil*.

TONGUE.

The tongue is a less deceptive organ than the heart.— ('Lord Cadurcis') *Venetia*.

TRADE.

Trade always comes back, and finance never ruined a country, or an individual either, if he had pluck.— ('Lady Montfort') *Endymion*.

TRAVEL.

Our first scrape generally leads to our first travel. —*Contarini Fleming*.

Every moment is travel, if understood.— ('Sidonia') *Coningsby*.

Travel is the great source of true wisdom; but to travel with profit you must have such a thing as previous knowledge.— ('Winter') *Contarini Fleming*.

Travel teaches toleration.— *Contarini Fleming*.

TRUTH.

When little is done, little is said. Silence is the mother of truth.— ('Sheikh Hassan') *Tancred*.

Truth is not truth to the false.— ('Brother Anthony') *Contarini Fleming*.

Sidonia was a great philosopher, who took comprehensive views of human affairs, and surveyed every fact in its relative position to other facts, the only mode of obtaining truth.— *Coningsby*.

After all, what is truth? It changes as you change your clime or your country; it changes with the century. The truth of a hundred years ago is not the truth of the present day, and yet it may have been as genuine. Truth at Rome is not the truth of London, and both of them differ from the truth of Constantinople.— ('Herbert') *Venetia*.

It is dishonest to blush when you speak the truth, even if it be to your shame.—('Winter') *Contarini Fleming*.

Time is precious, but truth is more precious than time.— *Speech at Aylesbury (Royal and Central Bucks Agricultural Association), September* 21, 1865.

TU QUOQUE.

A *tu quoque* should always be good-humoured, for it has nothing else to recommend it.—*Speech in House of Commons (Prosecution of the War), May* 24, 1855.

Turf.

That vast institution of national demoralisation.—*Endymion*.

Unfortunate.

The unfortunate are always egotistical.— ('Agrippina') *Endymion*.

Unhappiness.

There is no such thing as unhappiness.— ('Winter') *Contarini Fleming*.

Unobtrusiveness.

He (Premium) was an object of observation for his very unobtrusiveness.— ('Ernest Clay') *Vivian Grey*.

Variety.

Variety—that divine gift which makes a woman charming.—*Tancred*.

Variety is the mother of enjoyment.— ('Essper') *Vivian Grey*.

Vegetarian View of Animal Food.

The heresy of cutlets.—('Herbert') *Venetia*.

Vehemence.

Whatever they did, the Elysians were careful never to be vehement.— *The Infernal Marriage*.

War.

I hear of peace and war in newspapers, but I am never alarmed, except when I am informed that the sovereigns want treasure: then I know that monarchs are in earnest.—('Sidonia') *Coningsby.*

If there be a greater calamity to human nature than famine, it is that of an exterminating war.— *Speech at Mansion House, November* 9, 1877.

WEALTH.

After all, wealth is the test of the welfare of a people, and the test of wealth is the command of the precious metals.—('Neuchatel') *Endymion.*

Nonsense!—Great wealth is a great blessing to a man who knows what to do with it; and as for honours, they are inestimable to the honourable.— ('Neuchatel') *Endymion.*

WELLINGTON (DUKE OF).

He has been called fortunate, but fortune is a divinity which has never favoured those who are not at the same time sagacious and intrepid, inventive and patient. It was his own character that created his career—alike achieved his exploits, and guarded him from every vicissitude; for it was his sublime self-control alone that regulated his lofty fate.—*Funeral of the Duke of Wellington, November* 15, 1852.

The Duke's government—a dictatorship of patriotism.—*Endymion.*

WHIGGISM.

I look upon an Orangeman as a pure Whig; the only professor and practiser of unadulterated Whiggism.—*Coningsby.*

WHISPER.

A whisper of emphasis.—*Lothair.*

WILL.

Everything in this world depends upon will.— ('Lady Montfort') *Endymion*.

WOMAN.

The action of woman on our destiny is unceasing. —*Sybil*.

A reputation for success has as much influence with women as a reputation for wealth has with men.—*Coningsby*.

Where there are crowned heads, there are always some charming women.—*Endymion*.

Our strong passions break into a thousand purposes; women have one. Their love is dangerous, but their hate is fatal.—*Alroy*.

In the present day, and especially among women, one would almost suppose that health was a state of unnatural existence.—*The Young Duke*.

Woman alone can organise a drawing-room: man succeeds sometimes in a library.—*Coningsby*.

Male firmness is very often obstinacy. Women have always something better, worth all qualities. They have tact.—('Lord Eskdale') *Coningsby*.

The woman who is talked about is generally virtuous, and she is only abused because she devotes to one the charms which all wish to enjoy.—*The Infernal Marriage*.

There is no mortification, however keen, no misery, however desperate, which the spirit of woman cannot in some degree lighten or alleviate.—*Coningsby*.

Talk to women as much as you can. This is the best school. This is the way to gain fluency, because you need not care what you say, and had better not be sensible.— ('Baron Fleming') *Contarini Fleming*.

I believe women are loved much more for themselves than is supposed. Besides, a woman should be content if she is loved; that is the point; and she is not to inquire how far the accidents of life have contributed to the result.— ('Myra') *Endymion*.

Women are generous, but not precise in money matters.— ('Queen Agrippina') *Endymion*.

Women are the priestesses of Predestination.— *Coningsby*.

Perhaps he (Baron Fleming) affected gallantry, because he was deeply impressed with the influence of women both upon public and upon private opinion. — *Contarini Fleming*.

But they all agreed in one thing, to wit, that the man who permitted himself a moment's uneasiness about a woman was a fool.— *Henrietta Temple*.

One should always make it a rule to give up to them, and then they are sure to give up to us.— ('Lord Eskdale') *Coningsby*.

WORDSWORTH.

Gentlemanly man — but only reads his own poetry. — ('Alhambra') *Vivian Grey*.

WORLD.

The great world — society formed on anti-social principles.— ('Horace Grey') *Vivian Grey*.

To the great body, however, of what is called the world — the world that lives in St. James' Street and Pall Mall, that looks out of a club window and surveys mankind.— *Tancred*.

YOUTH.

Youth is, we all know, somewhat reckless in assertion, and when we are juvenile and curly one takes a pride in sarcasm and invective.— *Speech in House of Commons* (*Her Majesty's Speech, Amendments*), *June* 7, 1859.

The two greatest stimulants in the world are youth and debt.— ('Fakredeen') *Tancred.*

You know too little of life to think of death.— ('Winter') *Contarini Fleming.*

Oh! what is wisdom, and what is virtue, without youth! Talk not to me of knowledge of mankind; give me back the sunshine of the breast which they o'erclouded! Talk not to me of proud morality; oh! give me innocence!— *The Young Duke.*

The blunders of youth are preferable to the triumphs of manhood, or the successes of old age.— ('Princess of Tivoli') *Lothair.*

Almost everything that is great has been done by youth.— ('Sidonia') *Coningsby.*

There are few things more gloomy than the recollection of a youth that has not been enjoyed.— *Henrietta Temple.*

For life in general there is but one decree. Youth is a blunder; Manhood a struggle; Old Age a regret. — ('Sidonia') *Coningsby.*

Wealth is power, and in youth, of all seasons of life, we require power, because we can enjoy everything that we command.— *Henrietta Temple.*

The youth of a nation are the trustees of posterity.— *Sybil.*

A COMPLETE BIBLIOGRAPHY

CHRONOLOGICALLY ARRANGED

OF

THE WRITINGS

OF THE

EARL OF BEACONSFIELD, K. G.

CRITICALLY SUPERVISED BY THE LATE

MONTAGU WILLIAM LOWRY-CORRY
LORD ROWTON
*For many years Confidential Secretary
to the Earl of Beaconsfield*

———

NOTE : In this Bibliography, mention of the many French,
German, Swedish, Italian, Turkish, and Greek translations of
the various novels has been omitted.

BIBLIOGRAPHY

1826

Vivian Grey.

> 'Why, then, the world's mine oyster,
> Which I with sword will open.'

Vol. I. London: Henry Colburn, 1826. The Dedication is characteristic:

> 'To the best and greatest of men I dedicate these volumes. He for whom it is intended will accept and appreciate the compliment; those for whom it is not intended will—do the same.'

See also 1827, 1888, and 1892.

Nos. 2 and 3 of *The Star Chamber* (a monthly magazine) for April 26, 1826, contain notices of the volume of *Vivian Grey* just published, consisting of a long extract describing the castle of the Carabas family, and an equally long extract depicting Mr. Stapylton Toad. In No. 7, for May 24, appears a *Key to Vivian Grey*, the names of the originals having sometimes the first letter of the surname or title, and sometimes the last letter in addition.

1827

Vivian Grey. Vol. III. London: Henry Colburn, 1827. Vol. III. has pp. ii, 333; Vol. IV. pp. ii, 362; Vol. V. pp. iv, 324. These three volumes were issued in 1827. At the end of the British Museum copy of Vols. IV. and V. is bound a *Key to Vivian Grey* (tenth edition, published in 1827 by William Marsh). This gives the names of the originals of some thirty characters in the third, fourth, and fifth volumes, in the same manner as in the original Key.

1828

The Voyage of Captain Popanilla. By·the author of *Vivian Grey.*

'Travellers ne'er did lie, though fools at home condemn 'em.'

London: Henry Colburn, 1828. 12mo, pp. viii, 243. For other editions see 1890.

1831

The Young Duke. 'A moral tale, though gay.' By the author of *Vivian Grey.* In three volumes. London: Henry Colburn and Richard Bentley, 1831. 12mo. Vol. I. contains pp. iv, 300; Vol. II. pp. iv, 271, the last page containing the Notes. Vol. III. has pp. iv, 265. For later editions see 1888, and 1892.

1832

The Court of Egypt: A Sketch. *New Monthly Magazine and Literary Journal,* 1832, Vol. XXXIV., pp. 555–56. The little sketch is signed 'Mesr.'

The Speaking Harlequin: The Two Losses; in one act. *New Monthly Magazine,* 1832, Vol. XXXV., pp. 158–63. This little piece is in four scenes, and includes two stanzas entitled *Columbine's Ritornella.*

The Bosphorus: A Sketch. *New Monthly Magazine,* 1832, Vol. XXXV., p. 242. Signed 'Marco Polo, Junior.'

Egyptian Thebes. *New Monthly Magazine,* 1832, Vol. XXXV., pp. 333–39. Signed 'Marco Polo, Junior.'

Ixion in Heaven. By the author of *Contarini Fleming* and *Vivian Grey. New Monthly Magazine,* 1832, Vol. XXXV., pp. 514–20. Section VIII. is followed by the words, 'To be continued.' See 1833, 1890.

Contarini Fleming: A Psychological Autobiography. In four volumes. London: John Murray, MDCCCXXXII., 8vo. Vol. I. has pp. iv, 228; Vol. II. pp. iv, 247; Vol. III. pp. iv, 194, and two pp. of advertisements; Vol. IV. pp. iv, 230. See 1846, 1853, 1888, and 1891.

1833

Ibrahim Pasha, the Conqueror of Syria. *New Monthly Magazine,* 1833, Vol. XXXVII., pp. 153–54. Signed 'Marco Polo, Junior.'

Ixion in Heaven, Part II. By the author of *Contarini Fleming* and *Vivian Grey. New Monthly Magazine,* 1833, Vol. XXXVII., pp. 175–84. See 1832.

The Wondrous Tale of Alroy. The Rise of Iskander. By the author of *Vivian Grey, Contarini Fleming,* etc. In three volumes. London: Saunders and Otley, 1833. Vol. I. contains pp. xxviii, 303, the dedication, 'To —— ——,' being pp. v, vi; preface, pp. vii–xxv; half-title, p. xxvii; Notes, pp. 271-303. Vol. II. has pp. iv, 305, Notes occupying pp. 293-305. Vol. III. has pp. iv, 324. The tale ends on p. 106, pp. 107–112 are devoted to Notes. *The Rise of Iskander* begins on p. 113 and finishes on p. 324. For *Alroy* see 1846, 1888, 1890. For *Iskander,* see 1888, and 1891. Reprinted in 1884.

1834

The Infernal Marriage. By Disraeli the Younger, author of *Ixion in Heaven. New Monthly Magazine,* 1834, Vol. XLI., pp. 293-304. Section VI. finishes with the words, 'To be concluded in our next.'

The Infernal Marriage. By Disraeli the Younger, author of *Ixion in Heaven.* Part the Second. *New Monthly Magazine,* 1834, Vol. XLI. pp. 431-40. Section VIII. of the second part ends with the words, 'To be continued.'

The Infernal Marriage. By Disraeli the Younger, author of *Ixion in Heaven.* Part III. *New Monthly Magazine,* 1834, Vol. XLII., pp. 30-38.

The Infernal Marriage. By Disraeli the Younger, author of *Ixion in Heaven.* Part IV. *New Monthly Magazine,* 1834, Vol. XLII., pp. 137-44. Chapter III. is followed by the words, 'To be continued.' But no continuation was published. See 1890.

1835

The Carrier Pigeon. By the author of *Vivian Grey.* Heath's *Book of Beauty,* 1835, pp. 128-44.

1836

The Letters of Runnymede.

> 'Neither for shame nor fear this mask he wore,
> That, like a vizor in the battlefield,
> But shrouds a manly and a daring brow.'

London: John Macrone, MDCCCXXXVI., pp. xxii, 234. The Dedication to Sir Robert Peel occupies pp. v-xvii, and is followed by the contents. The nineteen letters which appeared originally in the *Times* occupy pp. 1–173. *The Spirit of Whiggism* runs from p. 175 to the end. See 1885.

The Consul's Daughter. By the author of *Vivian Grey*. Heath's *Book of Beauty*, 1836.

1837

Henrietta Temple: A Love Story. By the author of *Vivian Grey*.

> 'Quoth Sancho: Read it out, by all means, for I mightily delight in hearing of Love Stories.'

In three volumes. Henry Colburn, MDCCCXXXVII. The work is dedicated to Count Alfred D'Orsay, by 'his affectionate friend.' It was reviewed in the *Athenæum* for December 10, 1836. See 1853, 1888, 1891.

Venetia. By the author of *Vivian Grey* and *Henrietta Temple*.

> 'Is thy face like thy mother's, my fair child?'
> 'The child of love, though born in bitterness,
> And nurtured in convulsions.'

In three volumes. London: Henry Colburn. See 1853, 1888.

To a Maiden Sleeping after Her First Ball. By the author of *Vivian Grey*. Heath's *Book of Beauty*, 1837. A poem of four stanzas.

1838

A Syrian Sketch. Heath's *Book of Beauty*, 1838.

1839

The Tragedy of Count Alarcos. London: Henry Colburn, 1839. It is dedicated to the Right Honourable Lord Francis Egerton, and the opening words of the Dedication are:

> 'I dedicate to a Poet an attempt to contribute to the revival of English Tragedy: a very hopeless labour, all will assure me.'

The tragedy is in five acts. See 1892.

The Portrait of the Lady Mahon. By B. Disraeli, Esq., M.P. A sonnet in Heath's *Book of Beauty*, 1839.

1840

The Valley of Thebes. By B. Disraeli, Esq., M.P. Heath's *Book of Beauty*, 1841.

1841

Munich. By B. Disraeli, Esq., M.P. Heath's *Book of Beauty*, 1841.
Eden and Lebanon. By B. Disraeli, Esq., M.P. Heath's *Book of Beauty*, 1842.

1844

Coningsby: or, the New Generation. By B. Disraeli, Esq.. M.P., author of *Contarini Fleming*. Three volumes. London: Henry Colburn, 1844. It is dedicated to Henry Hope. In the 'Key to the Characters in *Coningsby*, comprising about Sixty of the Principal Personages of the Story,' published in 1844 by Sherwood, Gilbert and Piper, the names of the originals are indicated by the first and last letters of the surname or title; but in 'A New Key to the Characters in *Coningsby*,' issued by W. Strange (without date), the names of the originals are in nearly all instances printed in full, the names of the characters not being reprinted.
See 1888, 1889 (with Key), 1891.

1845

Sybil: or, the Two Nations. By B. Disraeli, M.P., author of *Coningsby*.

> 'The Commonalty murmured, and said, "There never were so many Gentlemen and so little Gentleness."' — Bishop Latimer.

Three volumes. London: Henry Colburn, 1845. 8vo. British Museum, 2474. Vol. I. has viii, 315; Vol. II. pp. iv, 324 ; Vol. III. pp. ii, 326. The inscription, to Mrs. Disraeli, closes with the words,

> 'The most severe of critics but — a perfect Wife!'

See 1853, 1888, 1890.

1846

Contarini Fleming. Alroy. Romances by B. Disraeli, M.P., author of *Coningsby* and *Sybil*. Second edition, in three volumes. London: Henry Colburn, 1846. 'vo. B.M. 2581. Vol. I. has portrait and pp. vi, 287; Vol. II. pp. ii, 370; Vol. III. pp. ii, 360.

Contarini Fleming ends on p. 285 of Vol. II.; the half-title (not counted) of *Alroy* follows, and the Preface to *Alroy* begins on p. 287. The Notes to *Alroy* occupy pp. 341–60 of Vol. III. For *Contarini Fleming*, see 1832. For *Alroy*, see 1833.

Shoubra. By B. Disraeli, Esq., M.P. *The Keepsake*, 1846, pp. 30–34. British Museum, P.P. 6670.

1847

Tancred: or, the New Crusade. By B. Disraeli, M.P., author of *Coningsby*, *Sybil*, etc. Three volumes. London: Henry Colburn, 1847. 12mo. Vol. I. has pp. ii, 338; Vol. II. pp. ii, 340; Vol. III. pp. ii, 298. See 1888.

1848

Sonnet on Wellington. *The Stowe Catalogues*, priced and annotated by Henry Rumsey Forster, 1848, p. xlii; British Museum, 786 k. 41. There is no title to this sonnet, which closes the *Historical Notice of Stowe*. Mr. Forster says:

'Mr. Disraeli, M.P., while a guest at Stowe, in 1840, composed the following beautiful lines in allusion to it [a silver statuette by Cotterell] ; they were written out at the time, and subsequently always placed on the table with the statuette.'

1852

Lord George Bentinck: A Political Biography. By B. Disraeli, Member of Parliament for the County of Buckingham.

'He left us the legacy of Heroes: the memory of his great name and the inspiration of his great example.'

London: Colburn and Co., 1852. 8vo, pp. viii, 588. British Museum, 10815 d. 10. The book is dedicated to Lord Henry Bentinck. The chapter on the Jews was translated into German in 1853. See also 1858 and 1872.

Address Delivered to Members of the Manchester Athenæum, on the 23d of October, 1844, by Benjamin Disraeli, Esq., M.P. This address forms pp. 49–67 of *The Value of Literature to Men of Business*, published by J. J. Griffin and Co. in 1852. The speech was delivered Thursday, October 3, 1844.

1853

Venetia. By Benjamin Disraeli. [Three lines of poetry, as in 1837.] A New Edition. London: David Bryce, 1853. See 1837.

Contarini Fleming: A Psychological Romance. By B. Disraeli. A New Edition. London: David Bryce, 1853. See 1832.

Sybil: or, the Two Nations. By B. Disraeli.

'The Commonalty murmured, and said, "There never were so many Gentlemen and so little Gentleness." '— Bishop Latimer.

A New Edition. London: David Bryce, 1853. See 1845.

Henrietta Temple: A Love Story. By B. Disraeli.

'Quoth Sancho: Read it out, by all means, for I mightily delight in hearing of Love Stories.'

A New Edition. London: David Bryce, 1853. P. iv has the following notice:

'This work was first published in the year 1836.'

See note under 1837 and also 1891.

Lines of B. Disraeli, Esq., to a Beautiful Mute, the eldest child of Mrs. Fairlie. Madden's *Literary Life and Correspondence of the Countess of Blessington,* 1855, Vol. I. pp. 383-84. Mrs. Fairlie was the favourite niece of Lady Blessington. Her daughter Isabella (the 'Beautiful Mute') died Jan. 31, 1843.

1858

Lord George Bentinck: A Political Biography. By the Right Hon. B. Disraeli, M.P.

'He left us the legacy of Heroes: the memory of his great name and the inspiration of his great example.'

A New Edition. London: G. Routledge and Co. Also New York, 1858. See 1852.

1870

Lothair. By the Right Hon. Benjamin Disraeli.

Nosse omnia haec salus est adolescentulis. —Terentius.

Three volumes. London: Longmans, Green and Co., 1870. 8vo. British Museum, 12627 i. 7, Vol. I. has pp. vi, 328; Vol. II. pp. iv, 321; Vol. III. pp. iv, 333. The book is dedicated to the Duke of Aumale.

Lothair. [As above, the same imprint.] Seventh edition. Vol. has pp. viii, 328; pp. vii, and viii are occupied by an Advertisement of the Fifth Edition, the other volumes are unchanged. Messrs. Longmans sold more than eight thousand copies of the three-volume edition, and more than eighty thousand copies of *Lothair* in cheap editions. See 1877, 1890.

1872

Lord George Bentinck. A Political Biography. By the Right Hon. Benjamin Disraeli.

> 'He left us the legacy of Heroes: the memory of his great name and the inspiration of his great example.'

Eighth edition, revised. London: Longmans, Green and Co., 1872. 8vo, pp. xiv, 422. The Preface of this eighth edition, occupying pp. vii–ix, is signed 'D.' See 1852.

1877

Lothair. By the Right Honourable Benjamin Disraeli.

Nosse omnia haec salus est adolescentulis.— Terentius.

New Edition. London: Longmans, Green and Co., 1877. 8vo, pp. xx, 485. Pp. vii–xx contain the General Preface, dated 'Hughenden Manor, October, 1870.' See 1870, 1890.

1880

Endymion. By the author of *Lothair*. *Quicquid agunt homines.* Three volumes. London: Longmans, Green and Co., 1880. 8vo. British Museum, 12640 bb. 3. Vol. I. has pp. iv, 331; Vol. II. pp. iv, 337; Vol. III. pp. iv, 346. See 1881 and 1891.

1881

Endymion. By the author of *Lothair*. *Quicquid agunt homines.* London: Longmans, Green and Co., 1881. 8vo, pp. iv, 474.

1882

Selected Speeches of the Late Right Honourable the Earl of Beaconsfield. London, 1882. The first speech reprinted was delivered at High Wycombe, June 9, 1832. Besides political speeches, there are included the Address at the Manchester Athenæum, October 3, 1844, on the Value of Literature; also the Speech on the Berlin Treaty, and the speech at the Carlton Club Banquet, after the return from Berlin, and other addresses.

1885

Home Letters. Written by the Earl of Beaconsfield to his sister in 1832.

> 'Absence is often a great element of charm.'— *Endymion*.

British Museum, 2410 a. Mr. Ralph Disraeli contributes a preface.

The Runnymede Letters. With an introduction and notes by Francis Hitchman. London: Richard Bentley and Son, 1885. 8vo, pp. xii, 292. The nineteen letters occupy pp. 1-242, and are followed by *The Spirit of Whiggism*, as in the edition of 1836.

1888

Tancred: or, the New Crusade. By the Earl of Beaconsfield, K.G. London: Longmans, Green and Co., 1888. 8vo, pp. iv, 487. See 1847.

Vivian Grey. By the Earl of Beaconsfield, author of *Coningsby, Henrietta Temple, Sybil,* etc., etc. Ward, Lock and Co., London and New York, 1888. 8vo, pp. viii, 9-247. See 1826.

The Wondrous Tale of Alroy. By the Earl of Beaconsfield, author of *Vivian Grey, Coningsby, Venetia,* etc. Ward, Lock and Co., London and New York, 1888. 8vo, pp. vi, 104. See 1833.

Contarini Fleming: A Psychological Autobiography. By the Earl of Beaconsfield, author of *Vivian Grey, Contarini Fleming, Venetia,* etc. Ward, Lock and Co., London and New York, 1888. 8vo, pp. iv, 130. See 1832.

Henrietta Temple: A Love Story. By the Earl of Beaconsfield, author of *Vivian Grey, Coningsby, Venetia,* etc. Ward, Lock and Co., London and New York, 1888. 8vo, pp. vi, 169. See 1837.

Coningsby: or, the New Generation. By the Earl of Beaconsfield, author of *Vivian Grey, Contarini Fleming, Venetia,* etc. Ward, Lock and Co., London and New York, 1888. 8vo, pp. vi, 7-191. See 1844.

Sybil: or, the Two Nations. By the Earl of Beaconsfield, author of *Coningsby, Henrietta Temple, Vivian Grey,* etc. Ward, Lock and Co., London and New York, 1888. 8vo, pp. x, 11-195. See 1845.

Venetia. By the Earl of Beaconsfield, author of *Vivian Grey, Coningsby, Henrietta Temple,* etc. Ward, Lock and Co., London and New York, 1888. 8vo, pp. iv, 193. See 1837.

The Young Duke. By the Earl of Beaconsfield, author of *Coningsby, Vivian Grey, Sybil,* etc. Ward, Lock and Co., London and New York, 1888. 8vo, pp. vi, 7-146. See 1831.

The Primrose Edition. George Routledge and Sons. [Pictorial cover.] London, Glasgow, and New York, 1888. Eight vols., 8vo. B.M. 12603 i. The volumes are not numbered, but are advertised on the back of the half-titles in the following order:

Vivian Grey, pp. iv, 5-245; *Coningsby*, pp. vi, 7-207; *Sybil*, pp. v, 7-192; *Contarini Fleming*, pp. iv, 7-195; *The Young Duke*, pp. vi,

7-154; *The Wondrous Tale of Alroy*, and *The Rise of Iskander*, pp. viii, 9-160 (*Alroy* ends on p. 124); *Venetia*, pp. iv, 5-185; *Henrietta Temple*, pp. iv, 188.

1889

Coningsby: or, the New Generation. By the Right Hon. the Earl of Beaconsfield, K.G. (reprinted from the edition of 1844). Edited, with a preface and elucidatory notes, by Francis Hitchman, author of *The Public Life of the Earl of Beaconsfield*, etc., etc. London: W. H. Allen and Co., 1889. 8vo, pp. xviii, 458. B.M. 12619 e. 2. The half-title is not counted in the pagination of the prefatory matter. There is also a frontispiece entitled 'A Cabinet Pudding.'

1890

Lothair. By the Earl of Beaconsfield, K.G.
  Nosse omnia haec salus est adolescentulis.—Terentius.
New Edition. London and New York: Longmans, Green and Co., 1890. 8vo, pp. viii, 482. See 1870, 1877.

Alroy. Ixion in Heaven. The Infernal Marriage. Popanilla. By the Earl of Beaconsfield, K.G. New Edition. London: Longmans, Green and Co., 1890. 8vo, pp. viii, 463. The preface to *Alroy* occupies pp. v–vii; *Alroy*, pp. 1–252; Notes to *Alroy*, pp. 253–266; *Ixion in Heaven*, pp. 267–97; *The Infernal Marriage*, pp. 299–362; *Popanilla*, pp. 363-463. For *Alroy*, see 1833; for *Ixion in Heaven*, 1832; for *The Infernal Marriage*, 1834; for *Popanilla*, 1828.

Sybil: or, the Two Nations. By the Earl of Beaconsfield, K.G.
New Edition. London and New York: Longmans, Green and Co., 1890. 8vo, pp. iv, 489. See 1845.

1891

Coningsby: or, the New Generation. By the Earl of Beaconsfield, K.G. New Edition. London and New York: Longmans, Green and Co., 1891. 8vo, pp. viii, 477. See 1844.

Coningsby: or, the New Generation. By Benjamin Disraeli (Earl of Beaconsfield). Cassell and Company, Limited: London, Paris, and Melbourne, 1891. 8vo, pp. iv, 5-382. See 1844.

Henrietta Temple: A Love Story. By the Earl of Beaconsfield, K.G. New Edition. London and New York: Longmans, Green and Co., 1891. 8vo, pp. viii, 464. The Advertisement, p. vii, says: "This work was first published in the year 1837." See that year, and also 1853.

Contarini Fleming : A Psychological Romance. **The Rise of Iskander.** By the Earl of Beaconsfield, K.G. New Edition. London : Longmans, Green and Co., 1891. 8vo, pp. viii, 461. The preface to *Contarini Fleming* is pp. v–vii; *Contarini Fleming*, pp. 1–373; *Iskander*, pp. 375–461. For *Contarini Fleming*, see 1832 ; for *Iskander*, 1833.

Endymion. By the Earl of Beaconsfield, K.G. New Edition. London and New York : Longmans, Green and Co., 1891. 8vo, pp. iv, 474. See 1880.

1892

Vivian Grey. By the Earl of Beaconsfield, K.G. [Two lines of poetry, as in 1826.] New Edition. London and New York : Longmans, Green and Co., 1892. 8vo, pp. vi, 487. See 1826.

The Young Duke : 'A moral tale, though gay.' **Count Alarcos : A** Tragedy. By the Earl of Beaconsfield, K.G. New Edition. London and New York : Longmans, Green and Co., 1892. 8vo, pp. vi, 451. For *The Young Duke*, see 1831 ; for *Count Alarcos*, see 1839.

There is a small pamphlet, consisting of thirty pages, which, though without the year of publication, must refer to an early time of authorship. The title is, *The Earl of Beaconsfield's First Novel : The Consul's Daughter. Hitherto unpublished.* 44 Essex Street, Strand. *The Consul's Daughter* appeared in Heath's *Book of Beauty*, 1836, pp. 74–113.